THE
LEGION
OF NOBLE
CHRISTIANS

Books by Gerald Green

Fiction
THE SWORD AND THE SUN
THE LAST ANGRY MAN
THE LOTUS EATERS
THE HEARTLESS LIGHT
THE LEGION OF NOBLE CHRISTIANS

Biography
HIS MAJESTY O'KEEFE
(*with Lawrence Klingman*)

Travel
THE PORTOFINO PTA

THE LEGION OF NOBLE CHRISTIANS

or The Sweeney Survey

GERALD GREEN

TRIDENT PRESS NEW YORK 1965

Perhaps we cannot prevent this world from being a world in which children are tortured. But we can reduce the number of tortured children. And if you don't help us, who else in the world can help us do this?

—ALBERT CAMUS
"The Unbeliever and Christians,"
Statement made at a Dominican Monastery

PART 1

BUCK SWEENEY

SWEENEY TIPPED HIS OLIVE-GREEN LINEN CAP TO THE STATUE ON the quay. "Old Rabelais," he said. "One of the all-time greats."

"I couldn't care less," the girl said. "This whole thing is a drag. Why don't you admit you're lost, so we can go back to Paris?"

She was a sullen beauty, a migratory parasite: tanned skin, elegant legs, lank blonde hair. Sweeney had met her sisters on the Hampton Beaches, in the East Sixties of Manhattan, in Greenwich Village. Her name was Dodie, but Sweeney kept calling her Dee Dee, and sometimes Weezy. She was a charter member of that band of good-looking women whose flesh exempts them from civil behavior. Thus, her rude rejection of the old humanist did not surprise him.

For more than an hour they had been blasting around the Loire Valley, crossing and recrossing the Indre, the Vienne, other lovely tributaries. They had stopped in Chinon so Sweeney could honor Rabelais, a hero of his boyhood. Years ago, he had furtively read *Gargantua and Pantagruel* in the Tremont Avenue Branch of the New York Public Library.

Communion ended, he bounced into the gleaming red MG, gunned it over the bridge, and headed south. The girl slumped unhappily in the tan leather seat; Sweeney sang. Although lost, he was joyful. It was fun speeding down rustic lanes and riverbanks in his nifty new sports car. His eyes gorged on color: black-green hedges and trees, yellow-green fields, red-brown farmhouses, and occasionally, the slate-gray roofs and lighter-gray façades of ancient chateaux.

Childhood memories of his father's tales of a bucolic Ireland came back to him. He sucked in spiritual nourishment from the foliage, the humming pastureland, the black earth.

His soul's peace reinforced his body's joy. He and his companion had dined in Tours at a two-star restaurant. Now, some hours later, cream sauces, melted butter, tender meats, velvety desserts, all solvent in a litre of Vouvray, had unified in an indigestible clot in his young man's paunch. Its persistency delighted him. Sweeney was an indestructible. Overeating, immoderate drinking, and long hours invigorated him. Oddly, he was forever fearful of imminent illness. Hypochondria and excess were the hallmarks of his disorderly life. Along with the massive lunch, he had eaten a half-dozen Rolaids, a Pan-Vita Fort tablet, two APC pills, and a stiff gulp of *Romilar*, a vintage French cough medicine, 18 per cent alcohol by volume.

4

Windy and sleepy, he was unperturbed that his search for the seminary (like most efforts of his life) was assuming a pointless, unfulfilled quality.

"I don't know about you," Dodie-Dee Dee whined, "but I'm ready to head back to Paris. This is *some* drag."

"Be patient, Weezy. Sweeney's taking the short cut. Through the lots behind the Castle Hill Pool."

The girl groaned. She was from Midland, Michigan, and she resented his arch references to his old neighborhood: *the Bronx.* At Westhampton Beach, *nobody* was allowed to be from the Bronx. But this clown! *Honestly:* to make jokes about it, to brag, as if it were a big deal, an *edge.* She wished he would forget his dumb trip and go back to Paris. There she would lose him and then try (as *he* had, and failed) to make it with the literary crowd. She stretched creamy arms, dangling bronze. Her scarlet skirt moved upward, exhibiting knees as smooth as a Gucci valise.

It occurred to Sweeney that he was *deliberately* lost. How could he have not followed the careful instructions he had gotten that morning from Brother François? But where was the dirt road leading off the canal? Where was the sign to the seminary? As a schoolboy, Sweeney had often taken the long way home, treading his sneakered feet through backyards, garbage-bright fields, coal and ice depots, in order to delay the drabness of his home. He hated going home to the bragging and criticizing of his older brother, Leo. Sweeney thought of Leo with his six kids and his wife in their big house in East Redfield, New Jersey, and he felt sorry for him. Leo Parnell Sweeney would never know the joy of being lost in the Loire Valley.

Random reminiscences of the Sweeney family disturbed him for a moment. Was he deliberately delaying his call on the seminary, in the same way he lingered in schoolyards and dusty lots to avoid his hearth? Sweeney was not certain. He liked the old Church; not in a fanatic, feverish way, as Leo did. (*That Pope John, they've gotten to him; that young Monsignor next to him, I hear tell, one*

5

of them. . . .) No, Buck Sweeney would never use his Church as a club. He was soothed and comforted by it, the cool cathedrals (he had swooned inside of Chartres), the dazzle of stained glass, the reassuring rumble of an organ. Religion's adornments delighted him. Once Allie Cooperstein took him into the Talmud Torah Tiphereth Hagro to hear the ram's horn on Rosh Hashonah. Sweeney had thrilled to its holy bleat. The Church—any Church Sweeney reasoned—in spite of all that guff about the *other* world, was like good food and good booze. Ritual had a substantive, tactile quality. Religion could be smelled, felt, stroked, tasted, digested—and stored away for future sustenance. Old tobacco leaves aging in mahogany casks; whiskey in oak barrels; so Sweeney conceived of his faith.

The girl, devoid of curiosity, asked again to be returned to Paris. Sweeney ignored her. He made a silent vow to avoid encumbrances from now on. Last night wine had undone him. A few clutches and grabs, a volley of wet kisses, a hand beneath the skirt, these were his rewards for dinner and a tour of Left Bank strip joints. *I will be punctual,* Sweeney told himself, *responsible, give a dollar's worth of effort for each dollar received, avoid dumb broads like this Westhampton Beacher, and do right by my patron.*

A teen-aged boy in minuscule shorts, pushing a bicycle, appeared on the winding road ahead of them. Sweeney brought the red torpedo to a rubber-scorching halt.

"*Hey walyo,*" he said. "Le Seminary?"

The lad's face was blank.

Sweeney made the sign of the cross. "Seminary. Students."

"Ah, *Le Seminaire.*" The youth flooded him with instructions; Sweeney understood nothing. He was cursed with a congenital resistance to foreign languages. High-school French, freshman Spanish, Berlitz Italian—all these had beaten at his unyielding mind, leaving behind a lonesome verb, an orphaned noun. Sweeney showed the boy the map he had scrawled on the back of his bill from the Ritz. The school was less than a kilometer away.

A few minutes later Sweeney saw the modest sign, and understood he had missed it because he had not looked hard enough. Partially hidden by summer leafage, it read:

SEMINAIRE ST. ÉTIENNE-SUR-LAC

He bounced the car down the dirt road. Behind him rose a volcanic cloud of red dust, and he had the sensation of entering a hideaway, of foxing pursuers.

A bell tolled four o'clock; he was an hour late. Presently the dirt road widened, and the bordering trees and hedges thinned and gave way to tangled meadows. Beyond he saw a blunted bell tower, a modest steeple, a green-bronze cross.

Sweeney wheeled the car into a gravel court, pivoted smartly around an old cistern, and parked alongside two old black Renaults. He vaulted over the door of the car, stumbled, and then extracted an attaché case and a tape recorder from the luggage compartment.

"I'll be a half hour, Dee Dee," he said.

"Half an hour? Oh, no. Why'd I let you talk me into this? Is there a bar around here?"

"I'll sneak you some sacramental wine," Sweeney said as a file of students with skirts flapping emerged from the main building. A few made comments about the car; others stared at the golden girl. Then they vanished around the courtyard. Sweeney rested a moment alongside the car. An hour's snooze under the chestnut trees was in order. Indolence and procrastination, old buddies, battled briefly with his new sense of duty. Duty prevailed. He walked to the gray stone pile, a loose-limbed, overgrown man in his middle thirties, dressed for a weekend at St. Tropez. Four young men in black crossed the court and he smiled at them.

"How ya doin' fellahs?" he asked.

"Bon jour," one said. "Américain?"

"You betcha." He envied them. "Hang in there, lefty," Sweeney called. They laughed: a comical American. Only an American would drive such a car, exhibit such a woman in a religious place, wear a lavender shirt, and carry such rich leather objects.

At the stone stairs, a dark, squat young man in a brown cassock was waiting for him. He extended a hairy hand and took the attaché case from Sweeney.

"I'm Brother François," he said, in undiluted Brooklynese. "Frankie Fellini from Borough Park. New Utrecht High School. I bet you didn't expect *that*."

"Can't say as I did, Frankie. I'm Buck Sweeney, Bronx boy myself, as a matter of fact. St. Nicholas of Tolentine. How ya doin' kid?"

Brother François shrugged. "It's a living. Only sometimes I wish I could have a Nathan's hot dog. Know what I mean?"

"Do I ever." Sweeney gave him the conspirator's wink.

"Ah—your wife. Maybe we could find a room where she'd be more comfortable. The rector's housekeeper has a room—"

"Nah. She isn't my wife. She's okay."

Brother François blushed. "I mean, it isn't often we see women, girls, and the students—"

"Hah, I getcha, Frankie. She's harmless. She won't give the boys any ideas they ain't rassling with right now."

Fellini grinned. "Come on." He led Sweeney through high wooden doors into a stone foyer. The old peace came over the visitor. St. Étienne-sur-Lac was an old, tired school—scarred benches, gloomy corridors, frosted-glass doors reinforced with chicken wire in penitentiary style.

They paused outside the last of the doors.

"The Rector's in there," Brother François said. "He's been waiting since two o'clock."

"I'm sorry. I got lost."

"Oh, well, he doesn't look at clocks anyway. Besides he had me get out the scrapbooks and the passports and the letters. And I had trouble finding them. . . . Nobody's asked about them for a long time." Brother François squinted at Sweeney in the gloom. "Maybe I'm thick or something, but I didn't quite get it this morning. Are you a reporter?"

"Ah—yes and no, Frankie." Sweeney yawned, stretching his

8

ruddy face, shivering until his tumbling black curls fluttered. He resembled a black Labrador retriever after a dip. "What kind of guy is he?" he asked. "Can I be informal with him? How's his English?"

Go back, go back! Some strangled voice pleaded with Sweeney. *Let it be, let it alone.* He scratched his temple. "Maybe I shouldn't bother him."

"He'll take you in stride," said the Brooklynite. "First off, he's an intellectual, one of the greatest linguists in Europe." The brother began enumerating the Rector's qualities on his fingers in a manner that Sweeney hadn't seen since his young manhood. "Second, his English is better than ours. Third, he isn't Barry Fitzgerald. Fourth, he's old and he's tired. Ask him what you want, he'll answer, and we'll all be happy."

The brother saw the hesitancy in Sweeney's red face. He wanted to comfort him, to be for one selfish moment part of the visitor's world of red sports cars, lavender shirts, and slender women in scarlet dresses. All hopes for that world had died many years ago on a cindery Brooklyn street corner. *Ay, Frankie, ya stink, ya lousy fairy, ya four-eyed sister-Mary!*

He opened the glass door and ushered Sweeney into the room, introducing him in excellent French. Sweeney mumbled a greeting to the old man behind the long, scarred table. The Rector waved a bony hand, motioning the caller to a high-backed chair opposite himself.

A carved crucifix was bolted to the stone wall behind Father Louis DesMoulins. Otherwise, the room was barren. The shutters were drawn. In the semidarkness Sweeney discerned some large cardboard boxes and several scrapbooks on the table.

"My eyes are bothered by sunlight," Father Louis said in a high, thin voice—an old man's voice, using itself sparingly. He dismissed Brother François.

"I can understand," Sweeney said with hypochondriac sympathy. "I got weak eyes myself. Twenty-two hundred in the right, and only partially correctible." He set up the tape recorder on the

9

table, placing the microphone at a polite distance from the Rector's gray beard. The biblical face studied the machine; it did not disturb him.

"First interview, Father Louis DesMoulins, Rector of the Seminary St. Étienne-sur-Lac, France." Sweeney spoke the words importantly into the mike, and then looked up at the priest. "They call that *slating*. So we know what's on the tape."

"*Slating*," repeated the Rector. "What is its origin?"

"I don't know, Father." Sweeney tried his boyish Irishman's grin. The Rector did not return the smile. For a moment a student terror gripped the visitor. He was back at St. Nicholas of Tolentine drowning in advanced algebra, losing the free-for-all wrestling match with Latin. There was an intellectual hardness in the Rector's face, and Sweeney was afraid of it. No Irish blarney, no Italo-American heartiness. Just a sharp intellect, and a pair of wise, cold eyes unblinking behind steel-rimmed glasses. Sweeney noted fearfully the large, domed head, the corona of gray hair, the prophetic beard, the thin nose, the unemotional mouth. A firm handshake was all you would ever get from him Sweeney realized. Not unless you were another linguist and dropped over to borrow an irregular verb.

"I guess we can start," Sweeney said cautiously.

The priest held up an arthritic hand. "Explain more fully who you are and why you are here."

Sweeney suppressed a nervous belch. "Ah, I represent an educational, an interfaith religious group, or more properly a research and statistical organization concerned with the matter at hand. You're one of the people on my list."

"You have explained nothing," said the Rector.

"Right! Right you are, padre!" And Sweeney wondered: how do I explain Sherman Wettlaufer's neurosis, his cringing fear of my brother, Leo Parnell Sweeney, and the Committee to Keep God in the Public Schools of East Redfield, New Jersey, to this old teacher?

"Well, padre," Sweeney tried, "there is this organization called the Wettlaufer Foundation. It's endowed by a wealthy American to document the deeds, during and before the last war, of people like yourself, to collect this data, and eventually to publish it and make it available to historians, scholars, sociologists, students of religion, and so forth."

"You are capable of clear expression, after all," said Father Louis. "Why were you so nervous?"

Sweeney gulped. "You scare me a little. I think I'm back at Fordham. That's a Jesuit school in New York."

Father Louis nodded. "I am familiar with it. Let us proceed."

Sweeney put his finger to the button marked *record*, then withdrew it. "Maybe some autobiographical data to start with, Father Louis?"

The Rector replied with a Gallic shrug, shoulders rising beneath the coarse brown cassock, mouth turning down. "I have lived eighty-three years, and I have forgotten a great deal. Wilfully perhaps."

"Well, just the basic facts of your life. If Father doesn't mind."

The priest nodded his agreement. Sweeney started the machine. The café-au-lait tape spun, the plastic spools rotated noiselessly. Father Louis wet his lips several times, in the manner of old men seeking verbal precision, wary of uttering anything indiscreet or inaccurate.

"There is nothing unusual about my childhood or my coming of age. My father was a greengrocer. I am lower middle class, a bourgeois. My family has lived in the village of Moyenne Terre, seventy kilometers from here, for centuries. The town clerk, the village butcher, the postmistress are all related to me. I was a studious child and was sent to the seminary at Les Marches. In time I was ordained and served a parish near Saumur, but soon found I preferred teaching and learning, particularly in the field of language origins. In a sense, I was a failure as a pastor. Too often I was more concerned with grammar than with souls.

"So I retired to a monastery and pursued my studies. Carlyle once said that language is the flesh-garment, the body of thought.

Reading and speaking Hebrew, I better understood Isaiah and Joel and Daniel. Knowledge of English took me, perhaps with too much joy for a priest, into Shakespeare's great heart. I learned German, and Goethe enriched my life." He held up a twisted hand. "But you did not come here to learn about my studies."

"Oh, please," said Sweeney—enchanted with the Rector's sweet and sensible words. "Anything, anything you want to tell me. Something that happened at the seminary that influenced you in the work you did later?"

"My student days. Yes." He shook his large head. "Oh, we were filled with *esprit*. Religion was simpler then. I can remember a bishop coming to address us. A stout man with a loud voice. He stirred us to cheers and shouts. I cheered also, although normally I was a shy fellow."

"What was all the cheering about?"

"Dreyfus, of course." Father Louis said this as if the captain's case were still pending, a matter of current interest, something of which the American would be fully aware.

"I bet it was a great speech," Sweeney said stupidly.

"Indeed it was. This bishop, and I cannot remember his name or his seat, made an interesting point. As nearly as I can recollect, he said that it was no longer a question as to whether the Captain was innocent or guilty, but only of who would win—the friends or the foes of the Church."

Sweeney shut off the recorder. The spools stopped. "Hmmm," he mumbled. "Hmmm. A fascinating point."

Father Louis closed his eyes. A breeze from the cloister infiltrated the shuttered windows and agitated his beard. *This survey,* Sweeney said to himself, *is not about the Dreyfus case. We got enough trouble with the six million we're working on without exhuming that fellow who was once portrayed by Joseph Schildkraut.* In his marbled mind, Sweeney recalled the actor clutching the bars of his cell and screaming: *Innocent! Innocent!*

"Ah, maybe we could skip right up to World War II, Father," he said. "Right to the heart of the matter."

12

But Father Louis appeared to have dozed off. His eyes were closed, his head drooped, and he was nodding faintly. Put a yarmulka on him, Sweeney reflected, and he could be in the front row at Talmud Torah Tiphereth Hagro, where once Sweeney heard them blow the ram's horn, and where, on occasion, he had worked as *shabbes goy.*

"You are right, young man," the Rector said faintly. "You wish to hear about the Jews."

"Yes, indeed."

"There is no avoiding them. They are our conscience."

"Oh, I wouldn't go that far, padre."

"You have not witnessed what I have witnessed. I will be pleased to talk about them. They have been a part of my life."

That was it! That was what Wettlaufer wanted! Sweeney almost leaped from his oaken chair. "Right, right, padre! Right on the button! You're a step ahead of me!" He turned the recorder on.

"I did what I could for the Jews. It was little enough." The Rector sighed, shaking his great head, a head crammed with Latin roots and Greek syntaxes and Hebrew conjugations, a head so loaded with knowledge that Sweeney marveled that it could also be filled with compassion and courage.

"Go to it, padre. Tell it!"

"We can begin my story on the 16th of July, 1942. Does that date signify anything to you?"

"No, sir. July 14 is Bastille Day."

"Correct. The Germans postponed it for two days so as not to hurt the feelings of the French, and in fact, to rally French support to their efforts."

"What did they postpone?"

Father Louis' eyes widened behind the functional eyeglasses, and gave dramatic emphasis to his words. "*Le grand rafle. Le rafle des Juifs de Paris.*"

"I am sorry, Father, my French is very bad. I just got something about Jews."

Again, he began that patriarchal nodding, and again Sweeney

saw him at *schul* on Friday night. He thought of Allie Cooperstein's story about the old Jewish grandfather complaining to his grandson that he could not hear the boy's mumbled prayers, and the child replying, *Who's talking to you?* He had the sensation that now Father Louis was not talking to him—that his ramblings were nobody's business but his own.

"The sweep-up. The big sweep-up of the Jews of Paris."

"I think we would say roundup."

"Ah! The exact expression." The linguist was alert. "Yes, an American western idiom having to do with the collection of cattle. This roundup took place on July 16. Up to that time I had stood by silently. What could I do? A penniless teacher of languages at a seminary? A man who had never performed a rash deed in his life? Oh, many had already acted bravely. The Archbishop of Toulouse, a noble man, ordered his clergy to preach against the arrests, and many did. Priests were arrested in Lyon for harboring Jewish children. My friend the Jesuit, Father Marechal, was among those jailed.

"In sum, and in comparison with many other countries of Christian Europe, I suppose we French came off rather well. We saved 275,000 Jews. We lost seventy-five thousand to the Germans. How terrible to think in these barren ciphers! What frightful arithmetic."

"You were talking about the roundup."

"The main collection point was a race course called the Velodrôme d'Hiver. The Germans were angered that so many Jews were still at large, perhaps twenty-two thousand. They caught approximately half of them. I regret to inform you that many French policemen, including many who heard our priests' admonitions, assisted the Germans. About seven thousand of these Jews were sent to the Velodrôme. Perhaps as many as four thousand were children."

The Rector paused; he was breathing unevenly. Finally he asked: "Mr. Sweeney, is it possible that the world is bored with these events? This organization you represent, is it possible it is mistaken in pursuing these stories? Much has been written."

"Oh, but not from your standpoint. I mean from the viewpoint of people like you, who helped. The good people."

"I am not that good. I do not know who can define goodness in such times. Perhaps what was demanded of us was *sanctity*, a state for which I am unsuited. Few of us achieve it."

"You were brave," said Sweeney.

"Perhaps I should have chosen to die with the Jews."

"No, no," Sweeney protested. "That would be carrying things too far."

"It is said that Paris is the most civilized city in the world," the Rector continued. "One must imagine then this Velodrôme, this sports arena, crowded with innocents. Seven thousand people with no food, no blankets, a single pump for water, no sanitation. Many people had been arrested in bedclothes, some were almost naked. The endless weeping of frightened children.

"At that time, I was teaching Oriental Languages at the École St. Blais. A Jewish family who owned a small *papeterie*, from whom I would buy journals, were among those arrested. One day they were there with their little inefficient business, living in a cramped room at the back of the shop—the next day swallowed up, *vanished*.

"On the afternoon of July 18 I wrote on the blackboard that I was ill, advised the Rector I would visit a physician, and walked across Paris to the stadium. I was two streets away when I heard the shrieks, the weeping."

He rested his forehead on his hand, shaking his professorial head. "What an odd recollection has come to me. On the street where I had stopped—it was lovely, shaded with chestnut trees, with a little park to one side, a row of shops—on that street where I first heard the cries, a little carousel was operating. It was one of those hand-cranked carousels with small painted horses. The children were all very young. Each child had a wooden baton, and as they rode around they tried to snatch a metal ring from a bar with their little sticks. It was so innocent! I saw the mothers laughing at their children and the children thrusting out their tiny fists to try to snare the rings!

15

"And rising above the happy music of the carousel I could hear the cries of Israel. What awful circumstances of history, I wondered, what terrible judgment, had decreed that Jews must die behind the walls of a stadium while Christians watch their children ride carousels?

"I argued my way past two gendarmes and presented myself to an SS sergeant who was guarding the main door. Even as I stood there, inventing a tale about a family of converts, Catholics I called Mulhous, who were personally known to me and for whom I would vouch, a truck stopped and unloaded new victims. Among them was a fat man in shirt sleeves who looked at me as if to say: *why me and not you?*

"I lied vigorously and protested with full moral fervor. Lies are potent when repeated often enough. My brown cassock, my crucifix no doubt helped. I was admitted."

The Rector sighed, shut his eyes, then resumed his narrative.

"Now, Mr. Sweeney, what I was to witness in the Velodrôme did more to educate me in the ways of our sinful world than all the years I had spent in libraries. More than half of these Jews were children. Many were infants. The filth was unbelievable, the stench appalling. It was the third day following the *rafle*. As yet no one had been fed. At the single pump, an endless queue stretched across the arena waiting to fill cans, old bottles.

"The SS man and myself wandered across the stadium asking for my fictitious family. As we walked the Jews clutched at my robe, grasped my hand, begged, pleaded, wept. Many were Eastern Europeans, people who had fled the Germans. They cried to me in Polish and Yiddish—both of which I speak. I dared not reply. In one row of the stands I could see an old man and an old woman desperately trying to temper the insane ravings of a young man in dirty pajamas. There was a bandage wrapped around this man's head and it kept unraveling, and the old woman would try to tie it. The young man kept screaming: *Ich vill essen! Daff aheim gehn!* I must eat! I want to go home! And the old woman kept saying to him: *Sha, sha, mein kind,* stroking his cheek. . . .

16

"I watched all this—the weeping, the terror, the murder of dignity—and I thought my heart would burst with compassion, and with fear. I pretended to search for my converts, conceded they were not there, and thanked the sergeant for his kindness.

"He smiled at me, and said, 'I am a Catholic myself, Father, from Nuremberg.' I said to him, 'Well, my son, be gentle with these unfortunates.'

"He was a beautiful young man with rosy cheeks and hair the color of cornsilk, and he smiled again, that strange flat smile of the Teuton. 'Oh, we will, Father,' he assured me, 'this is only a temporary arrangement. But anyway, they are not only enemies of the Reich, but also the cursed enemies of our faith.'

" 'No, no,' I said, 'they are only poor Jews.'

"And he laughed and replied: 'The same thing, Father.'

"I returned to the seminary and advised the Rector that we were being less than Christian if we did not aid the Jews. I hasten to add that many priests and nuns of France, especially in rural areas where it was easier to hide Jews, were already engaged in this work. Our tardiness embarrassed us, so after a meeting that lasted the night we decided that rather than attempt to sequester a handful of Jews in our small school we would undertake a wholesale rescue operation. We would become forgers and counterfeiters for the Israelites.

"One of the brothers was an expert engraver, another knew something about printing. In the cellar of the seminary we assembled printing presses, inks, papers, true passports, and cartes d'identité. I contacted Jewish organizations and secured more engravers and printers and professional counterfeiters. In a week's time our presses began to function. We tried our hand first at Swiss passports but botched them badly. Our inks were not true enough. But in time we learned, and soon the papers began to appear throughout Paris—reproductions of passports, cards of identity, baptismal certificates, wedding certificates, letters from employers, governmental documents, each one as precious as penicillin to a man dying of infection. Oh, how our lives are ruled by paper! What crimes are committed on parchment and vellum! And praise God, how many good deeds can be achieved with colored inks, cardboard, and the forger's steady hand!"

The old man's eyes were bright with memories of his deceits. He opened a large blood-colored box, the type used to store legal papers. "An example of our craft. Now, there is as perfect a Portuguese passport as you can find. It has done honorable service, a noble fraud."

Sweeney took the frayed booklet and opened its yellowed pages. A young woman's photograph, vague, smudged, stared at him. Beneath it was a signature: *Maria Pereira.*

"Who was she?" Sweeney asked.

"I do not remember. A Jewish woman marked for deportation and death. We got her into Spain and then to Portugal. She mailed it to me after the war as did many of the people. How I wish I had had a million of these instead of several thousand." He shuffled through the peculiar treasure and took out a dark-blue booklet.

"Here is a remarkable collector's item," the old man said. "It is our duplication of a German identity booklet, given to nationals of neutral states in occupied areas. We made so many of these on a yellow-gray paper that people holding the genuine booklets—on the original white paper—became suspect. Our forgery became more acceptable than the original document. Thus false became true, right became wrong."

Sweeney examined the documents, marveling at their power. He had a moment's vision of the priest deep in his seminary cellar cranking up the primitive presses, staining his cassock with red ink, painfully re-creating signatures, seals, perforations.

"You must have been in danger," Sweeney said.

"Now that is very odd," the priest said. "I myself was never in danger. Perhaps the Germans assumed I was a harmless old teacher. I had many dealings with them and I lied to them endlessly. Most importantly, I never failed to take the moral initiative with them. I made them feel I was their moral superior, that there

18

was something shameful about what they were doing. It is good to remember this when dealing with ideologues—Fascists, Bolsheviks, or racists. Make them understand, when all is said and done, that they are *inferior people*.

"We expanded our operations from mere counterfeiting to smuggling. We had liaison with Jewish groups in the south of France, in Italy, in neutral states. We were smuggling more and more contraband Jews, equipped with our false papers, into Spain, Switzerland, North Africa. I traveled a great deal, on the pretext of gathering information for a grammar on Romance languages. I carried dictionaries, notebooks, wherever I went. I am sure they suspected me, but I played the fool, the pedant, the mouldy scholar. I lied and dissembled perpetually. I committed a variety of dishonest, distasteful acts."

Weariness began to collapse Sweeney. The wine, the rich creamy foods, the useless woman waiting for him outside, and now the flood of information that he had listened to and recorded—all these conspired to enervate him. Worst of all (although he was only fleetingly aware of it) the blinding nobility of the old priest, almost too pure and too good for a wicked and cynical world, instead of inspiring him tended to wear him down. The world, Sweeney thought, respected only power and amusement; all else could be prudently ignored. Wettlaufer would never understand.

But Father Louis had warmed up to his subject. He was no longer tired. "Some time in 1943 I was denounced to the Vatican by a secret informant, and summoned to Rome to explain my activities. The Gestapo told the Holy See that I was helping Communists escape. There was some truth to that. Perhaps there were Communists among the many we saved. But to me they were suffering people—men, women, children. Ah, the children."

Again, he rested his head on his palm. "Many children died in the Velodrôme. Many were separated from their parents—forever. They were sent to a collection point at Drancy, and then to Auschwitz. At Drancy they were detained in filthy rooms, and then removed a roomful at a time to the goods wagons. Somehow, with the clear instinctive knowledge which is God's gift to children, and which so often reflects beauty and wisdom, these children *knew*, better than the adults, what was to happen to them. They screamed, they refused to leave the rooms. The Jewish adults who were ordered to bring them down refused. Soon the screaming became a frenzy. So the French police, under orders from the Germans, would drag them out, the children struggling and shrieking. Not all of them got to Auschwitz."

"They were rescued?" asked Sweeney feebly.

"No, no. Months later the goods wagons returned for new passengers. In Belgium, the railwaymen were cleaning out the vans. They found the crushed bodies of twenty-five Jewish children, tiny creatures aged two and three. They had never reached the chambers but had paid the penalty of being—*communists?*"

"How terrible," Sweeney moaned. "That's why what you did was so important!"

"I failed in many instances. We evolved a scheme for moving fifty thousand Jews from France to North Africa. When I was summoned to Rome for censure, I broached this to the Holy Father, an act of audacity on my part. He responded favorably. But the plan came to nothing when Italy surrendered and the Germans poured into southern France.

"By this time we were experiencing difficulties at the Spanish border. Many of our documents were suspect. So while in Rome, after seeing the failure of our grand plan, I prevailed upon the Holy See to appoint me *impartial arbiter* of refugees entering Spain from France. In effect I was passing judgment on my own forgeries. I found them all in order.

"Once a party of Hasidic Jews, awaiting secret entry into Spain and hiding in caves—no amount of false documentation could disguise the Hasidim—taught me certain rare Hebrew verb forms on which I later wrote a monograph. It was the first of its kind in any Western language."

Sweeney could think of nothing else to ask. He leaned toward the boxes. "May I look at them?" he asked.

20

"Please. The gratitude of these people sustains me in my old age. The poet wrote that old age hath yet its honor and its toil, and God has blessed me doubly in seeing that I may still toil and still be honored by these remembrances."

Sweeney picked up a letter written in French. The printed letterhead read:

Louis Salomon
West Cedar Road
Roslyn, Long Island

"From a family of Alsatian Jews," the Rector said. "They now live in a state called Long Island, which I am told is of great beauty. They have grandchildren and a son in the university. They send me letters at Christmas and Rosh Hashonah."

Sweeney thumbed through the letters, noting their geographical diversity—Buenos Aires, Tel Aviv, Brooklyn, London. . . . Outside, beyond the cooling shutters, bees and grasshoppers hummed a summer threnody. Thin shafts of light from the lowering sun slanted across the oak table. Father Louis clasped his hands on his cassock and shut his eyes.

As Sweeney riffled through the papers, some letters, filed separately from the rest, fell out.

"Do these belong with the others?" he asked.

Father Louis glanced at them. "No, those are copies of my own correspondence. This is one I wrote to Chambertin in 1941. He was the Vichy commissioner for Jewish affairs, an eminent anti-Semite of pure French origins."

"Why did you write to him?" Sweeney asked, recalling that the old man had not begun his counterfeiting until 1942.

"I suppose I saw what fate was in store for the Jews. I thought I would write to Chambertin, whose nephew had once been my student, to see if I might appeal to his sensibilities. I shall translate the letter."

Father Louis lowered his eyeglasses and began to read.

"Esteemed Chambertin, and so on. No Christian, and particu-

21

larly no Frenchman, should permit himself the error of hating and persecuting Jews. Pagans and atheists, understandably, may from time to time indulge this irrational passion. But it is illogical and ungrateful for a Christian to so act. First, the Jewish religion is the mother of Christianity. Secondly, the Ten Commandments are the charter of civilization. Thirdly, our Saviour and all his Apostles were Jews. M. Chambertin must realize, that in enacting anti-Jewish laws he is persecuting the people who founded Christianity."

"Attaboy, padre," Sweeney cried. "I bet you brought him up short."

"If that expression means that I changed Chambertin's mind you are mistaken. Let me read to you his response."

The rector unfolded a second letter, this one on official-looking stationery. "Chambertin waited several weeks before answering. By then the first anti-Semitic laws were in effect—expropriation of properties, travel restrictions, the usual. He acknowledged my arguments, and then sought to give me a lesson in history. Listen.

" 'Father Louis must know that these Jews of modern Europe bear no relationship whatever to the founders of our Faith. Many of them, indeed, are the scum of Eastern Europe, people with no ties with France. They are largely Bolsheviks, Trotskyites, socialists, and a variety of intriguers against the public order on the civil level and, on the philosophical level, atheists, materialists, and Gnostics, who gnaw at the roots of mystical Christianity. May I remind Father Louis that only fifty years ago our beloved Church led the crusade against the traitor Dreyfus, that symbol of Freemasonry and Jewish materialism, whose guilt is a matter of record.

" 'The good father must know that the Jesuits, whom I am proud to say educated me, led the battle against this Israelite traitor. Let Father Louis, whom I respect, direct his critical letters to his own Church, and not to me, a humble government servant.' "

Father Louis waved the letter. "Chambertin then concluded with a quotation from St. Louis, a much cited one, in which that

great man, in step with his age, and erring as even saints may err, advised his fellow Christians not to indulge in disputes with Jews in the fear of losing such arguments. Rather, St. Louis advised, they should drive their swords through the bellies of disputatious Jews."

"What did you do after Chambertin wrote you that letter?" Sweeney asked.

"Nothing, except pray. Until the rafle and the events at the Velodrôme d'Hiver. He disarmed me for a long time. He was a stupid man, a bigot, an opportunist, but he forced me into prolonged and pained meditation. Some equation eluded me, some formula which might embrace Christ and the Apostles, and St. Louis, and Dreyfus. I am too old to carry this exercise in historical accident, in theological marginalia, any further. You may continue to study the letters and documents. I will have Brother François bring us cognac."

Twenty minutes later, Brother François, the former Frankie Fellini of Brooklyn, eavesdropped outside the old priest's door. He heard no voices, only a rhythmic slapping sound and some heavy snoring. After a moment's hesitation, he inched the door open and entered.

He was confronted with this tableau:

Father Louis and the American visitor had both fallen asleep. The old man was sleeping bolt upright in his high chair, his arms locked across his chest. He was not dead, François assured himself, because his stertorous breathing fluttered his beard. Sweeney was noisier, more slovenly. He sprawled insensate, limbs outstretched, arms dangling, his yellow suede shoes pointing outward and upward. One of the scrapbooks rested athwart his abdomen, rising and falling with his snores.

In counterpoint to the snoring was a sharper rhythmic sound. It was the magnetic tape, which had run out but was still rotating, slapping its loose end against the plastic reel.

23

"Mr. Sweeney, Mr. Sweeney," said the brother, tapping the American's arm.

The visitor growled, then opened his eyes. "Hmmm? Whazzat?"

"You fell asleep."

"Jeez." A mammoth yawn distorted Sweeney's ruddy face. He raised his long body and turned off the recorder. "Holy smoke," he said. "The old guy conked out also. What a pair of sports. Couple of live wires." He replaced the scrapbook on the table and stood up. "Gaah. Yaaah." He stretched, and his overloaded gut protested. A headache pecked at his frontal lobes. He was intolerably thirsty.

"Hey Frankie," Sweeney said. "The old man was going to ask you for cognac. I sorely need some. Seems like I been asleep for hours."

Father Louis' eyes opened, as if he were a child who had been faking sleep. "My apologies, Mr. Sweeney. Old age has not only its honor and its toil, but its failings. François, some cognac. Our visitor will need sustenance if he continues these interrogations."

The old priest leaned forward. "What I have told you is a mere fairy tale compared to what you will hear about Eastern Europe. Poland, the Ukraine, Hungary. Arm yourself with the courage of youth. Pray. Attend mass."

Brother François departed. Sweeney sat down and opened his caramel-colored attaché case. From it he extracted a manila folder and from this he drew out an engraved certificate, suggesting a diploma or a municipal bond on the order of the City of Spokane, Power and Lighting Issue. It was tastefully printed in black and gold, with elaborate blue crosshatchings, Old English lettering, and rococo borders.

"Father Louis, this organization for which I am conducting this survey," Sweeney began, as embarrassment drowned him, "this organization has authorized me to present you with this citation, citing you as a member of an honored group of Europeans. With it goes a check for one thousand American dollars, which our

patron, Mr. Sherman Wettlaufer, of East Redfield, New Jersey, will send to you or to your favorite charity, or any other purpose you may designate."

He hurled a silent curse on Wettlaufer's head for having euchred him into this fool's role and handed the handsome paper to the old man.

"I am honored," said the priest. He raised his spectacles and slowly read the title at the head of the certificate. *"The Legion of Noble Christians.* That is very impressive. It flatters me. Please thank your patron. I cannot deny I am a Christian, but I wonder how noble I am. Who is this gentleman?"

"A rich American of my acquaintance."

Father Louis nodded and then began to read: *"The Wettlaufer Foundation cites Father Louis DesMoulins for his courageous assistance to the Jews of Europe during the recent . . ."*

"And the money will come in a month or so, when I wind up," Sweeney added lamely.

"Please thank the gentleman. I shall give the money to the orphanage."

Brother François returned with a decanter and two glasses. He poured and the old priest and Sweeney raised their glasses.

"To what shall we drink?" asked the Rector.

"I don't know, padre. I don't always dedicate my drinking."

"Well, then. To Malachi, a good old prophet. 'Have we not all one father?' "

"I'll buy it," Sweeney responded, and gulped the cognac, re-
joicing in its warmth. He accepted a refill, drank it swiftly feeling
liver and lights respond joyously, and packed his tape recorder and attaché case.

He shook hands with the old priest, thanked him, and walked toward the door with Frankie Fellini. Then he stopped.

"Maybe I'm stupid, Father Louis," said Sweeney hesitantly, "but I don't get it. I mean the basic thing. Why you did it. Risking your life. I mean, you could have got into trouble. All those forgeries and counterfeiting—oh, I don't suggest that was any *problem* to an intelligent man like you—but the whole bit. When you coulda played it *safe*. Most people don't take chances, most people play it safe. You could have gone on studying, and teaching, and said, 'I'm safe.' You see I keep asking myself, 'What would you, Bernard Kevin Sweeney, have done?' and I get the answer, 'Probably nothing.' Like most people. I know I'm being a pest—but, why? Why'd you do it?"

"Why? Recall, young man, what I wrote to Chambertin."

"Heck, it's no secret Our Lord was a Jew, or that Jews invented the Ten Commandments. In a sense I guess they invented God. If people realized that, there never would have been a Hitler. Or even if there had been, every single person in Europe should have stood up and said, 'No, *don't you dare*.'"

Father Louis closed his eyes. "It is a complicated matter, Mr. Sweeney."

Brother François tugged at Sweeney's lavender shirt and whispered, "Let him alone, he's tired."

"You need not mention this in your report," Father Louis said. "Scout's honor."

"I engaged in this work because . . . I was ashamed not to be a Jew." Then he seemed to doze off again, folding his arms on his brown cassock.

Sweeney passed through the frosted-glass door, ignoring a reproachful look from Brother François. His stomach churned, his brow ached.

In the courtyard Sweeney found that his car was gone. Dee Dee, or Weezy, or whatever the accessory's name was, had left a note with Brother François.

Dear Clown,
You made me late for a date with your dopey interview. I'll leave the heap at the Place Vendôme. It's been nothing.

That was more like it! Sweeney rejoiced in the girl's sturdy, dependable selfishness, the kind of brainless self-love that makes life worth living. Father Louis had been too noble, too good, to be subjected to for very long.

26

Brother François offered to drive him to Chinon where he would be able to catch a bus to Tours, then another to Paris.

Once more, Sweeney crossed the bridge over the Vienne.

"See that little island down there?" Brother François asked. "That's the Ile de Tours. I caught the old man praying there one day, all by himself."

Sweeney looked at the island—a sliver of shrubs and yellow buildings in the midst of the river. "How come?" he asked.

"Well, he wouldn't let on," the Brother said, "but I found out later it's the place where they burned a hundred and sixty Jews alive in 1317. Threw 'em all into a big open furnace."

"What for?" Sweeney was appalled.

"Oh, something about the Jews poisoning the drinking water or getting the lepers to poison it. They burned a lot of lepers, too. You know, it was the fourteenth century."

Several days after his interview with Father Louis, Sweeney lay on a bed of pain in the Amigo Hotel in Brussels. The previous night he had interrupted his pursuit of noble Christians with some frenzied eating and drinking; now he suffered. He was convinced he had contracted bulbar poliomyelitis, or perhaps bronchial pneumonia. His lungs felt constricted. His heart fibrillated. He breathed with rattling irregularity. "*Râles*," he said aloud, "the grim herald announcing my death. Come and get me, pal!"

Satisfied with this diagnosis, he staggered in jockey shorts from the luxurious Empire bed to a blonde coffee table, where were arrayed a variety of Belgian beers. He drained a bottle of *Trappiste*, thick, strong stuff brewed by monks. It set him to coughing. His face blossomed with crimson splotches. In the ormolu mirror he cringed at his piebald features and muttered: "I'm finished. As perfect a textbook case of *lupus vulgaris* as ever I saw. Goodbye, Buck."

Then he noticed he was running low on beer, so he telephoned for a half-dozen bottles of cherry-flavored *Geuze* and some wheat-based *Faro*. With them came a telegram from Sherman Wettlaufer. Sweeney, scowling at this intrusion, a burden to a dying man, read it with mingled disgust and pity.

DEAR BUCK YOUR FIRST REPORTS URGENTLY AWAITED STOP OUR PHONE RINGS EVERY MORNING AT FOUR AYEM THEN THEY HANG UP STOP I KNOW ITS YOUR BROTHER LEO'S FRIENDS STOP PLEASE PLEASE SEND ME FIRST INTERVIEWS SO I CAN PUBLICIZE THEM SOOTHE MYSELF STOP DO YOU NEED MONEY ANYTHING AT ALL JUST ASK REGARDS

SHERMAN

He crumpled it and tossed it in a high arc, banking it off a walnut escritoire and into a wastebasket papered with a view of Bruges. Guiltily he reminded himself to airmail Father Louis' tape to Sherman, aware that he would surely forget to do so unless he wrote it down. But he wrote nothing as he sipped at a fresh bottle of sweetish Geuze.

"Cherry-flavored beer, Jesus," Sweeney mumbled. "No wonder they blew the whole Congo."

Old habits engulfed him—sluggishness, boredom, aimlessness. *Story of my life,* Sweeney thought miserably. *Never finished anything I started.*

And so, he suspected, it would be with his current assignment. His eyes rested on the thick wad of traveler's checks—almost four thousand dollars worth—on the escritoire. Sherman's money, Sherman's gift. What have you bought, Wettlaufer old friend? To whom have you entrusted your money and your heart?

"I'll tell ya, Sherm!" he shouted hoarsely. "To old Buck Sweeney—king of the freeloaders!"

Still, Sweeney's mean estimate of himself was not shared by the Europeans with whom he came in contact that hot summer. His manner was polite, his voice loud but not overbearing, his attitude jocular, tolerant. Like most Americans, he often apologized in advance for imagined rudenesses.

In appearance he suggested any spoiled and stomachy American bachelor on holiday. "Yes, folks," Sweeney, in manic elation would shout from behind the wheel of his speeding MG, "I'm the young urban sophisticate! The whole world is for me, and I'm all for it!"

Had Sweeney been daintier and less boisterous he might have passed for a homosexual. But he could claim no credit there, even though his mode of dress and manner of speech suggested New York, show biz, advertising, and certain Third Avenue bars. Tall and big-boned, a thick-wristed, thick-ankled man in his middle thirties, he was more peasant than ephebe. Years ago, in a savage young manhood, Sweeney had conveyed a wild rakish quality—the hot-shot Bronx Irishman, the lean lifeguard at Orchard Beach, swordsman and wiseacre. Now he had settled flabbily into the style of a sharp ad agency or network Irishman, a buyer of long windy lunches for paint manufacturers from Akron, Ohio.

His face was a good face, a happy amalgam of Dublin, the Hampton Beaches, Fordham Road, Greenwich Village. A rich red coloration suffused the stubby features. Prolonged drinking or the strains of a starched collar intensified this redness, which would wax iridescent, purpling at the collar line, blending into scarlets, carmines, and vermilions, on up to a pale pink scalp.

Above this rufous face sprouted the lush black curls of an Eastern rebellion dynamiter. One raffish lock fell over the uncluttered forehead. The eyes were a guileless interrogating blue— as if Sweeney were forever posing a question or dubious of what he had just heard. This doubting quality was heightened by black eyebrows which pointed upward, forming a sable arch at mid-forehead. One could almost hear the questions being asked by these innocent eyes and raised brows: *Who did it? How come? What's the score? Where's the booze?* Most frequently they seemed to inquire: *Why me?*

Short-nosed, loose-lipped, white-toothed (two projecting incisors, more pronounced in boyhood, had earned him his nickname of Buck), the Sweeney visage advertised a compromise with life, an affection for its own skin, and a capacity to survive. There was no cruelty in it, and a fair amount of unused intelligence. It was not a face one would depend upon, but it was surely not a face to be feared.

Sweeney's career, prior to his present job, had been a tasteless salad culled from the poorer vegetable gardens of the talker world. For sixteen years following his discharge from the army, he had worked variously as a minor deskman for a press association, a poll taker, a press agent for nightclub singers, a writer for a junior encyclopedia, a promotion man for a firm manufacturing pet medicines. "I walked out," Sweeney would tell his Third Avenue friends, "the day they had me ramming Vitamin D suppositories up a Great Dane's ass in a goddamn demonstration booth at the Westminster Kennel Club Show. I mean, a man has to keep some dignity."

This canine association had been Sweeney's nadir. He envisioned his future grimly—a weekly slab in Bellevue, drying out after long, corrosive binges. His brother urged him to take holy orders—that was all that could save him. But Sweeney shyly demurred. "I'd do the faith no credit, Leo," he said. "They don't need the likes of me, although I sure need *them*."

But he was saved anyway; Bellevue was spared his sodden body. Sweeney discovered the magic of the free-load. He became a classic sponger, a man forever on the take. It was ridiculously simple. Invited to Westhampton Beach one weekend, he crashed a party high on the windswept dunes. The guests were parking-lot tycoons, rainwear manufacturers, vending-machine kings. At once they sniffed out that Sweeney was part of the *other* world, that happy valley of fags, pot smokers, writers who never wrote, wife beaters, all the important *inside* people. Fat men who were worth millions, and their clanking wives, women with cement-hard rumps in tight chartreuse pants, figured Sweeney for the *real thing*. A few ladies who knew about these matters thought he might be Dylan Thomas or Brendan Behan.

Soon he was tending bar (something he was genuinely good at—son of the late James John Sweeney, owner of an old-fashioned saloon in the Bronx). He told funny stories, he recalled how he put Norman and Jimmy in their place, and at three in the morning he wrapped a mink coat around his shoulders and sat in a deck chair listening to his host's confession.

The poor man hungered for better things. Father Sweeney absolved him. On the tongue of commerce he placed the wafer of art. The rich man (a cunning raider of shaky corporations) insisted that Sweeney move into the great glass house "to help me write my memories." In time the biography became a novel, a play, a movie, a magazine article. Not a word was written but Sweeney was brilliant; guests loved him. He had the best summer of his life. His host told him blushingly, "If there is one thing I seek, Buck, it is gracious living, and you have taught me to live graciously."

August ended, and Sweeney glided naturally into what seemed an inevitable destiny—emissary, counselor, guide, friend, collaborator to the newly rich. They cheered loudly for Sweeney—friendly Irishman, unmilitant Mick, writer, joker, bartender, a man without bias or anger. Most of his early clients were wealthy Jews, but soon he was fully nonsectarian and had several Gentile benefactors. Never had he lived so well, given so little in return for so much, and been so loved.

"But not you, Sherman," Sweeney said aloud, as his reminiscences ended. "Not you, Sherm. You're different. Jesus, I wouldn't dream of sponging off you."

Saying this, he wondered. Since leaving Father Louis at the seminary, his course had been erratic. He had attempted a second interview, with another elderly French priest. Father Gascar had organized a corps of young bicyclists who combed the countryside appealing to French peasants to shelter Jewish children. It was a marvelous story but the old priest was not as communicative as Father Louis. His memory wavered, his speech was hesitant, the interpreter was inept.

Sweeney shelved his survey and turned to the Paris literary

31

crowd, announcing himself as a "belle-lettrist" on assignment from the *American Scholar*. None of them was deceived. It took one to know one. They had begun their careers as Sweeneys. They wrote a magazine piece every two years, a thin novel, either self-pityingly biographical or consciously salacious or both, every six years. No parking-lot owners, they looked with glazed eyes at Buck Sweeney and cut him.

Guilt drove him out of Paris. He sped to Brussels in search of a woman named Huguette Pelletier, now married to a certain Pierre Roux. Through a Belgian journalist named Emile Gevaert, a fellow who spoke excellent English and hired out as an interpreter, he located her quickly. A meeting was arranged at a café in the Grand' Place.

Heavy with *waterzooi* (plump chicken afloat in creamy herb-laced sauce), Sweeney had sauntered from his hotel the previous night to the Grand' Place for the rendezvous. He was thrilled; a carnival was taking place! A bandstand occupied the center of the square, and four young Belgians, badly needing haircuts, clad in narrow suits, were thwacking electric guitars.

Around the square rose the splendid town hall, the old palace, the ornate guildhalls, rich with gold leaf and heavy sculpture. People with Memling faces jammed themselves against the stage and listened with Flemish impassivity as the boys shouted:

Cherry, Cherry bay-by!
Cherry, Cherry bay-by!

Sweeney, lugging his tape recorder and his attaché case, squirmed to the front of the bandstand. "Go, men, go!" he shouted. "Beat it out, kids. Yaaah!"

The sturdy burghers of Belgium laughed indulgently at this comical American. Women with Brueghelian potato noses, men with the indestructible look of Van Dyck saints, smiled and nudged one another.

Emile Gevaert, the journalist who had met Sweeney that afternoon, elbowed his way through the mob and waited discreetly until the musical selection was over. Cymbals clanged, the guitars shuddered in a long, sickly chord that echoed around the façades of the great guildhalls. Sweeney applauded. "That's America, boy! We sure got the inborn sense of rhythm!"

Gevaert greeted him. He said that Mme Roux was waiting at the café. They strolled across the floodlit plaza and Sweeney asked the journalist about the feast.

"It is the Brueghelienne. You will notice the stalls selling mussels and snails. The idea is to eat as much as you can. They are cheap and fresh, and are supposed to be good for one's sex organs. I myself abhor this kind of nonsense."

The square was lined with pushcarts heaped high with shiny mussels, enormous brown snails. Old ladies split them deftly, and sold them to the assembled celebrants, who sucked the live tissue from the shell noisily.

"Man, I got to try some," Sweeney said. Gevaert, a gloomy, undersized man in a lumpy black suit, protested. "Mme Roux is waiting."

But Sweeney was already on his first dozen mussels, slurping them from the shell, sucking them in quivering and alive. He put the first batch away faster than two snowy-haired old ladies could open them, then swallowed twelve more. There was a ripple of applause from the admiring Belgians, and Sweeney bowed. "The night is young, folks. Hang around and watch Sweeney set a new outdoor record."

Gevaert, as they resumed their promenade across the plaza, appeared disdainful of the gaiety. "I find these attempts to recover our past embarrassing. At heart we remain greedy and corrupt, betrayed by politicians and by America."

"Come on, Emile," Sweeney said. "You don't mean that, do you. What are you, a commie or something?"

"I beg your pardon?"

"A lousy Red? A Bolshevik?"

"I am a socialist, an intellectual."

Sweeney put an arm around the little man's shoulders. "So

what, Emile? Don't spoil other people's fun. I'll stake you to a dozen clams."

Gevaert disengaged his arm. "Please. I am a professional journalist. I do not accept bribes."

They found Mme Huguette Pelletier Roux seated alone in a crowded sidewalk café at the north end of the plaza. She shook hands with Sweeney—a swift, impersonal European handshake—and exchanged greetings with Gevaert.

"Mme Roux says she is sorry to make you come here tonight to meet her. She is here because her husband is playing first cornet with the railway workers band."

Sweeney waved his hand generously. "I wouldna missed this show for anything. You thank her for me, thanks from Buck Sweeney."

Gevaert translated, and the Belgian woman smiled. She was not a bad looking broad, Sweeney thought. She had clear skin and nicely done up brown hair, big bright eyes, and one of those remarkable tripartite Gallic noses. There was a little false start at the bridge, then the nose changed direction and went into a long slide, then changed the angle of descent *again*, and ended in an inviting tip. She wore a trim black coat, and her legs were slim and fashionably shod. She was middle class, but was was *with* it, Sweeney decided. Every time she tried a few English words, in that fruity accent, he experienced an innocent thrill.

"Explain to her I'm collecting stories of these people who helped the Jews, and she was on the list," Sweeney said. "Any way she wants to tell the story, with as much detail as possible. I'll interrupt for a question whenever I feel like it. We won't tape it, with all this racket here. I'll just take notes."

Gevaert translated and Mme Roux nodded. She began to speak, then stopped and opened her purse, extracting a creased photograph, which she showed to the two men.

The photograph showed a group of children. A class? A nursery? They were posing in three rows. Mme Roux was seated in the center, thinner and younger, but unmistakably the same pretty, dark-

34

eyed woman. As she spoke to Gevaert, she pointed to two of the children.

"She says these are two of the children who could not be saved. As far as is known they were killed at Auschwitz. They were named Aaron Bernheimer and Gaston Cohen. They were in Madame's reading club at the library. She carries it with her all the time."

In the half-light of the square, Sweeney studied the creased photograph, and promptly resented it. Bernheimer and Cohen stared at him with the trusting eyes of four-year-olds, two fat kids in smocks, knee socks, high shoes. They had long hair which fell across their foreheads.

In the square a succession of marching bands was parading in and out of the mussel vending stalls—*oompah-oompah-oompah*. People still could laugh, parade, get drunk, gorge themselves on shellfish, all those harmless Memling faces with bulging cheekbones, blunt noses, flat eyes.

Sweeney yearned to be part of it, to lose himself in mussels and strong beer, and perhaps a woman. But Bernheimer and Cohen stared at him accusingly, reminding him of the great cruelty, and his appetites shriveled.

He ordered coffee, set his notebook on the table, and asked Mme Roux to begin. Gevaert interpreted swiftly. His personality may have been obnoxious, but his English was excellent.

"She says," Gevaert began, "that during the German occupation she was the librarian of the children's section of the Boendal branch of the Brussels library. She still works as a librarian in the central office."

"Emile," Sweeney asked, "try it in the first person." Gevaert shrugged—no problem for an intellect like his.

"One afternoon I was reading from Grimm's fairy tales when a man from the Gestapo visited the library. He was a well-mannered fellow in a civilian suit. He said he used to be a city clerk in Wuppertal. He asked me to have dinner with him. I refused, and I also was reluctant to let him talk to the children. But he was charming and insistent. Besides what was to stop him? He joined in the singing and he held hands with the kiddies when they did ring-the-rosey.

"While the children took their milk and gingerbread, he explained to me that he was looking for Jewish children, especially the children of German, Polish, or Russian Jews who had fled to Belgium. He went around the room, after singing 'Two Little Blackbirds' with us. You know? 'Two little birds went out to play, over the hills and far away'—until he discovered Bernheimer and Cohen.

" 'They must come with me,' he said, 'to be registered and then taken into temporary custody. Nothing at all will happen to them.'

"I helped them into their coats, brushed their hair, and they left. Two little birds going out to play, *over the hills and far away.* That night their parents came to see me. I tried to assure them the children would come back, they had merely been taken away to be registered. How foolish I was! The parents thanked me and kissed my hand and told me I could not have done otherwise. But soon the parents vanished, too. Bernheimer owned a small fruit store and Cohen was a tinsmith."

She halted her story and studied the photograph again, shaking her head. "I sometimes think," Gevaert translated for her, "it did not happen."

In the Grand' Place a new band, its members dressed in the costumes of a medieval guild—broad felt hats, billowing white blouses, and blue pantaloons—marched by. They shook the Belgian skies with "On Wisconsin."

Mme Roux craned her neck looking for her husband, but the railway workers' band was not yet on the scene. She resumed.

"About a week after the disappearance of the children," said Gevaert, "I offered my services—the services of a frightened girl—to a secret organization called *La Comité de Défense des Juifs.* Our aim was to hide the Jews and perhaps resort to more drastic action if necessary. Had I known what kind of work I would be engaged in, I might not have volunteered. I am a coward. I have always feared for my life and my safety. As a child I refused to learn to ride a bicycle or skate.

"We discovered that many ordinary people—oh, by no means a majority of people, for who wants to run such risks?—were willing to accept children. We gave each child a new name, a new identity, creating false Catholic and Protestant children out of little Jews. They were hidden in convents, in churches, on farms, at schools, in private households.

"I remember once I made a trip to La Motte on an autobus with six children who were put under the care of Father Latour. He was a remarkable man. While the children were with him he did not sleep in a bed for two years. That is true. He would spend the night, fully clothed, napping in a chair near the door of the chancery, ready to move the children out through a secret passage should the Germans come. He saved all of them.

"Yes, and he had a ceremonial feast for them on Passover and did not try to convert them, returning them, still Jews, to their families. He told me once, 'I do not mind losing sleep—that is nothing. If I don't, they may lose their lives.'

"I became an expert in this business of transporting children to hiding places. It was very hard because I had to frighten the child so that he would understand and remember never, never, to give his right name. A child is trusting. He is innocent. He cannot believe that there are people in the world who want to murder him. How hard it was to convince Avrum Katz that he must say he is Jean Dumart! At first the child would remember to use the new name, to answer to it. Then after he was settled for a while on a farm, or in a Christian household, he would forget and tell somebody, 'I am now Jean Dumart, but once I was Avrum Katz.' And sometimes my own Belgian compatriots for money, yes, money, would inform the Germans."

Sweeney halted her. "Tell her," he said to Gevaert, "I can't believe that. Nobody would turn a kid in, not the biggest rat in the world. Not these people I see here with the bands and the costumes, eating mussels."

Gevaert translated the American's comment. Mme Roux smiled with a hard, intelligent cynicism. She spoke, and Gevaert resumed. "When your property or your neck is in danger, you will do anything. She asks you—what would you do, Mr. Sweeney? Are you ready to die for the blacks in Mississippi?"

"Foul!" shouted Sweeney. "No hitting below the belt! Skip that, Emile. Tell her to go on."

"In 1943 my fiancé, not the man to whom I am now married and whom you will meet later, but a man named Claude Dinant, asked if I would help in more hazardous work also for *La Comité de Défense des Juifs*. The committee had many members from our labor unions, and both Claude and my present husband worked in the Belgian railway system. For a long time the Belgian people had refused to co-operate in the arrests of Jews, and the Gestapo became impatient. By the middle of 1942, however, the trains with Jews were leaving regularly. So the railway workers decided to organize a resistance against these terrible acts.

"Claude was a despatcher. He got together some of his co-workers, including Pierre Roux, who is now my husband, to sabotage such shipments. I agreed to work with them.

"Our first attempt to help the Jews came, I believe, in April of 1943." She paused and conferred with Gevaert, apparently trying to confirm the date, but the journalist was no help. A veiled surliness had crept into his translating. Sweeney wondered why.

"No matter," the Belgian woman said. "A train on which the Germans had placed about fifteen hundred Jews had left the Caserne Dossin. My fiancé and his party secretly left the doors of the goods wagons unlocked—despite the presence of SS guards. The SS men were given gifts of whiskey from the grateful people of Belgium to make them less alert.

"Between Tirlemont and Vise, other railway workers lay in ambush. The Belgian engineers stopped the train at the head of a railway bridge. Shooting broke out immediately between the workers and the SS men. But the Jews were so frightened and so tightly packed into the vans, that less than one hundred and fifty escaped. About twenty were killed by gunfire.

"Claude, my fiancé, was shot between the eyes while trying to make some Jews run from the wagons. He kept screaming at them: 'Run, run! You will die anyway in the ovens! Run when you can!' But they refused to leave the old people or the children. As you know, Mr. Sweeney, Jews are very close to their families. They remained huddled in the wagon and would not listen to him. I think he knew he would die there. I can still see him, in his railway worker's blue overalls and his blue railwayman's cap, which he always wore since he was proud of being a worker and an official of his union, gripping the boards on the side of the wagon with one hand and waving his Sten gun with the other, and shouting over and over, 'Run, run! Run from the car!' At least he died quickly, a bullet through the head, and at least he saved some."

She paused to blow her nose.

"She doesn't have to tell me anything else," said Sweeney to Gevaert. "I got enough. Unless she wants to. I mean, I'm not here to upset people." But the truth was he was more upset than she.

Huguette Roux tucked her handkerchief into her purse and resumed.

"She says it's all right," the journalist said. "It was a long time ago."

Another marching band entered the Grand' Place. They turned to watch its loud entry. Sweeney saw a troupe of middle-aged cornetists and trombone players in baggy dark-blue uniforms and blue railwayman's caps, bright red kerchiefs knotted about their throats. They paraded with a stately, syndicalist cadence. Horns and woodwinds blasted forth the lilting airs of "Anchors Aweigh."

Huguette Roux stood up. She waved to a stocky cornetist in the first rank. His eyebrows arched as he returned the greeting while negotiating B-flat.

"Mon mari," she said to Sweeney.

"A swinger," he responded. "Man there plays fine cornet." Sweeney began to sing "Anchors Aweigh," to the amusement of the celebrants.

The railway workers' band stepped off toward the stage in the center of the plaza. People resumed their frenzied consumption of iced mussels. Sweeney, Gevaert, and Huguette Roux sat down.

"Later, there were other attempts by the railwaymen to free Jews," Gevaert translated.

"Once we released forty Jews and killed two of the SS. But if you are looking for some kind of cinema ending, some brave story of how I avenged my fiancé's death, I must disappoint you. I was terrified all the time. I was given a gun later, but I never killed anyone. Nor did I want to. I was sick and frightened and wanted the war to end. I was angry with everyone—all my fellow Belgians for letting this happen to our country. And even at the Jews for being such helpless victims that we all seemed like criminals if we did not help them.

"I suppose there were ninety thousand Jews in Belgium before the war. The Germans took away about a third and murdered them. Why did we not save them all? I don't know. I do know it is much easier to mind one's own business, to look the other way. If Claude had done so he would be alive today, not dead at the age of twenty-two.

"Mr. Sweeney, would you risk your neck for Jews you never saw in your life? Would you? Or would you say to yourself: *'Thank God it is not me! Yes, thank God, it is someone else!* Thank God, for example, it is the Negro in your country, or the priest in Communist China—anyone!—So long as it is not my flesh that is tormented!' "

The cornetist of the railwaymen's band—Huguette's husband—joined them. He was introduced to Sweeney, who bought him a beer. Sweeney liked him: a self-contained union man—one of Western Europe's better products. No resentment, no brutality: a man with a respectable niche in the social order, a sense of function.

Mme Roux touched Gevaert's arm and told him something. Again, the journalist began his expert interpreting. "She just remembered something: When the German took Gaston Cohen and Aaron Bernheimer away, he came back after a few minutes

40

with the children. I thought he had changed his mind or perhaps had made a mistake, and I thanked God for saving the children. But they had only come back to get Gaston's stamp album. He had brought it to the library to show to me that day.

"He had mentioned this to the Gestapo man, who escorted him back to our library. I looked at them as they left and could see little Cohen hugging his precious stamp album. The German was holding his hand and laughing. Once the child dropped the book and some stamps fell out. I remember him, a fat little boy squatting, encumbered by his leggings and high shoes, gathering up stamps while the German waited."

She began to weep. She cried with great dignity, her features undistorted, the tears flowing sedately. Roux put an arm around her and kissed her. Gevaert looked away.

"I'm sorry, gosh I'm sorry," Sweeney said. "She doesn't have to tell me any more. And what a dope I am! I got so wrapped up in her story I forgot to take notes! Emile, could you get it all down tomorrow and write it up for me in English?"

Sweeney extracted Wettlaufer's diploma and made his usual stumbling speech about the citation and the money that would be forthcoming. Huguette Roux wiped her eyes and thanked him. But she was upset by her recollections. She and her husband got up and excused themselves.

When Gevaert had left, the agent of the Wettlaufer Foundation sat ruminating in the café alone. A chill edged the night air, but the festival was in full swing. Couples twisted to the music of the shaggy guitarists. Mussels were devoured relentlessly. But joy eluded Sweeney. Who could dance, eat, drink, when Gaston Cohen kept rising from an unmarked lime pit in Poland to stare at Sweeney with dark victimized eyes? And whatever happened to his stamp album?

Sweeney was roused by a loud rhythmic chant and looked up to see a mob of young galoots charging across the plaza. They were long-haired and vaguely Bohemian and ran with their arms on each other's shoulders shouting: *Yan-kee go-home! Yan-kee go-*

home! If one listened long enough, it became: *Home-yan kee-go! Home-yan kee-go!*

Sweeney, gingered by this diversion from Mme Roux' burdensome memories, rose to meet this challenge. The Belgians appeared indifferent to the affront. Indeed, the twist music made more noise than did the left-wingers. (Sweeney saw in this a rude justice.)

He asked a few people what all the hollering was about, and got only shrugs, smiles, and a few comments to the effect that these were Communist students, out to ruin everybody's fun.

By now the galoots had swung once around the square and were clumping full tilt toward Sweeney.

> *Yan-kee go-home! Yan-kee go-home!*
> *. . . home-yan kee-go! Home-yan kee-go!*

"Hello there," Sweeney shouted, holding up his arms to confront the onrushing radicals. "Hello there, I'm Rex Marshall."

The Communist leader stopped. He was tall and gross and his hair grew in an uncut blond shock, covering ears, neck, forehead, and one eye. His flesh was a moist pink, like an uncooked veal roast.

"American?" asked the young man, as his cohorts gathered round. Sweeney noticed there was a Negro among them, probably an educated Congolese—very black, very handsome, in a tight black suit, white shirt, and black tie.

"You bet I am!" cried Sweeney. "I'm here to defend the Stars and Stripes. Now, just where do you want us to go home from?"

"Vietnam!" shouted the leader. "The Congo! Cyprus! Cambodia! Zanzibar!"

As he shouted out his roll call of marginal countries, of places where reason had died and where nonsense ruled, the demonstrators shouted after him in chorus. A considerable crowd had gathered to watch the confrontation, most of them intrigued by the tall American who stood like Gary Cooper facing off bad guys.

"You want to enslave the world!" Sweeney shouted. "Hell, all we want is for people to live in peace and freedom!"

"Yes!" the blond galoot yelled. "*Your* peace and freedom! Napalm! Germ warfare! Poison gas! Neo-colonialism! Hydrogen bombs!"

His troops took up the cry: *Yan-kee go-home! Yan-kee go-home!*

Sweeney, despite his Irish blood and the attendant myths that go with it, was an eminently peaceful man. He hated fights. He had a predisposition toward bloody noses. The first blow in the gut turned him yellow, and he had great difficulty becoming angry enough to hurt the other fellow. As soon as he threw a punch, a small voice would say—*look out, he'll hurt you worse!*

Still, something was expected of him. Burt Lancaster would never put up with such insults.

"I've heard enough!" Sweeney bellowed. "You there—you Sta-khanovite, or whatever you are! *I challenge you!*"

A few Belgians, evidently supporters of NATO, cheered. The youth's cronies pushed him forward; the Congolese gave him advice in guttural French. Would Sweeney be disemboweled, eaten? But the leader seemed hesitant, less sure of his ground. He was big, but he looked soft and slow.

"I'm a sick man," Sweeney told the gathering sincerely. "My gall bladder's shot. My doctor tells me I shouldn't fight, or get excited. But I challenge him, just the same! Come on, wiseguy!"

Goaded, the youth roared: "*J'accepte!*"

Another shout rose from the crowd—which now outnumbered the twist Daily. Two Belgian policemen walked over, conversed rapidly with some respectable Memling faces in dark hats, and began to herd the students away. Sweeney protested.

"My honor is at stake, fellahs! I demand satisfaction." He grabbed the cop's arm. "I didn't challenge him to *fight*, or anything. I just challenged him."

The students and the police halted.

"That's right," the American persisted. "It could be *anything*—rassling, dominoes, jacks. Name it."

"You are crazy," the Communist leader said haughtily.

"You're gutless, pal," said Sweeney.

As the police maneuvered them by a mussels cart, the American cried: "An eating contest! Come on, Trotsky, I can outeat any Communist on the block! I'll pay!"

The youth paused a moment, then, propelled by both his retinue and the two policemen, was shoved toward the nearest stall.

"I'll show you what it means to be an American!" shouted Sweeney, showering Belgian francs on the proprietors, an elderly couple. Two more pushcarts were wheeled close by to share in the largesse. Sweeney, elated, roared, "Make a circle! Women and children in the middle, and hold fire until the redskins are upon us!"

The great mussel-eating contest began—a memorable event. Communists, socialists, and other dissidents egged on the blond galoot, while the police and the middle class applauded the American. The first dozen went easily, as did the second dozen, and the third. Sweeney loved the mussels—tender, slippery, quivering with the mystic life of the sea. He felt his abdomen engorge and distend.

"Why not victory?" yelled Sweeney. "Why not victory? We want a man who'll face up to the Commies! A man who'll say: so far, no further!" He slurped a dozen more out of their shell. But his antagonist was no weakling. He was daintier and more deliberate than Sweeney, gently cradling the mussels and coaxing them off their shells, rather than tearing them off by suction the way the American did. Bravely he matched Sweeney on the first six dozen. Mounds of empty shells rose on the carts. A giant jar of hot sauce was emptied. Two more carts were summoned in reserve.

Belching, Sweeney kept a wary eye on his adversary. "Communism is my sworn enemy," he gurgled, as a particularly fat mussel made the glide down to oblivion. Now he noticed a hestitancy in the ringleader's movements, a slight shaking of one hand, a nervous smile betraying malaise.

44

But midway through the eighth dozen Sweeney himself began to sway. The mussels had united in one glob of pulsating tissue. He felt pregnant, about to give birth to a mermaid. When he placed his hand below his navel, he felt a convulsive jerking. "Nize baby," said Sweeney, "eat up all the mussels and grampa'll tell you about the Little Boy and the Stamp Album."

Bending backward to start on his eighty-ninth mussel, he hit the pavement. The Belgian police stood over him and whispered encouragement. Sweeney got up like an over-age middleweight and sucked in number ninety. Gratefully, he saw that the radical had slowed down. He was holding an opened creamy-white mussel, gazing glassily at his supporters.

"*Allez, allez!*" they cried.

"*À bas les Américains!*" another cried.

"*Nous n'oublions jamais Lumumba!*" cried the Congolese.

"Rat's ass!" cried Sweeney. "Either he outeats me or I outeat him." So saying, he thought he would faint. The mussels frolicked in his stomach. The Grand' Place turned sideways; floodlit guildhalls and palaces were aslant, lovelier than ever. Above him, canted, was the stage. Over its railings the hairy rock-and-roll band and dozens of young couples studied him with stolid eyes. The youth of Western Europe could not be let down. Sweeney passed ninety. His adversary pursued him, but with great reluctance. Fearfully, the Belgian stared at each mussel, perceiving in them fascist tendencies. Twice, he had rejected shellfish on the grounds that they were contaminated. Sweeney suspected this was a Red ruse to gain time, and to bypass jumbo-sized mussels

Both eaters rested in their labors. The Belgian's face was splotched with great red welts. He probed his bloated midriff. "*Assez?*" he asked Sweeney.

"He wishes to call it a tie," a policeman whispered.

"Hell no!" Sweeney shouted. "We make no compromises with evil! Eat on!"

Yet even as Sweeney picked up the ninety-second mussel, he felt the mass in his abdomen lurch, assume a life of its own and struggle to rise up his gullet. Reverse peristalsis convulsed him. Manfully he battled the sickening waves. But if Sweeney suffered, his enemy seemed ready to die. He was being supported by two galoots, his body slack, his face a lump of red swellings. The man was probably allergic to seafood.

"Down, Rover," Sweeney said, his voice strangling. The army of drowned mussels obeyed. He waved number ninety-two aloft as the Grand' Place whirled about him. The guild of the weavers, gold and dark brown, collapsed on him, and the guild of the brewers was ready to follow.

"When this is over," Sweeney whispered to the Communists, "we start on snails."

"Il a dit," one said with horror, "après les moules, les escargots."

The Communist leader freed himself and stumbled across the plaza. Halfway up the Rue D'Harengs he purged himself of mussels against the side of the Folklore Museum. A great hurrah went up. Sweeney triumphantly sucked ninety-two from its shell and fainted in the arms of the police.

The next morning found him dyspeptic and penitent in his suite at the Amigo Hotel. He was troubled by Wettlaufer's telegram. More than ever he was reluctant to pursue the survey. He was vaguely resentful of Huguette Pelletier Roux and her dead fiancé. They were all too noble. Too good for a rotten world. They made the Sweeneys look like heels and yellowbellies.

"Wettlaufer, do this yourself!" Sweeney roared from his bed. "Lay off! Take your money back!"

Sweeney turned to beer for solace, back to the Trappiste. It was heavy and sweet and tended to induce a mild, not unpleasant, vertigo. The door buzzer sounded. He sat up on the edge of the bed, a hairless herring of a man in jockey shorts, shouting for the caller to enter.

It was Gevaert, looking shrunken, sour, and disgusted. His cranky eyes were shadowed and peeked out from thick eyebrows grown together as if stitched over his nose. There were typewriter-ribbon stains on his fingers. "The ink-stained wretch himself," Sweeney said.

"I heard about your exploit last night," the journalist said. "You took advantage of that boy."

"He asked for it. Don't tread on me, Emile. That's Sweeney's motto. That'll teach them to holler about Vietnam. Lousy Reds."

Gevaert stiffened inside his lumpy black suit. "I am a left-wing socialist myself. I am in accord with them on many issues."

"Oh, brother," moaned the American. "You wanna try to beat me at beer drinking? Emile, I'm a sick man. I got a duodenal ulcer today. Maybe it's ileitis. Let's have the translation, then get lost. Or have a drink. But no arguments."

Gevaert placed a mustard-colored envelope on the coffee table, eyeing the beer disgustedly. Sweeney counted off a sheaf of franc notes and threw in fifty more than the agreed price. The journalist lifted the last fifty from the pile and gave them back.

"Go on, Emile, you did a great job. Take it."

"Only what I was hired for. Had I known the nature of this undertaking I would have refused to help you."

"You woulda refused?" asked Sweeney. "What's a matter? What's wrong with telling the world about Noble Christians?"

"Nothing at all. However, I am a socialist and an atheist."

"What else is wrong with you?"

Sweeney settled into a blue-silk armchair and invited the interpreter to sit down. Gevaert did so, sitting stiffly in the Empire chair, reluctant to soil his egalitarian purity with a touch of watered silk or polished fruitwood. His hands were clasped in his lap and his black eyes were hostile.

"Nothing is wrong with me. But I can tell you many things wrong with this report you are making for those rich Americans."

"Who? What Americans?"

"Do not deny it, Mr. Sweeney. You are a paid agent of the Roman Catholic Church in America engaged in a great campaign of what you would call whitepaint."

"Whitewash. You're a nut. My patron is an honorable, rich, neurotic American Jew."

Gevaert sneered. "I have found that there is always a convenient rich Jew to act as a front for Rome."

Sweeney, who had no heart for disputation after last night's encounter, thrust his naked limbs forward, scratched his belly, and yawned.

"Let's drop this particular line of discussion," he said. "Wanna beer? A big steak?"

"Typically American. Feed the flesh, ignore the mind."

"Just watch that, *walyo*. I'm as patriotic as the next man."

"Oh, yes. Churchgoing, hymn-singing."

"And watch *that*. I'm in the Faith meself."

"Are you, indeed? Quickly, now, Mr. Sweeney—what saint's day is it? When did you last confess?"

"Knock it off, Emile. I never discuss religion or politics with strangers." He drained half a bottle of Geuze.

"Do not deny it," Gevaert said, "this Legion of Noble Christians you are pursuing is a fraud, a deceit to make the Roman Catholic Church emerge as a great champion of oppressed Jews. Look at the people you have spoken to: two priests in France, now Huguette Roux, a narrow-minded Catholic woman with a lout of a husband who follows her to mass like a child. *C'est une blanchissage formidable*—a great laundering of the Scarlet Woman."

"Who?"

"The Scarlet Woman. The Whore of Rome."

Sweeney hauled his bulk from the confining chair. "Now, let's stop that, right now. I wouldn't insult your church, so you lay off mine."

"I have no church. I told you I am an atheist. You are all ridiculous to me, including those praying Jews. Politically I sympathized with them as victims. But their religion—*faah!* The Great Jehovah! Are you aware he had his origins as an elongated rock, a great stone phallus which they carried around in a box?"

The biological allusion reminded Sweeney his bladder was protesting. He lurched to the bathroom and relieved himself mightily.

When he came back, Gevaert was immobilized in the chair.

"I will expose you when you publish this report," the Belgian said.

"Nuts. Protestants and atheists get their innings later. The equal time provision. Now beat it. I got some letters to write. I got some Dutch contacts to line up."

Gevaert got up, one hand thrust in his black jacket, a frazzled Napoleon. Sweeney noticed that although it was midsummer he wore a frayed gray sweater in the manner of all impoverished Northern Europeans, people forever anticipating a severe winter.

"What eludes you, Mr. Sweeney," he said, "is that these heroic Christians you seek, and notably the Catholics, have acted as they have not out of any honorable impulses but out of *guilt*. A guilt so old and so deep it touches them all."

"Baloney."

"If you will come with me to Aarschot, near Brussels, you will find an interesting old church. Oddly it is the town from which Mme Roux comes. I believe she was baptized there. A religious woman. I am sure she has never noticed it but there is a wooden choir stool in that church dating from the fifteenth century. One may find similar stools with similar motifs throughout Europe—on altar screens, pulpits, pillars, and so forth."

"I didn't hire you for any lesson in medieval art."

"This carving depicts a man riding a goat. What a horrid man! He rides the goat backwards, grasping its tail. The goat is ugly, too. Its front legs terminate in claws. Look at the man! Long curls, a wide-brimmed hat, a hooked nose. He wears a cotton . . . In short, a hideous Jew."

"Listen, I know all about that jazz. So what? That was five hundred years ago. So Shakespeare wrote *The Merchant of Venice*."

Pacing the room, the journalist ignored Sweeney and continued. "Why does the Jew ride the goat? He rides the goat because the goat symbolizes *the devil*. But it also symbolizes the Jew. Why, you ask, does it symbolize both? Because, Mr. Noble Christian Sweeney, *the Jew is the devil*.

"If you will, follow this reasoning, if beer has not dulled you into insensitivity. Listen carefully. *The Jew is the devil.* The Church is engaged in eternal warfare against the devil. *Ergo, the Church must war on the Jew.* Each Christian must war on the Jew. I simplify all this in deference to your stupidity. But that is the basic formula.

"For example—ritual murder, of which even you should be aware. Who but agents of the devil would commit blood sacrifice on Christian children? Other evidence. The *foetor judaicus*, or foul odor of the Jews. Then the Jew as sorcerer, the maker of magic, of spells. Underlying all this nonsense is the Churchly conviction that the Jew *is the devil, the enemy, the antichrist*, or whatever else the Church Fathers decide is necessary to keep the organization functioning.

"The Spanish theologian de Spina, as a matter of record, proved beyond a doubt that the Jews were children of the devil. For, he reasoned, how could they prefer burning to conversion if they were not the spawn of Satan?"

There was a question in Sweeney's mind as to how to deal with Gevaert, so he delayed any precipitous action. Besides, he was exhausted, barely able to maintain a sprawling position in the armchair. He affected dignity. His eyebrows arched high and his querying, dubious expression became one of icy hauteur.

"Are you quite finished, my dear Emile?" he asked.

"I am not. Please understand. I tell you this not because I am a philo-Semite. Far from it. Their fables and superstitions offend me as much as the Mystical Body. It is merely that I detest hypocrisy. Moreover, your ignorance demanded that I educate you. Having taken your American bribes to assist in this falsification, I can do no less."

"You're a long-winded son-of-a-bitch," Sweeney said. "Sure, a lot of those fairy tales were believed. But man, the Middle Ages are over. Yeah, that anti-Semitic bit used to be okay to get the flock together on a friendly basis. I admit it, a couple of people got burned or skinned when everyone lost their tempers because

Yussel down the block was smarter than they were. But that's Christmas past. That's over. And it's got nothing to do with Father Louis or Huguette Roux or any other of my Noble Christians!"

Sweeney was on his feet, bellowing—an angry Harp in an Amsterdam Avenue bar, defending Pat O'Brien from the rude sneers of Columbia sophomores.

"And another thing! If this anti-Jewish idea was so important, how come you never, never see it in a famous painting? So what if they carved a stool in a church in Belgium? What about the great painters? Giotto . . . and Memling . . . and all the others? They could have painted Jews with big noses riding on goats—but they didn't. All their Jews look nice. Hah, answer that for me!"

"Precisely," Gevaert said. "The depiction of the Jew as devil and fiend was left to popular art—to woodcuts, prints, the common stuff which circulated among the people. No great artist would permit himself to despoil a canvas with horrid pictures of Jews. Have I answered you?"

"No, and I wish to hell you'd scram. Vamoose."

Gevaert strutted around the table, and with considerable courage, since the American was obviously losing his temper, pecked at Sweeney's naked shoulder with a dirty forefinger. "Insults are a mask for your own doubts. You and your pitiful survey. Admit it. 'The line though faintly drawn is right,' said Pope."

Sweeney pushed the accusing finger away. "Which Pope?"

"Alexander Pope, you fool. Whosoever does not believe in the Christian God, said the Church Militant, must believe in the devil. And since the Jews are the most stubborn unbelievers, they are the devil. It was foreordained that the antichrist must appear on earth. And he would come with claws, wings—and a huge Jewish nose. So he is portrayed in the vulgar iconography of the day. Satan-Jew, coming in one last insane effort to destroy God's world! Now what is the duty of the Christian, if this be true? Why, the Christian must resist him. Kill the devil, kill the antichrist.

51

What, I ask you, is more logical than a Christian upbringing to prepare a man for a job at Buchenwald?"

Some rejoinder was indicated but Sweeney, in his malaise, convinced that some of the mussels had been tainted and that he was incubating botulism, could summon up no energy.

"You cannot undo two thousand years of hatred. St. John Chrysostom told the Jews, 'God hates you' . . . and told his faithful that God destroyed the Jews, that it was God's will, His will, mark you, that they be slaughtered. Why is he not in the dock at Nuremberg?"

Sweeney leaped from his chair and cracked the back of his hand against the journalist's cheek. Gevaert, appalled, stumbled backward.

"You atheistical creep, watch your language around here! I may be a punk advertisement for my Church, but I'll listen only to so much, especially from your element! Nothing you said makes me less proud of Father Louis, or Huguette Roux, so just shut your trap!"

Gevaert fussed with his tie and shirt collar, tugged at his lumpy jacket. "Of course, they were brave. I acknowledge that. They are certainement more heroic than either of us, since I suspect that you are as useless and as rootless as I. I merely say that their efforts were attempts to atone for an ancient crime, a crime so pervasive that the Nazis only had to pick up where—"

"Give yourself at ease!" roared Sweeney. He clapped a hand over the journalist's mouth and wrestled him to the door. The Belgian wriggled and twisted like a beached trout. At the door he got a purchase on a gilt knob and wrenched free.

"Ignorant man! Drunkard, boor, glutton! Living off the doles of some millionaire! Sycophant, pimp, hypocrite, parasite! I dare you to undertake your survey of Noble Christians on my terms!"

Sweeney wobbled back to the coffee table, picked up a half-emptied bottle of Trappiste, stuck a thumb in the neck, and shook it. Swaying in his jockey shorts, he pointed it at Gevaert. "You asked for it, Emile. One more word!"

52

"Clown, imbecile, fornicator, forger, toady! You are all these—and worse! You do not remotely comprehend the fraud in which you are involved!"

Sweeney held his fire. "I give you one chance to apologize."

"Read Thomas Aquinas, read Albertus Magnus, my dear Mr. Sweeney. They saw the course of events clearly. Antichrist would rally the Jews to his banner—the false Messiah! Antichrist and his Jewish Army fighting God's emissaries to the death, until Michael conquers! Welcome to the Twentieth Century—for antichrist read Bolshevik, Capitalist, Cosmopolite! Read if you will——."

Sweeney's thumb popped off the mouth of the bottle. A jet of cold beer sped toward the journalist's face. It caught him flush on the nose and trickled into his mouth. He spluttered and coughed, but would not be diverted from his insane preachment. "I commend you to Hilaire Belloc, whom you probably read in parochial school——"

Sweeney shook the bottle and gave the Belgian a second shot of foamy beer. Gevaert caught this one in his opened mouth, spat it out, and fled down the carpeted hallway. Sweeney, a naked apparition, chased him a few steps as two prim chambermaids blushed.

"Goddam you, Emile, don't confuse me with your lousy lies! Any rat can make it sound lousy by quoting people out of context!"

He half-hoped the rude man would turn and resume the argument, but Gevaert, beer-drenched, had vanished down a stairway, leaving Sweeney alone, an angry nude American subjected to the stares of chambermaids and commercial travelers.

After a few hours of windy sleep, Sweeney tossed in his Brussels bed, unsettled by the Belgian's ravings. The man was a crank, a bigot, a pedant who scrounged around for obscure references and built an unfair case. Wistfully, Sweeney wished he had paid better attention to Theology or Church History in parochial school so that he could have knocked Gevaert down with solid argument instead of an old ginmill trick.

Gevaert temporarily eliminated from his fumed head, other

worries gnawed at him. It was bad enough for a man to suffer from chronic muscular fibrosis, to be prone to bronchial-respiratory ailments (he was convinced he had contracted ambulant pneumonia), but it was insupportable when in addition to perpetual illness you had no character. None at all. Grimly he accepted the truth that he was dreadfully inferior. Especially to people like Father Louis Des-Moulins and Huguette Roux.

On that coming day, he wondered, when they started rounding up the untameable *schwartzer*, where would he be? And surely that day would come. Surely the Negro would have to be rounded up and put away the way things were going. Suppose they even got around to the Jews? Impossible, he told himself. Not the good people of the Bronx. Not his old buddy, Allie Cooperstein, who could hit two sewers. Once Sweeney had looked, with a wrench in his bowels, at a photograph of Warsaw ghetto survivors being marched off, hands over heads, gray-haired men, dumpy women. When that day came, when the final barrier holding back the egregious *goyim* was lowered, when the last eight ball, snarling defiance and buh-buh-buh-ing his ultimate "mother fucker" was safely locked up, would Allie Cooperstein be next?

It was an interesting hypothesis. Still more disturbing was the question as to what he, Buck Sweeney, would do. Would he, like Huguette Roux and her fiancé, stage an ambush of militant Texans in big hats guarding a concentration camp on the shores of Lake Ronkonkoma? Would he die for Mr. and Mrs. Hyman Cooperstein, proprietors of a ladies specialty store on Castle Hill Avenue, and their no-good son Allie, and their nearsighted daughter Millie?

Like hell I would! shouted Sweeney, sitting up in bed. *Me die? Me get knocked off for Allie Cooperstein? Naaah! Sorry old punchball buddy, sorry old poolroom friend. I ain't you. And because I ain't you I will live to enjoy steaks and broads and a red sports car, given me by your co-religionist, Sherm Wettlaufer! It is dumb to die. It makes no sense. Buck Sweeney isn't ready for it. Not for you, Allie, or for all the stove-lids in Mississippi!*

He lay awake the rest of the night, filled with resentment against Father Louis and his co-workers, and Huguette Roux and most of the railway workers in Belgium. Twice he thought of cabling Wettlaufer that all bets were off, that the survey was ended. Then he thought of the wad of traveler's checks and the MG and the rest of sunny Europe (especially Italy), and he bravely decided to move on.

Wettlaufer had prepared an itinerary for Sweeney, but the interrogator was not compelled to follow it. "Please use it as a guide, Buck," the millionaire had told him, "merely a guide. Use your own good instincts and your heart to find these people. One will lead to another. Talk to only the most promising. I want a representative sample, if you will."

There were two names listed in Amsterdam. Sweeney secured the aid of a Dutch journalist and learned that one of the men, a baker named Wiegers, was dead. The other, a certain Willem Kruis, was working as a waiter at the restaurant in the Amsterdam Artis, or Zoo. Willem Kruis informed the journalist that he spoke rather good English—he had worked for many years in hotels—and would prefer to meet Mynheer Sweeney alone.

Having been a lifelong neighbor of one of the great animal collections of the world, the Bronx Zoo, Sweeney was a dear friend of all such places. He cried with joy when the taxicab dropped him at the entrance. The sky was bright and cloudless, the air dry. All the gloom induced by his despair in Brussels vanished with the first tiger. He strolled around smiling stupidly, greeting Dutchmen, Indonesians, Americans, a tall, red-faced man finding the world a decent place.

The restaurant was in a grove of elms and maples. At one side there was a glassy pond. Swans and geese floated by in Nederlandische stateliness. Sweeney settled at a lakeside table, ordered a beer, and asked a waiter to tell Mr. Willem Kruis that Mr. Sweeney had arrived.

The Dutchman approached him through the glass doors of the

café. He was wearing his starched waiter's coat, and he was a tall, broad-shouldered man. When he paused with unconscious dramatic effect on the cobbled path, beams of late afternoon sun slanting through the towering elms struck him on the face. Sweeney wondered: *Is he acting the part?* Or was this simply what Kruis was like? The Dutchman walked over, gripped Sweeney's hand powerfully, and welcomed him.

For a moment, Sweeney sipped his beer, studying the man's face. Surely Willem Kruis had been preordained to perform noble acts. One could not have predicted where Huguette Roux's life would lead, or what Father Louis would be doing in his old age. *But Kruis!* He was about sixty, but he was muscled and erect. The face was the face of an angry prophet—gray eyebrows projecting over eyes the color of the Zuider Zee, a square cleft jaw, a hard, short nose. His hands were like cinder blocks. Kruis could have been in Biblical robes and sandals laying about with a rod hitting sinners on the head.

Sweeney explained his mission, and the Dutchman nodded. He understood. He had been interviewed after the war by an Englishman.

"Whatever Mr. Sweeney wish. I tell." His voice was in accord with his appearance—a soft, authoritative voice, the Dutch accent endowing his English with a pleasant slurred quality.

Sweeney set up the tape recorder and asked Kruis to give him some brief autobiographical information. The Dutchman obliged. He was a native of Haarlem, Frans Hals' city, and came from a working-class family. He had had only a marginal education, going to work as a bus boy at the age of twelve, in the Schiller Hotel in Amsterdam. Later he learned the hotel-kitchen routine thoroughly—salad man, baker, soup man—and eventually, because of his aptitude for languages and his regal bearing, was transferred to the dining room as an assistant headwaiter.

Some gnawing memory of his mad interlude with Gevaert prompted Sweeney to ask if he were a religious man. He was relieved and almost felt impelled to write to the Belgian about it when Kruis disavowed any religious tendencies. He had been raised in the Reformed Church but had neglected it since his boyhood. Religion, he told Sweeney, meant nothing at all to him. He regarded all religions as meaningless. With some prodding he could have become an atheist.

"Why did you save Jews?" Sweeney asked him.

Kruis did not pause. "It is my business to help Yoosh people."

"How do you mean your business?" Sweeney asked. "Like a job?"

"No, no. Not yob like waiter or cook. Personal yob. Something tell me help Yews, I help."

But what this "something" was Kruis did not explain. Sweeney saw the mystic in him, a charismatic force, an absolute that propelled him to act virtuously and bravely—to risk his life and the lives of his frightened wife and four children. All this he had done without a rationale, without religious impulse, without political zeal.

Around Sweeney the late afternoon crowds milled and chattered and he had a sad awareness that this was what life was concerned with—Kruis knew it, and Huguette Roux did, but he, Buck Sweeney, would never know it. There were children in strollers, schoolboys in harmless wolfpacks, young couples, old men—all caressed by the great sun and the shading elms, all marveling at Noah's splendid animals.

"But how did it start?" Sweeney asked. "How did you get into it?"

Slowly, Kruis told his story. He explained first that the Jews' fate in Holland was one of the grimmest in Europe.

The Germans practically had had the Jews handed to them—not so much by the Dutch, although there was a considerable pro-Nazi movement, but by geography. The flat small country afforded few hiding places. Moreover, the Wehrmacht defeated the Dutch Army in five days, and a German civil government was put in charge at once. Of 140,000 Jews in Holland before the war, the Germans deported 110,000. Less than 6,000 of these survived.

57

Sweeney listened attentively. He watched the reels spinning on the recorder and wondered how Sherman Wettlaufer would act when he heard this. Would he run out and beg Leo Parnell Sweeney to come listen to it?

"We call general strike to protest what Yermans do to Yoosh people," Kruis said. "I help organize strike, all waiters, kitchen workers. But strike no good. Yermans too strong for us. Terrible what happen."

Soon after the strike the Germans seized six hundred Dutch Jews as hostages, as a warning to the Dutch labor unions. The Jews were sent to Mauthausen Camp to work in a stone quarry. There they were ordered to haul boulders up and down 148 steps of the pit, with no rest, no water. On the third day, when most of the Jews were assembled at the rim of the quarry, they dropped their loads, joined hands, chanted the Shema Isroel, and leaped over the side. The SS guards started shooting and turned the dogs loose, but they could not stop the Dutch Jews, who kept plunging into the quarry.

Kruis told the story stolidly, with no emotion. He had heard it from a Dutchman who had been released from Mauthausen. It was confirmed after the war. It occurred suddenly to Kruis, who at that time was working as headwaiter in an Indonesian restaurant, that he should be doing something. But what? How? He thought of his own secure house, his children, his wife, and refused to risk any action that would threaten them.

One day, walking across the Rembrandtsplein, he saw SS men herding Jewish families into trucks. The Jews went quietly. They did not cry or fight or scream. They stood in line and helped one another into the covered trucks. It bothered Kruis that the men had been separated from the women, and the children from both, since that meant that families were being broken up. He thought this was terrible but he had no idea what to do about it.

A few days later a baker named Pieter Wiegers, from whom Kruis often ordered brown bread, stopped him on the Lijnbaansgracht and asked him did he want to do something to help the Jews.

"Wiegers dead now," Kruis said softly. "Yermans find out he is hiding Yews in house. He die in prison here in Amsterdam from beating."

"What kind of man was he?" Sweeney asked.

"Yust plain man. Socialist like me. Married, two children. Little fellow, yust so big. Was once acrobat in circus. Nice man."

Wiegers had been contacted by the Jewish underground—what was left of it—and asked to bring any Dutchmen who would hide Jews to a house on Ceintur Baan not far from the National Gallery. Wiegers led him there that night. The house turned out to be a supposedly abandoned, boarded-up hotel, with no lights except candles, no heat and no water. It was a temporary hiding place for about fifty Jews, the ordinary people of Amsterdam— small merchants, teachers, diamond cutters. There was enough food to last two days. Unless they could be hidden they would have to take their chances roaming the street.

"Why'd Wiegers call on you?" asked Sweeney. "He didn't know you that well. Suppose you'd told the Germans?"

"Wiegers not know me well, true. But he knew I help."

Sweeney was unsatisfied.

"I walk in big room," Kruis said. "Dark, few candles. People sleep on floor, baby cry. All Yoosh people. I say to myself, 'Willem, why world so cruel make people hide like rats?' A Yoosh man walk up to me and take my hand and say he is Meier, the pharmacist, and will I help him and family?"

Kruis had told his story with a bland factual plodding, putting each unfamiliar word in order. But now he appeared moved. His square mouth drooped and he brushed a hand across his eyes. Then he braced his starched white shoulders, sat up stiffly in his chair, and said, "And I say to him, 'Yes I am Kruis of Amsterdam and I am here to save you.'"

The words came out clearly, shining in the summer air, as lovely as the yellow-green dazzle of leaf and grass. *I am Kruis of Amsterdam and I am here to save you.*

"And what did he say?" Sweeney asked.

"He tell me nobody will help them. Not priests or ministers or

59

city officials or even their own people, the *Joodse Raad*, who tell them—go, give names to Yermans, be nice, behave, go quietly when arrested, because you come back, only going for vacation. But Pharmacist Meier refuse and so do other people in big house on Ceintur Baan."

The waiter took a photograph from the inner pocket of his white coat and showed it to Sweeney—a dark solemn man and a thin woman photographed in street clothes standing beside a starved tree.

"This is Meier and wife. He say to me that night when he take my hand, 'No one help us, but you, Kruis of Amsterdam. Man we have never seen before in our life, you help us.' "

And so Kruis, under cover of night, spirited the Meier family, six people, to his house off the Amstel Dijk and hid them in his cellar. Later he built a sub-basement below the regular cellar. There they stayed for almost four years, in one room.

"All alive after war," Kruis said. "But poor Wiegers he die of beating. Some fellow down the street—ordinary fellow like us, no Nazi, no hate Yoosh people—he told on Wiegers because his wife was afraid. They say he was paid for it, also. I myself saw papers from Yermans to Dutchman who tell about Yews. Four Yoosh people in Wiegers house die for this money."

"But—but—why did *he* tell on them? And why did *you* and *Wiegers* hide them?" Sweeney was as plaintive as a boy who has missed a week of algebra and knows he will never, never, understand it as well as the rest of the class.

"I cannot say for Wiegers or for his neighbor."

"Can you say for yourself?"

The man's stolid dignity, that sense of rightness and honor that had so astounded Sweeney when he first looked upon the Dutchman's erect figure, asserted itself.

"I tell you. I, Willem Kruis, see fight in street. Big boy beat up little boy. I run to help. I stop. I see man beat woman, I run to make him stop. Wrong to hurt people, wrong. I saw Yermans hurt,

60

kill Yews, I must help. I should have help sooner, before Wiegers ask me. Yoosh people needed help, I help. Not matter I do not know who they are. I am man like that."

He made this speech without bragging, then sat back, as if all had been explained. He greeted a stout woman pushing ruddy twins in a stroller, he called to a waiter to ask if everything was moving along, merging into the warm afternoon glow of a place filled with good-natured people and laughing children who would never be separated from their parents and consigned to a shower room where no water flowed.

"My organization," Sweeney said, "wishes to present you with this citation for your work." He handed Kruis the embossed certificate of *The Legion of Noble Christians.*

"Thank your people," Kruis said. "This is great honor."

Moving his lips, the Dutchman read Wettlaufer's lofty prose and smiled. Sweeney explained that he would soon receive a thousand-dollar check in recognition of his deeds.

"Thank gentlemen. But money not needed. I take for grandchildren. But more important things than money." And for the first time in his soiled life that he had heard that hypocrite's cliché, Sweeney actually believed it.

Kruis reached inside his stiff white coat. "People I help send me this after war. More important than money."

He took from his pocket a yellow cloth star and held it against his chest. "They send me this, to thank me. I keep it close to heart, for I am Kruis of Amsterdam."

In a happier frame of mind, hungering for food, beer, and a fat Dutch girl, a blonde animated sofa built along the lines of a Rubens Venus, Sweeney returned to his hotel, where he was greeted with a letter from Gevaert. The Belgian had evidently gotten his address from the concierge at the Amigo Hotel and had lost no time in hounding the American. The letter was typed under a printed letterhead describing its possessor as: *E. Gevaert, Journaliste.*

My Dear Mr. Sweeney:

I hardly know why I feel impelled to direct you toward a true understanding of your mission or why I should concern myself so much about Jews, since they were not the only, and indeed were merely accidental, victims—and in some cases unknowing aides —to the virulent fascism that your country is now reviving.

"Old Emile," Sweeney snorted. "He kind of makes you feel good all over."

After some additional insulting comments about American foreign policy, the Vatican Ecumenical Council, and the Belgian monarchy, Gevaert got around to his reason for writing.

I did some research after leaving you and I found some interesting data concerning Nazi legislation against Jews. Terrible laws, you will agree. As would any civilized person. Please to note, Mr. Sweeney, the manner in which I have, at random, selected a half-dozen Nazi laws concerning Jews and—lo and behold!— discovered that these very prohibitions existed, in many instances identical in detail, in canonical, or church law!

Observe:
1. A Nazi law to protect German Blood (meaning no sex between Jews and Christians) enacted September 15, 1935.
Ancestor: *Enactment of the Synod of Elvira, 306, forbidding sex or intermarriage between Christians and Jews.*
2. Nazi law that allowed local authorities to keep Jews off the streets on Nazi holidays, enacted December 3, 1938.
Ancestor: *Third Synod of Orleans, 538, decreed that Jews cannot walk the streets or be seen during Passion Week.*
3. Nazi levy of special income tax on Jews in place of donations for Nazi-party donations. December 24, 1940.
Ancestor: *Ruling of Synod of Gerona, 1078, that Jews must pay taxes to support the Church, same as Christians.*
4. A Nazi law giving the Justice Ministry the right to void Jewish wills if they "offend the judgment of the people." July 31, 1938.
Ancestor: *From the Third Lateran Council, 1179, a law forbidding Jews to withhold inheritance from relatives who had been baptized.*

62

5. Nazi ruling: a Christian who turns Jewish runs the risk of being treated as a Jew. June 26, 1942.
Ancestor: Synod of Mainz, 1310, decreed that adoption by a Christian of Jewish faith, or return of baptized Jew to same, is heresy.
6. Book burnings—you know this well, Mr. Sweeney.
Ancestor: Synod of Toledo, 681, burning of the Talmud and other books.

Please note, Mr. Sweeney, that this is a haphazard selection. But I could burden you with more. Why? Even a foolish American like yourself must be aware that a historical process is at work here. One can only congratulate the German bureaucracy on its speedy, efficient legislation.

But may not the impartial student of history ask how in heaven's name were they able to accomplish so much so fast? The answer comes easily: they had fifteen hundred years of Church legalisms to guide them! Thus, the invention of new laws was unnecessary. There were precedents to follow.

So, the work went quickly, as all copy-work does. Mr. Sweeney, suppose you were assigned the job of rounding up, isolating, transporting to camps, and then annihilating the twenty million blacks of America? How would you start? Where look for models? Difficult, I suspect, in a problem of such a specialized nature. But the Jews—ah, that was another matter. Patterns existed and . . .

Sweeney read no more. He crumpled the letter, tossed it skillfully into the wastebasket, and turned to a bottle of Genever he had bought on the way back from the zoo.

He arose hours later, wobbling drunk, and prowled the alleys of Amsterdam peering at faded photographs outside strip joints. "Ugliest broads I ever seen," he advised passing tourists. "Fat and hairy."

Later, three sailors took exception to his derogation of Dutch womanhood. While an Indonesian bubble dancer screamed, they bloodied his nose, punched him around the dance floor of the Surabayo Inn, relieved him of a roll of guilders (luckily he had left the traveler's checks at the hotel), and left him to dry out somewhere on Prinzengraacht not far from Anne Frank's house.

63

He awakened, blood caked on his mouth, a lump as big as a gull's egg on his right temple, and his new trench coat motley with beer, gutter filth, and his own blood. He washed his face at a street pump and walked to the Rijksmuseum. There he wandered through Rembrandt's rooms, awed, silent, humble, thankful. At "Jeremiah Lamenting the Destruction of Jerusalem" he began to sniffle and at "Rembrandt's Mother" he openly wept.

"Ah, Jesus, it all can't be bad, it all can't be bad," he kept repeating. He stopped at "The Jewish Bride." "See, see, it can be good. Rembrandt knew. Oh, the faces and the light and the dark brown and the gold. Oh, it doesn't have to be bad all the time!"

He stumbled into the great gallery which has only the "Night Watch" resplendent on the distant wall. The militiamen, in full fig, strutted before him, the lights dazzled him, the glory touched him. "Ah, he knew, he knew. It isn't all rotten."

He turned to a troupe of Japanese travelers, miniatures in gray nylon suits, bullet-headed Disneykins laden with cameras. "You get it, walyo?" Sweeney asked. "You get it? It ain't all as terrible, as lousy, as dreadful, as they want us to think. Is it?"

The Japanese grinned, bowed, giggled, and walked away. Sweeney skidded on crepe-soled cordovans trying to follow. "Hey, Hey, walyo. What have you done with Amelia Earhart?"

Then as a museum guard walked purposefully toward the American drunk, Sweeney shouted after the Japanese: "Boy, if there's anything I hate, it's a sore loser!"

Sweeney moved on, finding solace in booze and new sights. He arrived in Hamburg with one side of the sports car stove in, the result of sloppy parking in a hotel alley in Groningen, Holland.

His list of German contacts was small. He discovered that one had died, another had left for East Germany and was unreachable, and that only a certain Dr. Ludwig Helms was still available for questioning. Helms was an engineer. Wettlaufer's sources held little hope of his co-operating. He was regarded as an elusive figure who had testified at a war-crimes trial and then vanished.

Through the help of a friendly concierge at the Guttmacher Hotel (Sweeney gained his favor by telling him that if the Germans would only stop murdering people, they would be the nicest people in Europe), he located Helms at the office of a British firm of civil engineers.

Helms' voice came over the phone as a ghostly whisper—a faraway voice, possibly an invalid's. He spoke flawless English, a bit stilted, with a British accent.

After Sweeney had identified himself and described his mission, Helms waited a long time before responding.

"I am afraid I cannot see you," he said.

"Why? The world should hear about people like you, doctor—"

A spell of coughing at the other end convinced Sweeney he was speaking to an ill man. "It will be impossible," Helms said. "I cannot talk to you about anything. I made my statement at Frankfurt and that is all. Thank you."

Sweeney studied the mute telephone in his hand and decided to leave Germany.

Two days later the agent of the Wettlaufer Foundation boarded a Danish ferryboat at Puttgarden, Germany, for a seagoing interview with the first mate of the vessel. He was a Danish mariner named Erik Allrup, a man who had transported several hundred Jews to safety in Sweden aboard a small fishing boat during the exodus from Denmark.

Sweeney was not on board three minutes, waiting for Allrup in the *Prince Hamlet's* pine-paneled dining room, when he became seasick. He sprinted to the men's room, disgorged, and minced back to the restaurant, where the headwaiter asked solicitously, "Are you all right, sir? Would you like a pill?"

"Nothing, nothing at all," Sweeney gasped. "It's terminal cancer of the esophagus. I never get seasick. Or else I'm hemorrhaging from a duodenal ulcer. Thank you just the same."

Allrup was waiting for him. The mate was a rosy, stocky man with a high forehead and a great, rising pompadour of brown hair.

He had brought along four other men who had also been active in the national effort that succeeded in saving almost all of Denmark's Jews from the Germans. There was a Lutheran minister, a tall bald man, chain-puffing tiny black cigars; a doctor, blond and boyish; a bookstore owner, an elderly man with a brown spade beard; and another member of the crew, a cadaverous stoop-shouldered fellow in oily dungarees.

Two things impressed Sweeney at once, as they insisted he have a few morning brandies with them before the smørrebrød. One was that these Danes—not just the men at the table but all the passengers and crew—were in some indefinable way *individuals*. Each seemed, at least physically, different in shape, size, form, or manner from the next. One might pass for a German, another an Englishman, still another an American, or occasionally even a dark Italian. But their variability went beyond bone structure and skin color. There was something about their dress, their mannerisms, their speech, that marked each as an *individual*, a man who went his own way.

"All this jazz about the welfare state making conformity," Sweeney said, "I don't believe it. You guys all look as different from each other as a row of freaks in a side show."

The Lutheran minister, whose English was excellent, translated the American's tribute. This set off unrestrained laughter. Allrup, the skipper, filled Sweeney's glass again. The brandy bottle went the rounds. Sweeney adored them. It was 11:30 of a weekday morning and they were well into a fifth of Flit! Cigars glowed like fireflies on a Catskill lawn in July. Sweeney accepted one and contributed to the general choking haze.

And at this time Sweeney made his second observation about his Danish hosts. It was this: although the group varied in professional skills, status, education, income, and background, they all accepted one another's company with ease and grace. The youthful doctor, for example, had no problem joking with the mate, and the skinny seaman and the minister conversed like old friends.

Professional men did not talk down to blue-shirted blokes, while the latter did not sneer at education or behave like serfs. The Danes appeared to have developed a society in which the classes had negotiated some kind of peace with one another.

He commented on this, Sweeney's second law of Denmark, to the reverend, who laughed and got another boisterous response when he repeated it. Ever the challenger, Sweeney asked: "Yeah, what about your high suicide rate?"

For some reason this provoked more hilarity, during which Sweeney was now shoved to the smørrebrød table. There his plate was heaped with four kinds of herring, smoked eels, pickled eels, lox, anchovies, sardines in mustard, spiced tongue, headcheese, cold roast beef, tiny hot meatballs, seven varieties of mayonnaise, innumerable salads, thick wedges of aromatic cheese.

The group ate voraciously, and eating called for more beer, more brandy, and more cigars. It occurred to Sweeney that Western Europe (which he was beginning to love) spent most of its life on its ass, eating or drinking. It was not yet noon, and the dining room was mobbed with these irregular Danes, no two noses alike, no two heads of hair identical, no set of gestures the same, all busy fressing, boozing, and incubating nicotine poisoning.

He was crazy about them even without knowing how they saved the Jews. As the party plunged into its second round of food (a great vat of simmering beef stew had appeared), Sweeney asked the minister if he would talk about the rescue.

The Reverend Niels Munk lit a fresh cigar (his seventh), sipped his *Tuborg*, and looked thoughtful. "I tell you, Mr. Sweeney, we have been asked about that so often we are tired of it."

"But my survey would be incomplete."

"You will make us look like heroes. We are not. Look at us—a bunch of Danes, doing what we like best—eating, drinking, smoking, joking with one another. I tell you, it is difficult holding down a parish in this country." He winked.

The young blond doctor (he was a gynecologist, Sweeney was

advised) nodded his agreement. Allrup, the seagoing hero of the rescue, wandered off to the duty-free tobacco shop for a few boxes of cigars.

"But it was a noble thing you did!" protested Sweeney.

"You are too dramatic," said Munk. "For us it was the normal thing. Everything was in our favor. First, we had Sweden across the water, a place to send the Jews. We were Hitler's prize conquest. Churchill called us Hitler's canary. We could get away with a lot of things the others couldn't. And our Jews were never thought of as Jews by us. They are *Danes*. They are not even listed as Jews. They are part of our nation, our life."

Coffee was ordered, and a selection of after-dinner drinks. It was now 12:30 and Sweeney had the sensation of having been feasting at some Roman Emperor's table for hours.

"Holy horror," he said, "I think I gotta throw up again. Doctor, could you examine me later?"

Allrup slapped him on the back and shoved a half-tumbler of *Akvavit* at him. "Wash it, wash it," said the mate. Sweeney drained it.

"Chaah, chaah," Sweeney gasped. "Yaaach. Look, reverend, what about your democratic traditions, your respect for people, for individuals?"

"All very true. We are proud of it. As a clergyman I am particularly proud. I merely say that given our fortunate geographical position, the favored role the Germans bestowed on us, the fact that there were only seven thousand Jews in our country and many of them intermarried and assimilated, one can understand why we acted as we did."

"Yeah, not many acted that way. I mean whole countries, right from the top, like the King or Prime Minister, down to the cab drivers. There aren't *that* many Noble Christians."

"True enough. But we are not the kind of people to point accusing fingers at others. Perhaps we felt guilty at surrendering so quickly. Perhaps that endowed us with a certain guilt when the Germans came to seize the Jews. I don't know. And then—odd

68

strokes of luck. The German shipping administrator here, a man named Duckwitz, who first got the orders to get ships ready for the transport of Jews—he came and *told* us, gave warning."

"A noble German, that guy."

"Yes, a good fellow," said Reverend Munk. "I would drink with him any day. Have another cigar, Mr. Sweeney. These little black ones have a nice Sumatran leaf."

Reconciled to a long, wasting illness, he lit up. The dining room was enhazed. Around Sweeney sat the stout, happy Danes, sated, half-bombed, puffing great clouds of smoke from black cigars. Two gray-haired women, one as pretty as a milkmaid, the other round and homely, inhaled and exhaled luxuriantly on petite cigarillos. If ever there were a people you could not begrudge the comforts of life, the pleasures of the flesh, it was the Danes, Sweeney concluded. They had earned the right to good chow, good booze, and a box of cheroots. They had earned it by being civilized, and good-humored and decent, and what more could a man ask?

Reluctantly, Reverend Niels Munk gave Sweeney a capsule version of what each man present had done to help the Jews escape. Allrup had run one of the best ferry services to Sweden, prowling up and down the coast to pick up Jews, running the German blockade, lying and bluffing his way across the channel for two years.

Dr. Nielsen had hidden fifty Jews in the basement of his maternity hospital. Sweeney learned from him that the Danish medical profession—to a man—had actively and energetically worked for the salvation of the Jews.

The bearded owner of the bookstore, Poulsen, had used his shop as a clearinghouse and headquarters for the exodus to Sweden. As the minister talked about him, Poulsen, a peppery little man, fell asleep.

The elderly sailor had also been active in the ferry service, first as Allrup's mate, then on his own, running a tiny motorboat into hidden coves and beaches to pick up "special cases"—Jews who were particular targets of the Gestapo. All had undertaken the job willingly, with a certain crazy daring, a wild humor.

"You must understand, Mr. Sweeney, that the pleasures of daily life are very important to us," said the Protestant clergyman. "As a man of the cloth I should be appalled by this, if you will, materialistic attitude. Yet is it so terrible? We have not produced much art or literature—frankly, I get a little sick of the way poor Hans Christian Andersen has to be paraded out for the tourists—but in the art of *living*, we have done well. Food, family, work, recreation, a warm home and a warm heart. We believe in these. I think we rebelled against the Germans' mad determination to deprive our Jews of these things that make life pleasurable."

"No, I don't get it," Sweeney mumbled, waving away the blue haze. "I mean, I can understand your philosophy—schnapps and friends and a lot of laughs—but that doesn't tell me why you risked your necks for the Jews. If you loved your pickled herring and your brandy so much, you'd have said, *nuts to the Jews, let 'em get theirs, we'll go on fressing and getting shicker!* Yes, you would have, if that's all that mattered to you."

"I did not say that was *all* that mattered," Reverend Munk said quickly. "The creature comforts, yes! But with them a sense of life, of work, of a society that is orderly but not authoritarian."

"You just won't accept any praise from me," Sweeney said plaintively. And suddenly he was filled with a delicious love for these people—originals, jokesters, nicotine addicts, two-handed drinkers, devourers of smoked herring and pickled lox and fried eels. They were unlike anyone he had ever met, a little bit nutty, a little bit off-center, yet somehow touched with a palpable, pulsating gift of love. He wanted desperately to honor them, to utter some comment that would not sound fatuous and superfluous, that would not have them nudging one another, laughing at him, blowing smoke in his face.

Clumsily, as a new wave of nausea rose in him, he leaned over for his attaché case as the *Prince Hamlet* lurched to starboard. He hit the floor, sliding a few feet into a mammoth Danish matron in

70

a green-tweed suit, who spilled a smørrebrød of brown bread, butter, lox, red peppers, hard-boiled egg, and mayonnaise all over him. Two waiters helped Sweeney to his feet. The laughter was general.

Wiped free of mayonnaise, dusted with talc to prevent spotting, Sweeney gasped for air, undid his attaché case, and took out one of Wettlaufer's embossed certificates.

"Reverend Munk," he said, "I am authorized to present to you, to all these guys, hell, to Denmark, this certificate making you members of the Legion of Noble Christians, and with it goes—"

His action touched off a wild argument among the party. The minister had been attempting to translate Wettlaufer's orotundities. Erik Allrup, questioning the reverend closely, suddenly displayed his annoyance and took the mate with him to help dock the ferryboat. The gynecologist, Dr. Nielsen, started shouting that he was no damn Christian, never had been, hated the Church and all it stood for, and would die an atheist. Poulsen, the bookstore owner, woke up and began arguing with the dining-room captain about the weakness of the coffee.

Reverend Munk finally gave the diploma back to the American. "No, Mr. Sweeney. My people would misunderstand this. And who would I give it to? This was a collective effort. I personally know thousands of people who helped. Thank this kind man, your patron. Perhaps you will find a noble Ukrainian or a brave Romanian who saved a Jew. Now here is what I suggest, since you do not look very well, Mr. Sweeney. Go ashore for a few days. Go to a fine hotel. Eat well, go to nightclubs, travel. Get to know our visit Elsinore, Odense. That will be good enough for us. We are tired of being honored by well-meaning people for doing something *that simply had to be done* if we were to retain our self-respect."

As the minister concluded, the *Prince Hamlet* bumped into the slip. There was a great tootling of whistles and blowing of horns. Passengers moved with leaden feet and glazed eyes toward the exits. How they had eaten! Tables sparkled with tens of dozens of empty beer bottles, whiskey bottles, coffeepots, teapots, glasses. And as the dining-room doors opened the impacted clouds of blue tobacco smoke billowed out and evanesced into the clear Baltic sky.

Sweeney appeared paralyzed. "It's muscular dystrophy," he whispered. "I always knew I was prone to it."

"Nonsense," said Dr. Nielsen. "Stand up, man, breathe the air!"

"Perhaps you should prescribe something," said Reverend Munk.

"A day at the beach and a blonde."

Erik Allrup returned from his duties to see if he might help the ailing American. He suggested a sea voyage, up the Kattegat to the Skaggerak.

But Sweeney did not respond. He lay there, inert, noncommunicative, hopelessly in love with these unexpected people, hopelessly sick on their food, their early morning sousing, their infernal cigars. He decided to return to Germany. Each man shook his hand warmly, wished him well, and departed. Reverend Niels Munk lingered, disturbed about Sweeney's condition.

"I'm sorry, Mr. Sweeney," the minister said. "Before I leave is there anything I can do for you? Or tell you?"

Sweeney managed to sit up. "Why'd you do it? Why'd you save 'em? In one short sentence, without the jokes."

"Because it was the right thing to do. Goodbye, my friend." He walked away, a wild ministerial fellow, with a wild compassionate heart.

So Sweeney returned to Hamburg, still sensing frustration in his search but feeling a little better about things. There was no correspondence from Gevaert, his nemesis, and no frantic cable from Wettlaufer complaining that some galoot had sneered at his children or painted a swastika on his garage.

Back at the Guttmacher Hotel he supped on *Arfensupp mit Snuten un Poten*, followed by a *Vierlander Mastente*, with a side order of *Birnen, Bohnen, und Speck*. The Danes had cheered him

72

and he felt expansive. In rapturous accord with his environment, he began to educate the dining-room captain.

"Sweeney looks at it this way, *walyo*," he began, as the captain stood by politely. "If you krauts would only stop murdering people, you'd be ace high with me. I mean it. Look at how you run hotels, so efficient. The johns work. The service is great. People are polite. I get smiles everywhere—"

The wine steward joined the captain. Both nodded in agreement. "Jesus, why do you have to go around stuffing Jews into furnaces when you're so nice otherwise? Fellahs, you got to get with it."

Two waiters joined the group. A girl from the newspaper counter wandered over. "You'd be the greatest bunch of walyos in Europe, smart, clean, hard-working, polite, helpful! Jesus, if you'd only stop murdering people!"

They all registered their accord. "Und Hitler nefer came up here," said the captain.

"Right!" shouted Sweeney, emptying his glass of *Pilsen*. "Now let's all make an effort, I mean a real team effort, to go out and win this one for the Gipper!"

"*Hah, das is gut! Der Kipper!*" cried the sommelier. By now, a dozen members of the staff had thronged around the American's table. There was much bobbing of heads, learned disputations on specific points he had made, but a general consensus on the gravamen of his argument.

"Ve haff always been different here!" said the captain. "Frie... und Hansa Stadt Hamburg, ja!

"Well, to hell with that," said Sweeney. "I can't get loused up in details. I merely ask you to go on doing the swell job you're doing and you'll make it. I have faith in you folks. The chambermaids are terrific. The cops know how to run traffic. You ask a guy a question, you get an answer. All of this tells me you people are part and parcel of a new era, and I know I'm right. *Just lay off murdering other people!*"

Inspired, they returned to their labors. The captain treated Sweeney to a brandy.

Exhilarated by these reformist exhortations, Sweeney wandered to the *Ankerplatz der Freude*, the Anchorage of Joy, in the St. Pauli Reeperbahn, where lurked congeries of whores, pimps, lesbos, fags, drunks, degenerates, and sailors. Sweeney made the rounds of strip joints (women almost as ugly as the ones in Amsterdam), fag shows, telephone clubs, and a streetful of beer joints where the amber flew in cascades, bursting his kidneys and bladder with tensile joy. His belly became a great hematoma of beer. He staggered into latrines, toilets, alleys, street drains, a sewer of a man, a Paris *égout*, making dross out of gold.

The night ended in the arms of a velvet beige vision, the German-speaking bastard spawn of some Hanseatic Sieglinde and Sergeant Willie Brown, night-fighter. She gestured to him from a clean, well-lit place, a dreamboat with frizzy hair, died rusty iron, pantherine features. Her skin had the texture of crême caramel. She was blue-eyed, red-mouthed, irresistible, the nineteen-year-old ripened fruit of the black American occupation and the penitent Boche.

Sweeney was an unabashed fetishist, and when she rose behind the flimsy nylon curtains, he got a glimpse of her in white lacy bra and garter belt, white silk stockings and white pumps with spiked heels. He felt faint and surrendered, disdaining fat blondes in black Merry Widows, dykes with whips, Junos in riding boots, French *bonnes*, Dutch milkmaids, and the Orientals who beckoned to him like a tray of assorted mixed appetizers in a Chinese restaurant. He went straight for Helga (for that was her name), Helga of the guttural voice, Bantu lips, and Zulu nose.

But the sex proved routine. His soggy body was awash with beer, weighted like a *baba au rhum*. He tired swiftly and fell into a drugged sleep. It was an honest house and the Madam, aware that Germans don't trifle with Americans, took only the basic fee—for the girl, the cover charge, recorded music, drinks, and a fixed service charge for the starched maid and the liveried doorman, plus a little extra for herself. *Service non est compris*, she informed Sweeney in the morning, and he replied, "Fair's fair, Mom." He slept another few hours on a bus-station bench, and was pleased to find his wallet intact, his gold tie clip in place, his watch telling him it was eight o'clock of a rainy windy morning in Hamburg.

The adventure pleased him; but he was man enough to admit it should have been more fun. Where were all the laughs? Where'd all the fun go?

An allergic lump, a scarlet swelling bloomed below his left ear. It itched fearfully. Scratching, he succeeded in enlarging it. He located a drugstore, purchased a bottle of benadryl in raspberry syrup, and drank half of it in one swig as the pharmacist goggled.

For an hour he sat drinking coffee in a rain-splashed café watching the people of Hamburg slosh through the morning downpour. Sweeney viewed them with pity, ordered more coffee, felt his allergic lump bloom into a second head, and thought about Dr. Ludwig Helms. A second try seemed to be in order.

He phoned Helms from the café, and again heard the faint voice. "No, no, Mr. Sweeney. I have told you I have nothing to say."

"What harm can it do, Dr. Helms?"

"It is not a question of harm. I have made my contribution to this—this—affliction of our times and I ask to be left alone. It is difficult for me to talk about it."

"Come on, Dr. Helms," Sweeney chided. "I was just up in Denmark. Those Danes are terrific. They gave me the whole story."

The Danes are a remarkable people and have much to be proud of."

"So do you! We want to set the record straight! Honest, Dr. Helms—just an hour. I tell you the Danes were great—talked a blue streak about it. Now you can't let a little country like Denmark make Germany come out looking so rotten."

There was an icy silence. Sweeney feared he had blabbered himself into a rejection. "The question of how rotten Germany looks or who makes her look rotten has long been decided. No invidious comparisons are necessary. You may come to see me."

Sweeney hurried to a stark office building, a prewar monolith untouched by RAF bombings. A creaky caged elevator took him to the sixth floor, where he found a frosted-glass door with the title:

FISHER & FROME, LTD.
Civil Engineering

He entered the reception room dripping buckets of rain from his trench coat. It was a great watershed of a coat, a madman's assortment of buckles, belts, straps, flaps, useless pockets and gas-mask hooks, and it had a remarkable capacity for storing water and releasing it at inopportune moments. Having flooded the room, he stood there stupidly, until an elderly secretary relieved him of the coat and directed him to Helms' office.

Sweeney introduced himself. The engineer got up woodenly and shook his hand with a single Teutonic jerk.

He was quite a bird, this Helms, Sweeney thought, as he unlimbered the recorder, looked for an outlet, and plugged in. A crane or a Malibu stork, some kind of tall wading bird, was what Helms brought to mind—stilt-legged, a rhythmic stiffness to his movements, a kind of starved dignity. Helms watched the visitor's movements with the cold eye of a doer, a man who dealt in measurable matters. The eyes that studied Sweeney were as gray as a Hamburg morning, retreating under gray furry eyebrows, masked with a filigreed gray skin. His nose was prominent, his cheeks hollow, his lips thin. There was an odd shrunkenness in his face, a face that had gone into retreat for dark reasons of its own.

Helms' slenderness and his faint voice made Sweeney wonder again if the engineer were suffering a chronic disease, a blood ailment, a malignancy feeding on his flesh.

Yet there was nothing of the invalid in Helms' manner or dress. His movements were crisp if sedate, his clothes were immaculately tailored and cut in the English style—a dark-gray suit, a white shirt with a soft collar, a black silk tie. When Sweeney appeared ready to begin Helms lit his pipe and spoke first.

"How did you learn about me?"

"The organization I work for researched this matter and found your testimony."

"I have said nothing since."

"I sure appreciate your willingness to talk now."

"Is it really necessary?" asked Helms. He puffed on his pipe. "Does the world need to hear this again?" He spun around in his swivel chair, and looked out to the shipyards, the docks on the Elbe. Sweeney waited.

"Why do you think I work for a British firm?" the engineer asked.

"Maybe they pay you more. I mean, you must be a valuable man, with your terrific English. It's better than mine."

"I have a minor job here. I am a trained civil engineer with much experience. At the age of fifty-six I could be earning twice what I am with a German organization."

Sweeney rubbed the pomegranate blooming below his ear.

"After the trials for a long time I was marked as a traitor."

"But you told the truth."

"The Frenchman Camus once wrote, 'again and again there comes a time in history when the man who dares to say that two and two make four is punished with death.' I received no death sentence but I was punished. I had told only a small part of the truth. The truth was so enormous, so horrible, so—so destructive of everything we want to believe that it can only be told slowly, in small drops, like intravenous feeding."

"You should have gotten credit for what you did."

"I will not burden you with the vicious telephone calls, the threats to my wife, to my children, whispers, rumors, obscene references. I attribute all that to the unrepentant, the unreformed, our *lumpen* lower classes. I was not prepared to suffer the rejection of the business community. I had served the *Wehrmacht* long and faithfully. Apart from my limited activities in behalf of the people

77

in whom you are interested, I was never anything less than a faithful servant of the Reich. Then came the trials.

"It was explained to me by an executive of one of our steel mills, a fellow who had used slave laborers. 'You see, Helms, we admire what you did and your willingness to talk about it, but it would be unpleasant having you around, flaunting your saintliness. By now the left-wing press has made a hero of you. The Jews have blown up your deeds so that you are the new Messiah. Well, Messiahs are out of place in a rolling mill and you'd only make the rest of us sinners feel uncomfortable.'

"He went on to tell me that the matter of war-crimes trials was being looked at in a new light, that even American jurists were doubtful about their legitimacy. And this fellow told me, 'But you, Helms, testified, told your stories which perhaps were true, but were they really necessary, when our major concern was rebuilding Germany?'

"So, Mr. Sweeney, that is why I work for less money for the British. Several Jewish gentlemen have asked me to come to America and work with them but I will not trade on that. I ask only to be left alone, to appreciate my home, my wife, my children, my grandchild."

"I'm sorry, Dr. Helms. You're sure that what you tell me, if it's published, won't make any trouble for you?"

Helms waved his hand. "I doubt it. There is a current vogue of philo-Semitism here. In any case my life has settled into a pattern and little can disturb me now. You may start your questioning with your excellent Swiss machine." He admired it with a technician's eye. Helms leaned back rigidly and Sweeney again had the sensation that he was favoring an old injury.

In unadorned engineer's language, as his voice became hoarser, he talked about himself. He was born in Bremen, the only child of a municipal clerk, attended public schools, then earned scholarships to technical schools. The early influences in his life were a mild Lutheranism, a milder socialism, a dedication to study and hard work, and deep family ties.

At the outbreak of the war he was in his early thirties, a skilled engineer, partner in a small firm. His talents exempted him from military service, since he was more valuable as a civilian. A lack of political conviction kept him out of the Nazi party. "I was always a bystander, an observer of politics," he said. "I trusted my slide rule but never a politician."

Civil engineers were an indispensable part of the *Wehrmacht*'s machine and Helms followed the victorious divisions into the Low Countries and France, building roads, improvising bridges, earning a reputation as a fellow who gets things done. He was self-effacing, quiet, a complete technician, and was soon in demand.

"I numbered a few generals as acquaintances. Not field officers but engineers and ordnance men, by and large. Yet I was never friendly with any of them. I have always kept a distance between myself and the next chap. My wife and my children I suppose are the only ones who have ever known me well."

Helms leaned back to refresh his memory.

"In the winter of 1942 I was sent to the Ukraine," he resumed. "The cold, the savage fighting, the primitive roads were delaying the *Wehrmacht*. Let me mention in passing that we used conscript labor. Slave labor. I make no apologies. It was a war. I was an engineer. My job was to build roads. Do you find this attitude deplorable in one of your noble Europeans?"

"Well, there was so much awful going on," said Sweeney stupidly, "that if you Germans went around apologizing for everything you'd never get done. I think you folks should only have to be sorry for the really lousy things you done. Did."

Helms paused a moment, as if appreciative of the American's analysis. It was crude but was it not without a certain logic?

"Perhaps. I have seen too many horrors to start quibbling over what was immoral, what was bad, what was vile, and what were the vilest of sins against humanity, against God. These slave laborers—Poles mostly, Ukrainians, Great Russians—one did not notice them after a while. They worked, sickened, many died. You are here to learn about the Jews. We are, you and I, studying a complicated map of evil rivers and mountains of sin. We must be selective in our reading of it."

The engineer poured a glass of water for himself, one for his visitor, and coughed softly. "A few preparatory remarks about my attitude towards Jews may be in order. I had never given them much thought. In Bremen, in my youth, there was some routine anti-Semitism. Not on my or my parents' part, I can honestly say. We were socialists, you know. But I do recall our neighbors discussing the notion that the Jews betrayed us in the first war. But not with any real conviction. The Nazis were never very strong in Bremen, certainly not in those early years.

"I knew a few Jewish merchants slightly, two or three students in the technical school. Fellows who kept to themselves, did not drink, and got good grades. After 1933, we saw less and less of them, and I thought about them not at all. As you see I was a neutral, a technician."

"But—the deportations. And knocking out store windows. And the old men with beards scrubbing the streets."

"What could one do? It was part of the new Germany. What are you doing, sir, about the black people in your country?"

"Excuse me, Dr. Helms, but everyone I meet in Europe keeps pulling that on me. It's the old gag 'What about the lynchings in the South?'"

"I do not understand."

"This American engineer, see, is taken on a tour of the Moscow subway by a Russian engineer. And when the American comments that he hasn't seen a train for half an hour, the Russian says, 'What about the lynchings in the South?'"

Helms did not smile. "I do not consider it an inappropriate comment. All I could have done in those years was to object, be jailed, and perhaps executed. Will you, Mr. Sweeney, go to jail—or death—in Mississippi?"

"Objection!" shouted Sweeney. "Our government is opposed to shooting colored people! Your government was in favor of shooting Jews!"

"Precisely. How much more difficult it was for us to resist—when government, police, army, local officials commanded our loyalty and fostered the persecution."

"Well, some people must have objected."

"You may count them on one hand. Most of us were indifferent. Some *applauded*. I, the neutral fellow, merely watched."

"The Churches?" ventured Sweeney hesitantly, feeling the dirty presence of Emile Gevaert at his elbow.

"Indeed? It now appears that our Catholic bishops were more than eager to support Hitler's race purification and all it envisioned. To be sure they used that circuitous clerical language which I, as an engineer, find repugnant, but what could be clearer than Archbishop Grober preaching that Germans had a *right* to maintain undisturbed their racial stock? *The right!* And we see where that right led.

"How clever Hitler was! Every time some goodhearted prelate, Catholic or Protestant, would question his Jewish policies he would hurl back at them centuries of their own traditions. That clever Austrian! He knew enough Church history to make them squirm. Had I time I could find for you a dialogue he had in 1933 with two leading churchmen in which he informed them he was merely attempting *to do more effectively* what the Church Militant had been trying to do for a long time."

"Oh no," protested Sweeney. "Maybe he fooled them at first. But they couldn't go along with that. Heck, who couldn't make a mistake as early as 1933?"

"Mistake? Perhaps. Policy? Perhaps. It is nothing for us to wax indignant over. We are talking about the results of a historical process. Now when these results became excessive, a little more than civilized people bargained for, particularly persons presenting themselves to the world as guardians of our morals, then there were some second thoughts."

"Such as?"

"Well—on the order of 'Naturally we don't like Jews, they are deicides and anti-Christian and should be kept in their place, but *perhaps shooting naked people in the neck is excessive.* By all means keep them apart, keep them from poisoning our precious national blood, but not quite so—so—*energetically,* you know.' "

A chill shivered Sweeney's hulk and he shut off the tape recorder. Helms did not notice and continued. His voice was growing fainter. "There were protests. It occurred to our clergy that what Hitler was up to was *not quite what they had in mind.* The Jew as a menace, enemy, money-changer was one thing, a handy adhesive to bind the faithful. But the Jew as a frozen corpse on some snowy field in the Ukraine? Well, there is always some fellow who takes things too literally. Henry II really did not want Becket murdered. But some bloody chaps will always take the cue and plunge the dagger. And the *moderate* hater is left with his mouth open asking himself how the devil it happened. Ah, I see you have turned off our Swiss witness."

"I'm not sure all this is part of the story," said Sweeney. "I wish I was smarter. . . . There were clergymen who objected. Bonnhoffer. Niemoeller."

"I do not deny that."

Sweeney sighed. Exhaustion devoured him. Helga's narrow bed and the bus-station bench were no substitute for a decent night's sleep.

"We got off on another angle, Dr. Helms," he said. "That's another story—what the Church *didn't* do. I'm interested in what people *did.*"

"Is it a different story? I often wonder. Suppose Father Senn, the Nazi priest, or all those Protestant divines who backed Hitler had been witness to what I saw in the Ukraine? What would they have said?"

"Tell me what you saw." He turned the recorder on.

The engineer waited a moment. "I shall omit a lot of my early observations—slave laborers and so forth. We were at Poldarenko, a village in the Ukraine. I was senior engineer in charge of a team of army and civilian personnel building roads. Although I was a civilian, in technical matters I held the highest rank.

"It was late November. Bleak, cold. Impossible to stay warm.

One would stand around a peat fire in a hut, venture into the open, and feel that icy wind inside one's bones in minutes. Snowfall every night—and an incessant wind screaming across frozen fields. Our task was difficult. There were shortages of labor, petrol, equipment. This place, Poldarenko, was at a crossroads where a secondary dirt road, knocked out by Red artillery, joined a major highway. We had been held back by Russian guns for two weeks, but the front had moved east again and we had orders to make a survey and get the dirt road into usable condition. Perhaps that was why the *Wehrmacht* engineers were willing to give in to me, why a certain laxity developed, why we traveled as freely as we did and were able to see what we saw.

"You see, Mr. Sweeney, such murder sites were usually in isolated, secret places. I have often wondered about that. If we really believed that the Jews *deserved* to be killed, that a Jew-free Europe was a blessing, why did we not murder them in public, with fanfare, as a great spectacle? We should have been eager to show the world what we were doing. Yet we tried to hide it. Is that a hopeful sign? That deep in our breasts we were aware of our own wickedness?

"We were riding along this dirt road, about ten of us in the survey party. We were a few kilometers west of the village crossing snow-covered fields as level as this desk top when we saw the Jews. I learned later this was the entire Jewish community of Poldarenko. They had been rounded up by the co-operative Ukrainians. They did not look like the Rothschilds. Poor people, cold, trembling, shabbily dressed. Hardly the kind who would represent a threat to anyone. There was a squad of SS men guarding them and perhaps a dozen Ukrainians.

"They marched by our vehicles and Papke, the engineering officer who was my counterpart, a good-natured sort, said to me that they were probably being *relocated* as a security measure. There had been much sabotage and some guerrilla action, although these miserable people hardly seemed the type.

"As they passed us the column turned off the road and plodded through the snow toward a long mound of earth, perhaps fifty meters distant. All were silent. Not a sound, except some coughing, the whimpering of a child, an infant crying. They made no protest. This mound was covered with snow and was about twenty meters long and three meters high."

Helms cleared his throat noisily and turned in his seat as if tiring. Again, Sweeney saw him as a man losing a battle against a wasting disease, an internal rupture that would bleed him white.

Facing Sweeney again, the engineer said, "I think you will understand all this better if I make a drawing. I wish to be precise." Helms took a yellow sheet of paper from his desk, and a soft red pencil from his pocket.

"Now here is the dirt road and here is where the column was marched off." He drew swiftly. "The mound was here, in this relationship to the road. This 'X' is where our trucks stopped."

Helms looked up. "Colonel Papke wished to move on. But I convinced him to stay. 'Herr Oberst,' I told him, 'you and I are blessed with inquiring minds. Perhaps we will learn something.' Papke, who never quite figured me out, agreed. As we got out of our vehicles an SS sergeant walked up and politely asked what we were doing. He was under orders to carry out his mission without witnesses. I told him that we had a divisional priority to survey the road and that we were not interested in his Jews. Before he could respond I ordered the enlisted men to set up the theodolite. The sergeant shrugged and returned to his column while Papke and I adjusted our field glasses. We pretended to be occupied with our job, but we could not take our eyes off the Jews.

" 'This does not appear to be a relocation,' I said. 'I have heard what we are doing with Jews.' 'So have I,' answered Papke, 'but we are at war. Jews aren't much good for anything. You can't get a day's work out of the parasites. And these Eastern Jews are the worst. Europe will be better without them.'

"The Jews were lined up in a ragged column facing the guards. The SS men moved them, rather gently, into an even line. Then the SS sergeant shouted an order, and they began to undress. I tell you it is a strange sight to see a hundred people, aged, adults, children, disrobing on a wintry day in the midst of an open field with the wind whipping their naked flesh. One is tempted to laugh. *Why are they doing it? And who would make them do it?* How ludicrous! The sight of ragged underwear, long hose full of holes, undone garters, dirty shifts, soiled vests. Soon the sense of embarrassment vanishes. One reasons thus: if these people are so poor and filthy they must *deserve* what is happening to them. Indeed, Papke was quick to state exactly what I was thinking. 'Jews are dirty creatures,' he said, with Bavarian simplicity. 'Look, look at that old man pissing his pants. And that little boy is shitting.' Papke laughed, the rich laughter of our northern race. Our enlisted men smiled and nudged each other at the sight of a breast bared, a patch of pubic hair exposed, a corset removed, a brassiere undone.

"I noted, too, the behavior of the Ukrainians, most of whom were drunk. Several of them had unbuttoned their flies and were flaunting their genitals at the Jews. I am convinced God gave us the Ukrainians and the Romanians and the Lithuanians so that we Germans might not be alone in our beastliness."

Without warning the engineer was convulsed with a racking cough. He held a handkerchief to his face, his eyes teared. "Once in a book on religious symbolism I read that the Star of David, the two triangles superimposed, represent the male and female pubes. The aimless thought occurred to me that when the Jews fell their private parts, those organs meant for love and creation, the sources of life, would fall on each other, dark triangles on white flesh, forming stars of David. Once I knew the Hebrew name—

"Mogen David," said Sweeney, shocked to find his own voice strangled.

"Of course. Let us return to my diagram." He began to sketch again. "All the Jews were naked now. About a fifth of them were separated and marched off at right angles, thus, around the mound. I told Papke to move our surveyors into the field, and engrossed in the sight of nude female bodies, that vision of freezing breasts and thighs, he agreed. We walked across the snowy

85

field, warm in our furry boots. The surveyors followed us. There was one questioning glance from the SS sergeant, but he was too busy to stop us. So we turned the corner of the embankment, thus.

"As I suspected, there was a deep trench there. The mound had been built with the excavated earth. 'I doubt that this is a relocation,' I said again to Papke. He was transfixed. Little bubbles of spit formed at the corners of his lips and his eyes were shining—a masturbatory experience. Finally he said, 'Oh, in a way it is. Jews believe in heaven and all we are doing is relocating them from their lousy village to a better place.'

"There was a delay, some confusion about where to stand the Jews, where to place the Ukrainians with the machine pistols. This may have been an inexperienced squad. Many of these execution teams were soldiers in trouble with their units—drunks, malcontents. They were given this duty as punishment."

"Fuck-ups?" shouted Sweeney, unable to suppress an intolerable urge to curse.

"I am not certain of the meaning of that expression, but I imagine it is accurate. Whatever the records of these men they *did* receive bonuses for their work, and were often allowed to divide the booty. In this there developed an argument over the discarded clothing, which had been neatly piled, shoes stacked with shoes, hats with hats, and so forth. True German orderliness, teaching those barbaric Ukrainians a few things.

"By now the Jews were shivering in the icy wind. A few of the women tried to cover their breasts and groins. Some adults were comforting the children. Papke and I moved closer. Now, as you may know, Mr. Sweeney, Yiddish is very much like German and I was able to hear the Jews quite clearly because only a few were speaking and there was very little crying or shrieking.

"There was a boy of ten, a skinny child with a shaven head and huge black eyes, holding his father's hand and repeating, 'Papa, will we go home soon? Papa, why did you bring me here?'—the eternal plaint of a child blaming his parents. 'Papa—why don't we go home, I am missing my school lessons. . . .'"

86

The engineer stopped. His starved hands sought the sides of his head, and he pressed palms and fingers against his cheeks and temples.

"You okay, Dr. Helms?" Sweeney asked. "You want to take a five-minute break?"

"No, no. I am all right." He stoked his pipe again and his hand was steady. "Back to my diagram. The rest of the Jews stayed here, behind the mound. They were very still. Then the SS sergeant lined up his squad at the edge of the trench, thus. I recall there was a very old woman in this first group of Jews. Her withered breasts were hanging like dried stalks. She held an infant in her arms—a granddaughter, a niece, who knows? She was *singing* to the child. *Singing.* It was a song about 'Raisins and Almonds' and perhaps it was my imagination but I could swear I had once heard it in the Bremen ghetto many years ago.

"There was also a little girl, no more than five, grasping her mother's hand. She kept asking, 'Mama, will you go to the hospital to get better? Will you be all better?' And the mother, quite ill, her eyes swollen, her skin splotched with a rash, kept nodding her head to assure the child that she would recover. She had red braided hair and I heard her say, 'Yes, my child, all of us will be better, we will be happy in a little while.'

"I had a strange sensation. Hearing that little girl asking her mother these questions I was transported to my boyhood, to those occasions when my own mother would fall ill. You know, Mr. Sweeney, in a child's world mothers are not permitted illness. We are selfish little beasts and mothers simply are not allowed this privilege. I can recall my mother in bed buried under the goose-down quilt and myself in a huge rocking chair, my feet off the ground, repeating these exact words to my mother, over and over, 'Mama, will you be all better?'

"That remembrance of my warm home, my parents, the sharing of simple pleasures, the mere *closeness* of the family, eating, sleeping, watching the sun rise and set, learning, talking to neighbors, reading books, all these recollections flooded over me in a great wave of guilt. I looked at the Jews again and discovered that terror has its own devices to cleanse the mind. Does life become unbearable? Then the mind rejects hope, sanity, compassion. Yet am I certain of that? How does one explain the old woman singing to the infant at the very gates of hell?

"I suspect my amateur philosophy does not interest you. Let us resume. The SS sergeant now ordered the Jews to descend a series of steps that had been cut into the side of the pit. They obeyed. Then they were ordered to lie down in the trench. Some couples embraced. The red-haired woman hugged the girl to her breast. The old lady had to be helped to the supine position. Not a soul begged for mercy. No one attempted to run. Papke, my fellow witness, noticed this and to him it seemed a justification for what was happening. 'See,' he said, 'the Jews expect this. It is inevitable. Human life with these Eastern people has little value. They are Orientals and they have no appreciation of life as do true Europeans.'

"This line of reasoning was cut short by the machine pistols. Massacre allows small room for discussion. There was some moaning. Some of the bodies in the pit twitched and moved. One of the Ukrainians was ordered by the SS chap to move into the pit and fire a few more rounds to make sure all were dead. He did so. Then the trench was silent, motionless. It was odd how the blood froze on their necks and heads as soon as it was spilled.

"The SS man shouted an order and another batch of naked Jews was marched around the embankment toward the trench. In this group there was one very old, extremely thin man with a long white beard. He was paralyzed, or simply frozen with cold, and two younger men were carrying him. 'It's all right, zayde,' I heard one of them say, 'you will soon be resting.' "

Irrelevantly, Sweeney interrupted: "Zayde means Grampa! I was raised in a Jewish neighborhood!"

"So it does. In this second group there was also a young woman, quite lovely. The sight of her naked figure aroused lewd comments from our surveyors, and one of them commented he had heard that Jewish women were savages in bed and how lucky the SS men were to have their pick of them. I found myself shouting at them to get to work, that they were not there to be spectators. As the girl walked by us—Papke and I were standing here and the Jews were marched thus—she turned to us and solemnly said, 'I am twenty-one years old and I am engaged to be married.'

"So this second group was ordered down the steps and made to lie on top of the corpses. Papke nodded to me. 'You know, Helms,' he said, 'after you see the first batch die it makes the second easier—like taking medicine. I'll bet these SS fellows get used to it in no time.' The truth was he was right. I had to fight the notion that we were not looking at people who once had had homes, jobs, hopes, religion, friends, and love—but at inevitable victims, beings whose only destiny was to be degraded beyond hope of salvation and then executed as barbarically as possible. Still, I heard the child's voice, 'Mama, will you be better soon?'

"The second volley exploded and there was the usual encore, the extra rounds to ensure that all were dead. And so a third group of Jews were made to lie down on the dead, and they too were murdered. In that group, or perhaps in the last, there was a father and a son, the boy perhaps ten, trying to hold back his tears, the father a stoop-shouldered man, stroking the lad's head and pointing to the bright wintry sky, reassuring him, smiling, telling him God knows what."

Helms suddenly looked challengingly at his visitor. "What do you think, Mr. Sweeney? What would your father have said to you?"

"I don't know," whispered Sweeney.

No, no I . . . I could not hear him. But did your father ever stroke your head when you were ten years old and frightened and assure you that all would be well? As mine so often did when I came to him weeping, perhaps over a spinning top lost in a drain?"

"You bet he did!" cried Sweeney. "My old man was a helluva guy! He never did a mean thing in his life—to us kids or anyone else!" And with that startling memory of James John Sweeney, as decent a saloonkeeper as ever lived and an indulgent and patient father, Sweeney began to bawl uncontrollably. He stuffed a handkerchief in his mouth and turned his swollen red face away from Helms. The engineer reached across the desk and turned the machine off.

"Perhaps you are hearing more than you want to hear," he said.

"Nah, nah, I'm okay," sobbed Sweeney. "Nobody should have suffered like that! Nobody should have to listen to it! Oh, that dirty Wettlaufer, what a friend. I'll fix him." His jaw trembling, he turned the recorder on and said, "Go on, Dr. Helms, I can take it."

"There is not much more to tell. With the last Jew dead the Ukrainians staggered to the edge of the pit and amid much laughter urinated on the bodies.

"Papke and I had turned to leave. I noticed that the trench had been dug too shallow and the pile of corpses was higher than the rim of the pit. The Ukrainians were hurriedly heaping earth on the dead. Now perhaps I imagined what I shall now relate to you, since after all that shooting, one would have to assume that the dead were in fact dead. But as we walked away I could swear that from that hellish hole *arms and heads* were gesturing toward the sky. I clearly saw them—bloodied, contorted arms—rising to— what? To their God?

"As you know, Mr. Sweeney, theirs is a very old God, much older than ours, and He is undoubtedly a busy one, perhaps even a tired one. I suppose we will never know whether He noticed them or not. But those waving arms and those raised heads! Reaching— like this——" The engineer lifted one lean arm, sleeved in dark gray, and stretched it not toward any Heaven but toward the fluorescent lights in the ceiling. "Reaching," said Helms in a whisper, "reaching to the sky, thus. . . ."

He lowered his arm. Sweeney's blubberings were under control. But his voice was damp, his face the color of a garden tomato. "That was quite a story. Now we have to get the other side of it, what you did to save the Jews. We have to end on a note of hope, Dr. Helms . . . somehow."

Helms crumpled his drawing of the execution site and threw it into a wastebasket.

"You're one of our Noble Christians," Sweeney said.

"A generous description," answered the engineer. "Before I speak of my work let me add that the massacre at Poldarenko was the last I witnessed. However, I heard of many more and on at least two occasions saw the naked bodies in the pits. A concerted effort was made to tighten secrecy and to make the business of executions less interesting. There was no undressing. Looting was forbidden, as were unseemly actions such as urinating on the dead. There was even a regulation that if a man were observed to be *enjoying* himself, he was to be sent to the front. Of course, the gas chambers and the ovens made all of this easier later on.

"In 1943 I was ordered to Galicia to supervise the improvement of roads leading to our airfields. I was given more and more authority because at this late date engineering officers were being transferred to the Eastern front in combat units. Thus I found myself signing papers, giving orders, assuming quasi-military functions, even when I was not authorized to do so.

"No one objected because I got the roads built. The security forces were so busy killing Jews, gypsies, the mentally retarded, political prisoners, intellectuals, and so forth, that I was left alone.

"There had been a particularly noteworthy massacre about ten kilometers from my headquarters. It was so cold that the Jewish women froze on the spot, their babies frigid in their arms—*before the shots were fired*. The graves were shallow, the bodies were piled high, and the Polish auxiliaries were so drunk that they neglected to finish off the wounded. Many people froze to death or were suffocated or drowned in blood.

"It may surprise you to hear this, but the efficiency of these activities varied from place to place. Through some oversight the Jews of the village of Szascina had been spared. In fact several of them, draftsmen and clerical people, worked at my headquarters and nothing was ever said about their presence. One day when I was alone in my office, a man named Avrum Label Flaum, who had once been an eminent Warsaw architect, came to me and said

91

that the Jewish underground had heard that the Jews of Szascina were doomed, . . . that the oversight had come to the attention of an SS colonel, and that they were to be 'relocated' within a week.

"Flaum asked me to help them escape. Ever since Poldarenko I had been filled with a sickening sense of defeat, as if aware that evil had won the world and that our lives were without meaning or dignity. So in choosing to help Flaum I was perhaps performing a selfish act: restoring my own faith.

"I told him that if he would spread the word among the Jews, I would arrange to send them to a remote construction camp where, disguised as non-Jews, they might survive.

"It was not easy. To begin with, only the younger and stronger, those with freedom of movement, could be saved. They were required to rip off the yellow badges and pose as Christians. The penalty for this was death. Little by little the braver ones fell in with our plan. Earlocks were shaved, badges came off. They attempted to assume the appearance of Polish laborers. They had no identity papers so I made up what I called an 'emergency-work card,' identifying them as qualified construction workers urgently needed. I was sufficiently respected by the Wehrmacht to be permitted a good deal of freedom. The ruse worked.

"Eventually, by truck, in my own car, with the help of a bribed Polish railway engineer, I transported about three hundred Jews to an isolated camp at Premz, a place which had been totally destroyed. The Jews were given Polish names and papers. They were put to work on a road that led nowhere. I got them a ration of food, browbeating the supply corps continually, a role for which I am ill-suited. All but three of them survived the war—as Poles. And that is all I did."

"Suppose they'd caught you?"

"I cannot say. I might have been shot. Jail, surely. I was past worrying about myself. Some gesture was called for, some indication that I was still a member of the human fraternity. But who is to say now who was more true to that brotherhood? Myself, hiding Jews in a work camp? Or the SS man giving the orders to shoot them?"

"You! You!" cried Sweeney. "Sure, there are murders committed, sure people can be criminals! But it goes against the grain to just kill, and kill, and kill without reason!"

"Under a given set of circumstances it need not, and given the historical processes of which we spoke earlier, who can say which action was more normal, mine or the SS man's?"

"Never! Murder doesn't come naturally!"

"Do not be so certain, Mr. Sweeney."

"Jesus, if only there had been a thousand guys like you. Ten thousand."

"There were some. A handful here in Germany. A woman in Dresden who worked for Catholic charities. A ceramics manufacturer in Berlin. Some priests."

That despairing sense of irrelevancy again surged over Sweeney as he reached into his case for one of Wettlaufer's diplomas.

"Dr. Helms, my organization is honored to present you with this certificate naming you a member of the Legion of Noble Christians. With it goes one thousand dollars for any charity you designate, for your own needs—whatever you want."

"I thank you, and I thank this mysterious donor. Who is he? What sort of man?"

"He's scared stiff," said Sweeney. He wound up the cord of the recorder, and packed it away. "I guess that's it. Unless you have something else to tell me."

Helms pursed his lips and shook his valetudinarian's head. He stared out the window at the interminable northern rain, at the damp gray of Hamburg. "A footnote, perhaps. Not part of your story, I imagine."

"Shoot."

"I would not bother recording it. It amounts to nothing more than some personal musings." He faced Sweeney and rested both palms on the desk top, a precise man assembling a new set of thoughts.

"I believe I told you," Helms said, "I was raised in a climate of rather indifferent Lutheranism. Christmas, Easter, weddings, funerals—that was all. But the mechanisms of religious experience have always intrigued me. Certainly I have never felt any hostility to the great faiths. Do you understand me?"

"I'm on your wave length, Dr. Helms. I'm a punk Catholic, I admit. But I like the old Church. Any church. I can get a lift out of a Quaker meeting or when I hear the ram's horn blow on Rosh Hashonah. It all kind of swings."

Helms ignored the visitor's barbaric locutions. "Some months after the shootings at Poldarenko I asked our chaplain to lend me a book of Luther's basic writings. Perhaps that inspired mystic, my countryman, had solace for me. For is that not one of the functions of religion? I needed something to make clear to me the meaning of those naked Jews. What was the significance of those arms reaching to heaven? Surely Martin Luther whose faith moved princes and nations would have an answer, something to illuminate that icy darkness."

"And you found it!" exulted Sweeney.

"I am not certain what I found." The engineer took a dark green volume from an old mahogany bookcase behind him. "Do you understand German?"

"Not a word."

"I shall translate. I almost know the passage by heart." Helms adjusted horn-rimmed spectacles on his nose, smoothed the pages, and began to read in a hoarse voice. "Written by Martin Luther in 1543, exactly 400 years before I witnessed the Poldarenko relocations. He begins thus:

" 'What shall we Christians do with this damned, rejected race of Jews?' "

"Oh no," Sweeney groaned. "Not him, too."

Helms continued. " 'Because they live among us, and we know about their lying and blasphemy and cursing, we can't tolerate them if we do not wish to share in their lying, curses, and blasphemy. In this manner, we cannot put out the fierce fire of divine anger, so say the prophets, nor convert the Jews.

" 'We must practice, prayerfully and with reverence, a kind of severity. Maybe we can save some from the fire. We must not seek revenge. They are surely being punished a thousand times more than we might wish. I shall give you honest advice.' "

"Well, that's not as bad as I thought it would be," said Sweeney, much relieved. "He says don't look for revenge. That should have stopped those SS guys. After all Luther was a pretty important cat."

"There is more. 'First, their synagogues or churches should be burned. Whatever doesn't burn should be covered with dirt so that no person can ever see a cinder or a stone that is left. This should be done for the honor of God and of Christianity, in order that God may see that we are Christians, and that we have not wittingly tolerated or approved of such public lying, cursing, and blaspheming of His Son and His Christians.

" 'Secondly, their homes should also be destroyed. For they do the same things there as they do in their synagogues. For this reason, they should be put under one roof, or in a stable, like Gypsies, for they must realize that they are not masters in our land, as they boast, but miserable prisoners.

" 'Thirdly, they should have their prayerbooks and Talmuds seized, because these are filled with idolatry, lies, cursing, and blasphemy.

" 'Fourth. Their rabbis must be forbidden under threat of death to teach any more.

" 'Fifth. Passport and traveling privileges must absolutely be forbidden to Jews. They have no business in the country, since they are not nobles, nor officials, nor merchants. Let them stay home.

" 'Sixth. They must be stopped from usury. All cash, all valuables must be taken from them and put aside for safekeeping.' " Helms looked up. "He makes no mention of wrenching the gold from the teeth of the dead as at Bergen-Belsen.

" 'Seventh. Let young, strong Jews and Jewesses be given the flail, the axe, the hoe, the shovel, the distaff and spindle, and let them earn their bread by the sweat of their noses, as was ordered by Adam's children.

" 'For as it has been said, God's rage is so great against them that they only become worse and worse through mercy, and not much better through severe mercy. Therefore, away with them! To sum up, dear Lords, who have Jews in your domains, if this advice of mine does not suit you, then find a better one so that you, and we, may all be free of this terrible devilish burden—the Jews.' "

A stupid glaze covered Sweeney's face. He blinked a few times. "Ah—rather strong stuff, yes it is. Has anyone thought that it might be a clever forgery?"

"I am afraid it is Luther's work."

Sweeney got up. "And what did this teach you about the naked people in the snow? The little girl who wanted her mother to get better?"

"I am not certain, Mr. Sweeney. If the God to whom Luther spoke is the same God to whom those wretched people raised their arms what response could He make? And would He be interested at all?"

"Out of my line, Dr. Helms."

"And leaving God out of this question—for I suspect He has been left out possibly by His own choosing—I am forced to speculate on the connection between our noblest religious personage, the most God-inspired man of his time, and the men pulling the triggers of the Schmeisser pistols."

"Don't ask me. I'm only interested in Noble Christians. The past is beginning to scare the hell out of me."

Helms appeared lost in his contemplation of the past. "The crime, the crime. Or was it a crime at all? I think we Germans understood the secret—that when one exceeds certain limits of human behavior one deals not in a crime but in godly power. Stalin understood this, as did Hitler and his associates. And this evil power has its own capacity for justifying itself. How else explain the acts I have described?

"Perhaps I am sentimental but I keep thinking of the ravished families. Mother, father, children. A house—walls, ceiling, floor, furnishings, protection from cold and rain, a community bound by love, by necessity. A father helps his son with his mathematics. A mother peels apples for dessert and gives a slice to a baby. Books, music, holidays, that exquisite joy of a daily routine, of the presence of children, for I tell you, Mr. Sweeney, no love on earth transcends that of parent for child. And all this denied to the Jews. Not merely to murder people but to say you have no existence, no right to live, you are as naked and powerless as plucked chickens, you have no homes, no warmth, no arithmetic lessons, no slice of apple—only the vilest of deaths. And as we give you this death we deny that you ever had any rights to any existence. We deny God's earth to you, because in God's name, we have seized the earth from Him."

"Aaah!" Sweeney cried. "It can't be! Dammit, the Jews won, the Jews won!"

Helms rose. With that stiff, storklike gait he walked toward the stricken American. "No, no, my friend," the engineer said, "there were no winners." He touched Sweeney's arm as if by some modest bodily contact—the wedded sorrow of two strangers—they might restore life to the bloody corpses in the Ukraine. "If you speak of winners look out the window and see us—fat and sleek with money and cars."

"Jesus, the old lady who sang to the baby . . . the two guys carrying the old man . . . the other guy who pointed to the sky. . . . Helms, you don't leave me *anything!* I need answers. I need someone to make sense out of it. You're no help. You made it all worse—with Luther and all that jazz!"

"I warned you when you first called me." Helms walked back to his desk, opened a drawer, and took out a folder. "If you are determined to pursue this, there is a man you should see. An Italian named Bolli."

Sweeney brushed a remnant of tears from his cheek. "Bolli? I got some Italians but nobody by that name."

Helms said, "It is not his real name. I think it is his mother's. They call him Franco Bolli, Italian for a postage stamp. It has, I gather, a double significance: he is a very small man, but it also symbolizes his efforts to effect communication between people. You will find him somewhere near Naples, engaged in a rehabilitation program with peasants."

"And he was a Noble Christian?"

"He and his brother were in charge of an escape program for Italian Jews. After the war he practiced as a draftsman. Later he began this social work. He wrote to me for information on roadbed stresses, cheap and quick methods of construction, and so on, so we have been corresponding. A remarkable man."

"Bolli," Sweeney repeated, and scrawled the name on the back of Gevaert's letter on canon law. Then he shook hands with Dr. Ludwig Helms and left.

From the nearest café Sweeney called the United States Consul in Hamburg. "This is Mendel Meyer Rabinowitz of Darien, Connecticut," he said. "I'm a big insurance man, member of the round-table, and my wife is loaded too. I got to find the synagogue. I think the *shamis* is a distant relative on my wife's side."

In a taxi, sloshing through flooded streets, he rode to a humble stone building seemingly deserted. The Mogen David looked out upon the harsh street—eternally triangulated, discreetly aged. Sweeney stood opposite the *schul* in the rain letting the cold waters soak his rakish beret and drown his useless trench coat, filling its secret pockets and flaps. He became some ancient Hibernian herdsman, silent in his wet goatskin.

For a long time no one left or entered the synagogue. After perhaps fifteen minutes a patriarch, a miraculous survivor of the fires, emerged. He wore a black undented Homburg. His hair was snowy, yellowing, as were his lush earlocks and rich beard. The old fellow wrestled with his umbrella and was suddenly terrified to find a hulking, drenched, red-faced *goy* trying to help him.

"Permit me, *zayde*," said Sweeney. "Let me help you."

"*Danke, danke*," muttered the ancient, trying to disengage. But Sweeney hugged him warmly.

"Lissen. Lissen to me. I'm Americanish. A goy. But I'm on your side, honest. I got to talk to you."

"*Bist a yid?*"

"Nah, nah, rebbi. But I was the *shabbes* goy. Ask anybody. Ask Allie Cooperstein, Talmud Torah Tiphereth Hagro. I know the score. I got to tell you something."

"Mil-vow-kee, Vis-con-tzin," the elder articulated fretfully. "Mil-vow-kee, Vis-con-tzin. *Mein ainikel hast* . . ."

"A great little place, Milwaukee. But to hell with that right now. Look, Dad, whatever happens, whatever, don't let 'em do it again to you, *never*. I mean, don't stand still for it—all the naked people in the snow and shooting the kids and Christ knows what else. Fight back! Fight! *Fight, team, fight!*"

Sweeney was roaring at the old man who kept struggling to release himself. "*Meshugeh. Du bist meshugeh.*"

"No, *I am not!* Nix! I'm the sanest man in the world. Tell 'em . . . collect guns. Grenades. Organize in paramilitary formations! Teach your children to make Molotov cocktails!"

"Pfui, Molotov! *Ferdamter* Communist!"

"Take one of 'em with you!" cried Sweeney, getting very confidential, speaking in a conspirator's low voice.

"When they knock at the door go for their throat. Kill at least one. Die like men! Not naked in the fields, or the chambers! Get it? Ounce of prevention worth a pound of cure. You can't win, so at least go out like a champ, go down fighting."

"*Gantze meshugeh!*" The patriarch clucked false teeth, yanked himself free of the American, and turning on rubbered foot sloshed off in the rain.

Sweeney stumbled after him, then stopped to scratch at his allergic lump. "Ah, what the hell. Too late now. All dead. Six million, give or take a million. Maybe only four million. Makes it easier to think about if we think the figures were rigged. Yes, that's it. It was okay. It wasn't so bad because the Jews had rigged the figures. Crime not so bad. Not so bad killing four million. Yes, sir."

With burned and bloodshot eyes he looked up at the six-pointed star and remembered Gypo Nolan, the informer.

"Frankie," he whispered throatily, in a fair imitation of Victor McLaglen, "Frankie, your mother forgives me."

And he fell on the steps of the temple, incubating influenza and an anguish which neither love nor money would be able to dispel for a long, long time.

PART **2**

A. C. STONEBREAKER

THE VILLAGE OF SAN PIETRO DEL GOLFO LIES SOUTH OF NAPLES AT the foot of the Amalfi Drive. It is a rocky, inaccessible place and has remained uncluttered and unexploited. Bohemia is nowhere in evidence. Efforts to cultivate a smart atmosphere have failed. Even the more obvious touristy shoddiness of, say, Sorrento is absent.

San Pietro has been spared this fate because it is too much

trouble to reach. Excursion boats from Naples and Sorrento make daily trips to the village, but they do only a marginal trade. Their customers are usually Germans, who eat an overpriced *fritto misto del golfo* at the only restaurant, sluice it down with harsh white wine laced with sulfur, swim from the hellish hot stones of the "beach," and then belch their way back to their pensiones in a trembling *vaporetto*.

There are no hotels in San Pietro. There is the aforementioned restaurant-bar, the Nettuno, a few antiquities. Only two are worthy of mention—the private chapel and tomb of the malignant Sfondrini family, ancient rulers of the Republic of Amalfi, and the tumbled ruins of an alleged temple of Poseidon. Both monuments, the temple and the Sfondrini buildings, can be reached only through an hour's climb up a goat path of coronary steepness. Each visitor must decide for himself if this exhausting hike is worth it. The antiquities are routine, except for the cloister of the Sfondrini Chapel, which is supposed to be an outstanding example of thirteenth-century architecture.

This same dirt road, too steep and rugged for automobiles, is braved by young Italian daredevils who on motor scooters transport food, services, and the like both from the coastal highway above and the harbor. The Naples boat brings in supplies for the twenty-odd families of resident fishermen and the dozen or so millionaires who nest on the green cliffs above the tiny harbor.

These grandees live in a variety of keeps, forts, and restored monasteries, which peek through the cover of parasol pines high above the iridescent wedge of Mediterranean below, now pale green, now dark blue, now stained with purple.

Here one may see a fluted tower once protected by Saracen crossbowmen, today the pleasure dome of a somnolent Milanese textile king. Some distance from this Islamic fort and cushioned by a green froth of leaves rises a yellow and white campanile. Once having summoned monks to their prayers, it tolls today for a Torinese maker of toilets.

The fishermen of San Pietro nightly cast their nets for the

elusive octopus, flushing him out with Hong Kong flashlights powered with West German batteries. Far out in the ageless sea the rowboats each night assemble, a new city of twinkling electric stars.

At the center of San Pietro's crescent-shaped beach of hot stones a decrepit wooden pier steps out nervously to deep water. It serves as an anchorage for small boats, a diving platform, a concession to the village's lazy efforts to attract tourists. To the left of the pier, under a bower of grapevines is the Nettuno. To the right of the dock stand a dozen peeling beach lockers and a stack of faded beach chairs. These are reluctantly put into service for a rare German or Swede.

Atop this wretched pier, its mossy pilings reaching into the water like a miser's hand in a coffer, slept Bernard Kevin Sweeney. More than a week had passed since his interview with Ludwig Helms. Now, in the early morning of an August day, the man charged with the documentation of Noble Christian deeds wallowed in a drunkard's coma, reluctant to face the cruel sun or his revolting lack of character.

Sweeney's appearance was much altered. He had not shaved for several days. The thick black whiskers covering his florid face gave him the look of a trombone player in a tramp band. Clownishness was emphasized by the bloody redness of nose and forehead, the filthiness of his clothing.

At his best Sweeney might suggest a Caravaggio Bacchus, all black curls, popping eyes, lush lips, and cute drinker's nose. Now he had degenerated into a Third Avenue stew-bum, at whom Jewish children, of a generation past, might chant, "*Oi, oi, shicker is the goy.*"

Two fishermen, swarthy fellows thickened with Arab and Greek blood, rowed past the figure on the dock. Sweeney rolled over and showed an open mouth to the burning sky. He snorted several times, ravaging the morning peace.

"*Guarda,*" said one fisherman. "*Americano.*"

"*Che mostro,*" said the other. They rowed by him, fluttering the blue-green water, in search of *dentice* and *dorato*. The soft voices roused Sweeney and he opened one eye. The fishermen vanished around a rocky cliff. Last night's sulfurous white wine still coated his mouth. He tried to ignore the throbbing in his temples. The question was would it be a migraine headache (left side of temple) or a regular headache (frontal) or one of those unclassifiable blasts that circled his dome, stung him with quivering darts, and convinced him he was developing a brain tumor? To reassure himself he thought of his medicine kit, his great bouillabaisse of pills, lotions, and liquids. There was something for each headache, some specific, nesting in that zippered pigskin bag. Then he groaned. "Jesus, I got no more medicines. I got no more luggage. I got no car. I got no money. I got nothing."

He slept for another hour, awakening once more to the sound of water lapping softly against the pier.

Sweeney sat up, favoring a right arm that had apparently atrophied during the night. He gazed at the sharp rocky cliffs, the lush foliage rising up their sides, the endless vista of the old Mediterranean. Then he saw the oarsman.

He was a shriveled old fellow resting on his oars in a flaking boat about two yards to Sweeney's left. A flopping straw hat covered much of his sun-roasted face, but the American could see a long nose, a drooping gray mustache, a sharp chin. The boatman's hands were hard with strength and even in his relaxed posture Sweeney could see a primordial power. There was also a certain *authority* about him—something in his manner that indicated he had special business with Sweeney.

"Hiya walyo," Sweeney said. He got no reply. He studied the shabby boat and discerned a small sign tacked across the bow. It said:

AL CRISTO

"Whaddya say, Al," Sweeney mumbled, resting his pained head in the crook of his right arm. "Al baby."

The boatman mumbled something in Italian, a few words strained through his mustache. Then he pointed out to sea.

"Sorry, Al. No spik-Italian."

"Cristo, Cristo."

"I know, walyo. Al Cristo. You're a helluva guy." An epiphany shivered him. Suddenly Sweeney understood that the oarsman's name was not Al Cristo but that the sign meant: *to Christ,* or properly, *to the Christ.*

"*To Christ,*" Sweeney said. Sweeney looked about him and his bowels fluttered. "I'm dead," he said. "Jesus, I'm dead. They told me it would be like this, and I didn't believe them."

The elements were all there: the dark waters, the old boatman, the cliffs, the scary silence. Shouldn't it have been hotter? Sweeney knew it would get hotter. *He was being taken to Christ, across the mystic lake. Into the great beyond. And one clear call for me. . . .*

"Do I have time to write a letter? Send a cable?" It occurred to him that he owed Wettlaufer some last words. Now poor old Sherman would have only Sweeney's obituary to read—*American Tourist Dies Mysteriously Near Naples.*

"*Viene,*" said the boatman. He helped Sweeney roll from the splintery dock into the rowboat, which rolled in protest. Sprawled on the thwarts, Sweeney began to cry softly. "I didn't mean it, God," he whimpered. "I tried to be a good egg, but I didn't have the will power."

Thrusting his arms out, Sweeney defiant, his left hand struck something metallic. It was a large empty khaki-colored can. It read:

LARD, PURE—U.S. ARMY QUARTERMASTER CORPS

"It figures. That's where they get their chow." He picked up the can and was puzzled to find that a circle of glass had been substituted for its metallic bottom. "Beats the hell out of me," he said to the silent rower.

Noiselessly the boat approached the end of the left-hand palisade, the point where it flattened out and the clear ultramarine waters of the cove mingled with the darker blue of the gulf. The boatman rested his oars and pointed to the water. "*Cristo. Il Cristo Sotto-mare.*"

"Nah, you're kidding. Come on, walyo, take me to Him."

"*Il vetro—vetro. Guarda.*" He kept pointing to the can with the glass bottom, and Sweeney picked it up. At length it dawned on him—he was supposed to look through the open mouth of the can, with the glass bottom resting below the surface.

"*Guarda, Cristo Sotto-mare.*"

Sweeney thrust his head into the open end of the can and stared. The play of lights dazzled him. Early morning shafts of sunlight slanted, then widened in the pale-green waters. Shadow and light mingled, assembled in wild patterns, scattered, as the movements of the boat, the light, the very air itself, created new forms and colors.

Small fish flicked past his window and then, as his eyes adjusted to the subaqueous glory, he saw the statue. It was indeed Christ under water, a great marble statue of Christ with his arms outstretched.

"Beautiful," Sweeney crooned. "It's beautiful." Aesthetic fulfillment mingled with the relief of not being dead. The mystic oarsman was just taking him to see a statue, not across the river and into the trees.

"*Nuotatori,*" explained the boatman. "*Cristo per i skin-daiversi.*"

"Skin-divers. I dig. They put it down there. What an idea."

"*Trecento lire.*"

"Musta cost more than that," Sweeney said, studying the bold lines of the underwater shrine. The marble glowed with iridescence —now the palest chartreuse, now grape purple. It stood in glory where the turquoise cove melded gently with the indigo gulf.

"*Signor, trecento lire.*"

"Oh, the fare. I get it. Well, easy come, easy go." With sluggish movements he searched the pockets of his black chinos and found a five-hundred-lire coin—his last. "There you go, walyo. Great thing to see. But it needs promotion."

"*E qualcosa di più per i bambini?*"

"Hah?"

"Some-a-ting more. For mai cheeldren."

108

"I give you something more already. Besides, there ain't no more. I'm broke, walyo. And come to think of it, your children are working the day shift at Fiat, anyway."

Business concluded, Sweeney stole a final look through the lard can. Several elongated, almost transparent fish darted by, followed by what had frightened them.

It was the slender gliding body of a woman. Sweeney could not see her face, but the figure was graceful, long of limb, wasp-waisted, no excess fat. She wore a silly bathing cap resembling a giant dahlia, and a striped bikini. With the sinuous movements of an expert swimmer, she skimmed by the underwater Christ and vanished.

"Don't go! Don't go!" cried Sweeny, trying to track her through the glass in the bottom of the can. She surfaced about ten yards from the rowboat and turned a tanned face toward him. She smiled and spouted water. In the clear morning light he saw that she was pretty, perhaps beautiful.

"Good morning, there," Sweeney said. "How's the water?"

"Fabulous." She spoke American—a firm voice. "This is the best time of day to swim. After ten the sun starts to burn. It's—it's—like cool silk now."

"And I forgot my trunks." He watched her perform a faultless surface dive and vanish. Inspired, Sweeney removed his shoes, socks, shirt, and undershirt, and clad only in chinos, rolled off the gunwale like a seal intent on a tossed sardine. The rowboat rocked perilously in his wake, and Charon, shaking his head, rowed back to the pier.

With the cocky strokes of an old Orchard Beach lifeguard, Sweeney caught up with her. She had emerged near the shore, wading up the pebbled beach. He rose, fell with a great splash, rose again, and ran toward her. She had yanked off the hat to reveal her thick shiny hair, the color of Coca-Cola, and was drying herself with a huge yellow towel.

"Hey there," Sweeney called. He stumbled from the sea—a shaggy creature in a science fiction film.

"I'm generally the first one down here," she said. "But I see you're an early morning dipper also."

"Yes, a hipper-dipper." He stood there dumbly, staring, saying to himself, "Ai, Sweeney, this is what it is all about, this is what you have been missing." She was lovely. The clean firm American look, the creamy tan of her flesh, the unsagging outlines of breasts, thighs, crotch—he was enraptured.

"I guess you're here for Andy's party," she said. "People just seem to turn up . . . at crazy hours, in crazy places."

"Ah, Andy's party," Sweeney mumbled. "Why, I certainly am here for it. I haven't been to a good brawl since McCarty's party."

She saw that he was joking, but the joke eluded her. Educated in Europe, she knew naught of Sweeney's Bronx nonsense, and the memorable jingle, *Balls McCarty had a party.* . . .

"I'm Melissa Davies," she said. She offered no further explanation, as if the name (as Andy's) was weighted with significance.

"I am delighted. Heard an awful lot of wild things about you." He started following her up a narrow path that wound up the rocky slope.

"Are you someone I should know about?" she asked. "I catch hell from Andy if I don't know everyone—what they've written—who they are."

"We'll fix Andy," Sweeney said, winking. "I'm B. K. Sweeney." He paused a minute. "The free-verse poet."

"Oh, of course. I *think* I've heard of you. You'd better tell me about yourself, so I won't seem so dumb."

Sweeney, staggering over rocks and twigs, obliged her. She had violet eyes and a large, full mouth. The lower lip was set back somewhat from the upper and there were small diagonal lines at its side. They were lips, Sweeney was sure, that would be responsive.

"Well, I've been kind of floating around Europe picking up background. I specialize in narrative free verse."

"Any books I should know about?"

"Yes. *Poems* by B. K. Sweeney. And one last year called *More Poems* by B. K. Sweeney."

110

"They seem to ring a bell. I'm sure I've *heard* of you."

The narrow path led to a rustic stairway constructed of fallen logs embedded in the earth and bordered by parasol pines. The ascent had been almost vertical. Sweeney could see below them the pale wedge of water, the pier where he had slept, the boat which had taken him *al Cristo*. He looked up and saw that the crude stairway was even steeper.

"I had a rough night. A rough *couple* of nights. Mind if we walk slowly?"

She laughed—a crisp sympathetic laugh. "It takes getting used to. Andy likes his privacy. You stop whenever you're pooped. We can't wear out our poets before the party even begins."

He followed her delicious back, hypnotized by the smooth machinery of hip, thigh, calf, and foot, barely capable of restraining himself. Oh, to touch her! Fatigue affected Sweeney that way; it intensified his sex urge.

"How did you get here? Are your bags at the villa?" she asked. They had paused to catch their breath. Groves of lemon trees rose on either side of the steps, fruits and leaves shimmering in a pointillist panorama.

"I drove," puffed Sweeney. He explained that he had had a little accident up the road—somewhere. Laughing, he confessed that he was full of the disturbance, as Mr. Dooley would say, and had run his car off the road into a ditch. "I'm not sure where it was," he said. "This side of Salerno. Or the other side of Salerno. Or in the heart of downtown Salerno."

"Oh, that's fabulous. And you don't seem to care at all. I guess that is why you're a poet. Did you ever read *clutch and differential* by e. e. cummings?"

A cautionary glaze covered Sweeney's eyes: on guard, be careful, don't go too far. "I'm no friend of *his*," he said haughtily. "I once called him an obscure and derivative writer, and he never spoke to me again."

"I thought he'd be bigger than that."

They ascended again, passing a few *contadini*, men in blue work clothing, women in black, farm workers poking around the roots

111

of the lemon trees. Melissa told him that if he had any valuables in the car, Andy would order the local *carabinieri* to recover them.

"Especially my tape recorder. It's worth over a grand."

"A poet with a tape recorder?" she asked.

"I'm also something of a folklorist. Make these random tapes as I rattle around. It would be tough to lose them."

"If anyone can find them Andy will. Where does he know you from?"

Sweeney thought: there's a hot grounder right through the middle. "I can't imagine. Maybe he saw some of my work in the *Paris Review*. I translated the Pugachev letters."

"Mmmm. I'm not sure Andy reads it. I do though, and I don't remember them."

Sweeney permitted himself to be convulsed with high-altitude coughing. "Winter is-is-is-issue," he choked out enigmatically.

That appeared to satisfy his Good Fairy. They now climbed a series of switchbacks hewn in the native stone, and emerged under a bower of pleached lemon trees. Beyond, across a series of terraced lawns dotted with ancient statuary and benches, he saw the pale-yellow walls of the villa.

"I guess this is your first visit here," she said, noticing that Sweeney was stunned, agape. "That's it—Villa Malerba."

"It's not to be believed. It's a gasser. The greatest. I mean, I've seen places, but this—"

Villa Malerba appeared to be built on several levels, conforming to the slope of the cliff. Sweeney guessed that the tower was the oldest part, a keep of great antiquity. Around the tower, walls, doors, windows, archways, paths had been built over the centuries, and the result was a splendid irregularity, an enchanting haphazardness.

Taste, money, and intelligence had been lavished on the Villa Malerba. Each succeeding terrace that brought them to the main building was a gem. The first was semicircular, bordered with pollarded lemon trees, and contained an authentic peristyle. The next was rectangular, hedged, studded with sarcophagi. The following level was bright with native tiles and included a glistening pool. Finally, a lush, immaculate lawn fronted the villa proper.

The vista at the summit was exhilarating. To one side there was a grand view of the Mediterranean beyond the cove of San Pietro and beyond the Gulf of Salerno, far across the venerable sea to a horizon as sharply drawn as a Van Gogh outline. To the other side marched an army of lemon trees heavy with summer fruit. And rising above all were the yearning pines, reaching out from the sides of the cliff for sunlight, balancing nervously over the gorge.

When they reached the lawn Sweeney sat on a marble bench. "Is it okay to sit on the relics? I gather this is all real stuff."

"That's what they're here for. Andy has a deal with the archaeological society. They give him leads on new stuff on the market. That's a child's sarcophagus, fourth-century Roman."

"Neat," Sweeney said, stroking the funerary lid. "Poor kid. Wonder what happened to him."

"A poet should be able to guess."

"Ah, like Sandburg said, 'let the dead be dead.' "

He shuddered, thinking of his abandoned survey, of the dead of Europe he had deserted, the tapes and notes and addresses he had banished from his mind after hearing the engineer's tale.

"Guess I should apologize for my appearance," said Sweeney. "Flit got the best of me the last few nights. Curse of the Irish."

"I'll get some clothes for you."

"And a razor?"

"I'm disappointed. I thought the beard went with the poems. Doesn't it usually?"

Sweeney got up and sucked in his paunch self-consciously. He did not resemble Charles Atlas. They walked across the summer lawn. "Actually beards are out this year. My whiskers are the fruit of sloth, madam, not fashion."

She stopped and offered him an appreciative smile, revealing strong white teeth. "That's positively Elizabethan! Andy will flip over you."

She led him through a crumbling tufa archway, through a

113

cloistered garden frantic with flowers and along a wall of *opera reticularis*. He smelled the stony aroma of centuries, the perfume of wildflowers. In the cool *atrio* of the villa there was a mingled scent of incense and Ajax.

"I don't know what housing arrangements Andy's made," Melissa said, "but we can always move a few people around or send them to the Nettuno. I'll give you the Paestum room—the least we can do for the arts."

Sweeney followed her up marble steps, intoxicated with the lilt of her hips. He would swoon, die, if he did not touch her. How better this was, how right and good for him, this great home, this kind and elegant and admiring woman! How better all this was by comparison to the horrifying tales he had been hearing! He was furious with the Jews of Poldarenko for spoiling his fun.

The Paestum room was minuscule, exquisite. It was so called because embedded in one wall was a fragment of a frieze—sea nymphs—from the excavations. There was a vast bed, a highboy, a tiled bathroom, and a balcony looking out over Homer's sea, where the morning sunlight turned blue to gold.

"This is much too grand for me," said Sweeney. The old joys of the free-load loomed. He only had to remain B. K. Sweeney, Irish-American poet and folklorist, contributor to the *Paris Review*. If necessary he would play the fairy, and that would clinch it.

As if to certify his dream Melissa kissed him on his bearded jowl and said: "I'll send someone up with clothing, shaving kit, the works. You probably need some sleep. The other guests won't be here until late afternoon so take your time—sleep, wander around, look through Andy's library, and if you're hungry, go to the kitchen and tell Augusta."

Augusta! All Sweeney's life he had yearned to be an honored guest at a rich man's villa with the prerogative of wandering into the kitchen and asking *Augusta* for a snack!

She left him and he collapsed on the bed recalling a movie with Dennis King—*The Vagabond King!* He had been the filthy beggar exchanging his smelly clothes for fine raiment, bathed, shaved,

114

perfumed, transformed from street bum to prince. So it would happen to him: Sweeney the bum into Sweeney the literary vagabond. Soon he was wallowing in a hot soapy bath. Fatigue and guilt drained from his pores. A sleek dark Neapolitan youth, a sorcerer's child, brought him fresh clothing, toilet articles, snowy towels, then returned with a tray of coffee, rolls, orange juice from local trees. Fed, scrubbed, shaven, at peace, Sweeney slept through the burning morning, the blazing afternoon (the same youth tiptoed through his chamber to shutter the obscuring blinds which cooled the room immediately), and well into the cocktail hour.

Awakening in the darkness, he was born again. Untroubled, he rose naked as Pan from the healing bed and opened the blinds. The westering sun was descending into the sea. To his right he saw the light glancing off another castle—a pink Moorish dome. Sweeney wanted to cry for joy. "And strikes the Sultan's turret with a shaft of light!" he intoned, trying to sound like Laurence Olivier.

There was crisp clean underwear for him, a loose white Riviera shirt, a pair of pale-blue denim slacks, a pair of matching blue espadrilles lovingly woven by some serf. He made a second voyage of self-love to the bathroom and admired his manly face. Better without the beard. Ruddy cheeks, black curls growing thick around the ears and neck, falling in a rakish lock over one eye.

Armed with self-confidence, Sweeney left his room and descended the stairs. He paused to admire a bust of Socrates in the hallway. He made his way back to the enchanted cloister and passed through the arch into the main section of the villa. He entered a small vestibule floored with Capri tiles and stopped in his tracks.

Two elderly men were leveling Thompson submachine guns at him. They were dressed almost identically: pearl-gray fedoras with wide snap brims, dark double-breasted suits with chalk stripes, bell-bottomed trousers, spats, patent leather shoes. They sported pearl stickpins and diamond rings. Frothy silk handkerchiefs peeked from their breast pockets. Their faces were cruel and cynical—professional killers.

"Handsa-up," said the taller one. Evidently he was the boss, a heartless mugg, with skin creases that began below his hooded black eyes and slashed his cheeks and jaw.

"No monkey-beezniss," said the other—a shorter, stouter chap. "You wanna I freesk him, boss?"

Sweeney, puzzled more than frightened, noticed that the short man was suppressing a fit of laughter. Little bursts would issue from the corners of his mouth. Finally he had to turn his back.

"Where you from, Mac?" asked the tall man. "Chicago? Detroit?"

"Shake hands with Machine-gun Sweeney, fellahs. The Bronx Bad-boy. Wanted for the stickup of Feinberg's Dairy on Southern Boulevard. What a haul! A million dollars in sour cream."

"What do you think, Mario?" the big man asked. "You like this kid's looks?"

The shorter hood turned around, pointing the Thompson. "No, I tink he lousy G-man. I tink he from Meesta Whiskers. He lousy spy."

"Yeah, I think so too," said the boss. "Turn around, big boy. Curtains."

"Hey, fellahs, this is too much," Sweeney protested. "Ask anyone. I'm a friend of Andy's. Melissa brought me here herself." He refused to accept the insane circumstance. Yet, what was mad, what was sane any longer? Was not Naples a haven for expatriated Mafiosi and Camorristi? Was it not possible that the mysterious Andy was an international hood, sheltering gunsels? "Honest, guys, I'm Machine-gun Sweeney—"

Without warning, the two guns, at a distance of less than a yard, blasted him unmercifully. "Yow! Yipe!" Sweeney screamed. "Cut that out!" His hands sought his back, his behind, his thighs, seeking gaping wounds, warm blood.

Then he heard the assassins laughing helplessly. He smelled the familiar boyhood odor of burned paper caps and turned around, humiliated, to see the hoods clutching one another. A haze of blue smoke lay listless on the hot air. Sweeney saw the strips of scorched red tape on the tile floor.

"Ah, for Chrissake," he said.

"Holy Jeez," the big man laughed. "Best yet, Mario."

"Machine-a-gun Sweeney," Mario roared. "Atsa so funny!"

"Balls," Sweeney mumbled. "Coupla jokers. You come around my block I'll mobilize you."

They hugged him, they pinched his cheeks. The tall man apologized. Little Mario offered to lend him his gun for a few practice blasts. Sweeney studied the weapons—American plastic, utterly perfect down to the last nut and bolt, the real item. A nice bit of mischief for the kiddies, guaranteed to produce one assassin every ten years.

"*Non se disturba*," said the big man placatingly. "*Siamo tutti amici qui.*"

"*Uguale*," said Mario. "Shake beeg-boy." He held out a manicured hand. Sweeney shook it, and the killers wandered off in search of new victims.

Normally Sweeney begrudged no one his prank, even if it were on him. But he was beginning to enjoy his role as poet-guest of Andy and it bothered him to be suddenly thrust back into the role of buffoon. Laureate was one thing, court jester another.

Adrift, he walked softly on his new espadrilles down the vaulted corridor. He heard a voice, a vaguely familiar one, and headed toward it. The corridor led him to four marble steps flanked by Greek amphorae, and he halted before entering the large room ahead. With a shiver, he heard once more the ghostly voice of Ludwig Helms.

". . . long hose full of holes, undone garters, dirty shifts, soiled vests. Soon the sense of embarrassment vanishes. One reasons thus: if these people are so poor and filthy, they must deserve what is happening to them. Indeed Papke was quick to state exactly what I was thinking. . . ."

"Steady there," Sweeney whispered to himself. "Don't let 'em fake you out of position." He summoned up courage, charm, deceit, and entered the enormous salon. Dr. Helms, of course, was not present. But Sweeney's tape recorder was. It spoke from a Florentine mosaic coffee table.

A stocky broad-shouldered man, wearing a pale-blue silk robe, sat listening to it attentively, his eyes hidden behind huge dark glasses, his figure comfortably ensconced in a black leather arm-chair, and his slippered feet on a matching ottoman. The man's head was shaved bald and his skin was so deeply tanned as to suggest he was colored. His face was hidden both by the great spectacles and his hands, which were folded over his mouth. Sweeney could not see him clearly. But he knew at once that this had to be his host, the Andy of whom Melissa Davies had spoken. He knew it because as a veteran freeloader he had grown sensitive to the attitudes of the rich. And no man could sit so possessively in a big leather chair, be so blissful in a silken robe, be so at ease with his property, his status, and his admirers, as a wealthy host.

". . . now ordered the Jews to descend a series of steps that had been cut into the side of the pit. They obeyed. They were ordered to lie down in the trench. Some couples embraced. The red-haired woman hugged the girl to her chest. The old lady had to . . ."

Ludwig Helms' thickening voice droned on. All in the great high-ceilinged room were still. Sweeney paused on the threshold, stunned by his imminent exposure. He remained silent, studying the people present.

Besides the egg-bald man (the presumed Andy), there was his good angel, Melissa, in tennis whites, cradling a racket, seated on a pouf to the right of the coffee table. To one side, in an alcove formed by a recess in the white plaster wall of the long room, two middle-aged women were playing cards. They looked to Sweeney like the types who would normally be gabbing their vain and foolish heads off—one redheaded, one blonde, both with var-nished bouffant hair-dos, layered make-up, lavish sports clothing, lacquered toes in gilt sandals. Yet out of deference to the host's engrossment in the recording, they played silently, deaf to the

118

engineer's recital of darkness. There was, lastly, a slender man in his thirties, in a light-gray suit complemented by white shirt and green tie, who sat in an armchair as if attending a meeting of junior executives at an Ohio bank.

Noiselessly Sweeney sat on a high-backed carved chair, some Norman baron's relic, and waited. He was within the field of vision of the man in the blue robe, but the latter made no sign of greeting. He was deeply absorbed in Helms' narration, immovable as a stone Buddha. Behind the protective glasses, inside that bald head, great thoughts were being nourished, Sweeney suspected. And with the thoughts would come exposure: he was no poet at all, he had never been invited to the party, he no more knew Andy than he knew Willie Mays. A bold voice within told him to be courageous. Not for nothing had he once been Prince of Free-loaders! True, he was out of practice. But when the tape ran out, he would be challenged. Then he would have to summon all the guile of the old Sweeney, the Sweeney of Westhampton Beach.

"... a particularly noteworthy massacre about ten kilometers from my headquarters. It was so cold that the Jewish women froze on the spot. ..."

"Shut up, Helms," Sweeney said to himself. "Just shut up and let me get on with my life, lousy as it is." Sweeney tried to shrink into the chair. He permitted his eyes to wander. To his left was a ceiling-high bookcase. The lower shelves held a series of tall, narrow volumes, custom bound in red leather, the titles incised in gold. He looked closer and read:

THE KILLERS AND THE SLAIN BY A. C. STONEBREAKER
HOMAGE TO KRONSTADT BY A. C. STONEBREAKER
WE OBJECT BY A. C. STONEBREAKER

At once Sweeney made the connection. Andy. Andrew. Andrew C. Stonebreaker. A. C. Stonebreaker. He was in the castle of one of the great American literary figures of the thirties and forties—playwright, screenwriter, polemicist, editor. Stonebreaker was a name out of Sweeney's youth when he had pined for the literary

119

life, scandalizing his brother Leo by bringing home *The Saturday Review*. He could not recall ever having seen any of Stonebreaker's plays, but he was certain he had seen the movie versions of some—possibly *The Killers and the Slain*, which he remembered as being about a coal strike. But the name thrilled him, evoking a time when giants walked the earth.

Stonebreaker's name had all but vanished from the press. Occasionally there would be a magazine piece, and Sweeney seemed to recall some nonfiction writing recently by his host. But the plays had ended in the forties, and he had not been in Hollywood for years.

"Well, anyway, he kept a lot of loot," Sweeney said to himself. "Maybe he don't work regular, but he lives good."

New courage came to him. Now he knew Andy's identity and could devise stratagems. Helms' narration was nearing its conclusion, and soon he would be on stage. Indeed, the notion of performance seemed implicit. There was something of the stage setting about the high-ceilinged lavish room. Even the placing of the people—the card-playing women, the thin man in the gray suit, Melissa, astringently sexual in her pleated white tennis dress, and the lordly host himself in communion with Ludwig Helms' weary voice.

With a decisive motion, Stonebreaker leaned forward and turned off the recorder. The room was silent. He removed his smoked glasses and smiled at Sweeney. "I hope you don't mind, Mr. Sweeney, our listening to your bit of . . . folklore."

"Help yourself," said Sweeney. "No secrets there."

"This fellow doing the talking. Is he an actor of some kind?"

"An engineer. Lives in Hamburg."

Stonebreaker reflected on this for a moment. His query appeared inane to Sweeney, but he was wary of any challenging. Politeness, charm, ass-kissing—these were the orders of the day. Melissa bounced up. "Let's get introduced—everyone. Mr. Sweeney—goodness, what do I call you?"

120

"Buck. As in Fast."

"Oh, that's *prima*. Buck Sweeney . . . Andy Stonebreaker . . . my Uncle Andy. This is Mr. Swanson, is it? Simpson."

The man in gray smiled and waved a hand. "Hi, fellah."

"And the ladies," Melissa continued. "That's Mrs. Ferrante, the redheaded lady, Frances. And Mrs. Halberstadt, Cecile."

They glanced at him incuriously and returned to their card game. Sweeney moved across the room and extended his hand to Stonebreaker. "Mr. Stonebreaker, it's a privilege to meet you. I'll never forget the night I saw *We Object*. I never had a serious thought in my thick Irish head until I saw that play. May I thank you?"

Stonebreaker winced. "Your thick Irish head may have been of more value to you."

"It's *still* a good play," Melissa said, as if reassuring her uncle.

Stonebreaker got up. "Technically, as good as anything of that period," he said. "Ideologically, garbage. A case of the man with the clap running the clinic." He gathered his robe around his stubby body with a kingly sweep. "Mr. Sweeney, I want to talk to you about these tapes. Inasmuch as you're sponging on me—I really don't care—I took the liberty of looking through your notes and I'm intrigued by whatever it is you're doing."

"Whenever you want, Mr. Stonebreaker. I'll do anything for a free-load. And thanks for finding my gear."

Stonebreaker excused himself; he was going to nap. He left them, walking in a peculiar rolling gait, his legs thin and delicate under the wide thick torso. The white jacketed ~~manservant~~ ~~ed, sinuous~~, swarthy, as handsome as a venial sin, and took orders for drinks. Sweeney had to keep from salivating; his starved gullet cried for alcohol. He asked for a scotch, and could barely wait until the youth returned with it.

While they waited, Melissa with a proprietary and somewhat sarcastic air tried to make Sweeney talk about himself. No fool, he realized that he had become her property, her discovery. Sweeney would raise no objection. Was he not accustomed to being owned, sponsored, displayed? And what better patroness?

"Mr. Sweeney does all sorts of interesting things," she said. "He's a poet, a folklore expert, and I think a journalist of some kind."

Simpson, the man in the gray suit, digested this information as he polished his eyeglasses on a square of silicate paper. "Quite a life you lead, fellah."

Sweeney fell into step. "And what's your line of work, friend?" he asked innocently. Brother Kiwanis to Brother Rotarian. *Give us a week and we'll be out there distributing eyeglasses to the Navajos.*

"I represent small business firms," Simpson said.

Melissa burst into laughter. "Come off it, Mr. Simpson. You're a spy."

The ladies at the card table looked up. Mrs. Ferrante, the tall redhead, lifted rhinestone-rimmed harlequins to examine the accused. She shrugged her shoulders at Mrs. Halberstadt, the short blonde. "He don't look like no spy."

"Couldn't prove it by me," Mrs. Halberstadt said.

"Now, Mrs. Davies," Simpson said, in pure midwesternese. "That wasn't a nice thing to say. I've heard many nice things about you. I'm surprised."

Careful of that one, Sweeney thought. *Right out of Cluett Peabody. Votes the Republican ticket and believes in tough immigration laws.*

"Oh, you're a spy, Mr. Simpson," Melissa persisted wickedly. "You say you represent small businesses. How small? Tiny? Teensy-weensy? Any American in Europe who wears a gray suit and a white shirt and says he represents small businesses is a spy. Admit it. It's nothing to be ashamed of. Who for, CIA? Army?"

"Jesus," said Sweeney, enchanted with her assault on Simpson. "Maybe he's working for the *other* guys."

Simpson smiled frigidly. "I see I'm being joshed."

122

"Did I hear you tell Andy that you lived in Rome?" Melissa asked.

"Correct."

"I'll prove you're a spy. You live in Parioli?"

"That's right."

"In a large, well-furnished apartment—seven or eight rooms?"

"Nine, actually," Simpson said.

"Two in help?"

"Yes."

"Wife and kids with you? Three kids? Four?"

"Three."

"You're a spy. Small businesses? Name one."

"Obviously, Mrs. Davies, you think this is comical and I'll play along. I represent a variety of small businesses—Acme Fixtures of Toledo, Ohio, for one. Apex Lighting and Heating, Canton, Ohio—"

"Phonies if I ever heard of phonies," Sweeney said. "Come on, Simpson, those are made-up names."

Melissa leaned forward and patted Simpson's knee. "Mr. Simpson, it's nothing to get angry about. I've been in Europe for the last four years. I was born in Paris and went to school in Switzerland and, I can tell you, I *think* like a European. We know who all the American spies are, and I think Americans *want* us to know Now in the last three months Andy's had four men from Rome down here as guests—you're the fifth—who say they represent small businesses, who live in big apartments in Parioli with large families, and wear gray mail-order suits. And every one of them was a spy of some kind. Did they give you a Chevrolet or a Ford?"

"As a matter of fact, I drive a Chevy. My own."

"That doesn't matter. It goes with the big apartment. And why we *bother* to spy on the Italians—" Melissa laughed. "They'll tell us anything we want to hear. Even the Communists. Nobody hates the Communists more than Andy—and they tell him everything."

"Well," Simpson said, "if I'm to be part of the weekend entertainment, I'll play along. Guess I'd better go to my room and get out the invisible ink and the itty-bitty camera." He grinned, a boyish grin from Toledo, Ohio.

"That's the ticket, Simpson!" Sweeney shouted. "Hell, if I can be a poet, you can be a spy!"

"Right, fellah." He drained his martini and left.

"Touchy kind of man," said Mrs. Ferrante. She had a neatly snipped nose. But there was a suggestion that the hand of the potter had trembled; the tip was slightly to starboard. Sweeney liked her looks—brassy, jazzy, lavish. He admired her hard-corseted figure, elegant legs. A lot of woman there, even if she was past fifty. Mrs. Halberstadt was smaller, quieter, a bit more class. Her features were round and soft, her lips moist and shiny, like cherry jello. They kept at their canasta, oblivious.

Melissa gestured to Sweeney. "Come along, Hart Crane, I'll take you on a tour of the grounds."

He followed her out a side door into an intimate bar, where he replenished his drink, then to a lawn-covered terrace, one of the many he had noticed on the hike up that morning.

"You passed the test with Andy," she said. "It was the recording that hooked him. He hasn't any idea what you're doing, but he's aching to find out. He's terribly political, you know. That's why he stopped writing movies and plays."

"I wondered what happened to him. Did I hear you call him Uncle?"

"He *is*. My mother's younger brother. The Stonebreakers of Denver, Colorado. Mean anything?"

"Nope. I'm strictly a New York City boy."

"Mining money. Not that Andy ever needed it. He's made it on his own."

"Does he know how to use it! I mean, this place. It makes Beverly Hills look like a slum. Class. Taste. Everywhere I turn . . . something new—it's the composition, the balance of art and nature."

"Andy's got the gift. He's spent six years working on this place.

124

It was a wreck when he bought it. It hadn't been occupied in twenty years, and it was a monastery before that. The tower and the east wall are just about all that's left of the original buildings."

Sweeney and his new friend sat in a small grape arbor. The plump, juicy clusters, palest green, dangled above him like the breasts of Diana of Ephesus. He could have kissed each grape in gratitude.

"Did I hear that spy call you Mrs. Davies?" he asked.

"That's right. I'm in the process of becoming the ex-Mrs. Davies."

"Sorry to hear it."

"Why are you sorry? You don't know anything about me or my husband. Divorce might be the best thing in the world for us."

"Middle-class morality. Behind the artistic pretensions, Melissa, Sweeney is a moralizing bore." He studied her calm, lovely face. She had a high straight forehead, a rather prominent nose, splendid cheekbones. Nothing was soft, unformed or uncertain—from her waved dark-brown hair to her slim ankles. "The guy I should feel sorry for is Davies. How could any man give you up?"

"It isn't difficult. He's the third one."

"Th-th-third?"

"Third husband. In a week or so, he'll be in the Melissa Henry Alumni Association."

Impulsively, Sweeney reached for her hand and squeezed it. It was a hard hand, a tennis player's hand. He was ashamed of his flabbiness. "Listen. It was all *their* fault, whoever they were. I'm on your side, Melissa, all the way." Knight-errant Sweeney, he would wear her scarf in battle, challenge anyone who would slander her.

"In fact, I am in love with you. Don't protest. Don't comment on it. We'll discuss it when we know each other better. I know I'm in love with you, and, as Dr. Johnson said, that's an end of it."

"Sweeney, you're good for me!" When she smiled, tiny wrinkles advertised that she was into her thirties—Sweeney wanted to stroke each wrinkle.

As they held hands beneath the fruited vines, Sweeney spied his two would-be assassins. They emerged sneakily from behind the yellow wall of the villa, padding across the lawn. They walked arm in arm, machine guns dangling from their free arms, two hoods from Cicero.

"Those two guys over there," Sweeney said. "Who are they? They tried to bump me off before. What's the joke?"

"I should have warned you. It's a costume party tonight. The theme is the Depression. Andy always has a theme. Last time it was World War I. I was Mata Hari, and Andy came as Hindenburg."

"But who are they? Those walyones. They pull those plastic guns on me again, I'll have to stage a little hooley of my own."

"The tall one is General Pandolfo and the little one is Air Marshal Zamperini. They live in Salerno."

"Retired?"

"By popular request. Former Fascisti big shots. Utterly harmless, both of them."

The general and the air marshal, having spotted a new sucker, quick-stepped down a flight of stairs. The tall one looked over his shoulder and winked at Sweeney, as if to say—don't snitch on us.

"No matter what the theme is Pandolfo and Zamperini always come as gangsters," Melissa said. "It's sad."

"You live here?" Sweeney asked. "All the time, in this castle?"

"I'm in and out. I have an apartment in Paris on the Champ de Mars. That's the nearest thing to a home I have, I suppose. My son is in school in Zurich."

"You have a son?"

"Why are you so surprised? Don't I look like good breeding stock? My son is seventeen years old—product of marriage number one. Not a bad kid, considering."

The offended voice of Bronx rectitude rose in Sweeney again.

126

"Why isn't he here? This is a great place for a kid. He should spend the summer with Mommy."

"I'm afraid Mommy and Jean Pierre don't get along too well. He's mad for sports cars and skin diving. In fact he's somewhere in the Greek islands right now with a bunch of other broken-home princelings, on a rented yacht."

"And where's his Daddy?"

"Daddy's been dead a long time. In fact, he never saw his son. Oh, I can see those big Irish eyes opening wide."

Sweeney's interrogating face, all candor and sympathy, was posing peremptory, compassionate queries.

"Yes, that was husband number one. I was seventeen when the marriage was arranged. La Comtesse de Camouillet. In fact, I still am—although there's a good deal of doubt whether the title is worth anything or whether Freddy, the count, merited it. Still, my mother wanted him in the family, and I guess I did.

"I was born and raised in Paris, Sweeney. A little Bemelmans' girl—what's-her-name, with the nice nun. But the family was deep, deep American. You have to understand why they craved a title. Mother with her Colorado mining money. Daddy, E. K. Henry, not exactly poor, but deep in sordid finance. He was the head of the Paris branch of a big U.S. brokerage house. So mother found me a real count to marry. Poor guy, I think he got the worst of it. I wasn't very nice."

"I can't believe it," Sweeney said. "Refuse."

"I was a horror. The lissome beauty. I had my first champagne hangover at fourteen. We moved to London during the war. Those Englishmen with the wavy hair that kind of grows down the sides of their heads—they're the world's most depraved men. And there was poor old Freddy, ten years older than me, going off to join the Free French. He was a true sad sack, un sac triste. Chinless, skinny, pale. Mama always said that proved he was real nobility. Anyway he fathered my child, and went off to get killed in the south of France, probably as a result of an artillery shelling by his own troops. He never could run very fast, and he wasn't

127

meant to be a soldier. Always blowing his nose, or getting pains in his feet. We never had a minute of genuine love together. We couldn't stand the sight of one another."

"No, but I bet you tried."

"That's what was so awful. I never tried. And as soon as Freddy went off to war there were those wavy-haired Englishmen. Ugh. They slobber with passion, those red-handed oafs, mumbling their demands, and then—no finesse, no tenderness. Not that Freddy was any better. He had skin the color of a *blanc mange*."

A look of terror suffused Sweeney's face. The bourbon tan, rising from his neck, up his jowls, to his forehead painted his face carmine, scarlet, fire-wagon red.

"I'm shocked. You-you-you were eighteen."

"Eighteen when I married and become La Comtesse. The Englishmen came a few years later. Sweeney, stop staring like that. Close your Irish mouth. Haven't you ever *heard* about me? Melissa Henry de Camouillet Breck Davies? You don't read the right sections of the newspaper."

"You got me there. I usually quit after Dan Daniel. I like when he lists the Jewish ballplayers in the big leagues. Or when he says, 'No, Arthur, no one has ever hit a home run outside the Yankee Stadium, but you win this year's prize for asking it first.'"

"I don't know what that means, but it's funny the way you tell it. You said it because I've shocked you, and you wanted to change the subject. Oh, my poet. You're a boy—an altar boy."

"I was that also. And a *shabbes goy*. And my brother Leo sold *Social Justice* and made speeches for Father Coughlin. Go on, you got two more marriages to tell me about. The count got knocked off by his own artillery, and there you were at the end of the war, a young widow with a little kid. Back to Paris, right?"

Marriage number two, she said, occurred some years after the war. She had gone to the States to find a career in the theatre, any career, and had surprised all her scoffing friends by doing rather well. She was a clean-limbed beauty, tall, intelligent enough to see through the vanity and fraud of most directors and producers, and

128

she soon learned that acting is largely mimicry. She played a few minor parts on Broadway and one supporting role, frequented the right bars, lived in a lavishly refurnished walk-up on Third Avenue, and developed a brittle, hard, East Sixties icing on top of her soft, continental manners. The truth was she was too cynical, too brainy for the theatre. She had too keen a tongue for the inanities and deceits of the stage.

She did not tell Sweeney two things. One, that she began to drink heavily, indiscriminately. Her capacity for alcohol was remarkable, a medical miracle, her physician told her. He counseled her to go easy on the stuff, but since it produced no painful effects, no hangovers, no weakness, no irregularities in her genito-urinary system, she kept drinking. It relaxed her. She also neglected to tell Sweeney that during this period of theatrical indoctrination, she required a reputation as "an easy lay." Sharp-tongued, well-bred, graceful, she possessed a knowing quality that created in men an irrepressible desire to subdue her, to force her into the supplicant attitudes of love, literally and figuratively, to get her on her knees. Many succeeded. She told Sweeney nothing of this, leaving him with the assumption that the ruddy-handed Englishmen of her youth were the last to win her extramarital favors.

"Of course," she went on, "husband number two *had* to be a stage type, and I picked a beauty. Hamilton Breck."

"The director! He's a genius."

"And he'd be the first to tell you that. What can I say about Ham? I was wise to the theatre from the first day I went to a rehearsal. All that endless jabbering that says nothing, means nothing. Good God, to hear Ham talk to a group of actors! I would defy anyone, anyone—Stuart Chase, Hayakawa, Korzybski—to make the slightest sense out of the garbage that was thrown around that empty hall. Yet it's what makes the theatre go. It has its own meaningless language, and don't ask questions, don't cry out that the emperor is naked.

"Now, assuming this, and assuming that I knew it from the start, how in God's name did I ever wind up with Hamilton

Breck? Would you think I were conceited if I told you that he had to have me, rather than the other way around? Yes, that must have been it. I couldn't have ever loved him."

Sweeney said softly, "That makes two you married and two you didn't love." He was disconsolate.

"Story of my life, Sweeney. I warned you."

"When we get married there'll be no misunderstanding. I won't have you unless you're mad for me, like I am for you."

Melissa laughed lightly. "Good man, Buck. Do you really want to hear about Ham Breck and his society wife?"

"Yeah. It beats what I've been listening to these last few weeks."

She went on to describe her second marriage, prefacing it with some biographical data on husband number two. Breck was a slumbred starveling, son of a Brownsville pushcart peddler. A stringbean of a child, nearsighted, splay-footed, he was always the butt of cruel pranks, sneers, the boy who was left out of the punchball games. When they would choose up sides for ringalevio or salugi, he was the odd man out, the one to whom the two captains would announce: "And you're playin' with ya muddah's broomstick."

Hymie Breck escaped to the quiet corridors of the New York Public Library on Watkins Avenue, where he read so much he ruined his eyes; great thick lenses distorted his pinched face from the age of fourteen. Penniless, undernourished, frustrated, he read endlessly, narrowing his interests to the theatre. There was no money for college, not even for the free city schools. Indeed, Melissa suspected that Hymie never finished high school, quitting after being humiliated in gym—the only boy in Thomas Jefferson High School who was not able to climb ropes.

Moreover, the neighborhood and the school were turning darker, Jews giving way to Negroes, and these new settlers took one look at Hymie and realized that here was the perfect patsy. He was waylaid and drubbed a half dozen times and he grew up in mortal terror of the dark brotherhood—not without good reason.

Melissa frowned. "Oh, poor Ham. Just about everything in the world was wrong with him. God knows, I didn't help."

130

"It can't be the same guy—not Hamilton Breck, the most brilliant young director on Broadway. It can't."

"I'm not doing too good a job of conveying Ham," she said. "Everything I told you is true—poor, skinny, undereducated, a natural victim, astigmatic. I left out one thing, and it's what made him a success. He had the gift of *tongues*. He could talk his way up and down the proscenium, wander around a piece of business or dialogue, make an actress feel that when she walked across the stage she was Bernhardt. He could work this magic on producers, backers, critics, composers, and on some playwrights. It wasn't just glibness. It was a talent for spinning words together, for cadences of speech, for crazy gestures, like little dance steps, for a kind of psychodrama that, God knows how, *worked*. He directed lots of plays. Many of them were damn good, and what was good in them was Ham's touch. And you have to remember he directed his first Broadway play when he was twenty-three—after six miserable years of sweeping floors and playing the banjo in the Borscht circuit."

"The boy had *chutzpah*," Sweeney said. "I kind of like him, and I can see why you went for him."

"I've already told you that he was a physical wreck. He had bad skin, weak lungs, no muscles, and a spastic colon. None of that was poor Ham's fault. But he also had a talent for *wrongness*. For example, he was also a Communist—but too late and of the worst kind. Up to his neck in committees to prove that Stalin was a humanist. And he had some kind of connections with the underworld. I think that dated back to his Brooklyn days, and I suspect it's how he sometimes raised money for shows. I remember meeting him once in a restaurant and being introduced to two stout, dark Sicilians with hooded eyes and thick lips. All very polite and gentle, and both murderers. So—he was a Communist, he played footsie with gangsters, and he had awful sexual problems, stemming from his ugliness and the way he was rejected as a child. I won't go into details, but he was an insane fetishist and lots of other things we'd better not discuss."

"And Jesus—you married him!"

131

"It wasn't all that bad. It put me right into the swim. I played a lead in one of his plays, and it was a semisuccess. We lived it up—a big glass house in Easthampton for the summer, a ten-room apartment in the Dakota, lots of theatrical friends. We made New York our living room. About that time the un-American boys and the McCarthy-ites descended on poor Ham and they just about destroyed him. He took the Fifth Amendment. He was very brave, read his statement, and was unable to work for a long time. The hiatus all but killed him. And it was during this period, when the rent went unpaid and we gave up the summer house, that I realized why he had married me.

"There he was—a Communist, a Jew, impoverished, an intellectual manqué, a striver, a rebel—and there I was—wellborn, well-bred, beautiful, snobbish, the slightly tarnished pot at the other end of Ham's rainbow."

"I get it!" Sweeney cried. "You fed his ego! You made him feel important!"

"Not *quite* that simple, Sweeney. It wasn't just ego-gratification. When Ham married me, it was his *revenge* on the whole United States of America. There he stood, the outsider, the foreigner, the enemy of the people, the disturber of the peace—but look whom he made love to every night, look who had to put up with his pornographic inventions—the wonder girl herself, Miss America!"

"It sounds grim," said Sweeney. "You must have been miserable."

"Oh, it had its marvelous comic aspects. I'll never forget the day Ham went before the committee and took the Fifth Amendment. There he was, in carefully rumpled worker's suit, from Brooks Brothers, his hair rising in two peaks from his temples, his eyes unfocused, his hairy hands unable to light cigarettes fast enough. You could see how those congressmen detested and feared him. And there I was, in the front row, cool, trim, American, Gentile, in my powder-blue suit, my pearls, my nyloned legs, things that even a congressman from Ohio could appreciate. Nothing too sexy mind you, just refinement and good breeding and charm.

132

"And when they'd got through lecturing Ham on his failure as a patriot, this saggy elephant of a Representative turned to me, and said, 'Miz Breck'—that was what he said, 'Miz Breck'—'Miz Breck, yoah husband has made some grave mistakes and has done some terrible un-American things, and for the life of me, I cannot understand how such a fine, intelligent model of American womanhood has not been able to change his attitudes towards his country.' I said nothing, of course, and merely smiled coolly, but I could see Ham suppress a grin. He was thinking, of course, 'You should see what I do to her in bed, you old futz!'

"Yet the nutty thing was, and Ham was too thick to realize this, *I* was really the rejected one. *He* had been accepted! Yet I served my purpose. Through some freakish reading of the law, or goodness knows what, Ham was never indicted for contempt. After some backing and filling, the committee forgot about him—but not the dozen or so others who had gone to Washington with him. My father, who made it a habit to know congressmen, learned later that Ham had gotten off the hook because of *me*, that the feeling was that no man who was married to Melissa Henry could be all bad. Indeed, marriage to me was deemed a patriotic act, just about the only honorable deed that Hamilton Breck had ever performed."

"So you divorced him?"

"It was inevitable. He got tired of experimenting with me. He never had any sustained strength anyway. We broke up quietly, politely, with no wild scenes. Ham took to wearing capes, and made an impression on some television executives. He's an executive producer now of several appalling series—he defends them as Pop Art—and terribly rich. He lives on Sutton Place with a young Italian hoodlum he claims to be grooming for a great career."

"As what?"

"Who knows? Way station number two. I suppose we had a few laughs, and if I saved him from jail or a longer time on the blacklist, I can't be surly about it."

Sweeney got up and stretched. It was dusk, and the light was charged with motes of gold and silver. The lemon trees no longer blinded one with their bright greens; in the shadows they were restful, somber. He was furious with the Ham Brecks of the world for having so much so quickly, for winning the Melissa Henrys, while he, Sweeney, was reduced to living on the alms of rich fools.

"Do you want to hear the rest?" she asked. "No matter, I'll tell you anyway."

She resumed—skipping over six months spent in a sanitarium for alcoholics in Stamford, Connecticut, where doctors warned her to level off because her blood pressure was alarmingly high, her liver and kidneys weak. She had been starting the day with an old-fashioned and a vitamin pill, moving on to a lunch that was preceded by two double old-fashioneds, and then increasing the ante as the day wore on. She was taking in almost no nutrition. She never, never got truly drunk, never lost control of herself. Freed of Ham Breck, who in fairydom found fame and fortune, she became a girl on the town—a smart apartment in the mandatory Sixties, a good-sized inheritance from a maternal grandfather, and a willingness to go to bed. She did not tell Sweeney that sex had become only *mechanics* for her. Repetition and alcohol had blunted the cutting edge. She was like a baseball pitcher in his forties who had all the right moves but no more curve, no fast ball.

"Davies is the most fun to talk about," she said. "I had always wanted to meet an out-and-out thief, though at the time I was the only one who would call him one. You must recall the Society Columns of about two years ago: 'Boy Financial Wizard Buster Davies at the Harwyn with lovely Ellen Glasgow' or 'Wall Street Whiz Kid Buster Davies escorting beauteous Gertrude Stein to El Morocco,' that kind of sewage.

"Every time I'd read these accounts of Boy Financial Genius Buster Davies, I would say aloud: 'He's a thief.' It was obvious he was a thief. Knowing nothing about him except those bits in the society pages, one *had* to assume he was a robber.

"Yet I couldn't help feeling that I was out of step with the world. You see, Sweeney, the world accepted Buster Davies, admired him, envied him, toadied to him, printed flattering lies about him in the newspaper, assumed he was important, relevant, worth knowing and worth reading about. Only me, Melissa Henry de Camouillet Breck, understood that he was, in point of fact, a *thief*. Eventually, I began to see that I *was* crazy. The Buster Davies of the world are objects of admiration and envy, and we are all constrained to read slavishly about them in gossip columns and to believe they are, indeed, financial wizards, boy geniuses, and so forth."

"So you married him. Abject surrender."

"You're rather bright, Bucko. I first saw him at a dinner party one night in Palm Beach. God, I always seemed to be in and out of Palm Beach, and Newport and Easthampton in those days, a kind of deluxe beachcomber. I took one look at this stumpy, ruddy, blond Texan, this little feather merchant with his wide grin and his silk shirt, and asked the hostess to seat us together.

"The joke was, *he* envied *me*. He was almost a Texas version of Ham Breck, except that his money—and on Wall Street Paper, at his richest, he was supposed to be worth fifty million—well, it provided a kind of buffer, gave him enough confidence to overcome the fact that he was the son of an itinerant shit-kicker."

"I wish you wouldn't use that word," Sweeney said delicately. "You're very articulate and you have an actress's talent for dramatizing a good story. Honest, Melissa, bad language doesn't go with you or with this lovely place we're in. It destroys the mood."

"Ochone, listen to himself," said Melissa, "sure the ould fellow wants the womenfolk pure as the Virgin's robes, he does. All right, Sweeney, I'll be careful not to offend your Bronx priggishness. That was Buster Davies, financial giant. He worshiped me, and who could reject that kind of worship? We had gold fixtures in the john, three Derains and two Vlamincks, and a yacht anchored off West 79th Street, where little Harlem children could watch us board and shout 'sheeet' at us."

135

"Now cut it out!" Sweeney cried. "I can't stand a woman cursing, especially the woman I love."

"But that's what they all yell."

"I know, I know. Jesus, I spent my youth listening to it. But for Chrissake, edit your copy for my ears, okay?"

"I got Buster interested in the theatre. God, did he have the touch. The first show he backed was a hit. He loved theatre people, rubbing elbows and behinds with them. I'm sure he did some tumbling with young actresses—the soiled, white-skinned, narrow ones. He liked girls with big moist eyes and small trembling mouths. Then he kept bugging me to introduce him to novelists—convinced his life would make the greatest book since *Giant*. It would have, except that the Securities and Exchange Commission would have needed a credit on the title page. Yes, they caught up with Buster, caught him with both hands deep in the till. Off he went to Brazil—where else?—where to this day he sits in a café on the Copacabana telling the world he was framed. He has a scale of prices for telling you this. Fifty bucks for a wire service reporter, up to four hundred for a filmed television interview."

"Good riddance, sez I. You're divorced, right?"

"The papers are in transit, Sweeney. I must say it was the vilest marriage of the three. Buster was loathsome. And of course, my instincts had been so right. He had to be a thief. A man can't keep getting referred to as a young Wall Street financial whiz kid genius without being a crook. Andy once explained to me—as nearly as I could understand—how Buster did it, and it was all so transparent, so patently dishonest, so utterly unbelievable. Just to *look* at Buster, just to hear him *talk*, you'd have to know that he was the fellow with the pea under the walnut shells. Yet, he did it. People gave him money. Corporations elected him president. The columnists printed all that crap about him, laying on their backs like cocker spaniels begging for Gaines dog meal. I could throw up.

"Am I being unkind? He left me pregnant, some future manipulator of over-the-counter securities in my tummy, and I had an

136

abortion—Sweeney lower your eyebrows—but I saved a lot of jewelry, furs, the paintings, and, the last I heard, the apartment, although by now the SEC probably has marshals stationed in front of it. Funny about that 50 million dollars. I always had the feeling that it never existed, really. That it wasn't laying in piles some place so that I could fondle it and stroke it the way Daisy stroked Gatsby's shirts. I also have the feeling that when the government blew the whistle on Buster and the castle tumbled no one really got hurt—that us taxpayers, or some kindly bankers, or the Ford Foundation paid everyone off, and nobody lost. It was like children playing cards for matchsticks."

"You sound like you wish you had the loot," said Sweeney archly.

"Shocked, Sweeney? I was furious when they caught Buster. As much as I detested him, after the first year anyway, I never felt more at ease, more sure of myself. It was nice to walk past Cartier's and say to myself: if I want it, I can have it."

"Yes, I know what you mean. As a boy, after me and Allie Cooperstein delivered a month's supply of old newspapers to Junkman John and we each got a quarter, I felt that way. I could walk into Rappaport's candy store and order a frappe."

"Oh, those log cabin origins! Anyway, your life story can be tomorrow's activity. At least you can tell us what you're doing collecting those interviews. Folklorist, indeed. Andy'll get it out of you."

While she had been telling him the story of her marriages, a wobbling, ear-blasting motor scooter, with a primitive bench bolted to its rear, had made three trips down the winding path, through the lemon groves, depositing shaken, dusty guests at the entrance to the villa. Others, all in costume, were arriving via the narrower path that wound upward from the beach.

"You need a costume," Melissa said. "Remember the theme: the Depression. I'm coming as Frances Perkins. If you need any props, ask Nino, the boy who served the drinks. *Ciao.*"

She left him to greet the guests. Voices—Italian, American,

English, a mélange of accents—rose on the caressing night air. Odor of lemon blossoms mingled with the distant pungency of the sea. He watched Melissa's departing form, the white tennis dress, the tan limbs. He yearned for the power of a Pope, the wisdom of Freud, the strength and beauty of Apollo, so that he might cleanse her of her sinful, indulgent past, then instill her with a new pure love, a union of their body, their blood, their spirits, at once fleshly and elevating.

He stumbled back to the Paestum room and found that his luggage had been placed there, though the attaché case and the tape recorder were missing. "Old Andy," said Sweeney. "He's listening to it all, the sneak." But he scarcely cared. The Sweeney Survey of the Legion of Noble Christians was a dead issue. He would have to notify Wettlaufer, apologize, promise to make up the money to him (fat chance; besides Wettlaufer didn't need it anyway), and recommend abandonment of the project. Tomorrow he would send a cable from Salerno.

Or better yet, he would write a long airmail letter to Wettlaufer, polite, funny, apologetic, explaining that the pursuit of the Legion was pointless, depressing, a raking up of old horrors which even the occasional acts of valor could not diminish. He would wash his hands, forever and ever, of the Legion.

Satisfied that all would be well, he settled back into accustomed indolence; his mind wandered, and he meticulously went over his duties for the morrow, the steps that would rid him forever of Wettlaufer's worrisome shadow. Yes, write the letter, get the boy to drive him up to Salerno or to the nearest post office, buy stamps—*stamps*. The Italian word for stamp? *Estampa?* No. A word that doesn't sound like stamp at all. Doesn't sound like anything.

"*Bolli*," said Sweeney aloud, jerking himself up in bed. "Franco Bolli. That's why I came here."

And his bemused brain made the connection. More or less drunk since his departure from Hamburg and Ludwig Helms, he had sped southward in a boozy stupor, not even aware of what was drawing him inexorably to Italy. He knew now: Bolli, the engineer turned reformer, the man who might answer his questions. *Franco Bolli*—somewhere in the hills in back of Naples. But he had been in Naples two days ago and had made no effort to find Bolli. Naples had meant a whore with the face of a goat, too much red wine fuming his skull, retching in alleys. His pocket was picked and the spare tire was stolen from the MG. Bolli had not once entered his mind until this moment.

He said aloud: "Nuts to Bolli and Helms and the rest. And nuts to Wettlaufer. I've had it up to here."

He buzzed for the manservant to assist in providing props for his costume.

Until Stonebreaker made his entrance, Sweeney's costume was the hit of the evening, even though nobody understood it. With absorbent cotton and Band-aids, he had fashioned a white beard and earlocks for himself. Out of a discarded umbrella silk, he had put together a yarmulka. From Nino the manservant, he had gotten a finger-length white coat, which he spattered with Mercurochrome. In each hand he carried a bamboo crate and in each crate were two scruffy chickens. On his back he wore a cardboard placard, hand-lettered with Magic Marker:

SCHECHTER'S KOSHER
CHICKENS

***

WE KILLED THE N.R.A.

There was general laughter from the assembled guests when Sweeney strolled out on the lantern-lit lawn, although none of them understood his significance. The costumes tended to be sedate. There were, of course, the Italian general and air marshal, as Italian gangsters, but there was also an American vice-admiral, a short, wiry man, who came as John Dillinger, in shirt sleeves, vest, gray hat, submachine gun, and snub-nosed .38 in his belt. The Italian gangsters resented him and kept trying to draw him into a shooting contest. The admiral's aide, a captain, came as an apple vendor, with papier-mâché apples in a wooden crate built by the ship's carpenter of the *U.S.S. Melville*. One woman was Aimée Semple McPherson, in flowing robes and long blonde wig, and another was Helen Wills Moody. A touring American banker who bore a startling resemblance to John L. Lewis—huge head, furry eyebrows, strong jaw—came as John L. Lewis, sporting a squashed black wide-brimmed Trilby.

"That's a great getup, son," the banker said to Sweeney, as the admiral, his apple-selling aide, and several ladies listened. "But what the hell is it supposed to mean?"

"Well, sir," Sweeney said, pushing aside his cotton beard, "there was this Schechter chicken case. The Schechters were small chicken dealers in Brooklyn, I believe, and they refused to abide by the NRA code covering such matters—ah, you remember the NRA— and when the case went to the Supreme Court the Schechter family won, that is they no longer had to abide by the code, and the whole NRA went right out the window."

"Commies," said the admiral.

"Oh no, sir, quite the opposite," said Sweeney, resting his chicken crates on a sarcophagus. "You see the Schechters were just little businessmen protesting the centralization and stifling of our national life by a greedy government. They were not only in favor of the Whole Man as the Senator says, but also the Whole Chicken, and they valued freedom more than this bureaucratic infringement on their liberties."

The admiral's eyes narrowed and he darted a look at his aide, as if demanding a full report on this nut in the white cotton whiskers. "What the hell is that getup?" he asked Sweeney. "Why the hell are you wearing a white beard if you're selling chickens? What's that black thing on your head?" He had a disconcerting way of snapping out his questions while never looking Sweeney in the eye; his own seafaring peepers were always a little to the right or the left. Sweeney had noticed this habit in many high-ranking military persons—an incapacity or an unwillingness to look the

140

lowly civilian, who paid the salaries of admirals and generals and did not have to obey them, head-on.

"You see, sir," Sweeney said, "I represent a *shochet*, a kosher butcher, a ritual slaughterer who supplies fresh killed chickens to persons of the Hebrew persuasion. At least I have taken the liberty of assuming that the Schechter family employed such a person. Your chaplain could fill you in more fully, you might ask him. . . ."

"Don't care for him either," said the admiral mysteriously. "Why is your coat covered with blood?"

"Mercurochrome, sir. It symbolizes the chickens I've killed. The *shochet* tends to get splattered with gore."

The sea dog's wary eyes sought refuge to Sweeney's right. "You know who I am?" he asked icily. The chickens squawked.

"Yes sir. John Dillinger."

"And don't ever forget it." He nodded at his aide, the apple vendor, and both marched off smartly to a long, lavishly furnished bar, attended by three of Stonebreaker's serfs.

Waiters glided noiselessly among the guests on the soft lawn, serving drinks, hot appetizers, artfully designed bits of bread and wafers bright with caviar and smoked salmon. On a section of the roof, behind the machicolations, under Japanese lanterns, a band began to play fox trots.

> *Every morning, every evening,*
> *Ain't we got fun. . . .*

Sweeney, happy with his noisy chickens, sat down on a marble bench beside a man in boxer's costume, with a Star of David on his trunks, obviously Max Baer. A tall, elegant woman, with the unearned hauteur of the well-bred English, sashayed by, presumably Greta Garbo—floppy felt hat, mannish suit, clodhoppers.

The presumed spy, Mr. Simpson, sidled up. The "representative of small businesses" wore a mortarboard, an academic robe, eyeglasses, and a sign on his back: *New Deal Crackpot*. He carried an axe labeled *Socialism*.

141

"Hi there, Sweeney," he said cheerlessly. "That's a clever getup, but isn't it a bit obscure?"

"I give a small speech with it, kind of a pre-recorded explanation. And I think yours stinks."

Simpson was not insulted. Spy or commission man, he never lost his head. "Oh, it all becomes evident when I go into my act. You see that big oak over there?" He pointed across the glittering lawn to a gnarled tree. "I put a sign on the tree, which says *Traditional American Liberties*. Then I go hack at it every few minutes with this axe, *Socialism*, and the story gets across."

Sweeney studied him closely. Was it a gag? Was he playing Sweeney's own game? Or did this bank clerk, this spy (according to Melissa), believe in his lunatic charade?

General Pandolfo, carrying his plastic Thompson at shoulder arms, walked up to them. He spoke to Sweeney, and the gangster locutions of their afternoon encounter were missing.

"Mr. Sweeney," said Enrico Pandolfo, former commander of the 75th Italian Armored Division, "may I speak with you?"

Simpson excused himself and hurried off, his academician's robes flowing, and began to chop at *Traditional American Liberties*.

"Sure, pal. Only don't ask about the chickens."

"Yes, some American humor that I do not understand. . . . Mr. Sweeney, I had occasion to hear your tapes. Mr. Stonebreaker was playing them again. The gentlemen telling about the massacre of the Jews. The part about hiding the Jews in the road-building camp moved me deeply."

"Yeah, yeah. Breaks your heart."

"I have no idea why you made this recording, but I have information on that subject which may interest you."

"General, I'm sort of finished with that. Thanks anyway."

Pandolfo grasped Sweeney's forearm; a glint of the old command presence lit his sad black eyes. No longer was he a fool in East Cicero clothing. "But I must talk to you."

"Nah, let's get drunk."

142

Pandolfo did not release him. Sweeney was on the verge of shaking him off when a round of applause and laughter signified the entrance of the host. Guests had gathered around the small tiled terrace leading from the villa to the main lawn. Sweeney picked up his clucking chickens. Followed by the General, he walked toward the excitement.

As the band struck up "Happy Days Are Here Again," Stonebreaker and Melissa made their entrance.

"How clever!" Sweeney heard an Englishwoman intone. Others voiced approval, surprise, envy, admiration. And indeed Stonebreaker had outdone all his guests.

He sat in a wheelchair. Melissa pushed him. She, as Frances Perkins, wore an enormous velour hat, a shapeless maroon velvet dress, a strand of heavy beads, and sported two large buttons reading CIO and AFL. But no one noticed her. Stonebreaker had hypnotized them.

Seated stiffly in the wheelchair, he wore a dark-gray striped suit, a red tie (Harvard Crimson?), and a cleverly dented gray fedora. He puffed on a cigarette in a long holder. A pince-nez balanced on his nose. The thrust of his jaw, a careful marking of his face with grease pencil had created an uncanny double of Franklin Delano Roosevelt.

There was a more enthusiastic burst of applause when the wheelchair came to rest under a moth-infested yellow spotlight. The band kept playing "Happy Days." People began to clap in time to the music. Max Baer and Helen Wills Moody danced the Charleston.

"Leave it to Andy," John L. Lewis said. "The guy kills me. A couple of years ago he was Booker T. Washington—you'd swear he was a boogie."

Stonebreaker thrust his chin upward, doffed his hat, and grinned—a frozen, heartless grimace, expressing equally his hatred for Roosevelt and his contempt for the people who were toadying to him. He signaled the band to stop, shifted in the cripple's chair,

143

and with his mouth distorted in cruel mimicry of FDR, began a speech.

"My friends," Stonebreaker said, "I am heah tonight to tell you that I hate waaah." There were squeals of delight from the guests, scattered clapping. "Yes, I hate waah. Sistie and Buzzie hate waah. Even Eleanoah hates waah." He paused, his ruddy, sly face eager for their reaction. "And I hate *Eleanoah*."

"Holy Jesus," Sweeney whispered to Simpson, "that act went out in 1940. The kids at Fordham thought it was hot stuff to pull that. Why that crap wouldn't even get a laugh at the Darien Country Club today."

"Sssh," Simpson said. The rest of the guests waited, a little frightened, a little ashamed, a little excited. Stonebreaker had filled some of them with a vague terror.

"I should like to tell you a little about my wife, Eleanoah," Stonebreaker said. His head moved in Roosevelt's familiar pattern—left, right, down, up.

"I should like to take a little of yoah time this evening," Stonebreaker went on, "to tell you something about my wife, Eleanoah. She's a grand woman, she is. Her heart bleeds for suffering mankind. The world is her slum, and she waddles around in it, that big, flat-footed, broad-bottomed, buck-toothed wife of mine, trying to raise every cannibal into middle-class respectability. That old bitch of a——"

The crowd had frozen into a heavy silence, except for a few foreigners—a Venezuelan diplomat, an Arab oil prince—who mumbled on in their native tongues, unaware of the harshness of Stonebreaker's speech. Melissa, Sweeney saw, had quietly left her place of honor at the back of the wheelchair.

". . . busybody of a wife of mine, I tell you, will end up mongrelizing the United States with her black auxiliaries, with whom, I suspect, she indulges in a lot more than social work. For, mah friends, make no mistake, Eleanoah is the be-all and end-all of liberalism. Whatever the old witch is, with her bad breath and body odor, whatever she is, stomping around the world and stirring up the savages, she is the liberal vision incarnate. Now all this may sound hypercritical on my part. I assure you, mah friends, it is not. I love Eleanoah the way she is, even though we haven't had a go at it for decades. She has her friends, and I have mine, and I'm sure you understand *that*. Of course I draw the line at coons occupying guest rooms in the White House although an occasional Communist doesn't bother me. But all in all, Eleanoah and I have achieved a tolerable truce. She is allowed to call me Moosejaw and I am allowed to call her La Boca Grande, or the Great Gabbo. But before doing so, we make sure to *clear it with Sidney!* So, mah friends, pity your poor crippled President who has to put up with an old bag like that. I thank you."

The applause was thunderous. The band played "Happy Days" again as Stonebreaker beamed, moving his large head in little semicircles, chin up, neck out, eyeglasses gleaming in the spotlight. Once more he stopped the band, wheeled his chair around crisply, and called out: "Perhaps the gentlemen of the Press would care to ask a few questions?"

Into the spotlight, bearing his drowsy chickens, stepped Sweeney, doffing his yarmulka in greeting. "Mr. President, sir?"

Stonebreaker's eyes were invisible behind his spectacles, two bright yellow discs staring blindly at Sweeney. Possibly he was puzzled by his visitor's rig. He could not see the explanatory sign on Sweeney's back, and no doubt the cotton beard and earlocks bothered him. "Yes?" he called.

"Sir," Sweeney said, "do you hate Mrs. Roosevelt more than you hate Adolf Hitler?"

"A good question, young man," Stonebreaker said swiftly—as if anticipating it. "Let me put it this way. We *knew* what Hitler was. A Nazi, a Fascist. And we were aware these were things to hate. But all we know of Mrs. Roosevelt is that she was a liberal. But what else is a liberal? Can a liberal be a Communist, or worse than a Communist? If we *knew*, we would be right to hate her as much as we hate Hitler."

"Tell us, sir." A small knot of puzzled guests gathered around

145

the kosher butcher. "You've read up on her a lot, so maybe you should know by now. Was she really a Communist? Or worse?"

"What newspaper do you represent, young man?" Stonebreaker asked. A little of his Rooseveltian cadence vanished.

"The *Jewish Daily Forvitz.*"

"Well, my Yiddish isn't quite up to a detailed response, so I'll see if Owen Lattimore can't work something out for you. Or Harry Dexter White. Or any of Eleanor's other liberal friends." He spun around and wheeled himself out of the spotlight and across the lawn.

A massive buffet had meanwhile been spread across yards of white tablecloth, and the guests moved among the shrimp, the baby lobster, and other exotic *fruits de mer,* the assorted Italianate cold cuts, such as mortadella, capicolli, salami Genovese, Siciliane, and Calabrese. Sweeney, former king of freeloaders, was among the first in line. He heaped high his paper plate, delighting in the scent of fresh, velvety mayonnaise, energetically whipped in Stonebreaker's kitchen by some dusky daughter of Poseidon using an egg whisk fashioned of the old man's trident.

Laying his chickens aside and adjusting his beard for the night's eating, he sought out Melissa Davies. She was standing alone at the steps of the villa. The flopping wide hat, the long, draped skirt, lent her an air of operatic melancholy. Sweeney wanted to sing to her something pained and heartfelt by Puccini, and to hear her high soprano's equally miserable response. But as she saw him approach she made a negative, keep-your-distance gesture, and went into the house.

Balancing his plate, the former agent of the Wettlaufer Foundation walked to a small ironwork table and chair. He was not especially intrigued with the guest list and opted for eating alone, happy with his *langostina* and *vitello tonnato.* Arm in arm, Frances Ferrante and Cecile Halberstadt, done up in sportswear designed by Simonetta for the party, wandered by, staring at him suspiciously. "What is with the chickens and the beard?" the short blonde, Mrs. Halberstadt, asked. "Search me," responded red-headed Mrs. Ferrante.

146

Sweeney's seat was at the edge of one of the terraced levels and, peering over the side, he could see lanterns hanging along the winding road. They were placed to mark the narrow path but Stonebreaker had added a unique touch. Under each sat a small Italian child. "His goddamn serfs," Sweeney muttered. He saw Nino, the all-around boy, smiling at him——that toothy insincere smile of the *meridionale*. "Hey walyo," Sweeney called, "bring me a bottle of vino. Da best."

Sweeney ate slowly, with dignity, distressed by the sight of Nino returning with an iced bottle of *Lacrimae Christi*—and General Enrico Pandolfo.

"Please," said the general. "Resume your dinner. This boy was good enough to tell me where you are."

"Awright. Siddown."

"Thank you, Mr. Sweeney. I did not quite understand what our host was trying to convey before. He is, I gather, an admirer of Mr. Roosevelt?"

"Well if you think so, it means the act is a bomb. So don't tell him or he might throw us all out."

"Please?"

"Yeah, please." He scanned the lawn, the terraces, the milling crowd around the buffet table. Melissa had vanished. The joyful person he had swum with that morning, the undefeated, thrice-married narrator who had beguiled him in late afternoon, had turned sullen. Perhaps she was a diurnal beast, unaccustomed to the night.

Pandolfo sat stiffly opposite Sweeney and was silent. The band had struck up a peppy medley of songs of the Thirties.

> *I can't give you*
> *Anything but love, baby. . . .*

Sweeney honored his mouth with the heady wine, whose grapes grow on the slopes of Vesuvius, and savored its harsh subtleties. He saw, diaphanous in a night haze, Mrs. Ferrante, artfully corseted, her years glorified by silk, and Sweeney, hopeless fetishist, felt faint. Oh, the nylon of her! High, high alligator pumps! He

147

ripped off his kosher beard and leaned back. Was he really happy? And who should it be tonight? No, it could not be Mrs. Ferrante, nor round Mrs. Halberstadt. Melissa, or no one. Yes, he would have Melissa, wipe away her unhappy memories of three lousy husbands. She had experienced a noble title, show business, great wealth. Now would come Sweeney, Sweeney, the poet, wanderer, and sage.

"I commanded the 75th Armored Division in Croatia," Pandolfo said.

"Your secret is safe with me."

"No, no. You cannot be a complete fool." The general gazed intently at Sweeney's flushed face. "If I knew why you are collecting those interviews I would know how to approach you. But you disavow them. You say you are finished with them. Why?"

"None of your business, General. Have some wine."

Pandolfo accepted a glass of *Lacrimae Christi*. He sipped it slowly, licking his dried lips. The creases ran deeply down his cheeks from the sides of his nostrils to his prognathous jaw, almost converging on the stubbled chin.

"Yes, I was a famous general. What were you in the war, Mr. Sweeney?"

Sweeney was about to invent some wild deed of valor to establish his essential superiority over this unraveled Fascist. But the fiction, half-formed, died in his mouth. There was a pitiful sadness about Pandolfo, a self-shame that gave the American pause. Why rub it in?

"General, I was a private in the U.S. Army Ordnance Department. I stacked boxes all through the war and the only shot I ever heard fired in anger was when I got caught with a Limey farmer's daughter in a haystack. He came after me with a Webley-Vickers. I hold the American record for drinking mild-and-bitter, and I was court-martialed twice. So don't feel bad."

Pandolfo managed a wry smile. "*Bene, bene.* I was fearful you had been one of those savage Marines who tore Japanese apart, or a courageous fighter pilot who shot up German panzers with your rockets."

148

"Not a chance. I'm gutless. Actually, limited service. I got a double hernia and a deviated septum, so I was kept out of combat duty."

"I admire your American sense of humor," said the general. "We Italians pretend to laugh, and are always smothering our guests—but it is dramaturgy, bad comedy. Our ancient past is so magnificent that the absurdities of the present force us into this role. How terrible, Mr. Sweeney, to be as I am, a descendant of Canaletto on my mother's side, and on my father's—in direct line from the Emperor Domitian."

"Cool it, Pandolfo. More wine? Tears of Christ, right?"

"Thank you. Tears of Christ. May I speak?"

"Shoot, Enrico."

"Do you wish to make a record of what I have to say?"

"Naah. My career as a folklorist is over. I think I'll open a chicken market. But I'll listen."

"You are very kind. As you may know the Germans and the Italians established what they called the independent state of Croatia under the rule of the Croatian Fascists, the *Ustashe*. The Germans occupied the northern sector and we moved into the southern area. They are curious people, the Croats. They are among the most cultured, the most charming, the most likable of Eastern Europeans. They are deeply religious Catholics. They are splendid family people. Yet they were so brutal in their actions against their Jews that even the Germans were aghast! It took the Croats, under the leadership of their noble *Poglavnik*, as he was called—a man named Pavelic—but four months to enact and carry out Jews which the Germans labored over for eight years!

"Pavelic! There was a fellow worth studying. His long sad face, huge ears, great hands, a man of dolorous ambition. Neither the Germans nor ourselves could manage him. And his wife was a Jewess! His anti-Semitism was without sincerity—he acted savagely against the Jews merely to curry favor with the Germans—and for plunder. Such cynicism ill becomes a head of state. When the Romanians hung the naked bodies of dead Jews in butcher shops they acted out of conviction. But not the *Poglavnik*. Do you know

149

the story told by one of our Fascist journalists about visiting Pavelic? He was in the Croatian hero's office. An aide entered with what appeared to be a pail of oysters. Our journalist asked the *Poglavnik* what they were. 'Eyes,' replied Pavelic, 'the eyes of our Serbian enemies, brought to me by my faithful Ustashe.' "

"Yaaach!" spat Sweeney. "Jesus, Enrico, not while I'm eating! A man can't enjoy a mortadella sangwich when you talk like that! I got a spastic esophagus as it is."

"My apologies," said the general. "Now, from the start the Italian Army was reluctant, and in most instances actively opposed to German policies against the Jews. Smile if you will, Mr. Sweeney, when I mention the Italian Army. I know what the world thinks of us—strutting fools commanded by braggarts, cowardly men who ran or surrendered at the first shot. That is not true."

"Yeah," said Sweeney, unaware of his own cruelty, "they say some of your guys are still running from Caporetto."

Pandolfo's weary face darkened. "I am too old and too fatigued to be insulted."

"Ah, what the hell, Enrico, I'm sorry."

"No, no. That is our reputation."

"Honest, I'm sorry. You're a good egg. I shouldn't insult you. Tell me about the Croats."

"There was nothing we could do about the German zone of Croatia. I leave it to your imagination as to what happened to the Jews there under the combined terror of Nazis and Croats. Indeed, the *Ustashe* was so vicious that a Nazi general protested! He believed in killing Jews, but not so brutally.

"In our sector we tried to prevent the Ustashe from committing excesses. About seven thousand Jews had fled from the German zone into our sector. We did what we could to protect them. It was not easy because the pressure from the Germans and the Croats was continuous.

"I shall tell you of an incident. I was accompanying a unit of my division as they moved out to subdue a party of Serbian guerrillas.

150

Our tanks and our accompanying supply lorries stopped in the square of a Croatian village, one of those miserable Balkan towns which seem to have no history, no future. Those graceless gray buildings, that utter lack of style, of gaiety! We arrived at a crucial moment. The *Ustashe* were dragging screaming Jews from the houses and assembling them in the square, to the applause of the villagers. There could not have been more than forty Jews in all— weeping, shrieking, well aware of what was in store for them.

"The *Ustashe* were drunk on *slivovitz*. I remember clearly those Croat irregulars taking liberties with the Jewish women—lifting skirts, fondling them in front of everyone, even in front of crying Jewish children."

"They sound like some Ukrainians I once met," Sweeney growled.

Pandolfo poured himself another glass of *Lacrimae Christi*. "I was a division commander, but I had only a lateral relationship to the military government. However, some action was called for. I told my adjutant, Major Pacetta, to break out our supply of *grappa* and brandy, and we asked the Ustashe to join us for a friendly drink in the town hall. When they were sufficiently drunk, incapable of standing, we told the handful who were left outside guarding the Jews that their orders had been countermanded and that we Italians would be responsible for the Jews.

"They argued, but finally agreed. We loaded the Jews into our tanks and trucks—the children crouching inside the tanks with our soldiers, the adults in the lorries—and instead of fighting the Serbs that day we returned to our base at Ragusa, from where the Jews were sent to an island off the Dalmatian coast."

Pandolfo smiled at some memory. "In my tank we had placed a little Jewish boy. He wore a round cap such as yours, Mr. Sweeney, and had hair growing in rings down the sides of his ears. His eyes were like a Raffaelo angel."

"What happened to the kid?"

"I do not know. But the manner in which these miserable people were pursued by the Germans and the Croats, the dedication of our allies in tracking down to the ends of the earth these unfortunates who could not fight back, is something for historians to study. As yet there are no explanations. Perhaps you, Mr. Sweeney, will find one.

"Imagine these penniless, sick Jews, hidden in our zone of Croatia. All this time the Jews in the German zone were being systematically arrested and murdered. Then the Germans became uneasy about the way we Italians were protecting the Jews. Can anyone explain to me such absolute evil? Can you?

"A man named Kasche, an old Nazi and a typical lout, was sent to Croatia to discipline us. He demanded our Jews. Listen carefully to this, Mr. Sweeney, when you think again of the Italian Army. All the commanding officers in our zone met and we decided unanimously against co-operating. Our answer to Kasche was: '*It is not consistent with the honor of the Italian Army to surrender innocent persons to be murdered.*' Remember the names of my comrades, Mr. Sweeney—Roatta, Robotti, Birolli, Pieche—Italian generals, some of them Fascisti. Would you judge their act as noble as any deed they ever performed in battle?"

"You bet," said Sweeney.

"I wrote a letter to my staff officers, in which I said: 'We must not permit the Italian Army to dirty its hands in this business. We will not be middlemen for the Croats and the Germans. We are filled with shame at having to watch these crimes take place, let alone participating in them.'

"But the German hunger for Jewish blood could not be appeased. Kasche complained to Ribbentrop and to Prince Otto von Bismarck. The latter called on Ciano. The matter went to Mussolini. Il Duce, in answer to Kasche's proposals for rounding up Jews in Croatia, scrawled on the paper: *No objection.*

"No objection, indeed. To Ciano's credit he tried to delay again, ordering an endless registration of Jews, exempting many. Ribbentrop was furious—he wanted to send two German divisions and an SS battalion to make sure no Jews got away. Imagine! Two divisions and an SS battalion to find that little boy with the ringlets of hair at the sides of his head!

"Pavelic now entered the scene, eager to catch the Jews before the Germans did. The noble Poglavnik, anxious to impress his masters, offered to pay the Germans thirty marks for every Jew deported. This angered other members of the Croatian government who had learned that they could make money by *saving* Jews for the Jewish Agency. *Che bellezza!* How quickly these noble Christians of Eastern Europe learned that their hatred of Jews could be turned to profit!"

"Yes," Sweeney interjected. "Boys, turn your spare time into cash. Like it used to say in *Boy's Life.*"

Pandolfo removed his Chicago fedora. He had a glistening bald pate; the hair circling it was gray, untrimmed.

"Between the pressure from the Germans and the eagerness of the Croats we Italians had a harder time hiding the Jews. I ordered the Italians under my command to transport, to hide, and to provision refugee Jews. If we had earned a reputation as poor fighters, perhaps we could redeem ourselves as decent men. We shipped many of the Jews to Istria and other Dalmatian islands.

"Somehow the Germans learned of this, probably through the Croats. 'No,' Von Bismarck said, 'those islands will not do. Trieste is a better place for Jews.' Trieste, Mr. Sweeney, has a direct rail link to Poland and Auschwitz. We told them we could not relocate the Jews again—we had no shipping.

"Imagine, if you will, all this fuss, this endless letter writing and bickering and cabling, and all the people involved. Hitler, Himmler, Ribbentrop, Eichmann, Bismarck, Mussolini, Ciano, Pavelic— all these people studying maps, making plans, going into rages, the hours wasted, the meetings held, the telephone calls made—all this energy and effort for three thousand poor Croatian Jews."

Sweeney blinked. "Yeah. Including a kid with *payes,* a kid you once took for a ride in your tank."

"For the blood of one innocent child. I regret to say, I do not know what happened to him. He may have been in a group we

153

sent to the island of Arbe in the Gulf of Cattaro for safekeeping. When Italy left the war, the Germans took over our sector. Even then Badoglio's government tried to save the Jews. But we heard no more of them. They vanished, swept up in the dimming years of the great Reich, some perhaps to safety in Italy, a few with the partisans, but most likely into the furnaces.

"I often think of these people and I am not satisfied with my role in their destiny, nor indeed the role of our beloved Christian Europe. These Croatian Jews were not cosmopolite moneylenders or Bolsheviks, as Jews are supposed to be. They were the simplest of people. They had lived, since their expulsion from Spain, in Dalmatian villages, working as shopkeepers, artisans, professionals. They were mostly poor and, this may surprise you, at peace with their Christian neighbors. Odd when one thinks of the savagery of the Croat leaders.

"I envision these Jews, in their haven on the islands, suddenly discovered, ferried away, packed on cattle cars and sent to starvation, asphyxiation, and the ovens. What in God's name could have passed through their minds? What would they ask of one another? What would my little friend with the skullcap ask of his Papa and Mama?"

"I don't know," Sweeney gulped. He emptied the Tears of Christ into their glasses. "I knew a German engineer once who was able to hear what the kids said to their parents. I don't think it made me any smarter or any happier for hearing it."

"I see him in the flames," the general said as he stood up with some of his old military dash. "I see my small friend, with his Raffaelo eyes—God-inspired. And they burn. They burn. He does not weep. Perhaps he has some intelligence that is denied us."

The Al Capone hat was back on Pandolfo's long sad head, the plastic machine gun held at port arms, and he seemed the ultimate in absurdity.

"Ah, come on, Enrico, it's all over. You came out all right, you did the right thing. You're ruining my weekend, pal."

"I have ordered the tombstone for my grave. It will stand in my family's *camposanto* in Salerno. Below my name it will read: *It is not consistent with the honor of the Italian Army to surrender innocent persons to be murdered.* I was perhaps an incompetent general, and an opportunist when I became a Fascist, but I hope I redeemed myself with those words and with the deeds that followed."

Sweeney patted his arm. "Sure you did, Enrico. Sure."

He strained his neck looking for Melissa. She was gone. Mrs. Ferrante was declared the winner of the Charleston contest and was performing an exhibition with the man who came as Max Baer. She danced with the long-limbed skill of an old professional. Sweeney got a glimpse of a white frothy underthing, a black garter, as her legs kicked and thrust. A passion tickled his toes and coursed upward, flaming at his groin, making his heart pump. Oh, Mrs. Ferrante, you are ripened, you are strapped and secreted in elastics and silks!

"I gather you are in search of something," Pandolfo said. "No man would go to the trouble you have unless he were looking for answers. I have none, but I am sorry you have given up your search. I have never understood Americans and I am at a loss to comprehend you, my friend, although I think you have a brave heart."

"Hah?" Sweeney had risen and was craning his neck, seeking a better angle from which to study Mrs. Ferrante's thrashing legs. But the Charleston was over. Max Baer lifted her high, to tumultuous applause. Her legs kicked in protest and the wide-pleated skirt traveled upward. Sweeney thought he would faint.

"Brave heart?" Sweeney asked. "Enrico, I am the yellowest bastard you ever saw. I am the original gutless wonder. And I'm through asking questions. Let the Jews solve their own problems. I got *tsuris* of my own."

"Pardon?"

"*Tsuris.* Troubles."

Frances Ferrante walked off, arms around waists with Max Baer. A soft mist rolled in from the Mediterranean. Each lantern nestled

155

in a silvery halo. Guests glided across the lawn, caressed by ghostly vapors.

"Oh, but they are your troubles, Mr. Sweeney, and mine. Auschwitz is part of us, and we must understand it and learn from it. I am too old, but you are not."

"Thanks a lot, Enrico, but I'm not in this line of work any more." Sweeney drained the last of the *Lacrimae Christi* and got up. Some prowling was in order. "Thanks for the story anyway."

"No," Pandolfo said mournfully. "I do not think you really are grateful. It does not matter." He turned away, carrying his plastic gun by the barrel, in search of Mario.

"Listen," Sweeney called after him, "don't let me spoil your fun. All this stuff is depressing. Go on and shoot up a few people for kicks."

But Pandolfo made no response. Sweeney had the sad feeling that he was an insulted child, a child who would hear no more excuses from the deceitful adult world.

The party had assumed a clotted, amorphous quality. It was by no means a wild affair. Mrs. Ferrante's energetic dance had clearly been the high-water mark. Now there was listless dancing, serious drinking, and a lot of arch conversation. Sweeney noticed that Simpson, Melissa's spy, was brown-nosing the American admiral and his aide. Mrs. Ferrante was gone—*strike two*—in the wake of Melissa's disappearance. A hellish fury welled up in him as he envisioned her spread-eagled on one of Stonebreaker's beds, giggling under the proddings of the man who came as the prize-fighter.

The old ennui troubled Sweeney. He had discarded his chickens and his beard. Now in the stained white coat he looked like a Fulton Fish Market Irishman, a rough handler of mackerel and cod. He walked into the vestibule of the villa in search of a woman—Melissa preferably, although Mrs. Ferrante, Mrs. Halberstadt, or even the lofty Englishwoman would do—and stopped as he heard Stonebreaker's firm voice.

"Give it to me, Melissa. Give it to me at once."

156

It scared Sweeney. It was the voice of a male nurse or a prison guard. Then he heard the unmistakable sound of a slap. There was a silent interval, then a second slap. "Jesus," Sweeney whispered. "He's going to beat the hell out of her."

He turned left at the end of the vestibule toward the unpleasantness. Sweeney walked softly into a semidark corridor which led to the kitchen, pantry, and servants' quarters. Too quickly, he blundered into a small alcove. His looming white-coated figure surprised both uncle and niece.

Melissa was seated on a stool. Her wide hat was gone, and her face was florid, yet bland, unemotional. Stonebreaker, out of his wheelchair, was grasping her left wrist firmly with his right hand. In his other he held a half-filled bottle of gin. Niece did not resist uncle. Her attitude was one of dignified surrender. Indeed, to Sweeney, she seemed almost the victor. Stonebreaker had the gin, but she had her serenity.

The host turned his large head and stared at Sweeney. FDR's pince-nez sparkled. A good deal of his presence, that talent for dominating and humiliating others, had deserted him. He had obviously anticipated no eavesdropping.

"Get out," Stonebreaker said. "Keep your mouth shut about what you've seen."

Melissa's eyes were flat, noncommittal. She did not acknowledge Sweeney's knight-errancy.

"I was wondering if Melissa would like to dance," Sweeney said. "I do a great Peabody."

"She is in no condition to dance. Melissa has a low threshold for excitement. She's going to her room now—to rest."

With a firm grace he forced her to rise, guiding her to a standing position with his right hand. She did not rebel, but her movements were drugged. Then Stonebreaker marched her off a few steps and whispering something that Sweeney could not hear directed her to the stairs.

"For Chrissake, Mr. Stonebreaker," Sweeney called out. "If you want to send the kid to bed early, okay. But at least let her take some Flit along." He pointed to the gin.

Stonebreaker watched his niece ascend the stairs. Then he approached Sweeney. For the first time, and with a rush of horror, Sweeney saw that he had mimicked Roosevelt down to the metal braces around his ankles.

"You will oblige me by saying nothing about what you have just witnessed," he said. His manner was cheerful, comradely. "My niece is a convalescent. She's under my care. Don't be misled by her healthy appearance. She has been extremely ill—no matter what she has told you."

"You klopped her a few times," Sweeney said. "I heard you. If she's sick why belt the poor woman around?" Manfully he tried to sneak an edge of menace into his voice and failed.

"Yes, I did slap her. I have to when she regresses."

"That's no way to treat a fine woman like Melissa."

Stonebreaker's hand locked itself around Sweeney's soft upper arm, bunching the sleeve of the butcher's coat. Just as a few minutes before he had forced Melissa to rise and to go to her room, he now reduced Sweeney to meek locomotion.

"Back to the revels," he said. "Sweeney, get drunk, eat well. I know *what* you are, and I suspect who's paying you. Store up food if you wish, like a good squirrel. I know you're penniless. And I guess you've abandoned this venture into slobbering liberalism. It's not for you, Sweeney."

The host's iron hand remained nailed to Sweeney's arm. The guest said softly: "You're wrinkling the merchandise."

Both men paused outside Stonebreaker's study—crammed bookshelves, a long antique mahogany desk, a goose-necked lamp, leather chairs.

"Honest, Mr. Stonebreaker," Sweeney said, "I didn't mean to come snooping around when you were smacking Melissa and taking her gin away. That's your business. She's kind of your ward, I take it."

"Don't presume too much, Sweeney," Stonebreaker said. "Inci-

158

dentally, those interviews of yours—I have a feeling they got Melissa back into bad habits."

"My tapes? Jesus, I'm sorry. I would never want to hurt her—I mean, I've only known her one day, but I admire her tremendously. I'm practically in love with her."

"You lout," Stonebreaker said. "My niece suffers from a common ailment. A sense of uselessness. I manage to keep it suppressed. But I could see the change in her as she listened. Touching stuff, Sweeney, especially that old priest."

"Yes, he's one great guy, Father Louis."

Stonebreaker was ignoring him with the admirable bluntness of a man who finds intelligence and wit only in his own voice, in his own ideas. "One more relapse may kill Melissa. She gives the appearance of health, strength, beauty. But her viscera are corroded, decaying."

Sweeney shuddered. *Gevald, geshriggen,* did he have to listen to this? A cold mist from the sea floated into the ancient villa. It filmed the stone walls with salty damp, penetrated flesh, muscle, and bone. Outside the band had ceased playing. Guests were bidding one another goodbye. He could hear the noxious bursts of the motor scooter, ferrying a terrified load of shrieking visitors up the goat path to the highway.

"That's sad," Sweeney said. "I'd love to help her, to make her happy. All those lousy marriages. And she has so much talent and good looks and a great sense of humor."

Stonebreaker guided Sweeney forcefully into the study. "Get in there. Sit down. Since you're being expelled tomorrow, I'd best talk to you tonight."

"About Melissa?"

"Forget about her. About this little campaign you're engaged in. Who put you up to it?"

"To what, sir?" The old Bronx caution warned Sweeney: play it stupid, know nothing, profess ignorance. Dumb Irishman. Stupid Mick. Hardheaded Harp. Mackerel Snapper. Sweeney settled deep in a black leather armchair. Stonebreaker sat behind the desk. He had removed the theatrical make-up, the pince-nez, and the cigarette holder. FDR had gone; he was now a burly tanned man in his sixties, with a large bald head and piercing eyes. Yet Sweeney could not dislike the man. He envied him, admired his mighty brain, his literary eminence.

"You know *what*, Sweeney. You're not terribly bright, but by the same token you're not quite that stupid. Who is financing this—" He indicated the tape recorder.

"Ah, I've never met the people."

"You're a tiresome liar. I've been through all your notes, all your letters, and I know it's a man named Wettlaufer. It's a name that's new to me, someone I can't find on my cross-indices, so he's probably fronting for someone else. Now, who are they?"

"Oh, you've got me wrong. Yes, it's a Mr. Wettlaufer, poor old Sherman Wettlaufer, my army buddy."

Stonebreaker shook his head negatively. "It isn't that simple, Sweeney. Still, you may be telling the truth. You're the perfect front man. Noisy, hard-drinking Irish Catholic lad. Who would ever suspect you?"

"Well, as a matter of fact, sir, that's right. That's just what Sherm said."

"Did he?" Stonebreaker asked sarcastically. "I'm sure he and I didn't have the same thing in mind." The owner of Villa Malerba sat back and made a tent with the points of his fingers. For an unguarded second, he was Roosevelt again. "May I tell you what you're doing? May I enlighten you as to the true nature of your survey of Noble Christians?"

"Yeah. I need enlightenment. But I have to warn you, Mr. Stonebreaker. Even if you do straighten me out, I still won't like your imitation of Roosevelt. I seen better imitations at the Fordham Dramatic Club. Yours stank."

"Sweeney, you're an agent of the *Hate Germany* plot."

"I am not. I don't even know what it is."

"In its essentials, the Hate Germany plot may be summarized as follows—an effort to keep the people of the world, but most

160

particularly Americans, perpetually aroused and angered against Germany, as a diversion from the spread of atheistic communism, the menace of Russia and the threat of China, thus permitting communism to expand and grow stronger, and at the same time, weakening the Germans, our most virile ally against the Reds."

"Holy smoke. Wettlaufer never told me *that*."

"I said it was a *conspiracy*. You were deliberately kept in the dark. Perhaps this Wettlaufer is being used also."

"Maybe I'm thick, Mr. Stonebreaker, but how in the world can stories by people like Father Louis and Huguette Roux be part of a plot?"

"You fool. By reviving and prolonging and repeating a lot of old exaggerated tales, stories that had their time and place but are all outdated now. The Hate Germany campaign will see to it that these stories are publicized—all that heart-rending stuff about Jews being murdered—and the American public will weep and forget the millions of innocent people slaughtered in Soviet concentration camps, the tens of millions murdered by the Chinese, the inexorable advance of communism in black Africa and brown Asia, and the liberal responsibility for all these unspeakable crimes. Americans will be asked to wring hands over Jews, long dead and beyond our help, instead of facing up to the real evil in the world.

"Now, let me make myself clear before that slum-nurtured tolerance of yours comes to the defense of dead Jews. I mourn, with all civilized men, their murder. I was horrified. I protested. I denounced the Nazis. I am well aware of the awful holocaust that struck the Jews of Europe. But when, when in God's name, will we be permitted to forget it? When will we be allowed to say, yes, it was awful what the Nazis did to the Jews but there are greater horrors in the world today, there are menaces threatening that require our attention and our strength, so enough of dead Jews! Enough! Six . . . five . . . four million, whatever the number was! We are sorry it happened, but on with the show!"

"Hmmm," Sweeney mumbled. "You may have a point, Mr. Stonebreaker."

"With what glee and enthusiasm the liberal establishment resurrects the Jews of Europe! Oh, the crocodile tears, the endless jabber about Auschwitz but not a word about Vorkuta! The interminable plays, movies, books, tracts, photo layouts, interviews, research, and now surveys such as yours, about the vile deeds of the Germans, as if the Germans were the only villains in the world, as if the Soviets never existed. Look away from the bloody hands of Stalin—and the equally guilty hands of the liberals! Nothing, nothing about the Communist evil! But floods of tears over the Jews, who, after all, were inevitable victims. . . ."

"Got what they deserved, Mr. Stonebreaker?"

"I did not say that. I made my position on the Jews clear to you. Don't you know anything about me? I'm practically a Hebe myself. Forget my Denver origins and the mining wealth. I went to Harvard with intellectual Jews. I did graduate work at Columbia with more of them, then Greenwich Village, Broadway, Hollywood. I walked the road hand-in-hand with Judaica Americana in all its artistic, intellectual, liberal, and creative permutations. I was a spy from the *goyim* in on their cabals, laughing with them, eating their rich food, stealing their ideas, and enjoying every minute of it. I would not trade my experiences for all the *goyim* in Darien, Connecticut. So I come to this argument shriven."

"I think I liked you better when you were imitating Roosevelt. You know the one about 'I have not sought, I do not seek, I repudiate the support of communism.'" Sweeney bobbed his head sideways twice and then downward on the last phrase, a better imitation than Stonebreaker's.

"I suspect that was a thrust, am I right? About my political past?"

"Heck no, Mr. Stonebreaker. I don't know what you were. Or are."

"Yes, Sweeney, I was a Communist. A Bolshevik. I was in the Party. I worshiped the God that failed. My past is on record."

"Oh, then that explains why you hate Communists so much. Well, they are a lousy bunch of mean bastards. Their suits don't

162

fit, and their women look like hell. No wonder the birth rate's so low in Russia."

"Don't play the fool with me. I stood well to the left of Trotsky."

"I thought he was as far left as you could go."

"Trotsky was brilliant in his way, but he was not ruthless enough."

"It sounds like you admired him. I mean, you hate all those people so much now."

"Yes, it is admiration of a sort. I admire decisiveness, dedication. I admired the way Franco put down the Reds. And I must say that apart from his excesses, his mistakes in arousing the Jews of the world, Hitler was a master tactician. Forget morals for a moment, and don't look so horrified. Hitler did no more than any routine German politician would have been forced to do in the Thirties. History propelled him into his acts. I don't mean the concentration camps. No sane or civilized man could approve that. Yet in foreign policy, in his relations with the West and the Soviets he was merely following a *logical* line, swimming with the stream of historical imperatives, and the day we admit this to ourselves we'll all be a bit better off."

"Ah, maybe," Sweeney ventured, "maybe he saw it a little different."

"How do you mean?" Stonebreaker asked—aghast that the visitor might have a constructive or original notion.

"I don't know how to say it. But maybe it was just as important, even more important for Hitler and all those people to murder Jews as it was to give Germany a favorable balance of trade." Sweeney paused, searching for words. "I mean maybe what the Nazis realized was that being a murderous son-of-a-bitch comes first, like shooting Jewish children in the head, and foreign policy grows out of it. Not the way you've got it—foreign policy and political aims first, and then like by accident murdering Jews."

"I'm not sure that weakens my thesis," Stonebreaker said,

163

somewhat surprised by Sweeney's observation. "I merely said Hitler's aims had a certain logic."

"Why near the end of the war those people loused up their own war effort: they used army transport and personnel that could have been fighting *just to keep killing Jews*. That was what really interested them. Not colonies or Danzig."

Stonebreaker nodded gravely, as if acknowledging that Sweeney had scored a point. In a sense he was pleased that his quarry had some spunk.

"Jesus, how can you say 'any routine politician,'" Sweeney pleaded, pursuing what he fancied was an advantage, "when what really mattered to that crowd was murder and robbery? They were a bunch of queers anyway, fuckups, and failures, all of 'em."

"Would you so characterize most Communists?"

"Sure. You'd know better than me, Stonebreaker. You were a Bolshevik once. I never was. My old man always voted the straight Democratic ticket, and he told me, 'Son, it's Tammany Hall or no Hall at all.' I didn't go to Harvard. I never knew Trotsky either, and I'm not sorry I didn't get a chance to kill a lot of people."

"A touching defense and a rather vicious assault. Not quite what I expected of you, Sweeney. I'd like you better organizing for the Christian Front."

"That's my older brother Leo. Hey, he does sound like you, only with less class."

"I think I'd like your brother," the host said.

"Stonebreaker, you'd hate him." Sweeney had slid easily into the use of his host's surname. Soon he might be Andy or Stoney. "Leo's a slob, a nut. You got class. You couldn't talk to him for five minutes. That's the trouble with all you hard-nosed conservative antiliberal ex-Bolsheviks. You're very big with the theories but you'd be scared shitless to get down there and slosh around with the people who agree with you. They're *really* rough. But I guess you need 'em if you're gonna have your revolution."

"Let's get back to Germany if we may," said Stonebreaker. "As a catspaw for the Hate Germany people, you should be obliged to know what you're being paid to hate. Admit something to me, Sweeney. Admit that if Hitler had left the Jews alone we would never have gone to war with him, that we would have permitted him for our own security and peace of mind to crush communism in Europe, and by extension world communism."

"Hah?"

"Had Hitler done all the terrible things he was supposed to have done—exaggerated, as usual, by liberals—but *not* touched a hair on a Jewish head, do you really believe we would have fought him? That France and Britain would have fought him?"

"Christ, you got history bass-ackwards. He started in with them."

"He did not. He went to war with Poland over an old grievance, to secure his eastern border against Russian communism. Britain and France, prodded by Jews—and dammit, I know they had a right to complain—foolishly contested him. They could have made a reasonable pact. They could have permitted him to go forth and destroy communism once and for all. And could have stayed out of it. And kept us out of it. But the Jews got in the way. . . ."

"Hey, hey, Stonebreaker. You're way out. Sure, the Jews in other countries got sore. You would too if your relatives were getting burned and shot."

"Hitler burned and shot Poles, Slavs, Dutchmen, Belgians, and many others. Yet they did not demand his destruction. *They* realized that in the long run he would have a cleansing action on the world—that communism could never recover from the blows ne would deal it. But we, of course, softhearted Americans, led by that softheaded cripple and his wife with the bad breath, King Franklin and Queen Eleanor, we rushed in to save Europe for the Reds. The liberals *meant* it that way, the Jews *forced* us into it out of self-interest, and those who were *both* liberals and Jews acted with an intent to save communism. Cruel, but true."

"Holy horror, Stonebreaker! Were they supposed to stand up and cheer when they got gassed?"

Stonebreaker ignored him. "Let us think in terms of *alternatives*, of historical possibilities. We admit the Jews were badly treated. But consider the alternative. The West lets Hitler attack Poland, attack the Soviet Union. The West lets Hitler set up his German hegemony in the East. Britain, France, Scandinavia, the Low Countries are allowed to run Western Europe. Once and for all, communism is crushed. I assure you some kind of viable, orderly Europe would have emerged. I am no friend of Hitler's, Mr. Sweeney. I detested him. But is not what we live with today more horrid? Europe under communism. All of Africa and Asia ready to succumb to it. China armed and antagonistic."

"So you think the Jews should have taken their medicine and shut up and things would have been okay?"

"Better than they are now. After all, there was nothing new about murdering Jews. It's been going on for two thousand years. The Jews should have been told by their leaders that their death would redeem Europe, just as Christ's redeemed the world. In that way they might have died happier. They die—Europe is free of communism. And Germany, a European *Christian* nation, when all is said and done, goes on to crush atheistic communism once and for all. But no, the insane cripple had his way and Hitler is dead and Germany is crushed. . . ."

"They don't look crushed to me. You been in Hamburg lately? I never saw so many fat-ass broads."

". . . and we are reminded daily about Auschwitz and Buchenwald, those awful Nazis, and poor Anne Frank, Ilse Koch and the alleged medical experiments, and now this sentimental pap you'll be disseminating. All it does is turn our minds and hearts and muscles away from the threat of communism. Let me tell you, Mr. Sweeney, we must be prepared to fight and die and *kill* to defeat communism. I am prepared to, and I hope you are."

Through all this peroration, Stonebreaker's voice was calm, firm, level. Apart from a slight hectoring tendency, an occasional rising of the voice to warn his audience of one, the man might have been discussing the values of a growth mutual fund.

"Ah, I suppose you might have a point." Sweeney yawned.

"Maybe I've been sort of brainwashed. I mean talking to people like Helms who saw it all first hand."

"I'll put it to you as simply as I can. Purge your mind of emotion, of sentiment. It boils down to this: *Yes, I am terribly sorry for little Izzy Cohen who was gassed at Treblinka. But was avenging him worth enslaving half the world?*

"Moreover, the world now must equate the triumph of Bolshevism with the Jews. I don't mean that old nonsense about Jewish Bolshevism. Not at all. But when comes the day of communism's extirpation, its destruction root and branch, the Jews, innocent as most of them are, will suffer again."

"Sounds like you can't wait."

"I am not sure that communism can be beaten any longer. The liberals have seen to that. They have so muddied the waters, blurred the arguments, that we are castrated. Western civilization is doomed by liberal guilt, by the liberal need to accommodate communism, to see in communism virtue. In their way the liberals are more insidious, more diabolic than the Communists."

"You should know, you used to be one. You hate liberals because they aren't Communists. You hate Communists because you used to be one. You're sore at the Jews because you think they got us into the war. Stonebreaker, who *do* you like?"

Stonebreaker seemed not at all insulted. He viewed Sweeney as such a total fool, so complete a parasite, sycophant, and sponger that insolence from him could not be seriously entertained. Indeed the evening's conversation was no more than an exercise for him, a sharpening of wit for more clever antagonists.

"I like generals, admirals, most businessmen, some Church people—fundamentalists and old-fashioned hard-line Catholics, not the trivial old fool they have running things. In short, *I like anyone who is willing to die.*"

Insulated to shock, Sweeney got up. He ached, his back and limbs were stretched out of shape. A yawn transformed his face into a rubber monster mask; he extended his arms endlessly, snapping two buttons on the white butcher's coat. Smacking lips, blinking pained eyes, he rubbed his hands over his face, yanking off the cotton earlocks. The NRA sign on his back was bent, and he removed it, tossing it on the floor.

"Beddy-bye for Buck Sweeney," he said. "Especially since I get the heave-ho tomorrow. It's been a ball, Stonebreaker. Or a stone, Ballbreaker."

"Sit down. I want to hear how this survey got started. I'm always intrigued with new aspects of the Hate Germany campaign."

"Ah, screw. I don't owe you anything. I'm not so sure I like your politics, whatever they are."

Stonebreaker smiled expansively. He turned and elevated his head, and for a frightened moment Sweeney noticed a bit of the old Roosevelt in him. The man was no longer acting, no longer had his make-up or props with him, yet the temptation to be FDR was scarily evident.

"I insist," Stonebreaker said.

"*Gotzongool*," Sweeney said. "I don't need you or your lousy house and your food. In fact, I'm going to say goodbye to Melissa, tell her I love her, and beat it. Like Looie that Dope used to say, I can get a room."

"Sweeney, Melissa is asleep, deep in seconal. You can tell her tomorrow. I'll let you stay a *full week*. Free. Food. Liquor. Melissa's company. We'll have another party next weekend. You and I can chat. I might finance you in *another* survey, a far more relevant one—noble Christians who fought communism."

The old Adam flickered and burned bright in Sweeney. A week's free-load. Like the good old days at Westhampton Beach. He slid, surrendering, into the black leather chair.

Stonebreaker called for Nino to bring coffee. Several guests poked weary heads in to say their goodbyes and thank their host for a marvelous evening. Sweeney nurtured envious lechery when Mrs. Ferrante walked by with Max Baer.

"Hey, who's she?" he asked Stonebreaker.

"One might call her the discarded wife of High Crime. Her husband is Feet Ferrante, the prominent Chicago entrepreneur.

Vending machines . . . white slavery . . . punchboards . . . wholesale market protection. I rather like Frances, and I liked Feet when I knew him. Two primitives, true vestigial types. Like finding a pair of Hairy Ainu or Bushmen. Feet keeps her in Europe for tax purposes."

"Yaas. Nothing like good old laissez-faire economics."

"And her friend Mrs. Halberstadt, Cecile. More of the same, but on a lower order. Feet runs the show, and Abe Halberstadt does the administrative work."

"How the hell would a cultured man like you know people like that?"

"Curiosity. You see, Feet and Abe, and their handsome wives, are among the few people who have remained outside the liberal establishment. I rather admire them for it."

"Right. Henry Ford always had a few hoods around for laughs."

The coffee arrived—steaming fresh espresso served from a gleaming silver pot. Enviously Sweeney watched his host rub a bit of lemon rind around the edge of the delicate china cup—a cup one was tempted to nibble à la Harpo Marx. Gracious living, that was what he sought—gracious living and no more massacres. And if the price was telling Stonebreaker about Sherman Wettlaufer and brother Leo, why not?

The coffee revived him—cleansed his mouth, burned through his alimentary canal like a spoonful of Drano, perked up his nerve endings. "A treat instead of a treatment," he beamed at Stonebreaker, and accepted a black cigar. They confronted each other once more—two men of the world. Round one was over, a draw. Now they were ready for a second encounter, and Sweeney, fortified, faced the prospect courageously.

"Tell me how this survey got underway," Stonebreaker said. "Skip nothing. Names, places, what was said, how you are paid, who is backing it. I am terribly curious. I thought I was well informed on the machinations of the Hate Germany campaign— all the weeping over Dachau, *The New York Times*, New York publishers, the television people—but this project of yours comes out of nowhere, and I must say I can't fit you into it. You aren't the type, Sweeney. I must assume you're being paid well."

"Not really. A nice expense account."

"Then you do this out of conviction?"

"Stonebreaker, I got no convictions. I believe in Sweeney. Besides, it's a dead turkey. I'm through with it. After you boot me out I'm gonna sell the tape recorder to make my way back to the States. It's insured, so I'll tell Wettlaufer I lost it."

"Wettlaufer. You keep mentioning Wettlaufer. That's a name I don't know. The Hate Germany people are so numerous I can't keep track of them."

"It certainly would keep a man busy." Sweeney felt superb. Second wind always exhilarated him. He leaned back in the chair, dragged deeply on the cigar (it was a chocolatey Havana in dark wrapper), and blew smoke across the study with baronial vigor.

"I'll try not to interrupt. You talk—fully. Tell me about this mysterious Wettlaufer."

"You got it, friend."

My older brother, Leo Parnell Sweeney, figures strongly in this story (Sweeney began) and before we get to Wettlaufer I must deal with Leo.

As a matter of fact, the Legion's birth is in part due to Leo and his friends, and a visit I paid to Leo's home last March. What can I say about poor Leo that won't make him sound like a turd? I don't know. He is your kind of hot-eyed zealot, Stonebreaker. He is four years older than me, much thinner, happily married to the former Midge Hanratty of Parkchester, has six healthy children and a job as an insurance examiner which pays him twenty-five grand a year.

Yet he is filled with hates and fears. He knows all the answers and he doesn't care for dispute. He hates UNICEF, fluoridation, Mrs. Roosevelt, *The New York Times*, Chet Huntley, Martin Luther King, and Milton Eisenhower. He is very suspicious of Pope John.

170

I could go on about my brother but why bother? In a way I've always pitied him. We never made it as brothers. He beat me up for years until I was a huge, husky thirteen, and then I rassled him to a draw. From then on we didn't talk much.

I had gone out to East Redfield, New Jersey, presumably to make my peace with Leo and Midge. She is not a bad kid, Midge. Indulges Leo, though she doesn't go all the way with him on the desirability of hanging Earl Warren. A long jail sentence would satisfy her. Preferably in solitary.

Actually, I had gone out to hit Leo up for a hundred dollars to pay my rent and escape eviction. I was living at the time in a room above a fish market on lower Hudson Street. Being a fastidious person I found my digestive system eroded by carp guts and cod entrails. Still, it was better than the YMCA, which was the next step down. Stoney, I was scraping bottom. The free-loads had ended. My last, literary advisor to a wealthy manufacturer of leathergoods, ended when he caught me sneaking out of his apartment with two unopened bottles of King's Ransom.

My credit, my reputation were shot. Nobody laughed at my jokes any more. I don't know, Stonebreaker, all the fun is over. As the fellow says in the O'Neill play, there's no life in the booze. On the one hand, it's people like you at the top telling us we all must die in a big explosion to save Cambodia from going Communist and, on the other, the rebellious *schwartzer* at the bottom threatening to slit our throats on the subway. Who can laugh?

Leo and Midge seemed genuinely pleased to see me. The kids fussed over their funny Uncle Buck, bon vivant, writer, traveler. We got to reminiscing about the old days in the Bronx, about Pop's saloon and some of his steadys like First Act Donahue and Spats Mulrooney, and we laughed a lot. May I digress, Stoney? I think I have just touched on why I shall never be a creative person, an artist. I had a happy childhood and parents who loved me. Why should I put the knock on my old man or my mother? May they have eternal rest, those two decent plain people. No, I cannot recall them ever doing an unkind thing to me or to Leo.

How strange, Stonebreaker, that all this became vivid for me and made me weep when that German Engineer Helms—the fellow you asked was he an actor—told me about the Jewish parents comforting their children as they waited for death in the snow!

But back to Leo. As the evening wore on things became strained. He accused me of being a wastrel, a liar, a parasite, and a hanger-on to liberal-socialist groups. I took as much as I could, thanked Midge for the roast beef, and started to leave. Leo halted me.

—Bernard, I want you to take a job. I want to change the direction of your wasted life.

—Loan me a hundred, Leo. That's all I want.

—This job will be good for your soul.

—That sounds as if it pays very little.

—It will pay you in inspiration. You will help save America from the rats.

I edged toward the door. He followed me, lecturing.

—Bernard, all your life you have evaded certain truths. You are a Christian American. You have deserted that heritage.

—Leo, I refuse to make obscene telephone calls in the middle of the night to admirers of Governor Rockefeller. I will not trample on sandwiches at the reception for Senator Clifford Case or sneak alum into the punch.

—You need not be sarcastic. Drastic means are needed to fight our enemy.

—I am a coward.

—We will make you brave. Bernard, I want you to manage the Manifest Destiny Bookshop here in East Redfield.

—Come on, Leo. I can't sell *The Supreme Court and Lenin* or *The Plot to Communize Our Schools*. I'd be giving it the needle all the time.

Leo thought a minute. In a sense I was a calculated risk. But he had a solution.

—Yes, perhaps you need indoctrination first. I think you are uninformed on communism and its methods.

172

He then suggested I sleep over and meet some of his supporters, who numbered one judge, a supermarket owner, and virtually all the members of the East Redfield Country Club.

It seemed that the following night, there was to be a big meeting of the East Redfield School Board. A vital issue was at stake, a confrontation as Leo put it, between good and evil. On Leo's side, the angels, the people who hated UNICEF, the backers of the Manifest Destiny Bookshop. In the opposite corner—*them.*

And that is how Sherman Wettlaufer, former commanding officer of the 997th Ordnance, under whom I had long ago served as Private B. K. Sweeney, re-entered my life.

As we drove out to the Thomas Jefferson Junior High School, Leo explained it all:

—The liberal-pinkos, most of them members of the chosen folk—he has a nice wit, my brother—have insidiously begun a campaign to de-Christianize the public schools. To remove the Nativity scenes, to ask equal time for Chanukah. Well, Bernard, they will hang themselves on this despite the communistic Supreme Court. Our people will be out in force tonight to smoke them out.

And Leo's friends were well represented. The group around Leo and Midge seemed eminently respectable—bourbon and scotch flesh tints, thick jowls, hard-corseted women, as sturdy a crowd of handicap golfers and power-boat pilots as you might find. Healthy, well-dressed, happy, upper-middle-class folk. And their kids! Pink cheeks, blue eyes, ruddy skin, button-downs and chinos. The auditorium was packed, and at the back of it there was a bunch of fat thick-necks in windbreakers loitering around. They didn't look quite as respectable as Leo's friends of God.

The school board trooped in. They were scared. The chairman was a chubby stoop-shouldered man, a certain Coccotello. There were two women, Anglo-Saxon Republicans, old family types, a few mild-looking men, and last, holding down the flanker-back position, who but my old buddy Sherman Wettlaufer.

Sherman had changed a good bit since I had last seen him in

the U.S. Army. He was fatter. His posture wasn't so good. His skin was pale and his wavy blond hair, which used to be neatly barbered and parted in the middle, was thinning out. The wide forehead gave him a perpetually worried appearance. He was, I might add, the only Hebrew on the East Redfield Board of Education.

—That Wettlaufer, he's the one to watch, he's in back of it all—Leo muttered to me as the routine business of the evening got on.

—He looks like a harmless shnook to me, Leo.

—He is rich and powerful.

So the board droned its way through police protection for a street crossing; a stipend for teachers who volunteer to stay late and to coach cheer leading; lunchroom decorum; and more footballs for the Negro elementary school—evidently on the theory that more athletics will make them model citizens.

Chairman Coccotello then raised the issue of how Christmas was to be celebrated in the school system, and I could sense a shiver, a thrill run through Leo's people. Sherman turned pale, and I faintly heard Thomas Jefferson snickering.

Coccotello called on Leo.

—I am Leo Parnell Sweeney, a taxpayer, a father, and a Christian, and I am the chairman of the Committee to Keep God in the Public Schools of East Redfield. Our committee has read the report of the board's Committee on Religious Observances, of which Mr. Wettlaufer is chairman, and has found it inadequate and un-Christian. We are a Christian nation, Mr. Chairman, and the framers of the Declaration of Independence put their trust in God. Despite the un-American rulings of the Supreme Court, which we know in our heart will be reversed by a patriotic Congress, we stand for (1) compulsory singing of Christmas carols of a religious nature, not merely clever evasions such as "Deck the Halls" or "Jingle Bells," which make no reference to the Christmas story; (2) the continuation of the Nativity scene on the lawn of Haym Solomon Junior High School; and (3) continuation of

174

the charming religious Christmas play *They Come*, written last year by the senior-class dramatic society.

Leo was rousing them. Sherman kept slumping lower in his seat.

—Now as for the requests of certain minority groups—Leo went on—atheists and others. . . .

—Name them, name them!—one of the big guys from the plaid-lumberjacket crowd yelled from back of the room. He was glaring at Sherman.

—Yes, name them!—cried a blue-rinsed old woman in front of me. Leo was a gentleman about it.

—That is not necessary—he said. —We know *who* they are, these people who want to abolish Christmas and God in our schools, to throw Christ out. They need not be named right now. He winked at the men in windbreakers, as if to say, all in good time, fellows.

—To get back to what these minority groups propose, such as equal time for their own holidays—and he just had to add—whose names I cannot pronounce—which got a lot of loud laughter from the back of the room. Let me say that I sympathize with them, but I must point out that we are a predominantly Christian nation, that in the battle to the death with the forces of atheistical communism we must recognize that fact. Celebrations of *other* rites would only dilute our basic strength as God-fearing, God-loving men. I might add that we respect and honor all religions—in their proper places.

There was more applause, and Sherman shifted in his seat as if he expected to be electrocuted.

—In short, Mr. Chairman, my committee will soon present you with a list of signatures of citizens of East Redfield demanding rejection of the special committee's proposals, and we ask that the Board of Education by-laws be amended to include a prayerful recognition of the proper place of God, Christ, and Christmas in the public schools. All who are with us are with us, but those against us (and he looked squarely at Wettlaufer) *will not be forgotten or forgiven.*

—Stand up if you're against God!—screamed one of the louts at the back of the room.

—That's it! Anybody against God stand up! Anybody against Christ stand up!

—Show your faces. . . . What are yez hiding? Stand up if you're antichrist!

They began racing up and down the aisles, three of these fat bums, guys with heads broader than they were high, pointing at people and hollering:

—You against Christ? You, buddy?

Coccotello pounded for order and advised these so-called religious activists that while they were undoubtedly sincere chaps this was a democratically run meeting and would they please abide by Robert's Rules and wait their turn.

—We're a Republic not a Democracy—shouted the first oaf, a fat crud with acne.

—Ha, ha, that is a subtle distinction that learned historians argue over, Mr. Kalber—said Coccotello, and you could hear his voice tremble.

You know, Stonebreaker, there is something to be said for your constituents: they do have a way of throwing scares into people, some hidden power which doesn't say out loud, but hints darkly that they're prepared to make it very hot, very uncomfortable for you if you cross them. Yes, you may smile, Stoney, and you know you wouldn't spit on these loafers but you need them if you wish to have your revolution.

—May we proceed?—Coccotello asked, and then turned to Sherman Wettlaufer. —I believe our board member Mr. Wettlaufer met recently with the special committee to review religious observances and perhaps he would care to present their latest recommendations now that Mr. Leo Sweeney has spoken out so frankly on his group's views.

176

They moved the microphone over to Sherman, who patted his soaked forehead. Again there was that sick murmur in the crowd, like when people are waiting for a man to be hanged or to jump from a bridge.

—Why ain't they all here?—one of the oafs shouted.

—Yeah, are they yellah? Let 'em show their faces, let's see who is really behind this antichrist agitation!

—Where do you stand, Wettlaufer? Are you one of them? Are you with us or are you against Christ and Christmas?

And with that, the clods again began running up and down the aisles conducting their survey as to who was or was not for Him. There were very few Jewish faces and they shrank into their seats and wished they'd stayed home and watched TV.

Amidst this furor Coccotello pounded his gavel and called for order. I noticed he signaled the secretary of the school board to stop taking notes. He wasn't going to have this scrimmage on record. Then he turned the floor over to Sherman.

Leo finally got his back-room bums to quiet down. Then Sherman got up and in a spongy low voice began to speak:

—Let me begin, ladies and gentlemen, by saying that we are all loyal American citizens.

—Prove it!—a loafer yelled. Then there was some real sick laughter.

—Yes sir, I'm an American just like you, I love my country as you do, I respect its cherished institutions, and I respect the rights of its citizens to different religious observances. . . .

—Then why don't you let us have ours?—the blue-rinsed lady screamed.

—No one, madam—Sherman said politely—is stopping you. You may worship in your homes, your churches, by yourself. But the public-school system . . . and the courts have ruled on this not once but several times . . . is not an agency of any particularized sect. . . .

—He's calling the Christian religion a sect!—the fattest of the lumberjackets piped up.

Now even Leo's respectable people were on their feet.

—We are a majority religion and you minorities had better watch your step!

—Next thing you people will want to take *In God We Trust* off the currency!

—But it isn't on there now—Sherman said weakly

—Atheist! Communist!

—Please—Sherman said—the committee of which I'm chairman includes some eminent citizens of East Redfield, professional and business men. . . .

—Name them! Name them! Name them!

The chant was taken up as Leo ordered his people to whip out ball-point pens and pads, presumably to make lists as Sherman mentioned the names.

—Mark them well—Leo said darkly.

—Their names are a matter of record—Sherman answered.

—Then name them!

—Well, they include Dr. Rosenfeld, Professor Malamud, Rabbi Gelbard. . . .

And a great wild shriek of laughter rose from the back of the room, drowning out Sherman's voice. He mopped his forehead and turned helplessly to Coccotello.

—He's yellow, like the rest of them.

—He can't take his medicine.

I watched Sherman's manhood being destroyed, and I suffered with him. Perhaps I'm a weak and devious human being, Stonebreaker, but I cannot abide cruelty. What is it about me, Stoney? Why am I fated to be standing up for the likes of Wettlaufer, a man who can buy and sell me a million times? Who appointed me his guardian angel?

And as I watched these people stomping on Sherman's soul my mind went back some eighteen years to a cold day in the muddy English midlands when once before I had rescued Sherman Wettlaufer. But that's another story. Suffice to say that as I rose to ask for the floor I was merely picking up where I had left off.

—Ah, the gentleman in the smoked glasses—Coccotello said.

Sherm had not recognized me yet. I took off the cheaters, and I thought he would faint. His lower jaw wobbled. A feeble smile curved his wet lips. I don't think that in his entire life he had ever been so glad to see anyone.

—Mr. Chairman, may an outsider say a few words? My name is Bernard Kevin Sweeney, and that should tell you where I stand.

Applause, cheers. Nothing like the old malarkey to get them on your side.

—I am a journalist, a Christian, a college graduate, but first of all a good American. And I wish to address my remarks to the school-board member who last spoke. Mr. Weinberger, is it?

—Wettlaufer—Sherman said, unable to suppress a kid's grin.

—Well, Mr. Wettlaufer, people like yourself who are not of the Christian persuasion must learn to shrug your shoulders and accept the inevitable where religion in the schools is concerned. Why make a fuss over it?

—Tell him, Sweeney!

—Teach him a lesson, Bernie!

—I would suggest to Mr. Wettlaufer that he take the following attitude in this matter. I shall tell a little anecdote to illustrate. There is a famous restaurant in the city of Detroit, Michigan, where the specialty of the house is carrying in your steak on a flaming sword. I am sure many of you have witnessed this elegant type of service. (I bowed toward the louts in the back, those pizza-and-beer fressers, and they loved this tribute to their gourmet tastes.) I once had occasion to meet the owner of this restaurant, and I asked him point blank what this business of carrying the steaks around on a flaming sword actually did to their taste. The owner looked around, to make sure no one was listening, and said: Sweeney, we figure it don't hurt the meat too much.

—And that is my advice to you, Mr. Wettlaufer. You must look upon these religious exercises in the public schools the same way. They don't hurt your kids too much. After all, your children, if they wish, can sing Hark the Herald Tribune Sings, or Know well, know well, Ben Gurion's the King of Israel, and so forth.

179

The lunkheads all laughed at my witticisms, not knowing the joke was on them and that I was on Sherman's side, although I still think he was a sucker for getting involved in a meaningless rumpus. But Leo was a little smarter than his roughnecks; he kept pulling at my pants to get me to sit down and as I did all applauded.

Coccotello closed debate and promised that a new committee would be set up to co-ordinate between the (let's face it) atheist-Unitarian-Jewish committee and Leo's and that this third committee would make its report to a fourth committee on extracurricular activities.

The subject of added police protection at the junior prom was then brought up inasmuch as at the last junior prom these fine Christian (and Jewish) kids from rich families in East Redfield, all from sternly moral homes, had smashed all the windows in the gym, spilled ink on a hundred library books, beaten up a male chaperone, and undressed a fourteen-year-old girl. Yes, that crusading religious atmosphere of which their parents were so zealous certainly turned out admirable children.

As the meeting ended Leo had a look on his face as if he had just stopped Attila the Hun dead in his tracks. He gathered up Midge and his retinue, and as we all started for the exits I could see Sherman making signals so I gave him the big wink, nodding toward the side door.

By the time I got there, one of those secret vestibules which school architects seem to supply as repositories for chewing gum, dirty scrawlings, and pupils with weak bladders, Sherman was in trouble. He was backed against a wall which read Suck Me, and was being firmly held in place by two monstrous cruds in plaid halfcoats and hunting caps.

—Gentlemen, this is idiotic—Sherman was saying—this is no way for civilized educated people to settle arguments.

They were not hurting Sherman, just kind of holding him against the wall with their massive shoulders, but one kept repeating:

180

—We'll get around to your kind, buddy.

—Yeah—said the other—you people think you can control everything, but we are wise to you.

—Gentlemen, this is ridiculous, I'm as good an American patriot as anyone here, and the question of religious practices in public schools is one to be honestly debated. I warn you not to threaten me or to continue those anonymous phone calls in the middle of the night or to hand obscene notes, such as the one calling me a Communist, to my children. I warn you. . . .

—Now would we ever do that, Al?

—Never, Pete.

But they would not let him pass and Sherman kept babbling on, making it worse:

—I'm chairman of the volunteer fire department committee, a school-board member, a Big Dad to the Little League of East Redfield, and chairman of the United Fund Drive last year, which as you fellows know set a record for this part of the state. I am a registered Democrat, although I often support Republicans for local office. Moreover most of my neighbors are Gentiles and we have lived in peace and harmony, each respecting the others' religious beliefs and showing a warm truly American interest in one another's persuasions. . . .

That Wettlaufer, he never would learn. With certain people all that avails are lies, deceit, and a clout on the chops, especially if they're smaller and weaker than you. A fight was out of the question with such insensate hippos, so lying was called for. I shuffled up and touched the biggest bum on the elbow

. . . . . . here, friend. Let me handle this one.

—Who are you?

—I'm from the big boss. The organization. Now go on home, fellas. I'm calling a meeting in a few days and I'll need you guys. The Commies may try to break it up, so we'll have to be prepared.

—You bet, Sweeney. Look out for this one.

And off they lumbered, great heaps of flesh disturbing the earth's peace.

181

I could see Leo and Midge walking up on this charming scene, Leo looking as if he was ready to murder me, caught in the act of fraternizing with the enemy. I explained immediately that Sherman and I had been in the army together, skipping the intricate basis of our relationship. Sherman was overjoyed.

—Mr. Sweeney—he said, bubbling to Leo—now that we have learned that your brother Buck is an old friend of mine I am sure you and I can sit down man-to-man and talk this over and reach an amicable understanding.

But Leo's face was colder than a cesspool digger's behind on a December day in Framingham, Massachusetts.

—Gosh, Buck, what a pleasure to see you—said Sherman—after all these years!

Well, nothing would do but that I go home with him for a long talk, for booze, food, and nostalgia. He invited Leo and Midge to come along, but catch Leo entering those vile precincts! He had apparently tangled with Sherman a few times at previous school-board meetings and was in no mood to smoke the pipe of peace with this pinko-liberal advocate of fluoridation.

I climbed into Sherman's Cadillac, letting the money envelope me like a warm bath. I could smell the gelt in the beige leather, the dashboard that lit up like the Ginza on Saturday night, and could hear it in the contented purr of that massive engine. We rolled off into the New Jersey night through wooded lanes and along stone fences, pastureland, and second growth forest, to the Wettlaufer estate. During the ride I leveled with him. I was broke, unemployed, at rock bottom. Sweeney was a failure.

Now I realized that Sherman had grown rich but I had no idea of the extent of his wealth. It filled me with a joy serene, a sense of rightness, for somehow I suspected I would be able to tap it, to drink deeply of that money and comfort and happiness that had accrued to my old friend.

We rolled up a circular driveway flanked with copper beeches and Norway maples, and stopped under a porte-cochere. The house soared above us like a Loire château—solid, indestructible,

182

a great stone palace built in the mixed suburban style of the twenties, the upper stories beamed and stuccoed in something resembling Tudor. There were elegant landscaped lawns and gardens at the sides and in front, and far to the rear I sensed a dark woods.

We entered a pair of doors that might have been stolen from the Cathedral at Rouen and progressed, like Virgil and Dante, through one room after another, each furnished with needlepoint Regency and Empire chairs, marble tables, sconces, fancy molded plasterwork on walls and ceilings, and more than a few French Impressionists. The living room was about the length of the Widener Chute at Belmont Park. I entered, dazzled by the logs crackling in the marble fireplace, the subdued blues and greens of the silk-covered walls, and two apricot poodles who snarled at me knowing I was poor, Gentile, and out of my element.

I felt ashamed of my scuffed loafers and wrinkled whipcord suit amid all that splendor. As Sherman went to the bar to fix me a long brandy I looked enviously at a huge photograph of his wife and kids. A good-looking broad—black hair streaked with gray, deep dark eyes, a wide sexy mouth. I wondered if she was the same girl Sherm wrote to every day when he was my old commanding officer.

—Yes, that is my beloved Lillian—he said, returning with the drinks. —I sent her to Bermuda for a few weeks until this mess with the school board is over. I don't want Lil upset by it. She worries terribly.

He looked at me warmly.

—My goodness, Buck, how happy I was to see you tonight. I'm sorry we've lost touch over all these years. It's my fault.

—Sherm, you're a big success, a millionaire. And I'm a bum.

—No, no, don't say that, Buck. I've always found something admirable in you.

—Jesus, I won't listen to this.

Wettlaufer got up, undid his tie, and began to pace the room. It was so big that if he wandered too far, like to the bar or the bookshelves, I sometimes lost his voice.

—How strange, Bucky! Society deems me a success yet I'm a bundle of fears, of terrors. I worry about atomic war, Negro rights, anti-Semitism, bad schools, juvenile delinquency. And you, with not a penny to your name, glide through life at ease with the world. Do I oversimplify?

—Yes, you do. I would love to have your money. And if I did I wouldn't waste a minute worrying about Negroes or teen-age galoots. I would have laughs and broads and good booze.

—Could you? Perhaps. Perhaps for the simple reason that you're not burdened with my Jewish sense of guilt.

—Christ, Sherm, can't we drop that once and for all?

I went after the Courvoisier. It was the dark old bottle, and it went down like a chocolate malted. By now all I wanted from him was the hundred bucks I'd never got from Leo. But Sherman was not in a listening mood. He needed badly to talk.

—Buck, what a stroke of luck this is. You're the only person in the world I can say this to: Buck, I am frightened, I am frightened to death. There is an illness abroad in our land, and I have the terrible feeling that this beloved nation of ours . . . don't smile, Buck, I mean it . . . this beloved country of ours is being threatened by evil forces. That meeting tonight. I am sure that was what they were like in Germany in 1933.

—Come on Sherman, Leo and his people are nothing more than extradevout Christians.

—That meeting was symptomatic of a larger illness. There is a kind of psychotic middle-class hate asserting itself here, exactly the thing that produced Hitler. It strikes out everywhere, at anyone, mindless, cruel, convinced only it is right and that all who disagree are traitors. Well, I have disagreed publicly, however mildly, and I am among the traitors. My name, Buck, is on a list kept by a semisecret group called the Sons of Wrath which drills in empty fields with mail-order rifles. I am listed along with the Unitarian Minister and the head of the local NAACP under a heading which

184

says *In the Cross Hairs*. Do you know what that means? It means the cross hairs of a telescopic sight are trained on me.

—That is lunacy, Sherman, the world is filled with screwballs.

—And I'm afraid they will take over. Anything that is anti-communistic must be good and hence these sick, twisted souls have a certain standing, a certain viability. Oh God, that our country should come to this!

—Sherm, you're distraught.

His voice was rising, semihysterical. I tried to calm him.

—Look at your neighbors, your position in the community. Aren't you accepted? Respected?

—Yes. That's the strange thing. There is warmth and friendship here. My neighbors give to UNICEF, they read Herman Wouk, they're interested in a friendly way in my observance of Yom Kippur. We discuss the New York Giants, and I've taken many of these good Christian neighbors to the Army-Syracuse game. In short they are kind people and I have every reason to feel secure.

—But?

—But I do not. I cannot help it.

—I oughta take you out and get you laid.

—No thanks, Buck, *that* wouldn't help. That's not my problem. Lil and I have a most satisfactory sex life.

—Yes, she looks like a terrific piece.

—For example—Sherman said, jumping up and ignoring my tribute to his wife—why were the Kennedy stickers ripped from our car?

—Jesus, what do you expect in East Redfield?

—And a woman came up to Lil once at a cocktail party and said, Tell me, dear, are you a Democrat because you're Jewish?

—Ah, the world is full of them.

—That is what I fear. It *exists*, it runs deep and dark, a black creeping river of venom. Oh, I tell you, Buck, I don't sleep anymore. Those phone calls!

—It'll all blow over, pal. Forget it.

—Will it? And what about my decent neighbors of American

Machine and Foundry and Revere Brass & Copper? What I mean is . . . if those bruisers in lumberjackets took over and got me in the cross hairs of their telescopic rifles, would they come to my aid and save me?

—I think they would, Sherman. Why the big corporations, which really run things, are falling all over one another trying to get Jews into their outfits, and they're even taking in the schwartzers. The liberals are winning everywhere, Sherman.

—I'm not so sure. This poison of distrust and fear is spreading, Buck. I often tell myself that the only reason we Jews have been spared is because of the 20 million black souls in our midst. All this secret hate has been unloaded on the Negro. He stands there in our midst, a great black buffer, taking blows and beatings and humiliations, and thus we Jews are spared. Without the Negro, where would we be? How would we fare? I shudder to think of it.

I realized then, Stoney, that without asking my permission Sherm had invited me into the whole Jewish persuasion, as he would put it, and I was being included as a full-fledged, circumcised, pastrami-eating member, in that editorial we. I raised no objection since I have always been partial to Jewish delicatessen, although I am hardly a philo-Semite and can take them or leave them. Allie Cooperstein was my boyhood chum not because he went to kheydr but because he lived around the corner and could hit a Spalding punchball two sewers. Yes, that allusion would be lost on you, you Denver zinc miner. Sometimes I think the whole war in the United States is between New Yorkers and everyone else.

Sherman charged on, a man thoroughly unnerved.

—And suppose the day comes when the Negro is crushed, eliminated? Who then will take the blows? Or suppose the violence of the Negro intensifies? Is it not conceivable that we will be blamed for it . . . and be called Communist liberal agitators who are inciting them? Are we not being blamed already?

—Yes, Sherman, you are, but the people who blame you are loudmouthed malcontents, the swinish sons of bigoted golfers at restricted country clubs. They are hot-eyed small-town turds, eating themselves up with self-hatred.

—And who is to say when they will become the majority? They have their heroes, their programs, just as Hitler did. You saw the mob tonight. I'm scared stiff of them. They protest about freedom, and liberty, but all they want is the privilege to hate and to kill. Can that be made any clearer? They shriek *we will kill them!* They do, Buck, and they scream *Hang Earl Warren!* This malignancy is growing, spreading its cancerous cells. The look of these healthy, scrubbed, pink children!

—Come off it, Sherman. Those people are chowderheads. We are a rich and complex people, easily distracted. The day those lunatics call for the revolution everyone will be watching pro football on television.

—Ah, Buck, you're not vulnerable the way I am. You can joke about it. You will be spared and I will not. Nor will my sons. Brian is thirteen and Gordon is ten. They are with their mother in Bermuda. You will think me a sentimentalist, Buck, but I tell you there is no greater love in the world than that of parent for child. I cannot articulate this, and I feel guilty gushing about it in front of you, a bachelor, but think back to your own father, Buck, and you'll understand. You often told me about him, that kindly saloonkeeper who never lifted a hand against his sons.

—Yes—I said—old Jim Sweeney was one of the best and he loved us more than we deserved. As good a man as ever dished out the disturbance to the East Bronx.

—I am the usual bragging father—Sherman went on—but they are special boys. Brian made his bar-mitzvah last month. He is very science-minded, very serious, yet with a dry wit. He refused to have a big affair at the country club. He wrote his own speech, about our responsibilities as citizens in an atomic world and what science could do for the emerging nations, and we had a small dinner at a local inn, with a few close friends and family. Brian invited several Christian boys and they were delighted to learn about our customs. Straight A's in school, a whiz in math, modest. And the little guy, Gordon, he's ten, all muscle, all heart. He has a battle every night with his homework. But a born competitor. A kid who will not quit. He played shortstop on a Little League team where the average age was *twelve*. And what an arm!

—Now I will tell you something about those two boys, Buck—his voice becoming strained, his eyes widening.

—Easy, Sherm.

—*I will tell you this. I see them naked. I see them weeping. I see them shivering in the snow. I see them walking to a great concrete room where they are asphyxiated with gas, and I see their lifeless bodies thrown into the ovens.*

—But you're safe here in America.

—I try to reassure myself all the time. And then I hear them scream *traitor*, or *antichrist*, or that I am soft on communism, or that I am a nigger-lover, and the nightmare comes again.

—But most of those people do not make an issue of anti-Semitism.

—Not overtly. But in their hearts?

—Sherman, you must get these notions out of your head.

—Suppose we have a depression? Or suppose an atomic war starts and the Russians drop bombs on us? Suppose the Negroes start murdering everyone? Who will be blamed? We will, of course. And then I see my sons, Brian and Gordon, going off to that hellish death. There is no Jew in the world today, nowhere, no matter how rich or powerful or successful or how well integrated, who does not think in those terms, who does not have those fears. The gas chambers and the smoking chimneys of Auschwitz have made us all aware that it can happen again. An evil deed once done merely makes it easier to be repeated. The pattern is set. All of us color our lives with this awful race memory. When? When will it happen? How? What shall we do when it does?

—First, you fight it all the way, Sherm, you don't give an inch.

—How easy that is for you to say. No, the terror is among us. It is small, it has lunatic aspects, and we are not its target now. We are rarely spoken of, and then by indirection, but it exists!

And then the telephone rang, with shattering pointless insistency.

Sherman began to sweat; his jaw shivered.

—See? See? You didn't believe me. It's *them*. This happens every night. It is a kind of revenge on me.

The phone kept screaming.

—Oh, if I could strike back, oh God, if I had some way of reaching them. . . .

He flew to a telephone alcove, me racing behind him, convinced he was as nuts as my brother Leo's stalwarts. He grabbed the phone and stood there, frozen, silent, his hand shaking.

—Hello? Hello?

Silence at the other end, perhaps five seconds of it, then the night ringer hung up.

—That is their technique. A call in the early morning hours, not a word, just long enough to make sure they have tormented me, and then they hang up. The perfect enemy. Anonymous. Cowardly. Malignant.

The phone blasted again. Sherman almost dislocated his right arm reaching for it, but I stiff-armed him and grabbed it myself. As soon as I had the mouthpiece to my lips, I spoke:

—This is Sweeney. Screw off.

Then I hung up. I turned to Sherman.

—Now was that so hard? Was that so terrible? Now for Christ's sake leave the phone off the hook at night.

—But I may get business calls. My mother isn't well.

—Any caller can wait till morning. I swear, Sherman, you have a need to stick needles in yourself.

—Buck, it's no picnic knowing that somewhere out there people hate you, people wish you evil.

—Screw 'em. Now let's go finish your brandy.

We were halfway across that Grand Central Station of a living room, when he grabbed me again, and if I did not know how square my old CO was, I'd have marked him queer. This time he got me in a bear hug and, for the first time in hours, he smiled.

—Oh, my best friend, my great friend! The only Christian in the world I have ever been at ease with! God, what a stroke of luck seeing you!

So we drank, and talked, and reminisced, and he expressed great sorrow at the way I had never made it. Old Buck Sweeney has never wasted any hours in self-pity, apart from my hypochrondria—as a matter of fact, Stonebreaker, if I don't get a glass of San Pellegrino water right now, I will contract cancer of the larynx and be unable to continue. No, I have never felt sorry for my lot, but Sherman fixed *that*. He thought it was awful that a man of my talent, wisdom, and charm could not latch on. He kept trying to ram me into slots where I didn't fit. No, I would not be public relations manager for Wettlaufer Industries; no, I was not interested in an interview with his brother; no, I would not talk to Lil's kid brother who was a TV producer at ABC.

—I will go my own way and ruin my own life—I told him.
—I cannot permit that—Sherman said.
Finally, I asked him outright to lend me a hundred bucks to pay my rent. Out came a fat black wallet.
—A hundred? Two hundred? A thousand? Buck, I would give you anything you want. But I must do more than give you cash, I must find a career for you.
My fingers were almost caressing those crisp bills when Sherman stuffed them back in, intent on saving my character.
—A magnificent notion has struck me, Buck. Something so marvelous, so constructive, and so good for both of us, it must happen.
—I will not accept the vice-presidency of your company. I know nothing about plastics.
—Now be still and listen.

190

He was up again.

—Some weeks ago our rabbi delivered an interesting sermon, growing out of all this fuss about what the Pope did or did not do to help the Jews. I must say I cannot get overwrought over his alleged failures, since he had other things on his mind.

—True enough: Monte Cassino and all that.

—What Rabbi Gelbard said was this: That while we were all aware of the horrible crimes against Jews and the complicity of Germans, Ukrainians, Poles, and many other Europeans—all presumably Christians of some kind or another—surely there existed many brave generous people who helped Jews during those dreadful years. And he said further that these people were worthy of being remembered in our hearts and our prayers. He cited the Dutch family who had hidden Anne Frank, and said there must be others, people like them who had done the decent thing and who indeed may have suffered for it.

—An unarguable point, Sherman.

—The sermon left us a little high and dry; we expected more, but I didn't press it since like all good Americans I had a golf game to run to after the service.

—And why do you bring it up now?

—I am not certain. But it somehow involves you, Buck.

—I am the most selfish Harp you ever saw. Saving you from my brother Leo does not make a hero out of me.

—I am just wondering how we might go about it. Suppose I set up a fund, a foundation, possibly a research organization? And I make you the head of it. Its purpose to find these people, wherever they may now be, people who protected and aided Jews, people who redeemed the conscience of mankind. Suppose we found them. . . .

—And then?

—We interviewed them, got their stories, documents, photographs, and then the foundation would publish them. We would be saying to the world: see, it is all not so terrible. We would set the hearts of many Jews at ease in places like Argentina and the

Soviet Union, and we would respectfully remind our Christian brothers that they have shown noble impulses.

—But what do I have to do with it?

—You, Buck, will conduct the survey. You will be my man in Europe.

—Well, I always fancied a free trip to the Continent under auspices other than those of the United States Army.

And he hugged me again, lifting me off the floor. Man, he was in good shape. Tennis, golf, swimming, and those Canadian Air Force exercises.

I spent the night in the guest room, on sheets so smooth they excited me. A colored maid served me a breakfast of canteloupe, soft scrambled eggs, delicate Nova Scotia salmon, and cream cheese with chives, toasted bagels, aromatic coffee, and three kinds of English jam. That breakfast told me something. Sweeney was back on the old free-load, and never felt better.

The Sweeney Survey of the Legion of Noble Christians was launched. I went on salary and expense account immediately—two hundred bucks a week and anything I'd put in for. But I didn't bleed Sherman. I like the guy too much.

But I wonder what he thinks of me now?

Convinced he had warped his spine after the long night in the leather chair, Sweeney stretched warily. Joints snapped, ligaments bent. He padded about the study, then threw open the high wooden shutters facing the sea, drinking deeply of the salt-laced morning air.

"Nicely told, Sweeney," Stonebreaker said. "I can see how this numbskull's exercise in distorting issues was born." The host was alert, sweatless, his voice clear. Years of irregular hours spent on movie scenarios, endless all-night sessions in hotel rooms rewriting plays, had inured him to this kind of sustained effort.

"It *would* be a dull naïve type like this Wettlaufer to embark on a destructive project like this. I would give a good deal to be able to convince these bleeding hearts that every tear they shed for

192

dead Jews only waters the seeds of communism. How many times can poor old Hitler be resurrected and slammed about?"

Sweeney did not hear him. The Mediterranean beckoned to him—a wine-dark sea stirring his Celtic blood.

"I've often thought that the very best thing that could happen would be for the Russians to murder a lot of Jews. Then the entire monstrous liberal apparatus of talk—press, television, books, and this alleged research you are engaged in—could be unloosed on Moscow."

Nothing Stonebreaker said could startle the agent of the Wettlaufer Foundation. Exhaustion owned him utterly, and he responded, "That's how I figured you, Stonebreaker. You're still mad it wasn't your revolution in Russia, that you didn't get to murder a couple of million people the way Stalin did. Maybe you'd have murdered more. So now you won't be happy until everybody's killing everybody else. Let the Russians murder their Jews. Then let us bomb them, and them bomb us, and kill everyone. Isn't that right? Know something, Stoney? You're queer for *death*."

"We're digressing," Stonebreaker said, not at all insulted by Sweeney's analysis. "What happened after you agreed to undertake the survey?"

"Sherman got a research outfit to dig up the names and addresses of the sort of people we wanted. We narrowed it down to a select group."

"Like casting a bad movie?"

"No, you son-of-a-bitch, not at all." Sweeney shuffled to a small bar, enthroned on one of his host's sarcophagi, and poured himself half a tumbler of brandy, diluted with San Pellegrino, and partook of it as a child would of orange juice. "Boy, if I wasn't broke and if I didn't want to make sure Melissa was okay, I'd split. I'd really insult you before I cut out."

"Back to Mr. Wettlaufer. He's financing this?"

"Completely. The research outfit wanted to do the interviews itself. But Sherm said no. Who else but me? Boy, did I fool him.

All that dough he laid out—the car, the recorder, expenses. It's over a week since he heard from me. I wouldn't know what to say if I got in touch with him."

"Try it on me. Pretend I'm your patron."

"It's hard to put in words. But this is part of it. I got so sick to my stomach listening to the lousy parts that the good parts didn't cheer me up the way they were supposed to. So Helms saved two hundred people. But the others. Millions. Shooting them in the head. In the snow. The Ukrainians pissing on the corpses. No wonder Helms didn't want to talk about it."

"You did the wise thing, Sweeney. Of course you are dropping this Hate Germany affair for the wrong reasons, but that's the way good things get done. I would have preferred for you to realize that this harping on German sins, this appetite for stories about Buchenwald, is nothing more than a plot against our inevitable confrontation with Marxism."

"Ah, screw you."

"These Wettlaufers—I see them in my mind's eye. *Nation* readers. Convinced of the innocence of Alger Hiss. Contributors to any and every group aimed at uplifting Negro muggers. Frothing at the mouth at mention of the House Un-American Activities Committee. Am I right?"

"Nah, nah. He's a millionaire, Stoney. Jesus, you never stop. Guys like you and Leo, you're like the Communists. You'll bore us to death before you kill us." He poured himself another dose of brandy and mineral water. "You know, Ballbreaker, there's another reason I blew this job. I got trouble putting my finger on it."

"Speak out, my boy. Perhaps I can help you."

"It's got something to do with religion. Now that's a frosty note. I'm hardly a full-fledged member of the faith, but I'm in it, and I like it. When they tinkle the bell at communion, my ticker beats faster."

"Good for you, Sweeney. I'm a firm Christian myself. An old-fashioned one. I know man is sinful, doomed, and weak. That is why liberalism and its permutations are so harmful."

194

"You're some help. Christ, a man tells you about his *faith* and you start yacking about liberalism. Now let's see if I can make sense out of this. Every time I interviewed one of these people there was a joker in the deck. It was like a—a—sanction, an okay, an approval—"

"For their noble acts?"

"*Hell no! For murdering Jews!* A kind of tradition, a policy. People in church robes, Stoney . . . nodding their heads and saying, *it's all right, it's all right.* I couldn't take any more of *that.* Some little bastard of a Belgian newspaperman got me started on it. A lousy atheist. Ah, the hell with all of it."

Through the opened shutters Sweeney saw the first shimmerings of dawn, the first brightening of the night-darkened blue waters. Streaks of rose and amber illumined the sea as the sun made its ascent. Sweeney wanted to laugh with joy.

"Oh look at it, Stonebreaker! It's too much, pal, too good for either of us!"

He trudged through the corridor, through the tiled foyer with its Roman antiquities, out to the terraced lawns. With affection the morning sun came gently upon the dark groves of lemon trees, the yellow walls of the villa, the green hillsides. Colors changed subtly, the air was charged with new life.

Unfortunately the emergent light also revealed the debris of last night's revels—soiled tables, ripped bunting, kitchen middens of paper cups and soft drink bottles, ruined Japanese lanterns. At the base of the great oak tree, labeled *Traditional American Liberties,* slept Mr. Simpson, either a spy or a representative of small businesses. He was wrapped in his academic cloak; his mortarboard covered his narrow face. The placard labeling him *New Deal Crackpot* lay athwart his chest, and the mighty axe *Socialism* had been hacked into the tree's bark.

"Sleep it off, pal," Sweeney chuckled, observing that Simpson, spy or agent, had vomited in his sleep. The sight pleased him, reminding him of the great slovenly brotherhood of which he was a member.

Wandering to the edge of the terrace, he heard Stonebreaker's steps behind him. The host, a barrel of strength on spindly legs, rotated down his hillside through the pale mist. He walked the earth giving notice: *I own all of this.*

At the limestone balustrade both men looked out over the platoons of lemon trees. Distantly, a rooster shattered the calm. A dog responded irritably. Sweeney heard footsteps, soft feet crunching on the gravel path that twisted through Stonebreaker's hillside to the tiny harbor of San Pietro del Golfo.

In a few moments he saw the pedestrian. It was a woman bundled in black rags and toting a burlap sack. Her face was not visible, but the splay-footed walk, the bent shoulders, the slow pace, suggested an old woman.

"Where's she going at five in the morning?" Sweeney asked.

"To work," said Stonebreaker.

"Work? What kind of work?"

"She's a *contadina*—a farm laborer. There's a little community above, but I can't hire all of them. So the excess workers do what they can. I would guess she's working over at the Alessandroni estate across the cove. She walks down to the harbor and with luck gets a fisherman to row her across for a hundred lire. Then she has to climb up to the other side. It takes her about three hours getting there, and three more getting back at night."

Sweeney looked at the black bent figure plodding purposefully down the path. Italy's sins wrapped up in one old woman with a burlap bag.

"It isn't that frightful, Sweeney. Rest your liberal conscience. They have straw huts at the groves, and if she's exhausted or if it's raining, she spends the night in one of them, happy with a flask of red wine and a loaf of bread."

"Yes indeed," Sweeney said, grinning. "Happy as a clam in red sauce. What does Alessandroni pay her?"

"Probably a little less than I pay. Maybe eight hundred lire a day. About a dollar and thirty cents. They make it go a long way. They do very little complaining. They're good country people, not like those thieves in Naples."

196

The woman's black form, an oversized bug, vanished into the foliage. There was no sense of apology in her painful passage down the hillside. Indeed there seemed to Sweeney a defiance, a pride in her warped body. As he watched her disappear, and as Stonebreaker went on to describe the lives of the *contadini*, both circumstances aroused a memory in the recesses of Sweeney's mind. It caused him to recall what had brought him to southern Italy, before booze had laid him low on the wooden pier.

"Hey, Stoney. You know a guy around here named Bolli?"

"I know about him. They say he's up in the hills."

"I got to see him."

"Another of your Noble Christians? I thought you were abandoning the project."

"Oh, I'm finished. Just for my own curiosity. Helms told me Bolli might be able to explain things to me. What is he? A kind of reformer?"

Stonebreaker put a fatherly arm around his guest's shoulders. "You are an innocent. Bolli is a Communist."

"Ah, come on."

"But he is. If not overtly, he is much worse than a real Communist. He is of that breed of self-anointed meddlesome fools, the archetype of the liberal humanist, convinced he can improve people's characters by raising their wages. He's the kind who makes the Communists' take-over easier. I know for a fact that he is being manipulated by them, perhaps financed by them, and he hasn't the faintest idea what this will lead to."

Sweeney blinked at the sun's risen face. "I better go see him anyway. Come along, pal. We might learn something."

"I think not." Stonebreaker turned, and with that stride that notified the world of his belief in the sanctity of private property, he walked back to the villa and entered it.

Sweeney drank deeply of the citrus-scented air and thought happily of the bed that awaited him in the Paestum room. He yearned for sleep the way he sometimes yearned for a double bourbon.

As he ascended the terrace, wallowing in the glorious fatigue that would help him sleep, he saw Simpson, the New Deal crackpot, snoring blissfully at the foot of the oak.

A pang of sympathy struck at Sweeney—that was where he belonged. In a generous gesture, a reaffirmation of the vast fraternity of drunkards, he stumbled toward the oak. Drawing his butcher's coat around him, he nestled in the mothering roots, and was soon snoring a rumbling counterpoint to his companion's manly snorts.

PART **3**

FRANCO BOLLI

ADREADFUL DREAM; HE WAS BEING CIRCUMCISED WITHOUT BENE-
fit of clergy or anesthesia. "Ouch, ouch," Sweeney protested.
"Watch it there, buster." He knew he was being circumcised because he could hear the surgical clippers going *snip-snip*. And as
much as he fidgeted, squirmed, tried to protect his vulnerable
private parts, his excellent manhood, the dreadful noise persisted,
informing him that he was being initiated into the club. *Snip-snip.*

"Nah, nah!" Sweeney cried. "I give up! No more! You don't leave a guy anything!" Surprisingly, it did not hurt much. What he had anticipated as a sharp pain came through as a dull ache in his loins, a shrinkage and shriveling, more embarrassing than oppressive. Still it was no party.

Snip-snip. They were insatiable, those fiendish snippers. But who were they? Who dared divest him of his manliness? He was not certain. There seemed to be two of them, each wielding the shears. Was one Sherman Wettlaufer? Was one A. C. Stonebreaker? Ludwig Helms? White-coated, bland-faced, they said nothing to him, moving with deft, experienced gestures, shears to his groin, trimming his precious jewel.

"Jesus, when I say quit, I mean it!" Sweeney roared. And he jerked upward from his slumber at the root of the great oak. Fully awake, shaken by the awful nightmare, he reached impulsively for his crotch. Saved. Safe. All there. No blood. Yet still he heard the chilling sounds. *Snip-snip.*

"They're after somebody else," Sweeney gargled. "They won't quit." His burning eyes scanned the bright green terrace, the silent villa, the lush lawns miraculously cleaned of debris during the morning, the shimmering pool, the citrus groves below.

A few yards from him two of Stonebreaker's indentured servants, sun-blackened *contadini* in faded-blue work clothes, were clipping the thick hedges. They worked silently, expertly, each with a gleaming pair of garden shears. *Snip-snip. Snip-snip.* Leaves and twigs fluttered about their bare feet.

"Scare a guy to death with that kind of thing," Sweeney said. Protectively he covered his vital zone, fearful of the flashing scissors. Delighted at this narrow escape he struggled to a standing position, and was pleased again by the absence of hangover, his clearness of head. He attributed this to the high quality of his host's brandy. "It pays to go first class, walyos," he informed the gardeners, and walked to the cool villa and his room.

Later, having showered, shaved, and finished a huge pitcher of black acid coffee furnished by the sleek Nino, he found Melissa

202

taking the sun on one of the recessed patios at the side of the estate. She was evidently the only house guest other than himself up at that hour—a little past noon. Neither Mrs. Ferrante of the magnificent cement corset, nor round little Mrs. Halberstadt, nor Simpson the spy-businessman, was in evidence.

"Hurray for Sweeney," Melissa called. "Sit down and get roasted."

If she had undergone some emotional turmoil the previous night, some crisis with her uncle—as Sweeney had deduced from the disturbing scene in the alcove—she betrayed nothing. In the noon glare, which her firm skin accepted without flinching, with healthy defiance, she seemed the world's best-adjusted, happiest young woman.

He sat beside her in a canvas chair, feeling privileged and proud to be the only one in her presence. In the yellow light of the southern coast he saw her more clearly than ever. She was thinner than he remembered—almost no waist, resilient as a dancer's, only the subtlest swelling of hips and thighs. Her ankles and wrists were those of a graceful child. Embittered, he thought of her three miserable marriages and the apparent dead halt at which her emotional life had arrived. "Oh, Sweeney, if you could help her!" he cried within his wastrel's breast. As he shielded his eyes from the sun, he told himself that he was hardly in a position to help anyone. Still, it made him feel estimable, worthy, that he could at least offer her his male chest to rest upon—and perhaps more.

"You didn't have a date last night?" he asked—as foxy an opening as he was capable of, considering the hour.

"Several. Let's see—Arnulfo, the motor-scooter king; he was the short fat one. And Nobby, the Englishman. He came as Neville Chamberlain. And a few others. I always carry spares."

"But I didn't see you dancing."

"I didn't care for the music. I danced professionally in New York, and I'm a snob."

"Hmmmm. Excuse my dumb Irish questions, but what went on

with you and Uncle Andy under the stairs? You remember. When I stuck my two cents in and asked you to Peabody?"

For the first time since Sweeney had met her she seemed to lose that enviable poise, that attitude of being at ease with all the world, all its people. Divested of this equanimity her face assumed a peculiar gravity—neither fear, nor sorrow, nor revulsion, but a kind of remote indifference.

"Oh, I got a reputation for asking nosey questions," Sweeney said quickly. "I don't get offended if people don't answer 'em or tell me to get lost."

She craned her lovely neck—not a wrinkle, not a sign of age or dissipation—and adjusted the sunglasses on her straight nose. "It's involved, Sweeney. Andy is the only person really close to me. My parents are dead. My three former husbands—one's dead, one's a fairy, and one's in jail. I have a son by the Count, but he's in school in Switzerland and really doesn't dig me. I have no brothers, no sisters, no close friends, just a lot of chatterers and flatterers like Arnulfo. So Andy, Uncle Andy, Mama's older brother, has taken over. He's appointed himself sort of a guardian; I can't say I've objected very hard. If you forget his nonsensical politics—and I often wonder how seriously he takes himself—he's a generous, good man."

"Yeah. He sure seemed like one last night when he was rassling you in the alcove, trying to get you to go beddy-bye."

"I was tired. I hardly remember." She said this quickly and Sweeney, old bar-room observer that he was, knew she was lying. "What did he say?" she asked.

"I promised him I wouldn't talk about it to anyone."

Swiftly, her hand reached out, as lissome as the hand of a posturing Hindu goddess, and stroked his bare arm. Her proximity made his blood sprint. "He said you were a *convalescent* and under his care. Then he told me to keep my mouth shut. He said you regressed sometimes."

"Is that all?"

"I didn't see, but I know he belted you. I heard it. And there's

204

one thing a Bronx Mick knows, it's the noise made by a person klopping another person." Suddenly, he was enraged with Stonebreaker, even more enraged by his supine cowardice. Knight-in-armor Sweeney should have dealt Stonebreaker a thrashing, such as an Horatio Alger hero would have administered to the town bully. But no. He had accepted Stonebreaker's harsh rules. The habits of the free-load were hard to shake; one did not strike the hand that fed and housed.

"And what do you, B. K. Sweeney, make of all this?" she asked.

"I'm not sure."

"Oh, be a sport. Let's see how many points you can score in psychological testing. Now, we've just flashed a photograph at you—older man dressed as FDR, holding arm of younger woman who is dressed in 1933 costume and is seated in alcove, and apparently ordering her to leave. His attitude, anger; hers, what? Resignation? Anything else? We'll do ink blots next."

"Yeah, something else," Sweeney said glumly. "He had a bottle of gin in the hand he wasn't using to slap you around."

He sat up in the deck chair and reached across to touch her upper arm. It was delicately muscled, alive with passion and a capacity to seize and appreciate the best things in the world.

"Melissa, he was trying to come between you and the Flit. As a saloonkeeper's son I recognized the situation. Either you'd had a few or you were about to, and you're under orders not to touch it. I guessed it when he said regress."

"Lush might be a modest word," she said defiantly.

Rather shocked, Sweeney's lower-middle class morals recoiled. Besides, he fancied he was in love with her and she was flawless in his eyes. "Nah, say it ain't so, Joe."

"I didn't tell you yesterday when we had our heart-to-heart about the drying-outs and the rest cures and the sanitariums."

"I don't wanna hear." They held hands, his sweating, seeking involvement, hers dry and unresponsive. "Hey, did that guy hurt you when he smacked you? I oughta go belt him a few times just for the record."

She laughed. "He can't hurt me. I've a very high tolerance for pain, to begin with. I never needed an anesthetic at the dentist when I was a child. And he doesn't hit me terribly hard. Andy just sort of cuffs and pushes—the way you hit a stupid dog when you want it to perform."

Some vague disgust ruffled Sweeney's stomach. He released her hand reluctantly.

"All I can say is I wish I was rich, smart, famous, aggressive, and that I appealed to you. I want to make it all right for you, Melissa."

"Sweeney, I've had all of that. Remember my husbands? And all the others who weren't husbands? With due respect to your big Irish heart, you won't succeed. Besides, that's Andy's problem now."

"Mighty thoughtful uncle, old Andy."

"You're hinting, Sweeney, you're hinting."

"Nope. I just think it's generous of him to want to put you back on the straight and narrow." He sneaked a glance at her unlined face with its sensual mouth neatly tucked in at the corners, and sought a betrayal, a secret disclosed. He found none.

"Andy's always been close to me. You know, he's still a hick at heart, a Denver boy with ill-fitting clothes. I guess I was a sort of continental hot-house flower to him—French education, a title when I was eighteen. You see being a famous playwright and a five-thousand-dollar-a-week movie writer was never enough for Andy. Basically he had contempt for everything he wrote and for all the people he dealt with. That's part of the reason he's up to his neck in politics now—a need to assert himself, to make up for what he regards as all those useless or mischievous words he once wrote."

"And what's the other part?" Sweeney asked.

"Oh, I've never gotten the whole story. During the war Andy volunteered to do some high-level speech writing, consulting, and so on for Roosevelt. Washington was filled with all sorts of famous writers pitching in. Well, he was turned down. It had to do with his way-out left-wing views. Andy wasn't a Communist any more, but he was some kind of wild revolutionary, all his own. There were lots of Communists floating around Washington and a lot of Soviet sympathizers and he suspects they blackballed him because he was a renegade. Left, but the wrong kind of left. He thinks the procommunist liberals did him dirt. His disenchantment dates from then."

"So he ended up hating FDR and Eleanor."

"Though he simply worshiped Roosevelt at one time."

"It figures," Sweeney observed. "But holy cow, that swill he preaches! That isn't politics. That's a curriculum for a funny farm." He leaned toward her. "Don't tell anyone, Melissa, but I think A. C. Stonebreaker is nuts. Only a little, but enough to sour the whole pail of milk."

"Perhaps. Actually, I pay very little attention to Andy's politics."

"How can you? That's all he ever talks about. Either he's sore 'cause I represent the Hate Germany campaign or he's imitating a Fireside Chat."

"There's more to Andy than that. Don't underestimate him. He's brilliant, Sweeney. And kind. And generous. He's helped an awful lot of people."

"Including you."

"Yes. And he's helping me now."

"I wish I knew what he could do for you that three husbands couldn't." Sweeney halted. "No, that sounds cruddy, I don't mean sex or any of that."

getting me off the Pat, as you call it.

"May not be a blessing. Take it from a club member. The hangovers get easier as you get older. I'm as bouncy as Elsie the Cow."

Her smile registered gratitude for his clowning. "No, I don't think we were in the same league. I needed it or I couldn't make it through the day. But you, Sweeney, you noble savage, I know you handle alcohol better. Andy's right about my problems."

"Wants you to get married again?"

"No," she laughed. "He's smart enough to know it won't work. Not again. He wants me to take a job. With some new foundation he's involved in—the Committee for National Revival, some such group."

"Buncha Commies, as the admiral said," Sweeney muttered.

"Quite the opposite. Some of Andy's oil millionaires, a few retired generals. The kind of people, oh hell, why go into it. They're so bloody predictable."

"Yes, the Ballbreakers, A. C. I know them well."

"Andy wants me to go back to the States and be sort of their Eleanor Roosevelt or their Jackie Kennedy. A kind of rally of the rich malcontents, but a bigger, more serious, and better organized one than any of the existing lunacies. The terrible thing is I might do it . . . out of boredom. They are a spooky bunch, and as I said, I'm the world's most nonpolitical creature. Still, one has to do *something*."

The morning was silent with heat, deadened with invasive golden light. Nothing stirred, except a suspicious solitary crow circling the tops of the yellow-green lemon groves. Sweeney knew that in hungry Italy, anything furred or feathered, anything that moved, was speedily shot, roasted, and devoured, bones and all, by the dark people of the earth. This crow would provide no *ultima cena* for some family of *contadini*.

The heat lay mightily on Sweeney, burning and fatiguing him, like cheap hooch. Pain propelled him into action. With surprising grace (normally he would have tripped and botched the whole enterprise) he sat beside Melissa, embraced her and kissed her long, lovingly. His tongue probed her mouth, one hand found the nape of her neck, a peculiarly desirable area to him, the other stroked a resilient thigh. He held the kiss for a long time, breathing in once to sustain his fluttering heart, his searching lips, and then released her.

There had been no response from her, nothing. There had been no resistance, no struggle, no words of caution. But once engaged,

208

she had remained lifeless, immobile on the canvas chair, disinterested in his passion, leading him nowhere, adding nothing to the venture, neither accepting nor rejecting the impertinence.

He held his roasted head in his hands. "Apologies. Didn't mean it."

"Sure you did, Sweeney."

"But you just sat there."

"I always do. Didn't I warn you?"

"Nah, nah, you're not a frigid woman. It's me. I'm a clod, a klutz, a big oaf."

"Not at all. You're an attractive and likable man. I'm pleased with you. It doesn't matter who'd do the kissing. I wouldn't respond. That's me. Or at least that's been me for the last few years."

"Oh, that's so sad," he crooned, stroking her smooth thigh again. "Oh, I want to weep for you. Why? Why? It's such fun."

"Not any more. I'm not sure I miss it that much. I had it all. So much of it and at such an early age. No aims, just appetites."

"You had it *all*? You mean . . . like in the sack?"

"Well, that and everything else that's supposed to be so terribly important."

"Why'd you rush things like that?" Sweeney was upset. How selflessly he wanted to help her and how unequipped for good deeds he was! "Nice and easy does it all the time, the song says."

"It just worked out that way. Beautiful young American girl in Europe—money, wit, long legs, quick with foreign languages, and no stability. Or maybe too much. The trouble was, Sweeney, and you must believe me, I was part of all that international nonsense, and later the theatrical nonsense and after that the quick-money New York nonsense—and yet I was wise to all of them.

"To really succeed in that kind of world you must *believe* implicitly. You must get drunk, trade bedmates, stay up late in night clubs, chatter a lot, do all those tiresome things, rub asses and elbows with alleged celebrities, but you must also *believe*. I'm afraid, Sweeney, I never believed. I participated to the limit, drank polo players under the table, wore out the great swordsmen of the West, yacked and glittered and giggled till dawn with fag playwrights and swish dress designers and paper millionaires, but I stifled my contempt and suppressed my wisdom, and I think that's what dulled my desires.

"You see, if I'd have *believed* I could have gone on making the scene forever. But some time after my thirtieth birthday, about the time I married my boy-wizard millionaire Wall Street financial genius—"

"The thief."

"Yes, the thief. I realized that it was all *schweinerei*. Nothing more, nothing less. Our world went round and round and it meant nothing at all, except in terms of our self-indulgence and self-importance. Out of all the long, wild nights I wasted, the parties, the champagne guzzled, the expensive clothes exhibited, the thousands of important people passing in and out of my life, and the smaller number in and out of my bed, I'll be damned if I can remember anything worthwhile ever happening, anything memorable ever being said.

"Do not misunderstand me, Sweeney. I loved it while it was happening. It's a good feeling to be envied, and I was among the world's most envied women. If you made out a checklist of what women—especially certain American women—attach importance to you'd find I'd had it all. A title, Europe, wealth, good looks, brains, wit, athletic ability, show biz, New York, money, high finance. Oh, and other goodies! Patrician decadence, faggotry, embezzlement. All enviable items, and I experienced them before I was thirty! I don't regret it at all, any of it. It was a ball. A swinging time.

"But the wine sours and the flesh fails to respond after a while. And here I am baking on this mountainside while poor Andy tries to cure me with the drying-out process and the new conservatism. Is that a laugh?"

Sweeney could summon up no laughter, not even a chuckle, a wry smile. He was shattered. The woman had seemed to him the ultimate in joy, in style, in possession of that desirable talent for conquering what the world deemed valuable, on her own terms. It was grievous to hear that she had rejected it after a too early surfeit of "goodies."

"Old Andy. Is he getting anywhere?" he asked.

"I'm afraid not. I'm in suspension at the moment."

"I guess the fun should have been doled out to you a little at a time."

"No. I know lots of women who thrive on it. Not just sex, mind you. The whole intricate complex. I told you what my failing was, Sweeney. I didn't *believe*. I knew it was asinine and harmful. It all was summarized for me one day when my name was linked romantically, as they say, by a gossip columnist with 'mysterious moneyman Gray Mandelstamm.' Good God, Sweeney! Gray Mandelstamm was the undersized, slack-jawed, lisping son of a rich manufacturer of medical elastic apparel, including jock-straps!"

"Yeah, and I bet I bought a couple of them that didn't fit."

She stretched her arms toward the sun—an Inca princess seeking life. "Sun, sun, put the good things back into me," she said softly. Sweeney, as gentle as a Jewish mother, bent over her and kissed her again. Once more she remained motionless, unresponsive. Not the slightest ripple of flesh, not the faintest twitch of muscle acknowledged his kindness.

"Okay, I surrender. Not that I'm such hot stuff. But I know when I'm not wanted."

"You are wanted, Sweeney. I like any man who makes a living out of a freeload. You're a little bit like me. Most spongers take their work too seriously, take themselves too seriously. But not you. I have a feeling you're wise to it also."

"Yeah, but I need it to eat."

"But I don't and that's why I'm rotten and you're not."

Nino, black and tan as a Manchester terrier, summoned them to lunch. Stonebreaker was ready to receive them on the dining terrace. They were neither of them hungry, but the host had spoken. It was clearly understood at Villa Malerba he was to be obeyed.

The dining terrace had eluded Sweeney the previous night. Villa Malerba had that enchanting capacity to produce new rooms, new vistas, new arrangements of lawn, trees, buildings endlessly—an architectural kaleidoscope. It was a more titillating corner than anything Sweeney had noticed the night before—a tinted glass roof, graceful iron railings and furnishings, marble planters abounding in purple and scarlet blooms. The floor was frantic with Capri tiles in lupine blues and daisy yellows.

Stonebreaker wore his blue silk kimono. His browned, round head and his disfigured eyes hidden behind thick sunglasses lent him the look of a Buddhist monk, a guardian of the Inner Temple wise with Dharma and Nirvana. He was cheerful, talkative, not in the least tired after the long night in the study. Melissa kissed him warmly on the cheek and he smiled—an annoyingly possessive smile as far as Sweeney was concerned.

The lunch was simple yet subtle, an amalgam of good judgment and the best local fare—an *antipasto del mare*, chewy morsels of squid, shrimp, octopus, and mussel, boiled, chilled, and delicately bathed in green olive oil and wine vinegar, kissed with parsley, basil, garlic, and love. This was followed by tender slices of cold veal in a tuna sauce and a salad of the world's sweetest lettuce and tiny bloody tomatoes, beneficiaries of an upbringing on night soil. The wine was *Lacrimae Christi*, more Tears of Christ.

Stonebreaker ate voraciously, but with elegant manners, great style. He practically finished the wine alone; for Melissa pointedly turned down her glass, as she and her uncle exchanged an understanding glance, and Sweeney could not stomach the fruity liquid. One drank Christ's blood in church; he had no desire to imbibe His tears in secular places. And he had had tears enough for a lifetime in the last few weeks. The kind sun, the gracious wealth that surrounded him, the terraces of citrus trees, the tranquil beauty of the sea below, none of these could dilute the testimony of those disturbing witnesses, Ludwig Helms, Father Louis, Mme

Roux, Kruis of Amsterdam, and the good General Pandolfo. Those people, Sweeney told himself, those people had done a rotten thing to him. The life had gone out of the booze, as Harry Hope had once said.

"I was wondering, could I have my tapes and my notes?" Sweeney asked abruptly. The conversation up to that point had been about Mrs. Ferrante and her clever husband, Feet, the vending-machine tycoon, whose exploits in murder and maiming filled Stonebreaker with a schoolboy's admiration.

"Why do you want them?" Stonebreaker asked cheerfully.

"Well, I oughta send them to Wettlaufer. He paid for them and all."

"I'll give you the recorder back, but I really think, for your own good, your own peace of mind—not to mention your benefactor's—I'd best keep the tapes and the notes."

"That's nuts. Even if you do what's to stop somebody, maybe not me, but someone else Sherman hires, from going back and getting new interviews?"

"Oh, he may try to. But you and I, Sweeney, we'll dissuade him. I know you've given up this foolishness, and we must now work on Mr. Wettlaufer to abandon it. I can think of better outlets for his money."

Melissa sipped at her aqua minerale. "Andy, aren't you carrying this too far? Those Noble Christians of Sweeney's can't hurt anyone. Publicizing their good deeds might do some good."

Stonebreaker shook his bald head emphatically.

Sweeney yawned. "Stoney, are you gonna give me them tapes?"

"No. You won't find them. I have locked them up. They have a symbolic value for me. You cannot have them, Sweeney."

"But I wan' 'em." He simulated a child crying for a hidden toy, for candy withheld.

"I don't think you do," Stonebreaker said. He helped himself generously to a cheese tray—creamy Gorgonzola, rubbery Bel Paese, a wedge of hard Provolone. Neither Melissa nor Sweeney joined him. He ate alone, just as he seemed to talk, act, and think alone, ignoring argument, objection, dispute, proof, evidence, anything that might deter him from pursuit of his intimate visions.

"On the other hand," Stonebreaker said, "I'm a little concerned about this Wettlaufer. I have a feeling he may be on your track, Sweeney. For all I know he may turn up here one of these days."

Blanching, Sweeney poured some white wine down his gullet.

"You're needling me."

Stonebreaker called to Nino for coffee. "I had a phone call from the Salerno *carabinieri* this morning. The American consul in Naples was in touch with them. He had your name and a description of your car—a red MG with French tourist plates. Since your car is the talk of Salerno—it's in DiGiorgio's *carrozzeria*—they had no trouble making the connection. The police called me, and since I am well known for my truthfulness in these parts, I told them that Mr. Sweeney was indeed my guest."

"Y-y-you told them," stammered Sweeney. "And they'll tell the consulate, and they'll tell Sherman."

"I only assumed that's who was looking for you. I could call the consulate and confirm it."

"Nah, nah, let's all be surprised." Sweeney got up and paced the tile floor. "Holy horror, Sherman is after me." Guilt coated his burning skin, aggravating his sun-poisoning.

What could he possibly say now to that decent man who had sought security, reassurance, peace of mind through him? Twice he had saved Sherman Wettlaufer from disgrace. Now he had betrayed him. And in the interim he was sure that Sherman's sorrows, real and imagined, had intensified. Was the crèche back on the high-school lawn? Was his phone ringing in the middle of the night, his children still the recipients of obscene notes? He had left Sherman in a state bordering on collapse, in full neurotic retreat. He had promised him mental health, love, a warranty that all was right with the world.

Noting his guest's unease Stonebreaker laughed. "I wouldn't be upset, Sweeney. I'd be delighted to meet the man. He seems an excellent subject for conversion. I guarantee you I'd have him on my side in a day or two."

214

"Sherm? Never, Stoney. No matter how much I kid about him I know the guy has got it here." Sweeney patted his chest. "In the old ticker. There's no ki-yi in Sherm."

He paced the wrought-iron confines of the dining terrace. "It'll kill him, kill him. And I blew the whole thing. Why me? Why'd he pick on me? Just because I saved his honor a couple of times?"

"He'll be a better man for having to go it alone," Stonebreaker said. "He can't have you fronting for him forever, Sweeney. And you've got to stop this masquerade."

Melissa came to Sweeney's defense. "That isn't very kind, Andy. I think Sweeney's quite candid in his blundering way. I have a feeling he went into this survey with a good deal of sincerity—not just for a free trip to Europe."

Sweeney patted her back—suppressing the thrill that leaped through his body and catching Stonebreaker's swift look of contempt. "Attagirl, Melissa. Nice to hear it from you. But I got to admit Stoney's right. I did it for the free-load."

"But you came to believe in what you were doing, didn't you?" Melissa asked.

"I don't know. I just don't want to hear anything else."

Below, on a winding limestone stairway wedged in the green hillside, they could hear Italian voices, liquid and clear in the noonday stillness. One was Nino's slurred baritone, sounding annoyed. He appeared to be pleading with someone, not angrily, but evidently disturbed. His *Vai vía! Vai vía!*—Go away!—kept recurring as the other voices persisted.

Like a mandarin Stonebreaker got up, gathering his kimono about his stubby figure, and walked to the edge of the patio. Sweeney, nosey as ever, followed. Melissa remained at the table. On the steps below Nino was barring the way to two men in faded work clothes. Host and guest, aware of the Italian rules which require several moments of silent observation of disputes prior to intervention, watched Nino grow angry as the two peasants stood their ground. The older of the two clutched a notebook to his worn shirt. He had one eye—the other was a yellow-white oyster. The second man was younger, a dark mixture of Arab, Greek,

Spaniard, and the ancient hill people of the Campania. His face seemed to have been hacked from olive wood.

"What do they want?" Stonebreaker called to Nino.

The servant jumped on hearing his employer's voice. He had been at pains to chase them away before Stonebreaker learned of their intrusion.

"*Loro sono di Bolli*," he called up.

"What do they want?" asked Stonebreaker.

Nino grinned stupidly. "*Non so, padrone*. I not know."

"Tell them to come up here and talk to me."

Nino translated. The two men plodded up the stairs and halted below the patio. The one-eyed man began to speak, not servilely but with a hoarse dignity. The young man remained silent. At the end of his brief speech the older man held the notebook toward Stonebreaker.

"He says they want my name on a petition to the government to help them get a road built," Stonebreaker said to Sweeney. "It's part of Bolli's uplift plan. These men are tenant farmers, a couple of his gullibles."

"It sounds great. You're gonna sign it, aincha?"

"Of course not." Stonebreaker, speaking Italian, lectured the visitors. They listened impassively. Neither anger, nor disappointment, nor sorrow showed in their faces. Sweeney wondered about all the claptrap about volatile, laughing Italians. The scorched men were as unresponsive as the hard earth they tilled.

When Stonebreaker had concluded his lecture—Sweeney understood none of it, except for an occasional *comunisti*—the men bowed slightly, the older one murmured a subdued *grazie*, and they descended the stairway.

"You straightened those wiseguys out, hey Stoney?" Sweeney asked as they rejoined Melissa at the table.

"I'm not sure how much good it will do." He overlooked Sweeney's sarcasm. "Bolli's been spreading his poison for weeks in the hills. Those two may be converts. Still, they'll repeat it to him, and it may shake him up a little to know that he isn't wanted around here."

216

Melissa laughed. "That was quite a lecture, Andy. A little rich for two illiterates, don't you think?"

"Not at all."

Sweeney, an expert on land reform and peasant labor, wanted to know more. "What'd Stoney tell 'em, Melissa?"

"He said that the temporary benefits they would get out of the road and the dam would be nothing compared to the slavery Bolli was preparing for them. Correct me if I misquote you, Andy—"

"On target, my dear."

"Andy said that Bolli was a Communist and an enemy of their religion, that he was opposed by all the important people around here and in all Italy. And that if they kept listening to him one of two things would happen. Either they would go to jail for following Bolli and bothering people for signatures, or if Bolli did have his way they would be slaves to a Communist government and would see religion die in this part of Italy."

"Well translated," Stonebreaker said. He popped grapes into his mouth.

"Yes," Melissa said, "but you missed what the one-eyed one said when he turned around—after you said religion would end. He muttered to the other one, 'Speriamo'—let's hope so. Andy, I'm afraid that delineation of the new conservatism didn't reconvert those backsliders."

Stonebreaker seemed amused. "That was just an exercise in reaching the masses. We're prepared for failures . . . at first."

"Seems to me you've had all you can stand," Sweeney said. "I mean you had some pretty big failures. Mussolini, Hitler."

The host rapped the table with his knuckles. "Come to order, Sweeney. You have no idea of our program. Since you are a professional ignoramus I excuse you. Equating us with primitive Fascists is a boor's argument. Our goal is quite the *opposite* of theirs, which was an extension of government power. We believe in limiting it *at first.*"

"Whaddya mean at first?"

"It's all right for the Senator and the other conservative voices to chatter about freedom, and less government, and less controls, but that's nonsense. What we seek is not some vague, catch-as-catch-can freedom, but a freedom based on honor. Society must be *honorable*, it must be dedicated to morality, orderliness, a respect for the sanctity of private property, profits, hierarchies, class distinctions. The only way to achieve such a society is through the establishment of firm standards of honorable behavior. And that, my friend, is exactly what we intend to do once we win a national election in the United States."

"Yaaah. You guys couldn't win a punchball game. How're you gonna take over? And who decides what's honorable and what isn't?"

"We will, of course."

"Who you?"

"More of us than you can imagine, Sweeney. Believers in the old Christianity of discipline, order, obedience, and original sin. Some businessmen and industrialists. The really creative people. The military. And indeed, for shock troops, the hardy Americans of the South. I guarantee you I could enlist a formidable citizen's army in the southern states, an army that no soft rabble of eastern liberals could ever defeat."

"Seems to me like your honorable society is a bunch of ridge-running pig-screwers. The Pellagra Athletic Club. Beating up *schwartzers* is a lot easier than taking over a country, Stoney."

"But that is exactly how we plan to do it. The first time we run a candidate we will lose by perhaps twenty million votes. *But wait, wait!* As the Communist threat grows, as the Negro horror worsens, as the false economy sickens, we will narrow the margin. Moreover, each time we lose, we crystallize, cement, and strengthen that hard conservative core of disciplined adherents."

"That's a great program. Kicking boogies in the keester. Letting oil millionaires in Texas cheat on their income taxes. And dropping atomic eggs on the Rooskies and Chinks. Very honorable, pal."

"In terms of the monstrous pinko-liberal-Communist conspiracy we are fighting those are modest actions. I will not sit by idly and let the Christian West slit its own throat."

218

"I bet. And you'd like to murder a couple of million while you're about it. Still sore because Stalin got to kill all them kulaks and you never had your innings, right, Stoney?"

"I would not shrink from killing, certainly not when the greatest cause known to man is in danger of extinction."

"What cause is that?" Sweeney's eyebrows arched upward.

"The Christian West, of which I am legatee and guardian. I am prepared for ultimate sacrifices. No matter what the liberals may do or fail to do I will not permit black savages to eat priests and nuns."

Stonebreaker was in full voice, walking the terrace amid the hanging grapes like a venerable Roman pro-consul sent to subdue the savage tribes of the Campania. "We are prepared to wait twenty, fifty years for our triumph. But it must come. We have three main hopes, any or all of which can result in the establishment of the world's first honorable society.

"First, a Soviet or Chinese atomic attack on the United States. Roosevelt maneuvered and lied his way into getting the Japanese to bomb Pearl Harbor. Surely we can be as intelligent as that disgusting paralytic and create a situation which will force Moscow to drop a megaton bomb on Washington or better New York. What excrescences, what garbage, what vomit would be cleansed in that purifying burst! In any event, one bomb is all we need. We would then respond and destroy *them*. But more importantly, at home the pinko-liberal left-intellectual conspiracy would be broken forever. Brutally broken.

"Method Two envisions a collapse of the economy. This is less likely, in view of the manner in which the octopus Federal government is empowered to steal my money and tax my income to support drunken Negroes and their bastard issue. Still, an atomic attack hand-in-hand with an economic collapse is a possibility.

"But in the meantime we intend to use an indigenous American sickness to advance the cause of the Christian West."

"Christ, you're a long-winded bastard," Sweeney mumbled.

"What is this sickness we can exploit? Why, the cancer of the

219

Negro. He has proven, I regret to say, that he is unfit for civilized society. One look at the Congo, at Malawi, at Zambia, at all those governments run by cannibals should convince you of that. New anthropological studies of colored peoples seem to bear out what conservatives like myself have long suspected—*he is inferior.* He can win the hundred-yard dash and the heavyweight championships, but he remains an emotional, intellectual, spiritual baboon.

"For conservatives this is a glorious opportunity to apply the rules of honor. The Negro has proved he is without honor. He is lawless, irresponsible, intemperate, uneducable. All the welfare work, all the experimental schools, all the scholarships and foundations have made him more of a sadistic killer, mugger, rapist, and thief. The male Negro is an animal who soils his own nest and leaves bastard children behind, the female a whore by nature.

"Be a good fellow, Sweeney, and stop grimacing. You are New York bred. You have run up against the Harlem syndrome. Your fellow Irish in the Bronx would be the first to agree with me."

"You stink."

"What then is to be done with the Negro?" Stonebreaker asked. "Clearly in our honorable society he will have no place. We can encourage missionary work among them but at the same time we will sternly enforce the law. Street riots will be rewarded with jailing of agitators, participants. So-called civil liberties will be suspended. The obviously guilty are in no need of complicated legal safeguards. The rest of society, decent Christian people, must be protected.

"It will be in our interest to permit these black wildmen to run their course for a while. We want more rioting, more sit-ins, more ranting speeches by the do-good breast-beating liberals, by the Negro's self-appointed literary spokesmen—and yes, more murder, rape, killing and vandalism! Only then can we arouse the anger and determination of respectable people.

"Mr. Sweeney, remember what I say, and tell your friend Wettlaufer. *Negro brutality will be the anvil on which we smash the spine of the liberals.* The maintenance of public order in the face

220

of the Communist menace is of paramount importance . . . and if that orderliness, that moral vigor is sapped by Negro brutality, Draconian measures are indicated."

"I bet," said Sweeney. "Like a barbed-wire fence around Van Cortlandt Park and inside the boogie population of New York. Ovens and gas chambers at the Bronx Zoo."

Stonebreaker walked jauntily off to the villa for his afternoon nap.

Sweeney and Melissa were alone in the stuporous heat. Sweeney looked at her helplessly. "You know something about your Uncle Andy?" he asked. "He's nuts. He's as crazy as Belfry Banahan, one of my old man's regulars. Belfry thought he was Sir Roger Casement and used to walk around with his neck crooked telling everyone the Sassenachs hanged him but never killed him. Only Belfry was nice about it. But Uncle Andy, he ain't kidding!"

"Sweeney, be a little tolerant. You don't think he's a clear and present danger, do you?"

He got up creakily, suffering equal doses of fatigue, burns, aches. "He makes just enough sense to scare the b'jesus out of me. It's like I'm understanding what Sherman was afraid of for the first time. It could happen and I'll tell you why. Nobody, nobody in our big country really likes the *schwartzer*. That's a fact. It's a built-in advantage for Stonebreaker, like the Jews in Germany. Built-in, expendable, guaranteed to produce results or money back in five days."

The old wanderlust prodded Sweeney. New sights, new faces, anything to dispel the despair with which Stonebreaker had filled him. "Hey, Melissa," he said, with a resurgence of buoyance, "let's go see this cat Bolli."

"The Sweeney Survey again?"

"Never. I just feel the need of a trip. We can check on my car at the garage so I can be ready to vamoose when your uncle boots me out, then go visit Bolli. I promised Dr. Helms I would."

She was delighted with the suggestion. "Wonderful. We'll go as social workers. I understand he's got more of them in his office than *contadini*."

The search for Bolli assumed a surrealist aspect which diverted Sweeney at first and then bothered him. For reasons which Melissa never made clear to him Mrs. Ferrante was included in the pilgrimage to Bolli. And since Mrs. Ferrante refused to ride in anything but her own air-conditioned white Lincoln Continental, Nino, who was her chauffeur, also had to accompany them.

In the withering heat of early afternoon Nino jounced them up the dirt path in the scooter with the passenger seat. Choking dust kicked up behind them in a high rooster-tail, coating the lemon leaves, settling softly on the sleeping workers in the groves. Mrs. Ferrante clutched a silk scarf around her face and whimpered. The rattling ride up the steep slope took less than ten minutes, but Sweeney was convinced it would end with a vertebra fractured, his pelvis dislocated. But he played the Spartan, particularly since Melissa laughed and moved expertly with each crash of the scooter, as cleverly as if she were riding a hunter.

The path widened near the summit, then connected with the Amalfi Drive just outside Salerno. Nino—he had exchanged his white coat for a gray chauffeur's uniform with a jaunty hat suggesting an Alitalia pilot—sped them along the blacktop for a few kilometers to a cavernous filthy garage run by several furtive brothers. Here Sweeney discovered his MG, its left flank smashed but with the engine in working order. A half-dozen dark gnarled elves were at work on the red gift, tapping at its mangled *corpus* with tiny hammers.

Sweeney protested to Melissa that he had not a nickel to his name. How could he possibly pay for the work?

"It won't cost much," she assured him. "Body and fender work is one of the biggest industries in the country. They have to keep the prices low. Italians are the world's worst drivers and most frantic car-lovers. They can't tolerate a dent or a scratch on that beloved *macchina*. DiGiorgio simply assumed that a rich American like you would want the work done."

"But who's going to pay?"

"I'll lend you the money," she said.

Nino wheeled Mrs. Ferrante's white Continental out of the greasy depths of the garage. The "discarded fruit of High Crime" was sitting up front with the chauffeur. Sweeney and Melissa got into the stateroom of a rear seat, and soon they were speeding through Salerno—a flaking, depressing place, giving the lie to travel-book mythology. The streets were all but vacant; it was the afternoon slumber of the *meridionale*.

Secure behind the closed windows of the cruising car, the air-conditioning blasting them with frigid waves, Sweeney had a sense of complete isolation from the sun-bright misery. Within the automobile they lounged on maroon leather seats, their arms at rest on plump bolsters, hearing nothing but the sound of their own voices. Outside, the eroded Mediterranean world saw them only as a dazzling white blur. With great clarity Sweeney understood how gratifying and how isolated it was to be very rich, and he enjoyed the sensation.

There was a sliding-glass partition separating the two compartments of the car and with a shy smile Mrs. Ferrante closed it so that she could enjoy Nino's company alone. The chauffeur had pushed the gray cap forward on his neat round head, and it gave him a hoodlumish air. Mrs. Ferrante nestled close to him and they held hands sweetly, his brown on her white, both at rest on her thigh. He flipped and swerved the Continental with one hand as they left Salerno and ascended a narrow road, rich in pot-holes and mule turds. Occasionally Nino bent his cunning face to hers for a baby kiss. Her silk scarf was removed to reveal a stunning head of red lacquered hair, frozen in a bouffant halo. The back of her neck showed a double strand of lustrous pearls.

"What is with her?" Sweeney asked.

"Frances? She's harmless—one of Andy's old flames. She was a showgirl in New York, years and years ago. Would you believe she's sixty-two?"

"I'd believe anything about her."

"She's very sad."

"And loaded."

"Well, the money really belongs to Feet—her husband. Feet lives outside of Chicago in a four-hundred-thousand-dollar house with barbed wire around it, Dobermans prowling the grounds, and four armed bodyguards."

"But he's good to the little woman, hey?"

"Generous. He's happier when she's out of the country. Andy sort of looks after her. There's nothing between Frances and Andy any more, but he likes to keep her around."

Once Mrs. Ferrante turned and twinkled her dark brown eyes at them, making a little *Hi there!* gesture with her fingers. Then she resumed her cozy game with Nino, who never smiled, never gave her more than his hand and an occasional peck.

"Frances is quite marvelous," Melissa said. "She's utterly fabricated, completely man-made—the hair, the skin, the eyes, the jewelry, the priceless French corsets and girdles, endless massages, sweatbaths, face and bust liftings, a wardrobe that would be the envy of any princess. Somehow Frances carries it off. You *believe* in her and you wish her happiness and success. It's like feeling good about a well-furnished apartment. No life, but lots of grand style."

"Hah. But Andy never goes to the post any more."

"I'm sure of that. Frances has Nino. He's *her* employee, not Andy's. In fact, she holds the mortgage on Villa Malerba. Andy isn't as rich as everyone thinks. He did make a pile when you paid no taxes but writers just aren't in the same league with punchboard kings and vending-machine barons."

The notion comforted Sweeney, who was in one of his more harshly materialistic moods. It occurred to him that Wettlaufer, whose plaintive presence he could not shake, was richer than A. C. Stonebreaker—possibly much richer. That would help. He was not sure what it would help, but it afforded him solace. As a last resort he could shout at Stonebreaker: "Yaaah, my friend's richer'n you!" Moreover, the knowledge that Stonebreaker, that moralizing defender of the Christian West, had to depend on the residual benefits of the exiled wife of a syndicate hoodlum was singularly refreshing.

The road kept ascending, flattening out after about a half-hour's driving on an almost treeless plateau. They sped through villages consisting of a single miserable store in a crumbling stone hovel, surrounded by a dozen equally appalling houses. The crops in the undulant fields were scorched and scant—grain, beans, grapevines. But much of the rockstrewn land was not under cultivation. Melancholy goats and starved sheep huddled in the sparse shade under the hooded eye of a neolithic shepherd, a burned scarecrow squatting beneath an outsized black umbrella.

"Hell of a life." More than ever Sweeney was grateful for the protective shell, the armor of the white gliding ark. How good to be inside, cool, resting on maroon leather while the horrid world outside sweated and stank!

"Andy says they're not unhappy," Melissa said. "They have their family, and the Church, and pasta twice a week and they love their children. He says the only unhappy ones are those that people like Bolli proselytize."

"I bet."

"It's all changing here anyway. All kinds of new industries are opening up around Naples and Salerno. The younger people get jobs there and earn more money. Andy says that isn't too good. In Italy when a poor man gets a little money he usually becomes a Communist, because he wants even more."

"What does Stoney have in mind?"

"Oh, some notion about keeping them on the land, telling them they're the heirs of Christianity and Western civilization, asking the absentee landlords to pay them a bit more."

Two aged men lugging burlap sacks on their shoulders looked up at them with the faces of misused animals as the car flashed by.

225

What, what in God's name, Sweeney wondered, could they be thinking of that white automobile?

Melissa consulted a road map. She had been told by one of the *contadini* working in her uncle's orchards where Bolli had set up his office. It was in a small agricultural community, a place of wrenching poverty where twice in the years since the war sporadic unpredictable riots had resulted in violent deaths. However, it had recently been quiet. A land-reform program was imminent. A few factory jobs were available in Salerno. Bolli's arrival there had thus been a source of distress to the government, the Church, and particularly the *carabinieri*.

"I like the guy better and better," Sweeney said when she had told him this.

A faded-blue sign at a crossroads read *Borracco*, and Nino, disengaging his hand from Mrs. Ferrante's thigh, turned the Continental onto a dirt road. The irregular bed barely disturbed the car. It continued its smooth untroubled passage, lulling the riders.

They came upon Franco Bolli faster than they had anticipated. Shortly after passing another directional marker, Nino squinted ahead, muttered a disgusted *Managg'*, and slowed the car. Beyond, the road was blocked by two olive jeeps, around which milled a half-dozen *carabinieri*. One of them gestured to the Lincoln to halt. Nino brought it gently to the side of the road alongside a parched irrigation ditch. A flock of meager goats scampered away from the intrusive car.

The chauffeur approached the policemen, chatted a minute or so, then returned. When he opened the door the dry heat rushed at them like the blast from an open-hearth furnace.

"He say Bolli making trouble on the road," Nino reported. "Some kind strike or meeting."

"Oh man, this we got to see!" Sweeney cried.

"No, plizz, Signor. *Carabinieri* say we stay in car. Maybe fighting."

"That's for me," Sweeney said. Stonebreaker's view of the world, the future he envisioned for the United States, had filled

Sweeney with an irrepressible desire to bust someone, anyone, in the snoot. "I been ready for a Brannigan since last night. Excuse me, Melissa, but I must go thrash a few rascals, preferably Italian fuzz."

He spit manfully on his hands and got out of the car into the blinding yellow light. The heat struck him full force and he swayed. Melissa followed him, but Mrs. Ferrante, sleek and silent, concerned only with her white skin and Nino's presence, demurred. "Come sit with me, sweetie," she said sadly to the chauffeur. "Don't get into no trouble."

Nino obeyed, displaying ivory teeth in a gentle grin. Sweeney watched them for a moment, envious.

"Francesca, *carina*," the chauffeur cooed. With the contempt of the impoverished youth risen to a rich sack he conveyed his hatred of both peasants and cops. "*Che gente brutta*—ugly pipple. Dirty farmer, lousy cop. Hate both."

Sweeney trudged happily toward the jeeps, feeling his heart dance. Melissa walked alongside him—cool, elegant in a white dress and leather sandals.

A *carabinieri* sergeant walked up to them and saluted. In slurred Neapolitan he told Melissa that they should leave. Bolli was up to no good. Melissa then explained to the officer that Signor Sweeney was a famous American journalist who had come all the way from the United States to speak with Bolli. This lie had a marked effect. Although still protesting the foolishness of their mission the sergeant stepped aside and let them ascend the roadway.

The scene that greeted them at the summit of the roadbed, some twenty yards beyond the parked jeeps, seemed hardly to contain the seeds of violence. It was an honored Italian tableau—a public dispute, nothing terribly serious, but a great deal of agitation, shouting, insult. Still, there was a curious sense of expectation, of the faint possibility of club on head, gun drawn, blood spouting.

A few yards to the left of the dirt road in a parched field, one so barren as to be bereft even of goats or crows, seven men in dust-covered work clothes were digging with shovels and picks, or smoothing the earth with long rakes. They had begun a primitive road—no more than five yards had been dug out and raked—that would lead from the main route to the grim yellow hills beyond. As they worked they kicked up puffs of straw-colored choking dust. They seemed to Sweeney to be at labor in hell or in some malignant penal colony. Yet he occasionally heard a laugh or a cheerful voice amid the *clump-clump* of the iron tools in the hostile earth.

To one side of the workmen stood four *carabinieri*, bemused apple knockers in tan uniforms drenched with sweat. They rested on their rifles guiltily. A fat young lieutenant, mopping his side-burned cheeks with a green handkerchief, was talking feverishly to them. The police seemed embarrassed by their superior's frantic behavior. Then the officer walked toward the digging men and shouted at them:

"Basta! Basta! Voi siete in contravenzione! Andante via!"

Melissa translated for Sweeney. "He's saying that they're breaking the law and they have to go home."

But the dusty men kept on hacking at the earth. Again Sweeney heard a low chuckle from their clouded ranks.

As Sweeney and Melissa approached the site, the sergeant who had stopped them hurried by and spoke to the fat lieutenant while pointing at the Americans. This agitated the officer further; he rolled his eyes and cursed. Somehow the intruders intensified his anger at the laborers and he stumbled back to them, shouting: *"Pazzi! Tutti Pazzi!"*

"Potsy?" Sweeney asked.

"*Pazzi.* Crazy. It's getting serious now. At first he told them they were breaking the law—that's nothing in Italy. Everybody breaks the law. But he's insulting them now. They'll insult back and there'll be trouble."

Sweeney helped Melissa over a dry irrigation ditch, which the diggers had bridged with planks, and as they crossed they noticed a second group of people, a small audience standing in the shade of deformed rocks. This party consisted of a half-dozen gnarled

228

women faceless in black shawls and black rags, a few barefoot children, and a priest. Through the dust-charged air Sweeney squinted at the *padre*. Although the prelate wore the long Italian cassock he was evidently a foreigner of some kind—a pale young man with Northern features and thinning red hair.

"*Bolli, tu sei criminale!*" the lieutenant was shouting as Sweeney and Melissa halted at the edge of the excavation. "*Tu sei comunista, tu sei socialista, tu sei nemico dello stato!*"

"That should do it," Melissa said. "It'll be every man for himself any minute."

But the worker to whom the *carabinieri* officer had unleashed his tirade, half-hidden in the dry asphyxiating clouds, made no response as he kept slamming a rusty pick into the ground.

This person whom the lieutenant had addressed as *Bolli* hardly appeared the type to foment revolution. To begin with, he was comically short, perhaps an inch under five feet. Moreover he was stout, his body a round hard sphere, his arms thick. Neckless, his ball-like head was crowned with a soaring mop of graying black Brillo. A pair of pince-nez balanced precariously on his short nose. He wore a white businessman's shirt coated with dirt. The shirt was buttoned up to its tight collar. A frayed black tie depended from it. This schoolmasterish rig was anything but appropriate for the labor, but Bolli flailed away merrily at the earth, setting a rugged pace for his co-workers. Their ranks, Sweeney noted, included the one-eyed man who had come for Stonebreaker's signature earlier that day and had gotten only a lecture. All had the look of the orphaned poor of the Italian south, people drenched in hopelessness and stupefaction. Yet oddly (and Sweeney sensed this at once but was hard put to explain it) they had a curious dignity. The presence of the professorial Bolli was not at all incongruous. One suspected that when they were finished hacking away they would rest in the shade and listen to Bolli read from Dante.

Sweeney touched the officer's arm. "What's goin' on, walyo?" Melissa, observing the lieutenant's distress and confusion, took over. She spoke her perfect Tuscan Italian and the officer removed his cap, bowed, and explained.

"He says they insist on building a road but they have no right to," she said. "This isn't their land, nobody hired them, and there are no funds to pay for the road, but Bolli has got them agitated and they're building it anyway."

"Great," Sweeney said, beaming, "just great." The oddball work party was right down his alley. Any minute he would grab a pick and join them.

"*Sciopero in senso inverso*," the officer said to Melissa. "*Che scandalo!*" He rattled on, pointing an accusing finger at Bolli.

"Bolli calls it a Backwards Strike. Instead of *refusing* to work the men are working without pay, because there is no work," Melissa translated. "The lieutenant is scandalized."

Again the officer walked up to Bolli and shouted at him. The reformer smiled, tucked his black tie between two of the lower buttons of his white shirt, and kept on working. When he responded, between thrusts of his pick, he spoke in a soft voice and smiled.

"The officer's furious now," Melissa said. "Bolli will make a laughingstock out of everyone by continuing this illegal work. The local government refused to build the road, the people in Rome won't listen to him, the Church has condemned him, everyone who matters around here, all the landlords, are against the road. Only Bolli is for it . . . and these farm laborers. I gather that what is particularly galling is that the men Bolli has working here are regarded as loafers; yet the government kept telling Bolli they wouldn't work for wages."

"And now he's got 'em working for nothing!" Sweeney cried.

Not a blade of grass stirred in the deadening heat. In the shadow of the rocks the black-hooded women stood as silent as gravestones. Only the fair young priest moved now and then, wringing his hands, making a few hesitant steps toward the diggers, then moving back to the shelter.

There was another furious outburst from the lieutenant. Bolli

230

smiled and nodded with a kind of Charlie Chaplin politeness. The irate officer retired to consult with his sergeant and his troops.

The police moved out of earshot, away from Melissa and Sweeney. It was apparent the officer was planning a move against the disturbers of the public order.

"Man, that's a gas," Sweeney said. "A backwards strike—working for no pay. Let's go up and talk to the guy."

Melissa greeted the men. In her fluent Italian she told Bolli that they were Americans and that Sweeney was a journalist who had heard about his work with the peasants of the Campania.

Bolli stopped momentarily. "Well you have seen me," he said pleasantly. Then he resumed raking.

There was nothing unfriendly in Bolli's response, merely the implication that while he was willing to let them ogle him he had more important matters on his mind than chatting with Americans.

"Mind if I help out?" Sweeney asked him.

"How?" Bolli asked, as if dubious that this well-nourished ruddy man had anything constructive to offer.

"I can swing a pick."

"*Prego.* Take one, go to work. It is hard work but you look strong."

Sweeney took a tool and posted himself between the one-eyed man and another burned peasant. They grinned at him, finding nothing exceptional in his enlistment. Their association with Bolli, together with the good manners of the Campania, had prepared them for the unexpected. Melissa retired to the shade of the rocks where the priest began conversing with her in English. Sweeney caught only an occasional word but the man's accent was unquestionably American.

It took three swings of the pick to convince Sweeney he had volunteered for more than he could handle. It weighed in his blistering hands like the *Queen Mary's* anchor. Each swing threatened to yank his dorsal muscles from their moorings. Immediately sweat broke out on his burned forehead and his hands cringed

231

with pain. Still he swung at the stubborn ground, winking at Bolli, trying to ignore the wrenching aches that threatened to pitch him into a dead faint.

"Aaaach! Oooopf!" He aached on the upswing and ooopfed when the steel pick struck home.

"Work, work," Bolli said to him.

Sweeney was certain he would fall down and die. Surely he was in better shape. How did these half-starved, bread-eating farmers, undernourished most of their miserable lives, find the strength to keep digging away at the unyielding earth? He felt infinitely inferior to all of them. He sniffed their sweat and their dirty feet and their garlic breath and envied them.

"I, ach, ach, heard about you from—aaaach—Ludwig Helms. Ooooopf."

"Ah, my friend, the engineer," Bolli said, not halting in his raking. "A fine man. He has promised to come down and help me with construction plans."

"Yes, I was—aaaach—very impressed with Dr. Helms. Oooopf!" Sweeney's heart thundered against his rib cage, frantic, shrieking for release.

"How is his health?" asked Bolli.

"Better than m-m-m-mine," Sweeney said. "He said—aaaach—I should talk to you if I needed—oooopf—answers."

"I have no answers. I only ask questions." Bolli paused in his raking, removed his glasses, and wiped them on a shirt-tail. Then he pointed toward the huddling police. "However, other people insist on supplying answers, as you will see, and they are usually wrong ones."

The carabinieri, in approximate battle formation and carrying rifles at port arms, were now trotting toward the work party. There was a new determination in the fat lieutenant's face. A decision had been made and Sweeney knew it harbored seeds of tumult.

"Non resistete, non disputate," Bolli said to his men.

"Hey, Bolli, a little hooley might do some good. I'll be your martyr." Sweeney was so heartened with the prospect of not

232

having to swing the hateful pick any more that he was quite willing to be beaten, manhandled, arrested, and jailed.

"No, no. That is just what we avoid. You must go limp, lie down, do not fight."

The priest cried out, but the cry was lost in the *clop-clop* of the hobnailed police boots on the dirt road. The priest and Melissa hurried toward the work party.

"*Per l'ultima volta, Bolli!*" the lieutenant cried. "*Cesserete?*

"*Mi dispiace, egregio tenente, ma non posso cessare,*" Bolli said, and kept digging.

"*Voi siete in arresto!*" He turned to his troop. "*Arrestateli!*"

The *carabinieri* surrounded the laborers. The sergeant ordered them to march off to the jeeps. But the workmen, with shrewd stupidity, laid down their tools and stood dumbly in the hot sun, scratching, spitting, glad for the opportunity to rest their weary arms. Sweeney stood in their midst, leaning on his pick, a fatigued WPA ditchdigger towering over their short figures.

No one moved, no one spoke. The sergeant appealed to the officer. Two of the *carabinieri* were smiling, and Bolli himself, at rest on his rake, seemed amused by the confrontation. "*Portateli!*" ordered the lieutenant.

At the command to carry off the violators of private property and public order the strikers and Bolli dropped their tools and sat down on the abortive roadbed. Sweeney joined them, squatting in the dust.

"Okay, gang, a little singing around the campfire!" he shouted. "Let's have 'I Got That Old Scout Feeling down in My Shoes!' "

The presence of the American journalist further unnerved the lieutenant, which led to another whispered conference with the sergeant. Everyone waited. When the meeting ended it evidently had been decided to pursue the arrests despite the presence of the foreigner. They began with the one-eyed man. Two policemen took his arms, two more his legs. They lifted him like a dead animal. The soles of his shoes, Sweeney noticed, were worn away, and had been replaced with chunks of corrugated cardboard.

"*Questa sarà una lezione per te, Bolli!*" the officer shouted.

"*E anche per Lei,*" Bolli replied calmly.

The priest and Melissa were at the edge of the work area. Sweeney waved to them. "Hi there, and welcome to Queen for a Day!"

"Oh, this is dreadful," the priest said. "They'll arrest Franco also. The people will be furious." He had a tremulous high voice, a midwestern accent.

"Good afternoon, *padre*," Sweeney called to him. "The name's Sweeney. Fordham man myself. Haven't you heard Bolli's a Red? You keep hanging around here I'll tell your Bishop."

"He is *not!*" the priest cried. "But if these stupid police keep arresting him they'll make him one!"

Franco Bolli slyly watched the *carabinieri* carrying off his limp workers. He spoke to Melissa through the dust. "*Signorina, non siamo politici. Non siamo comunisti, socialisti, fascisti. Niente.*"

"Bravo!" Melissa laughed.

To the wails and entreaties of the black-clad women, all relatives of the "backwards strikers" were toted to the jeeps. Bolli and Sweeney remained in the dirt. Bolli squatted cross-legged like a comic Hindu deity (Khashna, god of practical jokes?), and Sweeney, numb with exhaustion, stretched his body out full length trying manfully to avoid looking up Melissa's skirt. Her loveliness was his reward.

Gently the *carabinieri* lifted Bolli off the ground and stumbled along with him. The reformer's fat buttocks bounced on the ground and his neckless head wobbled.

"What happens now, *padre*?" Sweeney asked.

"They'll be taken to jail in Salerno and somebody will have to post bond. There'll probably be a trial. Oh it's awful, awful. I warned Franco not to attempt this crazy thing."

It appeared that the *carabinieri* were finished. In deference to Sweeney's status he would not be similarly manhandled.

"It looks like you beat the rap, Sweeney," Melissa said. "Preferential treatment for visiting newspapermen."

234

But Sweeney refused to be ignored. He recalled a newspaper account he had read recently of an angry, *avant-garde*, marijuana-smoking, image-smashing young novelist who had been arrested by the New York City Police for urinating in Herald Square. An embarrassing scene ensued in the police station. The cops, all City College English majors, began to light the irate author's cigarette, asked for his autograph, solicited his opinions on Hemingway and Faulkner, and otherwise brown-nosed and played the toady to this furious enemy of society. As Sweeney recalled the incident, the writer kept baiting the cops, daring them to slug him, inviting brutality—and reaped only more literary sycophancy. In effect, the whole New York City Police Department had become an arm of the *Paris Review*.

It appeared to the former agent of the Wettlaufer Foundation that similarly the *carabinieri* of Salerno were about to give him this same humiliating preferential treatment. He would be ignored! Bolli and his "strikers" would be carted off to jail, trial, and a niche in the history of Italian reform movements. And he Sweeney, lummox that he was, would remain flat on his ass on a dirt clearing near Borracco. Still worse, the only woman he had ever loved would be witness to his degradation.

"They can't snub me!" Sweeney shouted. He sat up. "Hey, lootenant! *Tenente*, you meathead!"

The demoralized officer turned from the overloaded jeeps. Two clawing crones came at him. The sergeant roughly shoved them away with the stock of his rifle. They keened and wailed. Oddly, their menfolk did not act distressed; a few days in jail appeared to be a welcome relief.

"Hey, *tenente*! You, you big crud! I can buy and sell a million cops like you! Yaaah—cops eat dirt! Cops eat dirt! *Gotzongoole! Fongoolate! Ufa! Mitagoolaqui!*"

This dreadful hash that Sweeney was making of classic southern Italian cuss words had its result. It struck the officer full face, like a plate of leftover pasta. Its ineptitude as much as its insult infuriated him.

235

"*Brutt' americano, mal'educato,*" he muttered, hitching his leather belt and striding purposefully toward Sweeney.

And Sweeney, anxious to ensure arrest, switched from verbal discourtesy to abusive gestures. These he had learned many years ago on East Tremont Avenue from Sal Pampitello and Vinnie Del Guardo. First Sweeney held his right arm out, fingers tucked in except for the middle digit, which was extended straight up. This was followed by a sharp slap of the cupped left palm against the crook of the right elbow, accompanied by a smart forward thrust of the right fist.

Finally, lest there be misinterpretation of his sentiments, he made the fearsome sign of the double horns, which said in effect: *your wife sleeps with everybody.* This Sweeney accomplished by extending the pinky and index fingers of each hand, tucking in the other digits.

"I gives you the double horns," Sweeney said darkly. Keeping his fingers delicately balanced, he struck his left wrist on top of his right wrist—the vilest of all Italian rudenesses.

"*Arrestarlo!*" shouted the lieutenant.

"That's more like it," said Sweeney happily.

The enlisted men trotted from the jeeps (the prisoners had no desire to escape and lolled about, placidly nonviolent) and surrounded the American. They were all smiling furtively, tickled with the abuse heaped on their commander.

"You're in for it now, Sweeney," Melissa said. "Italian jails are the worst in the world. I'll send you a file in a bowl of lasagna."

"Oh, this is shameful, shameful," the priest moaned. "My goodness, whoever you are, why did you butt in? Why? Isn't it bad enough Franco being arrested?" He ran to the jeeps to console the reformer—who hardly seemed in need of commiseration.

The *carabinieri* spit on their hands, listened for an "alley-oop" from their sergeant, and grabbed Sweeney—one on each flaccid limb—lifting him up like a sack of turnips.

"Easy on my keester, men," Sweeney said. "I may have a polynoidal cyst."

He was a lot heavier than the undernourished peasants or the minuscule Bolli. The policemen, weary from long hours in the sun, had difficulty hauling him.

"How do you feel?" Melissa asked, walking alongside them.

"If it wasn't for the honor of it," Sweeney said, "I'd just as soon walk."

The lead man, lugging Sweeney's left leg, stumbled on the timbering over the irrigation ditch. The human cargo hit the planking, and there was a moment of cursing, argument, discussion, and planning as to the best way to port the load to the jeeps.

They lifted him a second time; there was a loud, ripping sound. Sweeney's tight sky-blue denim pants had split up the back, dividing completely, fly to belt. His white jockey shorts peeked tantalizingly from the rear. Terrified, they dropped him again.

"Holy horror, you guys don't leave a man anything." He lumbered to his feet to inspect the damage.

The four bearers suddenly became convulsed, giggling like children in a tense, unhappy classroom after some miscreant breaks wind. As all teachers know and as the lieutenant quickly became aware, discipline is impossible under such circumstances. The carabinieri's hysteria spread to the men in the jeep; to the wailing women, who stopped weeping to chatter and point at the crazy American; to Melissa, who laughed helplessly; and even to the young priest, whose querulousness gave way to an indulgent smile. Only the lieutenant remained implacable.

Sweeney tried covering up his exposed rear, saw it was useless, tried shrinking his oversized figure, tried walking sideways, tried walking backwards, then gave it up. "Man, it feels better like this. Them fag pants like to have killed me."

With delicate mincing steps, daintily holding his split trousers together at the rear, he began walking toward the jeep. But the damage had been done, not only to his pants but to the officer's attempt to restore order to the Borracco road.

The enlisted men slapped one another, giggled, imitated Sweeney's crablike gait, and stumbled about like drunken adolescents. The laborers under arrest laughed softly. Bolli and the priest exchanged opinions on the identity of the ludicrous American. The black-clad women and barefoot children danced around Sweeney, taking him for some great wizard or benefactor, nicknaming him, *Calzoni-strappati,* or "Torn-pants."

"*Basta! Basta!*" shouted the lieutenant. But he had lost control.

"*Calzoni-strappati! Calzoni-strappati!*" cried the hopping children.

"*Su! Su!*" the lieutenant screamed at the prisoners. "*Fuori!*"

Puzzled by their liberation, the farm workers climbed slowly out of the jeeps. Bolli was the last to get out. He was a little disappointed at escaping jail. Scarlet with rage, the officer ordered his men into the jeeps, then shouted a final warning at Bolli. There would be no next time he warned. Next time, immediate arrest, if he kept up those funny tricks of backwards strikes and peaceful marches on the City Hall.

"*Tenente,* you're a sport," Sweeney said, full of compassion for the hot frustrated man. "I mean it, pal. I didn't mean for you to blow the whole gig. The way it looks to me, Franco *wanted* to get jugged. So you win anyway."

The jeeps vanished, obscured in their own eruptions of billowing dust.

It was agreed, as soon as the police had left, that Sweeney and Melissa would walk back to Bolli's headquarters with the reformer and the American priest. The unemployed *contadini* and their families were told by Bolli to return to their homes and to call at his office the following day for the next strategic step in getting the road built. Sweeney was convinced that the little man actively *desired* arrest, and had deliberately provoked the cops. Sweeney apologized for his split pants (now covered with Melissa's white silk scarf), but Bolli shrugged indifferently.

Mrs. Ferrante and Nino, who had been necking feverishly in the

238

Lincoln throughout the roadside drama, volunteered to drive everyone to the village of Borracco, but Sweeney would not accept the ride.

"It's like this, Melissa," he explained. They watched Nino back the white ark into a field and maneuver it around. "It's like a cartoon in the *Daily Worker*. You can't go riding into that poor, sick Italian village in that boat. I don't begrudge Mrs. Ferrante the car or her stud, but Jesus, let's not hang ourselves."

But Sweeney was wrong. The impoverished rag-clad farmers and their families had fallen in love with the Continental. The children skipped and danced around it. The men fearfully touched its sizzling white flanks and the women gossiped about its magical properties from a distance.

"Besides," Sweeney said when the Lincoln had vanished on its journey back to the villa, "those two are panting so hard they're ready to tear off a piece in a bean field. Let 'em be happy in a nice clean sack." He looked archly at his companion. "And don't think I'm not jealous."

"You'd be disappointed. You've been hero enough today, Sweeney."

After a fifteen-minute walk, during which Sweeney was convinced he had developed a spastic esophagus and sunstroke, they reached the hamlet. The country they had traversed was of a brutal barrenness that stunned them into silence. It stifled any concern with their own identities or their own problems. It was a land that sickened and disheartened.

The village of Borracco, where Bolli had established his office, was nothing more than several dozen flaking yellow-gray buildings grouped around a dismal square. At the center stood a hideous bronze fountain, the gift of some ancient Barone or Marchese. The sense of defeat and poverty was overwhelming, yet oddly the village was immaculate. It resembled a moribund hospital patient, corroded within, doomed—yet scrubbed, barbered, and spotlessly groomed by dutiful attendants. No scrap of paper, no morsel of refuse littered the crumbling streets.

"It's because nothing is ever thrown away," Melissa said. "Everything has a use of some kind."

The afternoon rest hour was coming to an end. The shutters of a few miserable stores were slammed open. Old men in black caps began a stately card game in front of a tiny bar. Over their ancient heads, in which coursed blood of Arabs, Greeks, Spaniards, Latin and Italian tribes, Sweeney read: *Bevete Coca Cola*. Two primitive carts—flat-beds on huge wheels drawn by mangy donkeys—moved lethargically across the piazza. A boy with the bland eyes of a half-wit shepherded goats down a dirt alley. There was not a single motor vehicle in sight—not a Fiat, not a motor scooter, not even a motorized bicycle. Sweeney was pleased with himself for having kept the mighty Lincoln from the village. "Start a goddamn cargo cult," he mumbled. "Great white car come to save poor benighted walyos."

They came presently upon a square stone house, surmounted by a flimsy second story of corrugated metal, and bearing the hand-lettered sign:

LA COMITIVA PER LAVORO E DIGNITÀ
NEL MEZZOGIORNO

"The committee for work and dignity in the south," Melissa translated. It hardly seemed proper headquarters for so noble an enterprise. It stood on packed yellow dirt. In front was an open drain through which trickled garbage, excrement, and discarded wash water. One side of the building was surrounded by a low wooden fence. Within the enclosure an effort had been made to set up a children's playground with dilapidated swings, a seesaw, a canted slide. A slender young woman in a cotton smock was watching four small children at play. Someone had attempted to plant grass in the area; a handful of withered patches advertised his failure.

They followed Bolli and the priest up a canted stairway to an oven-hot second floor. This consisted of one long rectangular

240

room, its harsh metal walls partially covered with unpainted beaver board. There were a series of long tables, cheap folding chairs, a mimeograph machine, and some handmade shelves laden with folders, office supplies, a meager library. At one of the long tables a slender bearded young man in khaki shorts and a white T-shirt was interviewing a peasant woman. At another table a chunky fair girl in a blue smock was typing on file cards with an old rattling machine.

One wall of the cavernous room had two windows carved into it and through these swarms of black flies hummed and circled incessantly. The other wall sported a series of lettered quotations, utterances by people who evidently were among Franco Bolli's heroes. They were in Italian and Melissa translated them for Sweeney. One read:

> *La supremazia dell' intelletto resta nella distanza molta lontana, ma, non probabilmente, infinita.*
>
> —*Freud*

"That's about the supremacy of the intellect," Melissa said. "Sigmund says it lies in the very distant future, but probably not an infinite distance. So we can all hope."

At the center of the long wall in larger lettering appeared the words:

> *Nella nostra epoca materialistica, i lavoratori serii e scientifici sono la solamente gente profondamente religiosa.*
>
> —*Einstein*

"Well, there's Einstein," Melissa said. "It's a materialist age, he says, and the only truly religious people are serious scientific workers."

In back of the long wooden table at which Bolli now sat with the American priest a final inscription appeared:

> *Forse, non possiamo impedire questo mondo d'essere un mondo nel quale i bambini sono torturati. Ma possiamo ridurre il numero di bambini torturati.*
>
> —*Camus*

241

"Perhaps we can't stop the world from being one in which children are tortured," Melissa translated, "but we can reduce the number of tortured children."

The two visitors stood facing Bolli, who without being impolite ignored them. He was engaged in energetic discussion with the priest, at the same time scribbling notes on a pad.

"But His Excellency doesn't approve of some of the people working with you," the priest pleaded.

"And he doesn't approve of *me*," Bolli said, in his brisk, impatient manner. "But that is not important. What is important is to have him support us to get the road built."

"He is in favor of the road in principle," the American prelate said cautiously. He had a fluty voice.

"Then let him be in favor of it in *fact*," Bolli said. "The Archbishop is a goodhearted man, but he must stop spreading these stories about me. I have never told our people not to go to Church. That is their affair. I am interested only in teaching them to read and write, to use fertilizer and tools, to act as a group, to develop a desire to improve their lives and educate their children. . . . "

"All of which sounds pretty subversive to me," Sweeney said, bending uninvited over the desk. "And how about that jazz from Einstein over there, hah? Where does that leave the Archbishop?"

The American priest was shocked by Sweeney's insolence—although the visitor's manner was enquiring more than minatory. Bolli was not at all insulted. His eyes, peering above the steel-rimmed glasses, were wide with interest.

"There's room for *both* Einstein and His Excellency," said Bolli.

"Oh, yes, yes, there is!" cried the priest. "Our beloved Pope John is proving that every day."

"Right!" said Sweeney. "All aboard! Come on, Franco, haven't you heard about how he's opening all them windows in the Church?"

"Of course," Bolli said bluntly, "but would it be impolite if someone were to ask why the windows have remained shut all these years?"

"Franco, that isn't fair," said the priest. "You know that is a very involved story and for you to simplify it like that is the same as people calling you a Communist."

Sweeney drew up two chairs for Melissa and himself. He introduced her as Mrs. Davies, himself as B. K. Sweeney, American freelance journalist. The priest's name was Father Henry Frade and he was from Toledo, Ohio. He volunteered little else about himself, and Sweeney, his nosiness piqued by the gentle young prelate, tried to draw him out.

"Father Hank, if I may call you that—"

"No one has ever called me Hank, Mr. Sweeney. Father Frade will do."

"No offense, padre. I'm the beneficiary of a good RC education myself. I'm just curious, before I get to asking Franco here a few questions. If he's supposed to be a Red, a lefto, a Commie and if the Archbishop doesn't like him . . . what are you doing here?"

"That is my affair," said Father Frade. "I'm doing graduate studies in the Vatican Library—twelfth-century texts, if you care about that kind of scholarship. I visit Franco on my own initiative and for my own edification. He and I have become close friends. It has nothing to do with my work in Rome."

"Little insurance on the side. If you can't lick 'em join 'em?"

"Quite the contrary. It is Franco who will eventually join us."

Bolli was indifferent to the mild argument that had developed. He kept making notes on his pad, occasionally referring to a fat red book, a manual of some kind. Perhaps, Sweeney reasoned, he was mapping out his next act of defiance, his next gambit in forcing the government to build the miserable road.

After Sweeney and Father Frade had jabbed and feinted at each other a few more times—references to Leo XIII, citing of the worker priests, discussions of the strenuous effort of the Church in America to help the Negro—Bolli looked up from his work.

"I do not mean to be impolite," the reformer said, "but I must tell you and *La Signora* that I have a full schedule this afternoon. In an hour I must look at a site for an elementary school, then I have a deputation of *contadini* from Alto Pazzolo calling. After that it will be time for our evening discussion group. You are welcome to stay and observe all of this but I am sorry, I won't be able to talk very much."

"Perhaps we'd better go," Melissa said.

"As you please, Mrs. Davies. Forgive me if I seem rude but none of us has much time."

Sweeney liked his matter-of-fact mien, his bland round technician's face, somewhat laughable with its great twin cones of wiry hair. His feet barely touched the floor.

"I tell you what I came to talk to you about," Sweeney said. "Not this work you're doing now. But about what you and your brother did during the war."

At the mention of his brother the reformer's brusque air vanished. Bolli's eyes blinked a few times. He leaned over the table, stroking his chin, evidencing no annoyance with Sweeney's request but rather a rush of nostalgia at old painful thoughts revived.

"Why are you interested?" he asked.

As vaguely as possible, Sweeney explained that he was engaged in taking down the personal accounts of Europeans who had acted as the brothers Bolli had. That, Sweeney said, was how he had come across Ludwig Helms.

"*Bene*," said Bolli, "since you have sacrificed a pair of pants in my behalf I will sacrifice a half hour in yours."

"Really," Father Frade protested, "you know how those memories upset you, Franco—"

"I do not mind." There was a framed photograph on Bolli's table and the reformer turned it around. "That is a photograph of my brother Massimo. It is perhaps the best likeness of him existing, which is as it should be because it was taken by some of the best photographers in the world, the Gestapo. He was not aware he was being photographed."

244

They scrutinized the faded picture: a street in an Italian city, a young man almost as short as Franco Bolli walking jauntily, a faint smile on his round face. He wore a floppy beret, a dark overcoat a size too large. Evidently it was winter but the coat was unbuttoned, flapping in the wind, and leaving him, it seemed to Sweeney, exposed and vulnerable. He did not look like a menace to the Third Reich.

"We were both students at the University of Bologna," Bolli said. "Massimo was two years older than me but we had been almost like twins—inseparable since our boyhood. Our father was an artist, a restorer of paintings who worked a good deal for the Bishop. You may see some of his work in the Churches of Santa Maria dei Servi and Santa Maria della Vita.

"I imagine that my father's technical skill, his knowledge of drafting, design, materials, and so forth, impressed me and led me to a course of study in civil engineering. Massimo, on the other hand, became infused with the *subjects* of our father's labors, the religious inspiration that created the paintings. So he became a passionate student of Christian rhetoric and Church history. Thus we followed our stars—mine that of the palpable physical world and Massimo's the so-called world of the spirit. Despite this divergence we remained fiercely loyal to one another.

"But you wish to know how we came to help the Jews of Bologna. One comes to these decisions abruptly, and with little forewarning. For some time we felt no deep animosity toward the Germans. Indeed, even after we embarked on our campaign to deceive them, I can truly say we did not hate them. We feared them, yes. But their actions against the Jews seemed so inexplicable, so far removed from either my own rationalism or Massimo's faith that we could not summon up any antagonisms. It would have been like hating a destructive storm or a flood."

The stout woman in the blue smock walked up to the table and whispered something to Bolli. He asked the visitors: "My wife asks if you would like to stay for dinner. We eat at seven."

"No thanks, Franco," Sweeney said. "We're kind of bushed, the heat and all."

"Very well, but you are welcome. There is a bus at five to Salerno." He looked reflectively at his brother's photograph and resumed.

"Must one look for turning points, for signs on the road which commit us to a course of action?" the reformer asked rhetorically. "Do we seek visions, portents? Perhaps my brother did. He often dreamed of a religious life, taking orders, a life devoted to prayer and contemplation. But he confided to me that he was too weak for such dedication, that his flesh would rebel. As for me, I have never felt the need of Christ rising before me in glory on some road to Damascus—"

Father Henry Frade interrupted. "That is not so, Franco, don't either of you believe it. I have known this man a month now, and he is one of the most religious persons I have ever met."

"Thank you, my friend Henry, but that is irrelevant. My impulses are practical impulses, and I think of our work with the Jews as the result of such practicality.

"We pursued our studies in Bologna, happy with our parents, a home where music, books, paintings, study supplied whatever money could not, indeed, much more. We were nonpolitical, indifferent.

"One day Massimo and I went to the post office near the University to purchase stamps. As we stood at the window a family came in to claim a package. There was a father, a small borghese with a big mustache and a black hard hat, a woman in a green coat, sniffling into a handkerchief, and two children, a boy of eight wearing long woolen stockings and a heavy coat, and a girl of five, similarly dressed in winter clothing. It was late afternoon. The children must have been met at school by their parents, for they carried briefcases slung over their shoulders with canvas straps.

"They were dressed shabbily but neatly, and they comported themselves with a quiet mannerliness. The man walked to the window and submitted a receipt for his package, as the rest of his

246

family waited at the writing desks. The clerk was in the rear of the office an unusually long time, and we could see the woman become restive, ill at ease.

"Suddenly the door at the side of the grilled windows opened, and two men in civilian clothes walked out. I needed no one to tell me that these healthy, ruddy men were our former allies, on some vital mission aimed at preserving the great Reich.

"The men walked up to the husband and presented themselves politely, showing Gestapo cards of identity and asking if the gentleman was not Alberto Terracina formerly of Ferrara. The man admitted he was, turning his eyes toward his wife and children, as if to say, 'Run, run, it has happened at last.'

"But the woman did nothing. She merely sniffled into her handkerchief, expressing a sorrow deeper than I can possibly describe.

"They did nothing this stricken family. Civilly the two Germans advised Signor Terracina that he was required to come with them to 'register,' that he was in violation of several laws for failing to do so, and that his wife and children were required to come, too. 'It is a routine matter,' one of the men said, 'and should not trouble you.' But this lie did not reassure the man. He suddenly had difficulty breathing. Seeing his bewildered children, those two laden with schoolbooks, staring at him, he gathered up his strength in a heroic effort, fixed his hat smartly on his small head, and nodded his agreement.

"And so they were escorted out of the post office, the smiling Germans flanking the four of them—Papa, Mama, two bambini. When they reached the door the man asked about his package, and the Gestapo men assured him that it would be forwarded to him. With that final comment, the poor man understood that he was to be arrested, shipped off, who knows what else. But he walked bravely, a hand on each child's shoulder.

"Massimo and I had seen all this, and with what we hoped the police would interpret as routine Italian curiosity, we wandered into the street and watched them depart. It was late afternoon of a winter's day; the streets were alive with shoppers, bicycles, peddlers, the whole joyous fabric of city life, the intermingling of shopkeeper and customer, policeman and driver, chestnut peddler and small boys, that marvelous warm rhythm of our Italian cities. And through it all marched *La Famiglia Terracina*, man, woman, boy, girl, escorted by two strange men, marching quietly, unresisting, into the gates of hell. *'Why them and not the others?'* I asked myself.

"Once I thought I saw the man turn and look at us—an appeal unspoken, a cry for help out of the dungeon, but I may have been mistaken. Perhaps he was only wondering about his package. But no one was interested. Is anyone interested today?"

"Yes! Yes!" shouted Sweeney. "Lots of people!"

The old despair, the wrenching sorrow he had sought to divest himself of forever, returned to Sweeney. Bolli was at him the way Father Louis had been, and Helms, and Huguette Roux, and Kruis of Amsterdam. The sides of the coin were unequal; you flipped the *head* of decency, and it was tiny, while the *tail* of brutality was enormous. A curious coin that changed dimension. He had the dread feeling that Bolli would have no answers, no solutions, no reassurances for him.

"Mr. Sweeney is right!" Father Frade said breathlessly. "People are listening. Oh, it will not happen again. I don't mean just to the Jews. I mean all those meaningless murders—Negroes, kulaks, all the awful crimes. And Hiroshima! That is what concerns our beloved Pope John. He is leading the world toward new love, new peace!"

Bolli patted the priest's hand. "Of course we must continue to be optimists, Henry. And as Camus said to his Christian friends, *"If you will not help us, who will?"* We must not lose hope. If I had lost hope I would not be in Borracco trying to build roads and dams. Still, one grows pessimistic as one gets older. . . ."

It disturbed Sweeney that this placid reformer, this petitioner and gadfly, should not exude optimism.

"Hey, Franco," Sweeney said, "you're the proof we're getting better and smarter. I mean it!"

"I appreciate your American enthusiasm. But you endow me with too much power, almost as much as the Archbishop attributes to me." Bolli winked at the priest, who smiled like an embarrassed boy.

"Let me conclude," Bolli said, somewhat impatiently. He glanced toward the front of the long room. A peasant couple, a knotty blackened man in rags and a woman in the inevitable black shawl, had entered softly and were sitting on a bench.

"What we witnessed at the post office," Bolli said, "convinced my brother and myself that we could no longer be neutral observers. So we contacted what remained of the Jewish community. We volunteered our services as guides to smuggle them into Switzerland, either at certain vulnerable points on the border or with false documents which we produced in the cellar of our home. We had no money, no resources, no organization. But we did the best we could.

"Since I was a trained draftsman I assumed the job of copying documents—passports, visas, identity cards. My father, who was unaware of the work we were engaged in, helped us get certain pigments for colored inks. Pretending to be engaged in a survey of medieval buildings in the ghetto, I undertook the contacting of Jewish persons who were willing to run the risks of escape. It was a grave risk indeed."

"They'd have died anyway if they stayed," Sweeney protested. "They all should have gone with you. Or at least fought the bastards and died fighting."

"That is easy for you to say, Mr. Sweeney." Bolli pointed toward the two workers who sat at the far end of the room, silent monoliths. "Paralysis in the face of evil is not restricted to Jews. Look at my two visitors. They each earn about nine hundred lire, less than a dollar and a half, for a twelve-hour day in the fields. They have been doing this for generations. Yet they do it quietly, raise children, attempt to keep them clean, and *do* keep them mannerly. They attend church, love one another, and die with dignity. But protest? Rebellion? Self-education? Nothing. It took me eight months to get the first children to attend our literacy classes."

"Don't say it, Franco," Father Frade said. Bolli looked puzzled. The priest turned to the visitors. "He always tells people that the reason he could not get anyone with his school was because the Archbishop warned people to stay away from Bolli, that he was worse than a Communist."

"What could be worse?" Sweeney asked.

"Well," said Father Frade, "he told people Franco was a *Protestant*."

"A shrewd move by His Excellency," said Bolli. "It certainly kept people away. You see the Communists, I am grieved to report, have an unfortunate good reputation around here for getting things done for people. If he called me a Communist people might have come to me."

"But they call you one now," Sweeney said.

"That is largely for national consumption, for Rome." Bolli called something to the people waiting for him, then resumed. "I had better conclude my story. My brother Massimo assumed for himself the most dangerous job of all. How strange for that gentle boy, that student of Christian Rhetoric imbued with medieval thoughts, a love of the twelfth century, old illuminated manuscripts. What an unlikely adventurer! He had always been a sickly lad, consumptive and thin-blooded. I on the other hand was a lump of good health, nerveless. Perhaps I should have taken the job of escorting the Jews to the border. But Massimo insisted, he would be the Virgil, the Moses. 'Everyman I will go with thee and be thy guide, in thy most need to be by thy side.'

"I see him in my mind's eye, Mr. Sweeney. A slender youth, starved in body but great in soul, his overcoat, once our father's, flapping in the January wind as he walks, somewhat abstracted, along the Strada Maggiore. He is hatless. The wind flutters his shock of dark hair. Massimo's skin is pale, almost translucent. The

250

blue veins in his temples are like the marbling in old tablets. He carries a bulging briefcase, his texts and his notebooks, since we must always pretend that we are students engaged in studies.

"At the end of the Strada Maggiore is the Church of Santa Maria dei Servi, where our father supervised the restoration. Inside one may see a Madonna of Cimabue, one of Massimo's favorite paintings. A woman and a child come out of the church, undistinguished ordinary people. Our Jews, Mr. Sweeney, are impossible to tell from Italians. Perhaps that is because we are all Mediterraneans. Most of them have been here since the Inquisition—forgive me, my dear Henry—and they are part of our lifeblood, our culture, our gifts, and our failings.

"The woman is perhaps forty, but she looks older. She carries a wicker basket. The girl is about twelve—skinny legs shivering in woolen stockings, her hair in braids, her eyes hidden by eyeglasses. They wait nervously on the steps of Santa Maria dei Servi. A *carabinieri* passes and they cringe; two German soldiers walk by and they retire to the porch of the church. And then Massimo, his oversized coat sailing behind him, his briefcase weighing him down on his right side, walks up and they chat briefly. He looks around—a very bad secret agent. He is nervous, apprehensive. Then he walks off in the direction of the railway station and after a few moments the woman and the girl disappear also, following his vulnerable figure.

"Later they will go to a certain car on a certain train. They will exchange no greetings, make no sign that they know one another. But shortly after the train departs from the Milan station the girl will come by Massimo's compartment, and he will give her a sandwich wrapped in newspaper. But there will be no cheese or salami or mortadella in this sandwich, just two false passports identifying them as Signora Colonetti and her daughter Regina, residents of Bologna en route to Locarno to visit their family.

"Massimo made these repeated trips into Switzerland under the pretext of doing research at the Nungesser Library in Lugano, which possesses one of the great collections of twelfth-century monastic documents. Soon he got to know the border guards well. While he never dared communicate with his wards as he led them into Switzerland, he could by a series of pre-arranged signals guide them to immigration officers whom he knew to be tolerant, or nearsighted.

"One finds it hard to see him as a hero; yet he ran far greater risks than ever I did. He had his Faith. I hope I had something that sustained me, too. Once I volunteered to change jobs with him, but he would not hear of it. 'No, Franco,' he said, 'there is something obvious about you, little as you are. You attract attention—your eyes, the way you look at people. I am a cipher, a pale student who could not possibly be engaged in such work.'

"And so he remained the Shepherd of the Jews as I daily went about Bologna contacting our people, laboring nights at forging documents, and worrying about Massimo. Of course they trapped him, finally. He was, I am certain, betrayed. To this day we do not know who was responsible. I have looked at much brutality and stupidity in my life, Mr. Sweeney. But it is hard for me to envision anyone wishing harm to Massimo, that pure and gentle spirit, that underfed weakling with his hesitant smile and shock of chestnut hair.

"He had gone to Piazza del Nettuno to meet a man named Alatri, whose wife had been deported in a sudden roundup. He had been in hiding in a convent. Alatri had decided he could not presume forever on the good will of the nuns nor run the risk of eventual arrest. So he decided to follow Massimo into Switzerland. But the Gestapo by now had learned from their informer that the brothers Bolli were engaged in this treasonable work.

"They waited until Massimo went up to Alatri and spoke briefly to him, then walked off with Alatri thirty paces behind. Both were arrested at once. I do not know what happened to Alatri. Probably he died somewhere in Poland or the Ukraine.

"As for Massimo, he was taken to the concentration camp at Fossoli for questioning." Bolli looked up at Melissa. "If Mrs. Davies will excuse me, what I have to relate now is indelicate.

252

Perhaps she would prefer to leave while I tell Mr. Sweeney what they did to my brother."

"Franco, this upsets you," the priest said gently.

"No, no. Mr. Sweeney deserves the full story for his survey or whatever it is."

"That's all right, Mr. Bolli," Melissa said. "I am not as delicate as one might imagine."

"I learned this after the war from a man, a socialist journalist who had been in Fossoli with Massimo. My brother refused to tell the Germans anything about our work. He protected me unfailingly, and all the others who had worked with us, the parish priests and the nuns who had hidden Jewish children, the brave *carabinieri* and courageous customs guards who had winked at our illegal operations. Not a word, not a sign, nothing at all did he tell them.

"So they tortured him. The ordinary tortures were unavailing, so they took him to the room for the defiant ones and undressed him. He was made to stand against a stone wall. A loop of metal was placed around his genitals. The Gestapo interrogator advised him that unless he revealed his associates they would pass an enormous charge of electricity through his private parts, never enough to kill him or stun him but sufficient to induce the most excruciating pain in the world.

"Massimo refused to speak. Oh, how I see that naked, starved body! As white as Christ's! An unmuscled, child's body, and a small, helpless face!

"On the interrogator's desk was an electric switch, and when Massimo refused to speak it was thrown. Oddly nothing at all happened, nothing. Everyone smiled and relaxed. The lieutenant lit a cigarette. The Gestapo sergeant tilted his chair back against the wall. And Massimo managed a faint smile. They were joking. They were not such bad fellows after all.

"And then, when he was utterly off guard, the electricity slammed through his genitals, coursed into his abdomen, and convulsed him. With noteworthy German ingenuity they had

253

constructed the electrical circuit to work on a delayed basis. Thus, when the victim was at ease and relaxed, unprepared, the pain would hit him with maximum force. I am told it is the most intractable, the most abominably monstrous pain in the world.

"The machine had a further refinement. The length of delay between the turning of the switch and the shock could be varied. Thus the victim never knew when to expect the frightful insult and to brace for it.

"But Massimo remained silent, and he was returned to his cell a whimpering wreck. The Jews at Fossoli soon knew about him, and they named him *Il Pastoruccio*, or the beloved shepherd. They came to him with gifts and prayers, for soon he was bedridden, unable to withstand the tortures, the cold of the barracks, the inedible food. I do not believe he was deliberately starved to death. His system merely became unable to absorb nutrition. He vomited perpetually and his bowels turned to water. The Jewish women in Fossoli would come to clean his bed. After a few weeks his body became a mass of suppurating sores, and he stank dreadfully. The Odor of Sanctity perhaps? Some of the other people in the dormitory, Communists who detested Massimo's religious dedication, threatened to throw him out, but the Jews would not permit it.

"He died in his sleep in April of 1944, his face as shriveled as a dried apple, his body a mass of vile sores. But his mind was clear and he called for a priest to perform the sacrament. He is buried outside of Bologna on a hill which affords a splendid view of our city."

For some time no one spoke in the hot fly-blown room. Only the noise of the typewriter punctuated the respectful silence. Sweeney wiped his forehead. His hand was coated with sweat and yellow dust.

"He was a saint, a saint," murmured Father Frade.

"You bet he was," Sweeney said.

Bolli called to his wife, who got up from her typing, went to a peeling wardrobe now used as a file cabinet, and took from it a cardboard box. She brought it to her husband, and returned to her work. Bolli took from it some letters, postcards, leaflets, some old scuffed notebooks.

"There is little else to tell you," Bolli said wearily. "Here is his last letter to me. 'Beloved brother, I die in the purest Roman Catholic faith, submitting myself to God's will, humbly hopeful that I have done the right things and that God finds some merit in my actions. I die as a sacrifice for our Holy Faith, for Christ Jesus, and all the Saints. I know, my brother, that you will shake your head when you read this for you are bored with my protestations of Faith and my love for the Mystical Body of Christ. But indulge me now, as I prepare to die, and convey my love to all who have known me—teachers, family, friends—'

"A pure spirit, Mr. Sweeney, but a naïve one. Still, his Faith may have been stronger than my disbelief. I do not know. He died, I live."

"Luck of the draw, Franco. It could have been you."

"Yes, I imagine it could have. Still, Massimo may have known all along that this would happen, he may have sought it. For strangers. Jews whom we scarcely knew. The man and his wife and the two children with the briefcases in the post office that day. . . ."

Bolli looked tired. That indefatigable stumpy body seemed to wilt, to turn to tallow. He rested his large forehead on one chunky hand.

"Saint or no, he was a brave guy," Sweeney said throatily. "I'd have been honored to shake that man's hand."

But Bolli did not hear. He was lost in some hazed recollection of his older brother. Father Frade looked helplessly at Melissa and Sweeney, shaking his head faintly. Bolli picked up one of the dog-eared notebooks in the box and opened it.

"These are Massimo's schoolbooks. At one time he was engaged in a study of Papal Bulls of the sixteenth century. He had devoted a great deal of attention to an analysis of the language used in *Cum nimis absurdum*, a bull issued by Pope Paul IV, Papa Caraffa, in 1555. You will not find it quoted these days, but it might interest you if I read some of it, merely to show you the wide interests of Massimo's young mind."

"I wish you would not," said Father Frade. "It would confuse our guests and it would pain me. These things are understandable only in their historical context. Pope Paul was fighting the divisive effects of the Reformation."

Bolli looked at him blandly. "Then he should have fought Luther and Calvin. He picked on the wrong people."

"A lot of that sort of thing went on," Sweeney said stupidly.

"*Cum nimis absurdum*," Bolli read. " 'Forasmuch as it is highly absurd and improper that the Jews, condemned by God to eternal slavery because of their guilt, should, on the pretext that they are cherished by Christian love, and permitted to dwell in our midst, show such ingratitude to Christians as to insult them for their mercy and presume to mastery instead of the subjection that beseems them—' "

"Hmmm," Sweeney said, "seems to me I've heard that song before."

" 'And forasmuch as we have been informed in Rome and elsewhere their shamelessness is such that they presume to dwell among Christians in the neighborhood of churches, without distinction of dress, and even to rent houses in the more elegant streets and squares of our cities, to purchase and possess property, to hire Christian maidservants and nurses and other salaried attendants and or perpetrate other misdeeds. . . . ' " Bolli's voice became faint. "It goes on, more of the same. Very fine rhetoric."

"What'd Paul recommend?" asked Sweeney.

"The usual prescription. Baptism. If they refused, eternal damnation in this world and the next. They were ordered by Papal Bull to wear the badge, forced into the ghetto, made to sell their property to Christian buyers. That was how some of our oldest Roman fortunes were founded. Well, we can argue about this forever. I merely cite it to show Massimo's range of interests. Sadly, there are no commentaries by him on *Cum nimis absurdum*."

256

"Then I should like to make a few," said Father Frade. "You are being unfair, Franco."

"Please correct me, Henry, if I have erred."

"What you have said about Paul IV is true, I cannot contest it," the American priest said, with some agitation. "But you know very well, Franco, that the Papacy was often the only shield the Jews had during the Middle Ages and into the Renaissance."

"True, true. The Vatican was decent about that sort of thing. Protecting Jews not from oppression, but from too much oppression. Condemn the Jews to degradation, to censure as deicides, well-poisoners, child-killers, yet try to prevent them from being slaughtered entirely." Bolli yawned.

"Yeah," Sweeney interjected, "they'd be without a good doctor if they killed them all."

Neither the reformer nor the priest paid any attention to him as Father Frade continued, "Whatever bad judgment the Holy See may have shown from time to time, it is also true that by comparison Jews were better off under Papal rule. They never suffered expulsion or violence or severe oppression. Why the Jews of Rome often came singing and bearing olive branches to greet Pope Julius II, and he was delighted to welcome them."

"I'm glad," Bolli said sincerely.

"Then why'd Caraffa blow the whistle?" asked Sweeney.

"Because of the Reformation, or as I prefer to call it, the *Protestant* Revolution," Father Frade said.

"But the Reformation was an argument among Christians," said Melissa.

"Exactly," Bolli said. "The Jews paid the price of being neutral."

"It is all changing, it is all changing," said Father Frade. "You'll see—all of you. There are no more references to perfidious Jews, we do not bend the knee to mock them. The entire relationship of Church and Jew is being re-examined, and we shall all be better men for it." With almost childish poignancy he appealed to all of them—Bolli, Sweeney, the American woman—to believe him, to have faith in *his* faith.

257

"Let us hope so," Bolli said, as he got up. "I am as much concerned for you, Father, and your faith, as I am for dead Jews." And with that enigmatic pronouncement the little man shook hands with his two visitors and advised them he was now required to meet with his colleagues—the patiently waiting contadini.

Melissa and Sweeney accompanied him down the room, walking past Bolli's wife, still at her typing, and the bearded young man. Melissa stopped and said to Bolli, "I should like to come here and work with you."

The reformer looked up at her. "What would you do?"

"Anything. Anything at all."

"Anything is nothing," Bolli said. "Do you have any skills? Are you an agronomist? A nurse? I have a staff of six people here, all volunteers. Our work is supported by donation. So the few people I employ must all be skilled. Kurt, the young man over there, an Austrian, is a soil expert. The woman you saw in the playground has had six years of experience as a nurse. My wife is a dietitian and a secretary. Two other men who are in the fields today are experts in animal husbandry."

"You make me feel useless," Melissa said.

"That is not my intention. I merely point out to you the realities of this kind of work. It is depressing, frustrating. I spent six months here before a farmer came to visit us. Eight months before any of these people would send a child to our school. We fight not only stupid governments, bad soil, venal police, two thousand years of ignorance, but worst of all, the resistance of the people we are trying to help."

"But I could do a lot of things. I can drive. I can take care of children . . . I could learn secretarial work." Sweeney was staring at her, his querying eyes popping from his burned face.

"I must be cruel with you, Mrs. Davies," Bolli said. "You are a woman of taste, good breeding, wealth. You are also intelligent, and your heart is not a selfish one. What you have seen today in Borracco, perhaps some of the things I have told you, have challenged you. You feel the need to help. It is a human, generous reaction. But your coming here, living as we do, spending each day in bafflement and defeat, this would do neither of us any good. Poor Schweitzer is forever besieged by rich ladies intent on cleaning up his operating room, and he is required to send them packing. I hope I am being politer than he generally is."

"Franco's right, Melissa," Sweeney said. "It ain't for us."

Never had she seemed more desirable to Sweeney. He wanted to cry for her, to offer his life to make her happy.

"Perhaps you're right, Mr. Bolli," she said. "An oversupply of fallen women coming to be shriven. Still, if you'd give me the chance—a day or two . . . a week with your people—"

"That would be impossible. If you wish, you and your friends may make a donation to our school program." He walked briskly to the peasant couple at the entrance.

As Sweeney and Melisssa walked past, the man, who had been seated with his arms tightly folded in his lap, rose and showed Bolli his right hand. It was wrapped in a blood-soaked rag. Bolli uttered a controlled gasp of disgust and with his wife's aid undid the makeshift bandage to reveal the man's mangled hand. The injury had evidently been sustained within the hour. Blood dripped onto the dusty floor in dark coin-sized pools. Bolli ordered his wife to summon the nurse. He shouted to the bearded agronomist to get the medical kit. Then he led the man to the back of the long room where Father Frade waited.

Bolli turned to face the departing Americans.

"He was injured by a thresher three hours ago and tried to take care of it himself. When he came here he would not interrupt us, but preferred, out of politeness, to bleed and nurse infection. Do you see what I mean?"

For a moment they stared at the serpentine line of dark bloodstains on the floor, then left to await the bus.

They rode back to Salerno across the same desolate hills, past the place where Sweeney's ripped pants had ended the attempt to arrest Bolli, then descended the parched fields into Salerno.

Melissa was silent for a long time. As they inched and honked through Salerno—it was early evening and the streets were jammed—she moved close to Sweeney. "Sweeney," she said, "I feel dreadful, put your arm around me."

"What's so bad?" he asked. "You should get a charge out of that guy Bolli. There's a man for you. Makes you glad you're alive."

"Does he? He makes me sick with myself."

"Ah, none of that, Melissa. You heard him. We can't all be like him, or his brother, or Helms, or the rest of those people."

"No," she said sadly. "But I wish to God we could be something *else*."

He held her tightly, Sweeney the comforter. But her sleek arms, her lean straight shoulders remained untouched.

It was dusk when they reached Salerno. Melissa suggested that they hire a motorboat to run them across the water to San Pietro del Golfo and then walk up to the Villa Malerba.

Already octopus fishermen were setting their nets across the sea. Their lights winked and glowed toward the horizon. The sky was mauve and maroon, ultramarine and turquoise. Sweeney thought the grandeur would make him swoon. He held Melissa's hand as they skimmed across the soft waters. Her palm was cold, inert. And so he retired, resting his suffering burned body against the thwart. For a while he wondered where he would light next, where he would secure finances, what he would tell Sherman Wettlaufer if and when his patron located him.

The skipper reduced the boat's motor to a decorous putt-putt as they approached the rickety dock. Sweeney looked at it with nostalgia. Once it had given him a bed for the night. He recalled the man in the rowboat who had taken him *al Cristo*. It seemed years ago.

"*Cristo Sotto-mare*," the boatman said, pointing below.

"He's an old friend of mine," Sweeney replied. "Me and the lady met down there."

The motorboat bumped politely against the wooden pier.

Sweeney knotted Melissa's scarf tighter around his ripped pants and jumped out, helping her to light.

Sweeney had never seen the little waterfront colony by night and the new vista charmed him. The Nettuno, the solitary café-bar, was open for business. Colored lanterns swung irregularly around its open façade, illuminating palms and sea-shrubs with lavenders and oranges. A few people lolled on the stony beach around a small fire, singing softly. A guitar twanged gently. Several fishermen awaiting an occasional tourist sat about their overturned craft.

"This is great, great!" Sweeney cried. "I love this place!" His elation melted the glacial gloom that had overcome her. "Hey!" he said, noticing her smile. "Let's have dinner here! On me!"

"On what, Sweeney? You're a gem. You can pay me back. It's my dinner. I know the owner and he'll make something special."

In Sweeney's marbled mind the world turned hopeful and happy. There would be dinner and wine with Melissa, a long night's untroubled sleep, and a bright new day. Perhaps he would bribe Nino to tell him where the tape recordings and the notes were hidden. Yes, he would find the tapes and the notes, send them airmail to Sherman with a long, explanatory, apologetic letter, resign from his post and look for a job or, better, another free-load. The future glowed—as uncomplicated and cheering as the gay lanterns festooning the Nettuno.

"Buona sera, buona sera, Signora Davies!" The owner, a stout man in a stained apron, was ecstatic. He knew class when he saw it. Melissa was proprio elegante, the kind of straniera he adored.

Waltzing, he escorted them to a table overlooking the harbor, from which they could gaze on the glory.

"A special dish for you, Signora!" the owner chortled. "Dentice aglio e olio—"

"Does that sound good, Sweeney?" she asked as they sat down.

But Sweeney was deaf, senseless. He was staring at a table opposite them. There was a lone diner seated at it, his back to them. A huge black American briefcase rested on the adjoining chair. One almost got the impression that the briefcase was his

261

dining companion, that he would slip it bits of *linguini marinara* or *calamari fritti* and pour red wine down its leather maw. The man was rather heavy-set, blondish, not at all dressed for the zestful informality of San Pietro. He wore an iridescent dark blue suit, a white shirt, a pale blue tie, black shiny pumps. With his heavy briefcase, his sedate dress, he might have been a lost insurance salesman.

"Sweeney, what are you goggling at?" Melissa asked.

But the former agent of the Wettlaufer Foundation was retreating sneakily toward the trellised archway at the entrance to the restaurant. He tippy-toed backwards, a finger to his lips warning Melissa to be silent.

The solitary diner turned to summon the waiter. "Ah . . . waiter . . . garçon, if you please?" he asked pleasantly. "A little butter and a bit more bread?"

And he saw Sweeney skulking off—Sweeney his beloved friend, his agent, his saviour. The diner rose—puzzled, delighted, fulfilled—and Melissa knew at once it was the magical Wettlaufer, the great benefactor. Only Wettlaufer could have had that pained, winsome look, that attitude of apology, explanation, forgiveness.

"Buck! Buck, my buddy!" he cried.

"Nope. Wrong person." Sweeney kept retreating. "No spikka da English." He raced under the trellis and across the stony beach, past the fishermen. A mighty leap propelled him onto the dock. The motorboat which had just brought him to San Pietro was pushing off with a passenger for Salerno. Too late, Sweeney shouted at the skipper to wait.

"All out for the running broad jump!" yelled Sweeney. But track and field had never been his forte. He missed the boat by a yard and hit the soft loving waters with less grace than the diving horse on the Atlantic City steel pier.

262

PART 4

SHERMAN WETTLAUFER

A BOLD SUICIDAL IMPULSE SENT SWEENEY FREE-STYLING OUT TO sea. That was it! He would die rather than face Sherman, die as Melissa looked on weeping. Ah, the glory of it! They would lay his waterlogged body on a slab in the Sfondrini Chapel and the little children of San Pietro would place palm leaves on his chest.

Although the Mediterranean was as warm as mulled wine, and the night clear and gentle, he quickly tired of both swimming and his conceit. His lifeguarding days at Orchard Beach were far behind him. After a dozen Australian crawl strokes (he was just short of *Cristo Sotto-mare*) he surfaced, gasping and spewing water like a whale calf.

"Buck! Buck, you crazy Irishman!" He could hear Wettlaufer calling for him—not angrily, not hurt, but with bald delight. Melissa was standing next to the benefactor, and the sight of her cool white figure propelled Sweeney into a few show-off butterfly strokes. The exertion brought him to the pier in so weakened a condition as to preclude lifting himself up.

In the moonlight he saw Wettlaufer's monstrous silver cufflinks winking at him with glandular initials: SSW. *The good ship Wettlaufer.* The freckled hand of the millionaire hauled Sweeney topside. He cowered on the dock, his lungs heaving.

"Oh, you nutty wildman," Sherman laughed, hugging Sweeney's quivering form to his blue silk suit. "What a stunt to pull on your best friend!"

All three walked back to the Nettuno to finish their interrupted dinner. When Sweeney introduced Melissa to Wettlaufer, his patron burbled with admiration. Leave it to that operator Sweeney to come up with a connection like *that!* The long day's journey to Bolli had not diminished Melissa's loveliness. Her skin was unmarred, her features fresh.

As Sweeney excused himself to borrow the proprietor's bathrobe (he had left a puddle the size of Lake George on the restaurant floor) Sherman tried to identify this handsome companion of his old friend.

"Ah, Melissa Davies. Yes, I have certainly heard of you. In fact I was once approached by your husband—Buster Davies, isn't he?—to participate in a syndicate he was forming. Natural gas. I'm sorry to say other obligations prevented me from accepting."

"You were lucky, Mr. Wettlaufer," she said.

"Was I? Buster Davies was the man with the golden touch. The boy financial wizard of Wall Street."

"Mr. Wettlaufer, he was a *thief,*" Melissa said smiling. "You knew that all the time. From what I've heard about you from Sweeney you'd be much too honest and intelligent to throw in with Buster. And he isn't my husband any longer."

"*Touché*, Mrs. Davies. Forgive me. I remembered you from the society pages and made the connection with Buster, and in my eagerness to impress you I forgot all about his, his, ah, irregularities with the SEC."

"I think you were trying to be kind."

Wettlaufer blushed like a flattered child, then beamed as he saw Sweeney return, cocooned in a white cotton robe. The field agent sat down and Wettlaufer grabbed his arm.

"Dinner's on me. I want to hear everything. Buck, right off, no hard feelings because you haven't been contacting me. I know you've been so busy you just haven't been able to organize yourself. Right?"

"Not exactly, Sherm. Jesus, I need a brandy. That water was colder than I thought. I got a bad chill."

"Yes, yes, waiter, *garçon!*" Wettlaufer cried. Linguistic failings undid him, and Melissa's impeccable Italian rescued him.

"It would be rude of us to get right down to business," said Sherman, "especially with such charming company. Are you on vacation here, Mrs. Davies?"

"I'm staying at my uncle's villa. Sweeney's our guest."

For some reason this tickled Wettlaufer, who nudged Sweeney in his aching short ribs. "Still the old hell raiser, hey, Bucky?"

"As a matter of fact, Sherm, I'm getting to be a drag."

"Don't needle your old CO, pal." He punched Sweeney playfully, almost knocking him from his chair. "When you hit the water out there, I swear, I was back in England. Oh, those nights, giving the MP's a run for their money—running across cabbage fields with a bottle of hard cider in one hand and a ground sheet in the other!" Sherman laughed uncontrollably, until tears flooded his tanned chubby face.

Glum, pained, Sweeney could not share his remembrances. To begin with he was in agony, convinced he had dislocated his spine in the leap from the pier. His sunburn was obviously more than sunburn—perhaps a severe case of *herpes zoster*. In addition, Sherman's camaraderie was pumping him full of guilt. Never had it been more evident to Sweeney how much he—bootless, undisciplined, penniless—meant to that terrified rich man.

"I'd better get up to the villa," Melissa said. "I know you and Sweeney have a lot of ground to cover."

"Do stay, Mrs. Davies!" Sherman was on his mannerly feet. "Has Buck told you about the Legion? It's very thrilling, isn't it?"

"It is. One finds so little in the world to admire wholeheartedly, without reservation. All of those people, like that man Bolli we met today, they rather convince you there's hope for all of us."

"Precisely! Precisely!" cried Sherman. "Mixing work with play, hey Bucky?"

Melissa excused herself. Wettlaufer looked at her slim figure as she departed for the footpath and sighed in admiration.

"Ah, to be single for a little while—not that I don't love Lil more every day. Buck, I have to hand it to you."

But Sweeney was having none of his patron's praise. He had retreated deep within the old white bathrobe like an invalided pensioner in a Veteran's Hospital. "Sherm," he said hoarsely, "I'm gonna break your heart."

"Impossible." Wettlaufer was chewing on a crispy *fritto misto del golfo*. "What is this stuff?"

"Squid."

"Wow! Lil should see me now. She'd hit the roof. You know she keeps a kosher house?"

"Sherm, I've blown the survey. It ran away from me."

"Nonsense." Wettlaufer did not seem at all perturbed. "Why you were out seeing someone today, Mrs. Davies said, somebody named Bolli. I have absolute confidence in you."

Sweeney put a hand on Wettlaufer's dark blue shoulder. "I just can't convince you I'm a no-good bum. Allie Cooperstein's mother would call me a *trombonik*."

268

With another belt of brandy in him he proceeded to outline his adventures from the day he had talked to Father Louis Des-Moulins, the old forger, to his current impasse at Villa Malerba.

"I am more inspired than ever to consummate this project," Sherman said firmly, when Sweeney concluded. "This man Stonebreaker who has impeded your progress can be handled."

"I ain't inspired any more, Sherm; there was this painting I saw in the museum in Amsterdam. It was called 'Christ Preaching in the House of Mary and Martha.' And the whole foreground of the picture, maybe three-fourths of the canvas, is a kitchen in one of them Dutch houses, and there's a cook plucking chickens. All around her there's dead rabbits, pheasants, turkeys, ducks, sides of beef, six kinds of fish, clams, oysters, potatoes, apples, eggplant, kohlrabi, rutabaga, carrots, Swiss chard, and God knows what else. Food, food, food. And where's Christ? Well, way back in a little alcove off the kitchen, there He is, with the women, preaching. Who cares about Him, when everyone wants to stuff their gut with rabbit and turkey? Who hears His sermon, when there's lots of roast duck and fried oysters?"

"What in the world has that to do with our survey?" asked Wettlaufer.

"Sherman, you and me and this survey and these people like Huguette Roux and Willem Kruis—we're preaching way back in the corner to two people. But most of the world is in that kitchen drooling over those rabbits and geese!"

"I happen to disagree, but, even if that were true, it would not deter me. All the more reason for making known the good of which men are capable. But go on, tell me why you've lost heart in the survey."

"It was after I talked to Helms. He made my flesh creep. All the decent things didn't balance out the lousy things that got done."

"But that is always the case, Buck."

"Nah, not like this deal. Sherm, I know we been killing Jews for a long time and I ain't responsible for every guy who gets *kike*

269

hollered at him, but look who thought it up! Look who invented it and kept it going!"

"Who, who?" cried Wettlaufer.

"Sherm—the *organization*, the old Church! All of 'em—popes, bishops, St. Louis, and Luther, and a whole bunch of cats who should have known better!"

"*I reject that out of hand!*" shouted Sherman, so explosively that the Nettuno's waiters and guests stared. "I do not accept that, and it is not part of our survey! All such opinions, Buck, are to be kept to yourself. They are never to find their way into your reports to me! How in heaven's name did such an issue ever arise? I did not send you out to condemn the Christian religion! Quite the opposite."

"Ah, I'm sorry, Sherm," muttered Sweeney. "Some little rat of a Belgian atheist started me off. He kept bugging me. I hired him as an interpreter, but he kept sticking his two cents in."

"Whoever he was he did you no service. What a fantasy! Now I forbid you, Buck, in the name of our old friendship, to accept this notion. There is nothing in Christianity that can remotely be connected with Buchenwald, and that is an end of it."

"Yeah, if you say so, Sherm."

"History says so."

"Right. Well, by the time I got through with Helms I'd heard enough. So I went on the booze and I lost a lot of your money shooting craps in a joint called San Remo, and here I am Stonebreaker's prisoner, with him keeping the tapes and telling me I'm part of the Hate Germany plot."

Wettlaufer dabbed at his lips. "I am at a loss to understand Mr. A. C. Stonebreaker's attitude. He was one of the great radicals of my youth. A Communist, it was said. I assume the man is unbalanced. To think . . . he was once the voice of Marxist revolution! But if you think he'll deter us, Buck, you're mistaken. We can always get those interviews taped again."

"Except Helms. He'll never talk again."

"No matter. You will recall his testimony and dictate it."

Sweeney shook his wet head. "Nope. I'm out. I can't take it. I mean, who'd have thought all that harmless stuff about killing Christ would have led to Auschwitz?" A deep original thought struck Sweeney and he sat upright. "Hey, *somebody* had to kill Him. I mean the Jews kind of performed a historical function. Like, He couldn't have died of old age sitting around like a genial Senior Citizen with a long white beard. There'd never have been a Christian religion. So why get sore at the Jews? They helped make the scene."

Wettlaufer was shocked, indignant. "You are a dreadful theologian, Buck. What a nonsensical notion! I must ask you to cleanse your mind of these wild dreams of yours. They are irrelevant and harmful and untrue. Besides, I am reliably informed that the Vatican will soon absolve us of this old charge. As I suspected all along, we certainly did not kill Him. At least most of us didn't."

"Yeah, but the pardon's too late for a lot of people."

"*Stop that!* I insist, Bucky, for your own peace of mind, that you abandon this foolish theorizing! I want you to remain with the survey. But you will make it difficult for me if you keep harping on this subject."

"Sherman, lose me. I caused you enough trouble."

Wettlaufer called for a check. He was pensive, mapping a new move. "Now, then, how shall we proceed?" he asked. "We shall meet Mr. Stonebreaker forthwith and demand the tapes and the notes. Whether he returns them or not does not really concern me. But I will certainly threaten him with legal action. Then you and I shall proceed to Rome."

"And my home," said Sweeney.

"Oh no. To summon the Legion of Noble Christians."

Sweeney reached for the brandy and drank deeply. *The Summoning of the Legion of Noble Christians.* It had a cockeyed unbelievable quality like the memorable sign in the Sherlock Holmes story: "The Redheaded League is Dissolved."

"How are you gonna summon 'em?" Sweeney asked. "By blowing the *shofar?*"

"Let me be candid, Buck. During your absence, when you failed to write me or to report on your progress, I grew uneasy. I decided the survey needed reinforcing. So I engaged a research and polling organization, Whitlock & Gates, to take over the survey on a professional basis. Buck, you will of course be retained as a consultant. Jerry Whitlock is in Rome right now making arrangements. He's really a swell guy, a down-to-earth chap, even though he's a Ph.D."

"You should have done that in round one," Sweeney admitted sadly. "I'm an amateur, Sherm."

Immediately Sweeney resented that Protestant-sounding bloodless organization that would pick up his flickering torch. Whitlock & Gates, hah! Would Jerry Whitlock, Ph.D. (probably a pipechewer), ever challenge the head of the Brussels Communist youth movement to a mussel-eating contest? Would Mr. Gates ever fall down in the dirt with Franco Bolli's workers and get carried off by Italian cops? And would either of those two gents, Whitlock or Gates, ever lay on the steps of the Hamburg synagogue and remember the punch line from *The Informer? Never!* But they would do the job for Sherman, whom he had betrayed.

"Yes, after summoning the members we are calling a press conference," Wettlaufer said, "to announce the formation of the Legion. We are getting wonderful co-operation from a lot of people, including the Eastern Europeans—the Soviets, Hungary, Poland. Many of your old friends will be there."

Sweeney sulked. He had abdicated, but he resented his successors.

"Don't look so glum, Buck. Every scrap of information you gathered will be useful. I'm working on a title for you—Chief Consultant or Managing Director."

They began the trek up the path to Villa Malerba. Wettlaufer marched fiercely, inspired by the soft beautiful night. He never stopped for breath. Sweeney, burned, battered, brimming with self-pity, had to plead for several halts along the way.

Wettlaufer availed himself of the ascent to fill Sweeney in on events in East Redfield. The dispute over the presence of God, religion, and nativity scenes in the public schools was only simmering, apparently far from boiling. Advisory committees had been set up and were hard at work keeping everyone happy. For example, the committee on Christmas music had come to a brilliant solution. Christmas songs were to follow a 5–3–1 ratio on the order of the London Naval Disarmament Conference. That is to say, for every five truly religious songs ("Hark the Herald," etc.) the children would sing three nonreligious songs ("White Christmas," etc.) and one for Chanukah. Admittedly there weren't many Chanukah songs available, but some were being written.

"This seemed to please most parties," Wettlaufer said. "The funny thing is Chanukah is a minor holiday. Nothing compared to Yom Kippur or even a Sabbath. And I am wondering myself, why holler about it in school? If the Christians wish to observe these diluted semireligious affairs in school why complain? It has no real religious intensity and I think it even tends to generalize and to blunt the religious impulse. So I am not opposing it. Let them have their way."

"Yeah," gasped Sweeney, "and don't I know where them intense ungeneralized impulses lead."

As for his persecution at the hands of Leo Parnell Sweeney's associates it had died down. There was a spell of it after the frenzied meeting that lasted a month or so—obscene calls, false fire alarms, hate letters. "It is odd, Buck, how these people who protest their belief in God, their deep religious dedication, find it necessary to use the vilest language imaginable to argue their points."

Certain local ministers had become outraged when they learned of the attacks on Sherman, and they had spoken from the pulpit denouncing them. A few of his Continental Can and Cluett & Peabody neighbors had rallied to his side. The local newspaper, a conservative Republican journal, ran an editorial condemning the people who were after him. "But I bet none of 'em told you to tell 'em screw off in the middle of the night, hey Sherm?" asked Sweeney.

Wettlaufer smiled sheepishly. The old fears still agitated him. But he was not afraid the way he once was. He had a deep and abiding faith in America and was prouder than ever to be an American. He had been overwrought, distracted, the night he had confessed his fears to Sweeney, but he was calmer now, more sure of himself, his country. Still . . .

And he told Sweeney that sometimes in the middle of the night he would tiptoe into the boys' room to make sure they were still there, his happy American boys, not seized and taken off to some terrible death. "It is stupid of me, Buck, but I shall be like this all my life."

They reached the last terrace. Through the aromatic groves, dark blue-green in the night, Wettlaufer saw the villa. He was impressed, a bit apprehensive.

"We come to beard the lion in his den," he said.

Did Sweeney detect a note of querulousness in his voice? A hesitancy to confront the Grand Reactionary? All through their conversation that evening he had been impressed with Wettlaufer's firmness, his decisiveness. His steel had been tempered in the fires of the East Redfield School Board. But could it withstand Stonebreaker's savage intellect? It occurred to Sweeney, with a coward's intuition, that Stonebreaker might destroy his friend. Leo Sweeney and his supporters were fools and bumblers after all, and they had almost carved out Wettlaufer's heart. How much more vulnerable he would be to A. C. Stonebreaker—glib, convincing, assailing him with his relentless knowledge of history, of great events, of the grim future course of the world! And for a moment Sweeney was frightened also, fearful that he was not much of an ally.

"Sherm," he said, "you got to be careful the lion don't eat you up."

"I have no fear of Mr. A. C. Stonebreaker. After all the man is an intellectual, a creative person. I am sure I can reason with him."

274

A bad sign, Sweeney realized. Wettlaufer would be rational and therefore would anticipate a rational response. He would be skewered and flayed by Stonebreaker's lunatic intransigence.

They padded across the lawn to the great villa. It was a peaceful dome, a palace designed to give the heart rest. At the doorway Sweeney paused. He turned to Wettlaufer.

"Sherm, before we go in, I got to ask you to remember something. How long has it been since you thought of Sergeant Garvis Turpin?"

Wettlaufer frowned. "Who?"

"Garvis Turpin, one-time head of your motorpool in the 997th Ordnance Company when we were in England and you were Captain Wettlaufer and I was Private Sweeney."

"Oh, that Turpin! Yes, the fellow from Alabama who ran the crap games and the bootlegging until we stopped him."

"You stopped him, but that is not why I brought his name up. Don't be evasive, Sherman. I want you to remember what happened one cold day in the English midlands. I want you to recall a small drama involving you and me and Garvis Turpin."

"It hardly seems necessary at this moment."

"It is obligatory," Sweeney said. "And since you seem hesitant I'll recall it for you. Sherman Wettlaufer, you were the most unhappy, miserable, persecuted commanding officer in the United States Army. You were humiliated every day by enlisted men from Bat's Ass, Mississippi, and Warm Crotch, Georgia. You were insulted by your fellow officers and ignored by First Sergeant Phipps, a tobacco-chewing possum-eating drunkard from Raccoon Dropping, South Carolina. Do not deny it. You sat in your tent all day staring at Lillian's photograph and wondering why they all hated you. I will tell you why. Because you were polite, considerate, helpful, friendly, from New York, and Jewish."

Wettlaufer flinched. "All that may be true but I see no reason to revive old—"

Sweeney ignored him, maneuvering him against the yellow stuccoed wall. "You will listen to me exorcise these old devils, Sherm. The worst rats in that company were the drivers, led by old

Garvis Turpin, a conniving ridge-runner who once proudly told me he had a Bertillon on file in six states.

"May I set the scene for you? It was a bitter cold March in rural England. I was digging a latrine near the motorpool, by order of the first sergeant who realized that since I was from New York, like you, I was not to be trusted.

"Enter Captain Wettlaufer, a man ostracized and browbeaten daily by illiterate sons of the soil. He asks Sergeant Turpin for a jeep. Turpin allows as how the jeeps are all out of commission. Captain Wettlaufer replies that cannot be because he just saw a company jeep leave the post and there were two English girls giggling in the back. At which point Turpin, to the accompanied sneers of his motorpool drivers, says in flawless Appalachian, 'Yew callin' me a liar, Cap'n, and whaar ah comes from, yew call a man a liar, yew better git ready to fight him.' "

"Yes, yes, I remember that whole unpleasant business, Buck," Sherman said sadly. "How could I forget it?"

"You stood there and let them snigger and snort their folkloric obscenities. Of course you would never fight an enlisted man. Not you. Not honorable, decent Captain Wettlaufer. And as you turned to walk away, a ruined man, I heard Turpin advise his associated pellagra sufferers, 'He's chicken, plain chicken-shit, lak all his kind.' "

"He was not a nice person," Sherman said weakly.

"And now," said Sweeney, "you finish the story. What happened then?"

"Oh, it's all clear as day," Wettlaufer said. "I walked past you, down in that hole digging a latrine. I barely knew you then, Buck. You were just a private, a faceless man named Sweeney. And you came clambering out of the latrine and stopped me. I must say I was surprised."

"You remember what I told you?"

"Of course." Sherman grinned. "You said I had to go back and belt Sergeant Turpin on the chops, not because you cared about me especially or wanted to help poor persecuted Jewish officers, but because we were both Bronx boys, New York innocents surrounded by sheep-screwers. You convinced me with your last admonition: I had to fight Turpin, for *the honor of the block*."

"Right!" Sweeney cried. "Jesus, I never did see a guy fold the way he did. You slapped him once and he cried a little, and then you slapped him again harder and he went down. Sherm, I knew you had the moxie all the time. I'd of never sent you into the ring unless I knew you were a sure thing. Turpin'd had the clap twice that month and was obviously the victim of a bad childhood diet. And I'd seen you run around a basketball court without getting winded. Sweeney don't back losers."

"Ah, that was so long ago. Buck, I would be the last to deny it changed me, changed me completely. They respected me in the 997th Ordnance after that."

"You're damn right they did. Thanks to Sweeney."

They entered the tiled foyer.

"And one more thing I want you to remember before we sit down with Ballbreaker," Sweeney whispered.

"I fail to see why you keep connecting this old incident with our mission tonight, Buck."

"Never mind. Leave it to Father Sweeney. Do you remember what I told you to do before you socked Turpin? Do you recall the ritual I prescribed?"

"No. I just remember you practically shoving me by the seat of the pants back to the motorpool. . . . Wait, wait! I remember!" Wettlaufer laughed softly. "Oh, how comical, what a notion! Yes, I remember!"

"You bet your mutual funds you do."

"Yes, just before I hit Turpin, you made me tap him on the shoulder and recite an old Bronx street rhyme, one that summoned up all kinds of marvelous memories for me—

> "Three, six, nine,
> A bottle of wine,
> I can fight you
> Any old time!"

Sweeney nodded his approval. "Now you're ready," he said. "He can't hurt you, . . . I think."

In the living room Mrs. Ferrante and Mrs. Halberstadt were playing canasta. A copy of the Pompeian bronze of Mercury, god of thieves, stood watch over them.

"Hello there," said Frances Ferrante. She was as edible as ever, if a bit worn. Nino had done his duty after they had returned from Borracco. Yet even in her weariness Sweeney found her sensual. He spent a moment in admiration of the emphatic white bags under her eyes, as synthetic as her nose, eyes, mouth, hair, bust, behind. The pouches looked like two uncooked supermarket frozen blintzes, attached with Scotch tape. How he envied that serf Nino!

"Hi, girls," Sweeney said. "Like you to meet an old pal, Mr. Sherman Wettlaufer, a big man in Wall Street. Sherm, say hello to Frances Ferrante and Cecile Halberstadt, a couple of great broads from Chicago."

Wettlaufer greeted them. The exotic grandeur of the villa, the high charm of Mrs. Davies, neither of these meshed with the two aging cosmeticized canasta players. The villa was romance, adventure. These two looked like his wife's relatives in Newark.

"Where's Stonebreaker?" asked Sweeney.

"He don't want to be disturbed," Frances said, not looking up.

"That ain't what I asked."

"Oh, upstairs."

"Well, I got to change from this Salvation Army bathrobe. Sherm, grab a sofa and a magazine but not the girls. A few dirty jokes are okay but no passes."

As he trudged up the stairs, Sweeney's terrible exhaustion devoured him. He was not merely tired. He had contracted some wasting disease—muscular dystrophy, myasthenia gravis, maybe acute infectious mononucleosis. He craved sleep—dumb, drugged, snoring sleep.

In the dark corridor he was seized by vertigo, so he rested

278

against a stuccoed wall and then stumbled toward his room. The narrow hallways confused him. As in all Italian homes—rich, poor—the maximum wattage for hallways was fixed at 15. He could barely see.

Blundering about, he heard voices. The voices were low, conversational. A moment's concentration, the practiced listening of an old Paul Pry, enabled him to distinguish first Stonebreaker's firm baritone, then Melissa's softer voice.

Sweeney followed his pointing ears to one of the great wooden doors. The transom above was open; a faint light issued from it. His ears quivered trying to catch words, but they came to him mashed, indistinct.

". . . no right to take advantage . . . we won't . . ."

". . . to act reasonably . . . you did promise, Melissa . . ."

An incurable snoop, Sweeney was ravaged with curiosity. After all, the conversationalists were deeply involved with him. He was certain he was in love with Melissa (a hopeless love, but all the more romantic for that). As for her uncle, he was about to challenge him to a few more rounds of gab. His schemer's eye searched the corridor and discovered an antique wooden chest. Tiptoeing in his soaked espadrilles, he attempted to lift it and felt something snap in his spine, something stretch in his bowels. A vertebra had separated; hernia of the sigmoid flexure was indicated. Quietly he removed the wooden drawers, then summoning up his last fraction of muscle lifted the antique and lugged it, lungs afire, heart blasting, to the door.

The coronary he had long feared had come at last. He rested on top of the chest, attempting to suffocate his monstrous windy gasps. Then he climbed the chest. It was not quite high enough for him to see through the transom. But he heard more clearly now.

". . . we've discussed this so often, Andy . . ."

". . . have gone running off and tiring yourself to see that fellow Bolli . . . get rid of Sweeney . . ."

". . . blame him, it was my idea . . . nothing to do with . . ."

". . . forget everything and try again . . ."

By stretching his right leg as high as he could, standing on his toes like a male ballerina in a PTA musical, Sweeney was able to anchor the side of his left foot on the upper hinges. This purchase permitted him to grip a side of the transom with his left hand. It was a position calculated to torment every moving part of his body from his sternocliedomastoid to his Achilles tendon. But he clung to his perch with grim courage, and was rewarded with a clear view of Melissa's room. He could also hear the conversation.

Melissa was resting on her bed propped against the bolster. She wore a white dressing gown, her feet were bare. Her face was bland, noncommital. If she were upset she betrayed her unease only in her hands, clasped severely below her breast. In the half-light her marvelously proportioned face, with its emphatic angles and planes, was more dramatically charged with beauty than ever.

Stonebreaker was seated in a wing-backed chair to her left. As usual he had that capacity for advertising his patronality by the very manner in which he occupied a chair. But he was also some-what tense, strained. He wore his pale blue kimono and sat well forward in the chair. His large bullish head was thrust forward, too, and his barrel of a body seemed ready to spring. In one arm he cradled a bottle of gin, holding it like a halfback starting an end run. A momentary fear shivered Sweeney. He was not especially proud of his peeping.

"Andy, I'm leaving," Melissa said.

"I won't let you. You know what will happen. You'll be in the hospital in a week. Hysterics, withdrawal symptoms. It almost killed you last time."

"I'm not sure I care."

"You can't go to Paris or New York. You're better off here."

"I'll go to work with Bolli."

"That is insupportable nonsense. You'd last a day up there in those hills. He won't have you anyway. Give the Communists that much credit—they know who can help them and who can't."

"But I won't stay here."

"You'll destroy yourself if you leave."

"Maybe that's inevitable. For God's sake, Andy, turn me loose, let me drink all I want and let's have an end of it."

Stonebreaker drew his breath in, his pigeon's chest inflated.

"You are too precious to me. I've told you that so many times, my darling. You're the only woman, the only person that's ever mattered to me."

She turned her head away—a wan hopeless gesture. Sweeney called some gods unknown for help, any kind of help.

Melissa sat up in bed, swinging her legs over the side. "Andy, let me have a drink. One."

The calf muscles in Sweeney's tortured limbs shrieked. But with a courage that amazed him, he clung to his perch.

Stonebreaker inched forward. His voice was thick, frosted. "I will, darling, if you honor our agreement."

"I'm sorry, Andy. I can't. Not any more."

"But you agreed. We've been through this a dozen times, and it's been satisfactory to us both. I must insist that you honor it."

"It hasn't been satisfactory to me. At least not the part that satisfies you."

"Did it disgust you?"

"No. It does nothing to me. I have no reactions to anything except alcohol . . . or on very rare occasions, like this afternoon, my conscience."

"I should have prevented you from going there."

Melissa held a pleading arm out toward her uncle. "Andy, don't sit there cuddling that bottle as if it were a child. Let me have it."

"Only if you agree."

"No."

Sweeney's throat constricted; his bowels gurgled.

"Melissa, Melissa, you've always been my little child." Stonebreaker's words came out blurred, strangled. "Always. You sat on my knee and stroked my head—and with such knowing hands, such wise, warm hands for a child. There were no secrets from you. I've never loved anyone but you, and I shall always love you. I ask you only to return that love."

"I can't."

"But you have already, many times."

"Andy, how you deceive yourself. *Love.* It was a favor returned for your boozy bribes, for doling out to me what I need more than anything. Andy, I'm so far gone I can't even feel disgust for us. You sit there dangling that bait in front of me like an old pervert showing lollipops to schoolgirls so he can pet their fannies. I'm worse. I'm the child who willingly, wantonly accepts the arrangement. Andy, how foul and rank we both are. And worst of all, how useless, aimless. . . ."

"I beg you. You can have all you want." It was a high-class English gin, Sweeney noted, as Stonebreaker held the bottle up. He had an impulse to shout at Stonebreaker: "You'd get the same results with Sterno!"

"Please, please, Melissa. I need you."

"Oh, to hell with that, Andy. Give me my drink. Just enough to let me sleep."

"I will if you agree."

"Tell that pot-bellied old bastard no!" Sweeney said to himself. "Let him go get his ashes hauled in Naples! Throw the Flit in his face! Break clean!"

Telepathy failed. She put her hands to her face and said, "What's the difference? Just let me drink. . . ."

Stonebreaker, with a mandarin flourish, stood up and walked toward her. "I knew you would, I knew it. Why do you resist me all the time? Haven't I made my love for you apparent, admitted it, confessed it?"

At that moment Sweeney's racked limbs surrendered. His left foot slipped from the hinge and his hand lost its grip on the transom. He hit the top of the chest like a bag of cabbages. Fearful that his criminal eavesdropping would be discovered he adopted a quick course of action, an easy one for him: he would

282

play the drunken fool. Rolling off the chest, he shoved it down the corridor into the gloom.

He hitched the belt of his poorhouse bathrobe and pounded his rope-soled feet on the stone floor, singing:

> Lulu had a baby
> She named him Sunny Jim
> She threw him in a piss-pot
> To teach him how to swim!

Then he pounded his fists against the door, singing loudly, yet on key, straight into the chorus:

> He swam to the bottom
> He swam to the top
> Lulu got excited
> And pulled him by the
> Cocktail, ginger ale
> Five cents a glass . . .

"Anybody home?" Sweeney bellowed. "Whass goin' on here? Sweeney's home. Ole Sweeney, Christian Noble Legion. Noble Goy."

He rattled the great bronze knob, kicking the door. The kicks seemed to fracture several toes; he had forgot he was wearing soft espadrilles. "Slips!" shouted Sweeney. "I'll be in a cast for weeks. Hey, Stoney! You got a guest. Colonel Wettlaufer, Chief Legionnaire, is here. Up and at 'em Stoney!"

He sang again:

> I only want a discharge . . . 'r'furlough
> Furloughs only make me blue
> Furloughs are great, but they bring back
> Memories of a life that I once knew . . .

A fine tenor, as good as one could hear in Jim Sweeney's saloon of a Saturday night. Sweeney sang fully, open-throated, thinking of James Joyce joining in the "Marseillaise" in a French café during the war, his clear Irish pipes drawing applause and admiration from the natives.

The door opened and Stonebreaker appeared. Sweeney had read somewhere that all writers are frustrated actors. The actor in Stonebreaker was ascendant. He was calm and aloof, skillfully hiding whatever malevolence he felt toward the intruder. Melissa sat on the edge of the bed. She was smiling. Sweeney twinkled two fingers at her in greeting. It was a small victory, or as the New York *Daily News* might have put it: *When Justice Triumphed.*

"Stoney, I hate to butt in but Mr. Wettlaufer wants his tapes. Ah, caught you with the Flit in your hand. A solitary gin drinker! My old man used to call them the real professionals."

"You lout," Stonebreaker said. "Get out of my house at once."

"Andy, Sweeney's broke, he's got no place to go," Melissa said.

"His friend Wettlaufer can take care of him. Go on, leave, or I'll call the *carabinieri*."

"Wettlaufer's got to see you," Sweeney insisted.

"I've got no business with that moron. Both of you go."

"Gimme the tapes."

"I've destroyed them. Burned, buried."

"Don't believe you," Sweeney said. "But if you have, be advised that Mr. Wettlaufer is initiating legal action against you. You will be sued from beam to butt. Let me tell you about Sherman, Stoney. He's a lot richer than you. He's got a company full of high-priced lawyers whom he hasn't used yet. You'll get hit with all of them."

"You're a liar. He wouldn't dare sue me. And for what? A lot of sob stories?"

"Come on down and find out. I know you're loaded, Andy, but he's got more. Besides, he owns his own home. He don't need no hoodlum's wife to set him up."

Without a word to his niece Stonebreaker closed the door and stepped outside. His eyes were flat, cold. "How did you know I was in here?"

"Sharp ears."

Sweeney twisted his mouth, like a Tammany Hall doorkeeper imparting secrets to a newspaperman. "The old hipper-dipper,

Andy. A little foghorn to warn ships that pass in the night. I wanted you to come out but didn't want to embarrass nobody. Catch?"

But Stonebreaker had walked away from him briskly down the stairs. He went at once to his study. Sweeney summoned Sherman from the living room.

Wettlaufer was introduced. Sweeney observed a curious tilt to Stonebreaker's jaw, a firmness in his posture, a swiftness to his gestures. He was saying to Wettlaufer: "Me arts, you trade."

"I've been a great admirer of yours for many years," Sherman said. "I'll never forget that poem you wrote about Sacco and Vanzetti in *New Left Ideas*."

"They were both guilty, those wops. There's new evidence that seems to clinch that. What were you doing reading *New Left Ideas?*"

"What were you doing writing for it, Mr. Stonebreaker?"

"I've reformed. I doubt that you have."

Sherman laughed noisily. "I was in high school then. A lot of radicalism was going around, not that I was ever a Red or anything. I guess someone lent it to me."

"I see. An early infection. I'm afraid it's still in your system. That's a shame."

The man was as nutty as a crate of Goldenberg's Peanut-Chews, Sweeney thought to himself. Having just been deprived of sex he was invigorated by the prospect of holding audience once more, of terrorizing, enlightening, dominating Sherman Wettlaufer just as he had manipulated Sweeney the night before.

"Mr. Wettlaufer, since you are my guest may I make a request of you before we get down to the matter of those tapes?"

"I am at your disposal, sir."

"I'd like to run a saliva test on you to determine where you stand. You won't be insulted?"

Wettlaufer drew himself up in his chair. Sweeney was never prouder of his old commanding officer. "Mr. Stonebreaker, I am chairman of the board of a prospering corporation which I built with my own energy and imagination. Our assets are well over twenty million dollars and our products are sold in forty-two foreign countries, at the last count, with branch offices in eight including West Germany, with whose government and business community I have enjoyed most amicable relations."

"Atta baby, Sherm!" Sweeney cried. "Hit 'em where they ain't! Throw him the hook!"

"Good. Now if you'll prevail upon your rude friend to control himself we'll proceed."

"Please, Buck," Sherman said.

"Now I realize you're a man of wealth," Stonebreaker said carefully. "But that hardly means you are free of the liberal virus. It infects the rich, too. Virus *liberalis* makes no distinctions."

"You regard liberalism as a disease?"

"A malignancy. A cancer eating us away. But let's move on. Now, this is almost like a free-association test. I'll shoot certain questions at you and you answer with the very first opinion that comes to your mind. Ready?"

"This sounds like fun," said Wettlaufer.

"Hell, I'm insulted," said Sweeney. "You didn't give me a test."

"You weren't worth it." Stonebreaker leveled a finger at Sherman. "Here we go. First. What was your opinion of Senator McCarthy?"

"Wh——" A vague caution impeded Wettlaufer's response.

"Faster, faster. Liberals never think, they just react."

"All right, he was a dangerous, reckless man who smeared people's reputations. Oh, basically he had a point. There were Communists in government and labor—"

"Stop. Never hedge that first liberal reaction. Now then, is censorship wrong?"

"Yes. If one believes in a free press—"

"Next. Do you approve of the United Nations?"

"Of course. I think it has its limitations, especially with all the new Afr——"

286

"No, Mr. Wettlaufer, never qualify your response. I liked that 'of course.' That was genuine liberal certainty."

Sweeney shifted anxiously. "He's putting you on, Sherm."

"Not at all," Wettlaufer said. "Go on, sir."

"Now, does everyone have the right to form a union or join one?"

"Certainly. It is one of the—"

"Stop right there. Should hotels and restaurants be forced to serve Negroes?"

"They should. There is an issue of property rights, but where human r——"

"Is colonialism wrong?"

"Ah, it had certain good aspects but in the over-all I am sure it was destructive. Besides, it just isn't workable any more whether the European—"

"Hmmm. A little off the mark. Does everyone have the right to vote?"

"Absolutely."

"That's more like it. There's the true liberal tropism, a blind wiggling toward the light. Try this. Should we seek accommodations with the Soviet Union?"

"I would think so. But we should keep our heads clear and our powder dry, and try to get a quid pro quo with—"

"You're hedging again. I'm disappointed. Do you believe in academic freedom at all times?"

"Certainly. When I was an undergrad at Syracuse—"

"No evidence needed. You're doing better. Try this. Is it government's responsibility to take care of the poor, aged, and unemployed?"

"Surely, if private groups can't."

"Perfect. Are quota systems for university admissions wrong?"

"They are. Gosh, when my wife's cousin wanted to go to med school—"

Stonebreaker held a hand up. "Are there differences in intelligence between the different races?"

"Well, I'm no expert, but—"

"That never stopped a liberal. Go on, Mr. Wettlaufer."

"—evidence from anthropologists seems to show that all races have the same potential, that culture and environment are—"

"Spare me the jargon. You've done wonderfully well." Stonebreaker's eyes twinkled. "Now for the clincher. Ready? What do you think of Mrs. Roosevelt?"

"She is the greatest woman of her time," Wettlaufer said.

"Bravo!" Stonebreaker pounded his desk. "Passed with honors! You're a true specimen of the genus *Liberalis*, with all its symptoms. All of which goes a long way toward explaining this blundering survey you've invested so much money in."

Sherman shifted in his deep chair. "It does not. My political views, which are not nearly as dogmatic as you assume, have nothing to do with the formation of the Legion. I launched it because the world needed an example of unqualified goodness."

"Why not a survey of Noble Christians who are resisting communism and are being murdered for their bravery?"

The query gave Sherman pause. "There is a lot of evil in the world, Mr. Stonebreaker, and it is not my responsibility to engage all of it. I have contributed to many worthy anticommunist causes such as Radio Liberty, Radio Free Europe, and missions of the Catholic Church, so I owe you no apologies. I am every bit as anticommunist as you are."

"Well, then, join me. Change the direction of your survey."

"No, sir. You are not merely anticommunist. You are against humanity."

"Humanity in the form of liberated cannibals eating White Christians?"

A formidable determination hardened Wettlaufer's normally lax face. "Yes, it would be typical of you to accuse me of favoring cannibalism and savagery. I assure you I do not. But as horrid as those black Africans are, as disgustingly as they have acted, they can at least plead ignorance. What, Mr. Stonebreaker, is the plea of the White Christians of Warsaw who came from mass on Sunday and cheered as the SS shot down the last of the ghetto Jews?"

288

Settling back in his tribunal chair Stonebreaker smiled, not without warmth. He had not anticipated such spunk. From Sweeney's descriptions he had conceived of Wettlaufer as an equivocating weakling, a man ashamed of his money. But this same Wettlaufer now sat before him unruffled, ready to dispute him through the night.

"Let us re-examine your survey," the host of Villa Malerba said. "I have no doubt that many Christians did applaud the murder of Jews and indeed actually committed the murders. But what good can repetition of such facts do?"

"We are not interested in bad deeds. We are concerned with the acts of noble Christians. Many were clergymen, sir. Our early research, as Buck knows, has revealed a very high percentage of priests, nuns, ministers among their ranks. But there were also lay persons, socialists, atheists, all sorts of people united only by the impulse to act decently."

"Communists, too?"

"I am certain there were. Mr. Stonebreaker, if you were being shipped to a gas chamber and a man offered to save you would you ask about his politics?"

"That's understandable. But I'm afraid it's put people like you in an embarrassing position."

Wettlaufer's cheeks pulsed faintly. "I beg your pardon?"

"Now don't misunderstand me. I've been through all of this with Sweeney. I am without prejudice, etcetera, etcetera, admire Jewish brains, creativity, and so on and so on. What I say I say honestly. It boils down to this. If atheistic communism is our sworn enemy, and pinko-lefto-liberalism is its cunning agent, we need every ounce of strength and intelligence to fight them. The only real ally we have is Germany. The rest of Europe is weak, its will killed by liberalism.

"So if people like you keep assaulting the public ear with these horror stories of babies being used for target practice by SS men how in heaven's name can we ever use the Germans to crush communism? No one will believe us."

"Who needs them?" Sweeney interjected. "Man, we got enough

nuclear stuff to kill every Roosky and every Chink five or six times. Who needs the Krauts for that?"

The host, shaking his round head sadly, ignored him. "How different history would have been if Hitler had only left the Jews alone! Then we would have let him crush Bolshevism. The Holy See was right in counseling moderation toward Germany. The choice was clear. Destroy Hitler and avenge the Jews, expose Europe and the world to the ravages of communism. Or, as it might have been, let the Jews serve as the *kippuroth*, the sacrifice, and save the world from Bolshevik tyranny."

A gasp came out of Wettlaufer as he tried to speak. Stunned, he looked helplessly at Sweeney who opened his palms, equally helpless.

"You . . . you . . . you are saying the Jews should have accepted their deaths . . . the furnaces . . . the naked women . . . the children shot in the head . . . and died happily? You can't mean it!"

"I do. A cruel judgment, but history is full of horrors which nonetheless brought about worthwhile results. Any sane person's heart goes out to the Jews. But look where it led. In our eagerness to crush Hitler . . . we reaped the whirlwind."

"I see. I see!" Wettlaufer cried. "We are guilty of rejecting a historical role!"

"Precisely." Stonebreaker spun about in his chair. "There's still hope. Now, if the Soviets were to murder several million Jews we'd be able to destroy them!"

"Sir," said Sherman coolly, "you are in need of medical help. With all due respect for your past achievements and intellectual attainments, you require psychiatric attention. I have never heard anything so disgustingly brutal in my life."

"I intend to upset you further. I must convince you to abandon this survey. Your own salvation, nothing less, is at stake." Stonebreaker turned sideways in his chair. One eye, merry as Santa, winked at Wettlaufer. "People like yourself should buy a little insurance."

"What do you mean by that?" Sherman asked.

290

"I get it!" Sweeney shouted. "He wants you on his team!"

"Your parasitic friend is right," Stonebreaker said.

Wettlaufer sucked in his breath. "I would die before I associated with persons of your stripe."

Stonebreaker turned, clasped his hands professorially on the desk, and lowered his head. "You will be more likely to die if you spurn us. Ribbentrop once advised German diplomats and businessmen in the United States to spread the word to influential Jewish groups that if America, through Jewish prodding, entered the war Jews would be beaten to death in the streets of New York by indignant Americans—"

"It never happened!" Sherman cried. "I have more faith in my country than you. I am proud and grateful to be an American. You cite that conniving, cowardly wine salesman who got his just desserts on the gibbet!"

"You're too emotional," said Stonebreaker. "Look at this calmly. True, anti-Semitism was not noticeably intensified as a result of King Franklin's war, . . . but are you so certain you'll be saved *next time?*"

"No!" shouted Sherman, jumping to his feet. "You are insane! You are a monster!"

"I cased him last night, Sherm," Sweeney said. "He's queer for death. He ain't happy unless a couple of million people are getting it."

"There's still hope," Stonebreaker said. "Particularly for men of wealth like yourself."

"Indeed?" Sherman's voice quivered. "Like marching my family into the gas chambers? Dying to redeem the world from communism?"

"Much simpler, more exhilarating. Something that will open your heart and your mind, free you from your liberal chains. Join us. I'm calling a conference here in a few months, a rally for the creation of the first honorable society. A check for five thousand dollars will enroll you."

"Yah, I knew it!" Sweeney leaped to his feet. "He's a sponge, like me! A freeloader! Hiya pal!"

Stonebreaker ignored the insult but he was not entirely at ease. "I repeat, Mr. Wettlaufer, a little insurance now, a lot of protection later."

"Man, it takes one to know one," Sweeney taunted. "Stoney, I knew you and me had something in common. Sherm, don't give him a subway token."

"He shall get nothing from me but my contempt," the benefactor said icily. "But I must demand something of him. My tape recordings, sir."

"I have destroyed them."

"I shall sue you. It was a childish thing to do."

"It was a symbolic gesture, a manifestation of my opposition to the Hate Germany campaign, this eternal wailing to turn our attention away from the sworn enemy."

"You are hopeless," Sherman said. "One thing has nothing to do with the other. I am as opposed to communism as you are. I would be the first person they would shoot. I am a capitalist, an exploiter of the working man. I am religious; I attend synagogue regularly. It is quite possible, sir, that you would survive them. After all you were a Red once. You speak their language in your contempt for human life. You might even applaud when they start shooting capitalists like me."

Stonebreaker nodded, spoke softly. "We shall try to arrange it so that we do the shooting first. I must ask you to consider carefully whether you want to be shot at or on the side of the shooters. If you join us now, a small contribution of five thousand dollars, you can when the time comes say, see, I am Sherman Wettlaufer, rich Jewish manufacturer, former liberal but staunch patriot today. I am one of you. I do not want to make a college professor out of every Negro drunkard.

"Then, you would be saved. Certain wealthy coreligionists of yours are already working with us. I burned your tapes as an act aimed at convincing you of your errors, but I can see you're intent on pursuing your own doom."

"You are a shrewd one," Sherman said. "There were certain, as you put it, coreligionists of mine in Germany who thought they'd

292

get along with Hitler. They ended up in the furnaces, too. All I can say, sir, is that you have come to a sorry end. What a creative life! To have to rise every morning and hate Mrs. Roosevelt!"

Stonebreaker looked at Sweeney. "Tell your friend how we intend to smash the liberal conspiracy in America. The way I told you last night."

"It's involved, to say the least," Sweeney said. "Basically, Ballbreaker here is going to get Americans so angry at the *schwartzers* —you know, muggings, sit-ins, forced bussing of kids—that all these decent white Amurricans will go out and murder the *schwartzers*, and incidentally all the rat liberals who kept prodding them into committing murders. That would include you and your family, and possibly me."

Wettlaufer smelled the old fear. A terrifying racial memory almost made him flinch.

"And you presume to speak for an honorable society!" said Wettlaufer. "You presume to speak for the Christian West! Yes, you will cheer when they shoot Negroes in the street!"

"Don't let him bug you, Sherm," Sweeney said reassuringly. "He ain't with us. I mean the old Church. They got him outvoted a thousand to one. Father Louis, old Pope John, they got the right idea. Why, there's priests and nuns working with the NAACP all over America. You can't even find a migrant labor camp without a minister. They're way ahead of him. He don't count at all."

"A temporary aberration," said Stonebreaker. "We can safely ignore *Mater et Magister*. They will soon tire of putting red hats on African witch doctors. Moreover, we aren't quite the minority you regard us. Lenin and Hitler represented minorities at first— but dedicated, uncompromising ones. Not that I compare the nature of our mission with theirs. In the honorable society—"

"How's this for honor, Stoney?" asked Sweeney, bending over the desk. "How about holding back booze from lushes, and then doling it out for favors? Like favors the lush don't want to give?"

Stonebreaker stood up with a military snap. Arching his roosterish neck, he looked not a little unlike Mussolini.

"You are right, Buck," said Sherman. "He is insane. But it is an insanity that is contagious. Do you know something though? I am not afraid of him. Not a bit."

"Queer for death, Sherm. He loves it."

"It will be appalling when the first Soviet megaton is detonated over Chicago. But what follows will be worse. Windrows of dead, pyramids of corpses."

"The son-of-a-bitch wants everyone dead because he's dead already, only he don't know it!" Sweeney hopped joyfully. "Queer for death, queer for death!"

"All I ask is five thousand dollars—"

"Still panhandling!" shouted Sweeney. "Man, I got to hand it to him!"

"You've wasted easily that much on Sweeney's interviews, and it would seem that for your own peace of mind—"

Sweeney would hear no more, nor permit his patron to listen. He herded Wettlaufer to a corner of the study, while Stonebreaker continued to build his case of horrors, and whispered something in the millionaire's ear. Then the two of them walked up to Stonebreaker, flanked him, and began tapping their index fingers on his shoulders chanting:

> "Three, six, nine,
> A bottle of wine,
> I can fight you
> Any old time!"

Thus having reaffirmed old bonds the two former members of the 997th Ordnance Base Depot Company left the Villa Malerba. They walked into the moonlight, through the scented groves, down the steep path to the timeless wonder of the old sea, Celt and Hebrew, men of two ancient races.

For a fretful moment Sweeney felt the need to run back to Villa Malerba and make his farewells to Melissa Davies. Perhaps he would console her with a brotherly kiss and promise to return rich and famous to save her from her avuncular dragon, the man with the tempting booze under one arm. But he understood his limitations, and her unwillingness. By now Stonebreaker was surely in her room again with his bait. And perhaps that is the way she really wants it, Sweeney reflected miserably. But didn't she once say, "Sweeney, you're good for me?" Yes, he was good for her. Like Prince Myshkin was for Nastasya Filippovna.

Jerome B. Whitlock, Ph.D., certainly smoked a pipe, a great gnarled blackened puffer which he crammed with Barking Dog tobacco, stoked, patted, tapped, reamed, and frequently emptied, using gross lots of safety matches and a variety of cunning tools. Occasionally he would rub the handsomely burled bowl against a nostril and admire the oily sheen resultant.

Each puff of that professorial pipe (Whitlock was not only a partner in Whitlock & Gates, motivational researchers, but taught Social Psychology at Columbia General Studies) blew the last vestiges of energy and self-respect out of Buck Sweeney.

He had gone to the first meetings in the Hotel Duchi d'Aosta, where Sherman had taken over an entire floor and a large conference room, and it soon became apparent he was out of his class. Whitlock not only smoked a pipe, he wore rumpled pale seersucker suits and had a long balding red head, freckles the size of nickels, and red tufts on his long, strong hands. He was a Unitarian.

Withal, Sweeney admired him, was rather jealous of him, and soon found himself deferring to him on all aspects of the Legion and the press conference that would announce its formation. At first Sweeney affected a moral superiority, the disdain of the field soldier for the high command. But Whitlock was a generous and sincere man and did nothing but praise Buck's dictated recollections of his interviews with Father Louis, Huguette Roux, Kruis of Amsterdam, the Danes, Dr. Helms, General Pandolfo, and Bolli. Soon Whitlock was calling him "Bucky" and he was calling the professor "Jer" or "Jer baby."

But once Sweeney had performed this function he found himself a fifth wheel, a silent clod sitting around Sherman's busy headquarters in everyone's way. To avoid this he lolled in hot baths for hours. Or he would frequent Turkish baths hopeful that the whipping branches and the masseur's cruel hands could beat spirit into his flagging limbs.

With unseeing eyes he wandered past the imploring whores and pimps who knew a customer when they saw one. Rome's healing grandeur did not rouse him—the tangerine and melon buildings, the dry invigorating heat, the sun-painted monuments, the sky bluer than any blue that Perugino ever dared suggest, the black-green cypresses, and the protective parasol pines. The old Sweeney would have gamboled and clicked heels at such intense beauty. Now he gazed on it through the gray gauze of melancholy. Sluggish of eye, fatigued of brain, he had no appetite for the city's loveliness, that hot casual marvel of Rome in summer.

"It's that bastard Stonebreaker," he murmured, sprawled on a bench in the Villa Borghese. Italian children wheeled about on junk-heap bicycles. "Old Stoney took all the laughs away. Can't even get Sherman to go out on the town with me."

Worst of all he found it difficult to be stirred (as was Sherman) by the deeds of the Legion, by the brave stories he had heard, those courageous acts so rare in a brutal world. *I got mine, pal, you worry about yours. Others may be looking for theirs, but I got it made. Haul up the ladder, Sweeney's on board.* Wasn't that the way most of us saw it? Especially when things got hairy—for Jews, kulaks, black people, yellow people, white people, whose ever turn it was to get the big *ootz?*

Sherman's Legion had a gift so rare and glowing that it should have filled Sweeney with joy. He had undertaken the survey riding the great free-load again. He would have undertaken it just for that red MG. (It was repaired, and was to be a gift from Sherman to his buddy.) He had not even looked forward to the interviews.

Yawning in the sunlight Sweeney remembered the day he had willingly got lost in the Loire Valley near Chinon looking for St. Etienne-sur-Lac and Father Louis. There had been some indifferent broad with him—Dee Dee? And a statue of Rabelais. And then the awesome dignity of the rector, the master counterfeiter, the Father of the Jews. The priest's decency had been almost painful.

296

And so it had gone—Huguette Roux, Kruis, the others—filling him with dumb admiration, reminding him of his own inadequacy. Didn't they realize that not everyone could be a hero? Sometimes they didn't even know *why* they did it. Like Kruis, whose identity alone seemed reason enough.

Then to compound his confusion he had fallen into Stonebreaker's hands—that madman imitating FDR and cursing Eleanor, plotting his lunatic schemes to free America from the liberals by getting everyone mad enough to kill Negro muggers. What if the creep had something there?

"It ain't my worry," said Sweeney. Above him the pines formed a lacy roof. Through shimmering green needles the hot blue wash of the Italian sky glowed. About him the children of Rome wheeled noisily on their junky bikes, heedless of the worshipful admonitions of mamas and nannies. *Fausto! Basta, basta! Giorgio, guarda, non troppo rapido!*

Ah, that was what life was all about. Kids riding bikes in a sunny park. Mamas hollering at them. An old man on a bench reading his *Paese Sera*. Young couples, those handsome Romans, strolling up a sunny path thinking maybe of the Fiat they'd buy after they were married. Jesus, it wasn't so bad. Why was it so hard to get? He was piqued at the Italians for making it look easy. He had heard they play-acted all the time, that they were really frustrated, unhappy. Nuts to that. If it was acting it was pretty good acting. Sweeney would settle for it any day.

Weltschmerz led him to a doctor's office. His hypochondria needed indulging. Why not admit that he was a wreck, a sick man, a fellow on death's doorstep, and have an end of it? The doctor was a slender young man elegant in a fawn-colored narrow suit. He had been educated at Bellevue and wanted to talk to Sweeney about automobiles. Still it was worth having to venture opinions on Thunderbirds and Corvettes to have one's prostate artfully massaged by the probing rubber finger of fate. Dr. Ricardi had good news for him. "You have a nice small prostate," he said warmly. Sweeney was proud of his small prostate. He was not a complete failure.

The doctor rapped at his chest, thumped his back, cradled his scrotum while he coughed, shone a light in his bloodshot eyes, X-rayed his lungs, tapped his arm for blood and his bladder for urine. Sweeney loved every minute of it.

"You have nice dark blood," said Dr. Ricardi, "I doubt there's any anemia. How did you like your little MG? Have you ever driven a Triumph? I once had an Austin-Healey. My wife has a Giuletta Sprint. Clench your fist and don't look at the needle if it bothers you. I love my Alfa Romeo."

But how, how could he ever describe truthfully to Dr. Ricardi what ailed him? The doctor would laugh at him as had dozens of medics in the past. How explain to the man that he suffered three distinct varieties of headache: migraine, regular, and a terrible insistent pinging which he knew was the onset of a brain tumor? Surely he was the only man in the world who was cursed with constipation and diarrhea *simultaneously*. The fierce sunburn he had contracted in Bolli's village had left his skin peeling in mammoth swatches like a Paris sycamore. All over his flesh itched, shriveled, turned pink and brown. Climbing stairs he was short of breath. Three steps and his heart raced around his chest in a frenzy. If he sat too long his ass ached, if he stood too long his legs were semiparalyzed. In elevators he was the only passenger to lean against the wall. The middle of the night found him awakening with strange new pains in his fingers, harbingers of rheumatoid arthritis. When he leaned over the sink in his hotel bathroom something in his lower spine went *knack*, and when he lunched in the Duchi d'Aosta's luxurious restaurant the *pasta e fagioli* constricted his stomach. Wine was vinegar in his mouth.

In fine he was finished, through, *kaput*, burned out. The lights in Sweeney's castle were all going out, thanks to Sherman's plans for him, thanks to Mrs. Melissa Henry de Camouillet Breck Davies, who at that moment probably lay on a sinful bed in Villa Malerba deep in gin and her uncle's embrace, joined to a man who was queer for death.

298

"I find nothing irregular," Dr. Ricardi said, "so it must be your liver. Have you seen the new Lotus? That *is* a car. We'll give you something to pep up your liver, new stuff. In a week or so it should give you a lift. That's the national disease, *mal di fegato*, so you're very Italian already. I like the lines on that Caravelle the French put out, but you can't beat the Mercedes. Call me if you don't feel better."

He did not let the doctor off so easily. Having heard that drugs were cheap in Italy he insisted on prescriptions for headache pills, tranquilizers, sleeping tablets, sinus decongestants, and something to regulate his frantic bowels which were either in watery retreat, cementlike fixity, or both at once.

Thus laden with delicacies he retired to his hotel room and doused himself liberally with everything. Soon he felt better. He saved the liver tonic for last, approaching it as if it were a virgin bride. It came in giant glass ampules, large enough to hold a bullfrog in formaldehyde. The glass had to be broken at either end with a small metal file that came with the box. One end had to be notched and snapped off, then held over a glass as the opposite end was broken, releasing the elixir. His fumbling hands botched the procedure mercilessly. First he used the blunt side of the file, failed to notch the glass and snapped it off jaggedly, cutting his thumb. He again cracked the opposite end of the ampule, slicing an index finger. Blood mingled with the chocolaty liver stimulant. He drank it all, suddenly realizing he had probably imbibed glass chunklets along with the tonic. Frantic, he tried reaching Dr. Ricardi, but it was two in the afternoon, the time of the long, hot, winey, food-heavy midday snooze of Italy. He lay whimpering on his bed, convinced that bits of ampule were carving their way down his alimentary canal.

An hour later, with his heart still beating, he revived. A mouthful of tranquilizers helped. A litre of San Pellegrino mineral water was even better. Comforted, he read and re-read its encouraging label, which advised him it was good for arthritis, rheumatism, diseases of the lung and heart, ailments of pancreas and spleen, and other organs, all sworn to by a famous Doctor of Physiology.

"That's a good man there," he said. He slouched out of his room to Sherman's command post on the second floor.

A happy, diligent group filled the headquarters of the Legion. Sherman was on the phone shouting to an operator in Belgrade. "Hallo, hallo, Mr. Dusan Primich, please! Yes, Primich!" Jerome Whitlock sat at a long table sorting out dossiers, making notes on a pad, and dictating to one of four girls hired to do the secretarial work. Two others were typing feverishly and the fourth was operating a humming mimeograph machine in the corner. At Sherman's elbow, in a black suit, sat the inevitable accessory to official business in Italy, a man-of-all-work. His name was Claudio, he spoke six languages, and he served as fixer, arranger, press contact, chauffeur, authority on restaurants, and payer of bribes.

Whitlock waved a hand at Sweeney. "Make that read 'these ordinary people who performed extraordinary deeds, Luisa.' Hey, Bucky, we've missed you. How'd the medical go? Doctor cheer you up?"

"He admired my prostate," Sweeney said wistfully.

The Ph.D. tossed his head back and laughed approvingly. A Unitarian with a sense of humor. His teeth bit at the monstrous pipe. "I've been meaning to tell you, Bucky. You did a helluva job on those interviews. Terrific stuff. And some memory you have! It's a shame we don't have them *in toto*."

"Oh, you'll get them again," Sweeney replied wanly. He felt out of place in the busy room. "Except Helms. I think he's had his last say."

"Don't tell me," agreed Whitlock. He had taken off his seersucker coat. Ivy Leaguer's twisted tie, washable button-down shirt—it was all there. Sweeney cringed with jealous admiration. Somewhere along the line Whitlock had connected; and somewhere B. K. Sweeney had missed, missed by a mile.

"Close-mouthed fellow that Helms," Whitlock went on. "Polite, approved of our project, but not a word out of him."

"Darn shame." Sweeney nosily thumbed through the manila dossiers in front of Whitlock. *Mezhnev, Marushka, USSR.*

300

"Belgrade? Is this Belgrade, Yugoslavia?" Sherman was at full throttle. "Thank goodness, at last! I want Mr. Dusan Primich. He's with the Small Industry Planning Council, something like that. Louder please, I can't hear you. I don't speak Yugoslav—"

"It's called Serbo-Croat, Sherm," Whitlock said gently.

"Serbo-Croat!" Sherman shouted.

"Helms wouldn't play," Whitlock said. "He asked to be remembered to you, Bucky."

"He did? Me?"

"Yup. Said he was very impressed with you. You seemed a fine American with a good heart. *Ein gut herz,* he said."

"Mr. Primich?" shouted Sherman. "Mr. Dusan Primich?"

"Gosh," Sweeney said. "Old Helms." Hearing this tribute from the gaunt engineer, that citizen of Bremen who had tried to save the doomed Jews, that sombre witness to the practices of hell, Sweeney nurtured a memory of the morning in Helms' office. How he had wept at the terrifying connection he had made between his dead father Jim Sweeney and all the dead fathers and sons in the snowy field! He had cried that day for all parents and children seized from the warm routines of life, the risings and goings to bed, the meals, the magic of learning, music, art, play, the texture of joy and oneness. Helms had made him see the naked bloody bodies and hear the rat-tat-tat of the machine pistols. And so he had bawled in front of the engineer because he knew Helms would understand. Then he and Helms had touched one another, as if to affirm something, to recover something lost, to redeem the dead. He snapped smoked glasses on his face to hide his eyes from

"Is that you Mr. Primich? Mr. Dusan Primich?" Wettlaufer was yelling wildly. "Do you speak English? How about German? *Sprechen Zie?* This is Mr. Wettlaufer. Did you get my letter? It was all cleared with the Foreign Office. Ah, you don't understand me? Wettlaufer. W, e, t . . ."

Typewriters clattered. The efficient A. B. Dick machine rolled on, turning out neat summations of Sweeney's interviews and other dramatic stories. Slouched in front of Whitlock the original agent of the Legion felt ignored. Worse, he knew he deserved to be. Drunken bum, whoremaster, *shicker goy*, petty liar. But Dr. Helms had liked him, and Helms was a real man.

"Italian! You speak Italian! Oh, that's marvelous!" Sherman crowed in triumph, covering the mouthpiece and directing his shouts to Claudio, the Italian man-of-all-work. "Claudio! He speaks Italian, come here quickly!" Trotting like a Bersaglieri, the little fellow in the black suit was at Sherman's side rattling away in Italian to the elusive Primich, one more of Sherman's people. Immediately Wettlaufer seized a telephone from one of the secretaries and started talking to Warsaw.

"Operator, it's a village south of Warsaw, Przyzk I think, a man named Krakowski, Stanislas Krakowski. He has no phone but he is awaiting this call at the town hall in the mayor's office. Thank you, thank you. The mayor's name is Rotkewicz."

Whitlock jabbed the stem of his pipe at Sweeney. "You know, Bucky, you'd have a great career in this business, motivational research, opinion polling. You've got a knack for making people talk. I hope we do as well. Of course we'll approach it differently— control groups, sampling, weighing evidence."

A messenger entered with a handful of telegrams for Sherman. He left his Warsaw call to rip them open. "Oh, great, great! Huguette Roux is coming . . . and she's got the old priest, the one who hid the children!"

Wettlaufer had shouted the good news to the room at large and Sweeney was hurt. Huguette Roux was *his* friend. He mumbled something to Whitlock (Sherman had not even noticed him except for an offhand "Hi, Buck") and left for his room.

There he gulped down a parfait of multicolored pills. Having mastered the technique of the file and the glass ampule, he drank a double dose of liver stimulant, half a litre of San Pellegrino, and called Villa Malerba.

Frances Ferrante answered the phone. Hearing her sleepy voice he imagined her in the hay with dark disdainful Nino. It was late afternoon, a good time for it, although any time probably sufficed. "Oh, Sweeney," she said vaguely.

"I want to talk to Melissa."

"She isn't here."

"Where is she?"

"In the hospital in Salerno."

Even as Mrs. Ferrante said the words he had a premonition of disaster, a psychic warning. "What's wrong? What happened?"

"Oh, I don't think it's serious," she said. Her speech was slow, searching, the speech of a determined ignoramus, a woman who had gotten a great deal without the need for any mental expenditure, any curiosity. Even talking was an effort.

"Well for Chrissake, Frances, what is it?"

"The doctor says she's just rundown. Tired. She went back to that village the other day."

"Where? To Bolli?"

"Yeah, back to that dirty place. She spent a whole day there and she got sunstroke, or heat exhaustion, or who knows what, the poor thing. She came back that night and had to go to bed. And the next day she was in a coma. She took a lot of drugs and got sick."

"A coma?" Sweeney shivered. People went into comas for a variety of reasons—heat exhaustion did not seem to be one. An overdose of drugs, of booze, of booze *and* drugs, what the doctors called the *synergizing* effect of the two. Sweeney knew about synergizing. Once in a prolonged period of alcoholic indulgence it had been explained to him.

"Is Stonebreaker around?" he asked.

"No, he left yesterday, after he made sure Melissa was going to be all right. I mean, after they took her off the oxygen."

"Oh Jesus," moaned Sweeney. "But what the hell is wrong? Can I talk to her? What's the hospital?"

"Salerno, Salerno. She's better now. Listen, I can't talk to you all day."

He could only guess. Melissa up in the hills with Bolli's ragged,

303

dedicated crew—a day of remorse of conscience and hot, dry sun, then back to another game of cat-and-mouse with Uncle Andy. Then what?

"They pumped her stomach," Frances Ferrante whined on, "and then she felt better. I don't know, the doctor said her kidneys weren't too good, she needed a long rest. Who can figure these things? I never knew anyone healthier than Melissa."

"Tell her old Sweeney called. I'll be in touch again." As they mumbled insincere goodbyes it occurred to Sweeney, chillingly, that he did not want to talk to his recent love. He was afraid to learn any more about her. It would accomplish nothing, do nothing for her or for him.

Some months ago, Sweeney remembered, a vivacious young Broadway actress, a girl of talent, beauty, a girl on the "inside," had committed suicide. For a long time after her death Sweeney kept meeting men, at least a half-dozen, who were convinced they could have saved her. A long fatherly talk, a happy sex life, a family, a recommended reading list—the solutions were varied, yet each man was firm in his conviction that he alone held the touchstone. What arrogance! What consummate vanity!

Sweeney realized that he, too, had been party to such arrogance. Whatever Melissa Davies' brink-of-horror status, nothing that Sweeney could offer would serve as palliative or panacea. Whether she was ill with the Flit, drugs, heat exhaustion, bad kidneys, or revulsion with her life and the people she had so long associated with, Sweeney could not help her. Not Prince Sweeney, the idiot. For that matter neither could Franco Bolli.

He brimmed with pity for that handsome unhappy woman and tried hard not to feel noble. Well, he had given her a few laughs. And in a way she had let him down. People were always letting him down, especially the rich, the wellborn, the cultivated and envied. They were all supposed to have wit, charm, grace. The clever things they said were in the newspaper columns. They were quoted. They could ski, sail, shoot, race horses, and were supposed to screw better than anyone. But up close they usually confirmed all the Marxist lies about them. No matter what envious novelists wrote about them they were pretty much a tiresome, self-serving bunch. If they excelled at anything it was boredom.

There was Melissa, his bright star, wallowing in that fearsome relationship with Uncle Andy. Money, opportunity, high style—none had helped. Where was that special luminosity he kept reading about? Start peeling the layers off, fellahs, Sweeney wanted to tell them. Up close the privileged had a talent for souring one's stomach. If not rotten they were surely dull. If not harmful at least noxious. Of course Melissa's real trouble was she knew all this, knew it better than Sweeney. She admitted as much. The girl who had it all knew that the mere having wasn't enough.

Sweeney was tempted to call the hospital but his coward's hand recoiled from the hotel telephone. He envisioned a blurred, semi-comatose voice, a sound of defeat, surrender, and he could not face it. His relationship with Melissa had been what the anthropologists called a joking relationship—kidding, asides, nothing serious. So he would let it rest.

The whores on the Via del Tritone beckoned. That night he reviewed them like a general, made his selection like a child picking a goldfish from a Woolworth aquarium. Like that same overeager child he was sorry as soon as he had made his choice. She was a great big one with a huge whore's head—enormous black eyes, a banana nose, wide thick lips. Her hair was black, lacquered, and enclosed in a snood. Mammoth breasts thrust forward like the continental shelf. A bottle of *Punt e Mes* could have rested on their upper plane. Her behind was thick and round as a Percheron's. Fresh from some Sicilian slum she wobbled amateurishly on spiked heels as she led Sweeney down a back alley to a narrow hotel, which has served the same purpose since the Renaissance. Sweeney expected to see a plaque on the door: *Bernini Got His Here.*

There was something aggressively horrible about his lady. She was a sex monster, a wild witch out of some damp cave. As they

305

lurched arm in arm down the alley Sweeney regretted turning down the thin sad blonde, the busty Nordic with braided hair, the phthisic waif with the face of a she-goat. But there he was, hotshot Sweeney, with his earth mother. They hated each other. Once she tripped on the cobbled street and grimaced viciously at him when he tried to help her. "*Brutta strada.*" The grimace embodied all her contempt for him, for Rome, for everything. *You made me what I am today.* A gold molar winked in her powdered yellow slab of a face and he winked back.

In the dim foyer of the "hotel" a crone in a nurse's uniform demanded his passport. He refused. "I'm an American, that's enough," Sweeney said haughtily. "Blood type A." The whore and the old woman argued; the whore won, and kept her client. She led him to a vile yellow room (bed, dresser, sink, plastic bidet) in which a lone 15-watt bulb spread a bilious haze over the squalor.

"Ten t'ousan' lire," she demanded. Up close she was magnificently disgusting. A half inch of caked powder covered her exorbitant face. If he jabbed her, Sweeney felt, she would spout powder.

"Jesus, that's sixteen bucks," Sweeney complained. From his pocket he lifted a fat roll of orange notes and gave her one. She nodded and pulled her basic black dress over her head, careful not to disturb her varnished hair. Sweeney, normally an insatiable fetishist, a man to whom accouterments were stimulating and refreshing, sensed naught. She wore the standard accessories, black lace predominating, but her giantess' thighs and butt, the great ledge of her bosom, absorbed everything. She lay in wait for him, a *strega* hungry for tender Argonauts. Sweeney cringed. Her belly was swollen with the livers and lights of old lovers.

She mistook his terror for a debilitating passion and wrestled him to the bed. "You like? Ten t'ousan' more lire, I let you in."

"Whah? What the hell was the first ten thousand for? A cover charge? You're crazy, lady."

She undid his pants, yanked them over his loafers, and helped herself to a second orange note. *Thirty-two dollars!* How he detested her, feared her! He wanted to run into the warm Roman night to a quiet church.

Manfully he tried—sweating, churning, grunting, laboring to arouse himself with her straps and lace, her heaving flesh, her aroma as pungent as an open drain in downtown Palermo. He failed. They lay apart, truce declared, nothing accomplished. Cursing, she reached into his trousers for another ten thousand lire.

"Hey there, hands outa my pants, Dee Dee."

"You steenk. Big-boy steenk. I take ten t'ousan' pay for you insulta me."

"Come on, let's have it. I'll go for thirty-two bills, not forty-eight. That's inflationary."

She hauled her pillowed body off the bed and Sweeney almost fainted at the sight of her rearing can—a zebra's, a wild mare's. She began to get dressed.

"No you don't," said Sweeney. "Gimme that last ten grand."

"You steenk. Pay for insult."

He was up against some venerable Sicilian concept of honor. "I'll insult you for real, Weezy. Where is your heart of gold? Don't you read books or go to plays? You're supposed to be kind and lovable."

"Put on you pants," she sneered. "Maybe you like better little boy, hah?"

Slow to anger, a man who avoided fights, Sweeney could not let this ultimate abuse go unchallenged. The words gnawed at his last remnant of pride. He threw himself upon her, grabbing one fat wrist, the other arm around her girdled midriff.

"Gimme the gelt, kiddo," he muttered. "I'm lettin' you off easy. You get thirty-two bucks just for five minutes work."

"Leggo, figgin Yank."

"Nah, gimme the last ten thousand you lifted. You stuck it in your brassiere, right down there between the Grand Tetons."

He let go of her wrist and thrust his hand into the valley. She was a Fury, a Gorgon. Nurtured on pasta, hard bread, and beans, she was solid muscle beneath that yellow-brown fat. They waltzed around the dim room a few minutes, contestants at the Harvest Moon Ball. She did not shriek (apparently the girls were supposed to handle their own rebels) but kept hissing wicked noises through clenched teeth.

"Over you go, Dodie." Sweeney huffed. He flipped her backwards using all his strength, tripping her legs over his knee. They hit the bed thunderously. Writhing, hissing, she jammed her thumb into a buzzer on the night table. "Feex you, beeg figg," she snarled. Now her teeth dug into his shoulder. He roared in agony.

Howling, he bounced off the sagging bed as the door opened. Two blunt-faced hoods in dark suits were looking him over. They exchanged information with the sobbing whore.

"She cheated me, men," Sweeney explained. "Can't let her do that to an American. Give Italian tourism a black eye. Louse up the favorable balance of trade."

They shut the door softly and circled him, one to each side.

"Ha!" gloated Sweeney. "Come and get me, coppers!" He almost relished the prospect of a beating. What else did he deserve? He did a James Cagney, hitching up his underpants, sneering, curling a lip, hands wiggling at the level of his navel. "Awright, Jocko, you're the guy who killed my brother."

The two galoots advanced cautiously. They had no foreheads, tight black curls—cheap labor from the south.

Once again he was Sweeney the barroom battler from Fordham Road. Stupidly he had left his rear unguarded. As the two toughs moved in, the harlot, with feral shriek, hurled herself on his back, nails, teeth, and shoes working.

"Stand back, men!" shouted Sweeney. "I'm the young urban sophisticate, a subscriber to *Playboy* magazine!"

The taller of the two hoods wielded a short length of metal pipe. The first blow missed and Sweeney got in a few wild licks. All four combatants hit the deck. They milled about a few seconds, then the lead pipe found Sweeney's left temple. "Young urban sophisticate," he muttered as the darkness blanketed him and he threw a last desperate punch.

The press conference had been called for five in the afternoon. Several members of the Legion would not be arriving till midday or later, and Sherman wanted as full attendance as possible. Claudio, the interpreter-assistant, warned against the late hour. "A bad time, Signor Wettlaufer. We are still asleep then. In Italy if you want anything done, do it between nine in the morning and one in the afternoon. After that we eat, sleep, then after that we yawn, scratch, taste the wine, and think of the wife or mistress we just left. We cannot be expected to pay attention."

On Claudio's recommendation a lavish buffet and bar were set up in the room adjoining the conference chamber. However, it would not be made available until *after* Whitlock had conducted the conference. The bait, Claudio explained, would draw a good representation of Rome's native and foreign press.

The conference room had a riser at one end, in front of a kingly maroon drapery. On the riser had been set a long table at which would sit Sherman, Whitlock, Sweeney, and the members of the Legion. In front of the riser and the table twenty rows of folding chairs had been placed, and at the left-hand side of the room there was a second table stacked with mimeographed handouts in different languages. These summarized the general aims of the Legion and contained accounts of the experiences of Father Louis, Mme Roux, and the others.

At 5:15 the room was less than half-filled with journalists. Most were Italians but there were several Germans, Frenchmen, and two Americans—a man from the Associated Press, and one from a network. There were also a few merely curious people who had heard there would be free food and drink, a few hotel guests who had wandered in, and a group of coarsely dressed, heavy-faced men who clustered in a rear row around one of Rome's leading Communist journalists.

Whitlock had decided that apart from a brief question-and-answer period speeches would be of a rather formal nature and would follow the information in the multilingual mimeographed sheets. If questions were asked Claudio would act as French-English-Italian interpreter, while some girls from the University of Rome had been engaged to handle the rarer tongues, such as Polish and Serbo-Croat.

The Duchi d'Aosta was a new, sterile, air-conditioned hotel. The meeting room was surgical white, brightly lit to advertise its modernity, and was not an altogether homey place for Italians. By 5:30 a few of them were dozing, and some had asked when they would be fed.

In one of the front rows the people of the Legion waited nervously for the signal from Whitlock to take their seats on the dais behind the long table. Huguette Roux, in a new green dress, sat with Father Latour. The latter was a feathery, stooped ancient, the legendary priest who had spent two years half-sleeping in a chair at the door of his chancery awaiting the Gestapo's knock. He had saved the lives of dozens of Jewish children. Deaf, trembling, he held Mme Roux's hand.

Willem Kruis of Amsterdam was present. He stood at a window exchanging cigars and conversing in German with the Reverend Nils Munk, who had come as representative of the Danes. Alone at the end of the front row in a shiny suit, his hair needing trimming, sat General Enrico Pandolfo.

There were also four people from Eastern Europe. One was the hard-to-find Yugoslav, Dusan Primich. The others were from Poland, the Soviet Ukraine, and Hungary. All four sat quietly, uncommunicative, somewhat confused.

Sherman looked worriedly at his witnesses and turned to Whitlock. "I guess we'd better get the show on the road. Too bad there's such a meager turnout of the press."

"Afternoon bad time," said Claudio.

"I wouldn't worry," Whitlock said crisply. "We'll have other shots at it. We'll hit the New York press hard when we get back. We're just getting our feet wet today."

310

"Yes, yes," Sherman said. "Jerry, please run the show. You're less involved emotionally than I am. Take the center chair and Buck and I will sit on either side. . . . Buck? Have you seen him?"

Whitlock stoked his pipe. "Looks like he's a no-show. Let's get on without him. The natives are restless. I saw one of the Communists sneak in and steal a few canapés."

"I wonder where Buck is?" Sherman mused. "But you're right. Let's do it."

He, Whitlock, and Claudio herded the honored guests to the riser. For a brief, terrorized moment Sherman felt helpless without his old saviour Buck Sweeney, who was after all the living link with the good people. Would it be official without Buck? This fear was reinforced when Huguette Roux, speaking English in a delightful accent, asked, "And where is M'sieu Sweeney? Such a nice gentleman. My husband and I speak of him always."

"He was detained," Sherman replied. "He's working for us right now."

Mme Roux smiled as they approached the table. Father Latour followed her.

"You know, M'sieu Sweeney is a hero to us."

"Sweeney? A hero?" Sherman was confounded.

"Oh, yes. He had a big fight with the Communists in Brussels. *La grande lutte avec les moules. Sweeney a vainçu completemente les communistes.*"

"I don't understand."

Claudio stuck his head between them. "Sweeney had a big fight with the Communists, a fight with cozze—mussels. And he beat them."

"Muscles?" asked Wettlaufer in wonderment. "He wrestled them?"

"No, no," Claudio said. "Like oysters, clams."

A chilling vision of Sweeney and some Communist toughs hurling shellfish at one another romped through Sherman's head. He was afraid to ask for details.

Whitlock and Sherman took the center seats. To Whitlock's left sat Huguette Roux, Father Latour, Kruis of Amsterdam, and Munk. To the Dane's left, apart from the others, totally ignorant of what was transpiring, sat an ancient gnomish Ukrainian woman named Marushka Mezhnev. She was surely in her late eighties, although she herself was not certain of her age. Stooped, frail, in a black shapeless dress and a black cotton babushka, she was out of Russia's dim past. Her coarse face swarmed with wrinkles so intricate and multiformed as to hide her tiny amber eyes. But the eyes saw, the ears heard, and one sensed an indestructible strength in her.

To Wettlaufer's right sat General Pandolfo, rubbing his chin and gazing at the ceiling. To the right of the general were three other late arrivals from Eastern Europe. These were a Hungarian doctor named Tibor Jekely, a stout man with drooping, flaccid cheeks and the expressive features of an actor; the Polish farmer Krakowski, blunt and potato-faced; and the Yugoslav official Dusan Primich. This Primich was quite a bird, a dark hairy man with the savage look of a mountain Serb or a Montenegrin. Out towards the audience he thrust a hooked nose, a nose for impaling Turks and Nazis. Over the bridge of this beak, black furry eyebrows met thickly. He sat a pace back from the table, legs apart, prepared for a fast exit if necessary.

Jerome Whitlock surveyed the room (a bit more than half-filled by now) and rapped for attention with his pipe.

"I think we can begin," he said. He identified himself modestly, introduced Sherman, and asked Sherman to say a few words of welcome.

Nervously Wettlaufer stood up. Why wasn't Buck here? Buck's presence would have calmed him. "All of you have access to the mimeographed material which sets forth the aims of the foundation. Dr. Whitlock will enlarge on them in a moment. I only want to welcome all you gentlemen of the press and other friends and say that we are all honored and humbled by the presence of the nine persons who symbolize this undertaking, the first members of the Legion of Noble Christians. That's all I have to say, since Dr. Wh-Wh-Wh-itlock is much bett-bett——"

His voice putt-putted to a halt, like a cheap outboard motor dying of bad maintenance. His eyes were transfixed on the rear of the room. Sweeney had arrived.

But in what condition! A cluster of Band-Aids was pasted to his right temple. His left eye was a rich blue-black, like spilled Schaefer's Quink. The Sweeney face over-all was pale and mis-shapen. He looked hung-over, mishandled. Higher than ever arched his questioning eyebrows, demanding of a hostile world: *Why me?* But most distressing to Sherman was the presence at Sweeney's side of a short pompous Italian in a bulky gray suit and a wide-brimmed white hat. The man's bearing said: *police.* The manner in which his left arm adjoined Sweeney's right said: *handcuffs.*

". . . bett-bett-better equipped to summarize our aims and methods, so I-I-I-I turn the meeting over to him."

Fortunately no one had noticed Sweeney's entrance. Wisely the former agent of the foundation slumped deep in his seat. The gesture convinced Wettlaufer that the right arm was harnessed to the short man. Bending to Whitlock, Wettlaufer whispered, "Buck just walked in. He's sitting in the back. For God's sake don't call on him, don't even mention him. I think he's in terrible trouble."

Whitlock nodded and began. "My comments will be brief," he said, "because the deeds of our guests speak for themselves. I invite you to read the summaries of their acts on behalf of the victims of Nazism. Their stories and thousands of others will be documented, researched, and published by the Wettlaufer Foundation. No amount of discussion and elaboration on our modest aims in establishing the Legion of Noble Christians can render these people—people of our time, of our common heritage—any more admirable than they are.

"On my left is Mme Huguette Pelletier Roux, a librarian in Brussels. She is a housewife and the mother of two children. Next to her is Father Jean-Marie Latour of the Church of St. Martin in LaMotte, Belgium, an unexpected guest. We're honored, Father. Then Mr. Willem Kruis of Amsterdam, and next to him the Reverend Niels Munk of the Evangelical Lutheran Church of Kroge, Denmark. Reverend Munk has emphasized to me that he is here not in witness to his own deeds but as representative of all the people of Denmark who helped save the Jews of that country."

This was the first overt reference to Jews that Whitlock had made, and it drew a sprinkling of applause. The fact was most of the audience had failed to read the handouts, and many had come only in the expectation of food and drink. Like Sweeney's vision of Christ preaching in the House of Mary and Martha they were after the turkey and lobster in the foreground, not the sermon in the rear. But with the reference to Munk's work in behalf of Jews there was an embarrassed hurrying to the mimeographed sheets, a murmuring, as in a class required to catch up on missed lessons.

"Next to the Reverend Munk is Mrs. Marushka Mezhnev, I hope I have pronounced her name correctly, who is from the Ukraine in the Soviet Union. She is eighty-eight years old, and I'm told she still sews, cooks, and gardens."

This shriveled bent woman, a buglike creature out of a Chekhov tale, nodded her head once. What in heaven's name, wondered Sherman, did she understand of all this? But what a great soul she had! She had been employed as a maid in a Jewish household and had saved all eight members of the family during the German invasion by spiriting them to her own family's village where they miraculously survived the war.

"To Mr. Wettlaufer's right, a man well known to our Italian friends, General Enrico Pandolfo, former commander of the 75th Armored Division, Italian Army."

En masse all the Italians except the men around the Communist journalist rose and applauded, whistled, and stamped enthusiastically. Waiters and busboys edged up from the adjoining room and joined in the tribute to the doleful general. As the cheers died, a single sneering word could be heard from the leftist group:

314

"Fascisto." This in turn touched off murmurs of disapproval from the rest of the Italians. No reaction was evident in Pandolfo, whose long-creased face kept studying the ceiling, perhaps in search of some revelation, some clue as to why all that fuss had been made over the Croatian Jews or the fate of the small boy with earlocks he had once hid in his tank. A vagrant thought passed through his weary mind—in one village the *Ustashe* hanged all the Jews, and their dogs and cats as well. A terrifying sight, a hanged dog.

"Next to the General is Dr. Tibor Jekely, a physician from the city of Budapest, and next to him Mr. Stanislaus Krakowski, a farmer from Przyzk, Poland, and at the very end, Mr. Dusan Primich of Belgrade, Yugoslavia, an economist."

Primich acknowledged the introduction by lifting his great beak. When the applause came, it came largely from the Communists, who appeared to know him or at least knew about him. The leading Red journalist waved at Primich and called out something in Serbo-Croat. Primich raised a hairy hand. There was a hint in the gesture of some dark brotherhood.

"Several of the original members of our group were unable to attend," said Whitlock. "They include Father Louis DesMoulins of St. Etienne-sur-Lac, France, Dr. Ludwig Helms of Hamburg, Germany, and Mr. Franco Bolli. Mr. Bolli said he would be here but was evidently detained by his work in the Campania—"

A young fair-haired priest raised his hand. "I am a friend of Mr. Bolli's," Father Frade said softly. "He wanted very much to attend. But he was arrested yesterday and is in jail."

An unmannerly guffaw went up from the Italian journalists—both the Communists and the conservatives. The two American newsmen immediately left their seats to sit in back of Father Frade.

"Jail?" Whitlock asked.

"Yes. He was arrested for attempting to build a road without a permit. He asked me to attend in his behalf, although I am hardly worthy to join your guests. I am merely here as Franco's colleague.

315

He sends you all his good wishes, especially his friend Mr. Sweeney."

This cryptic reference evoked nods and comment from the people on the dais. Huguette Roux, smiling, whispered to Father Latour. Reverend Munk rapped the table twice, as if to say, *hear, hear!* Kruis of Amsterdam bobbed his large gray head affirmatively. Even the General managed a thin smile. Perhaps he was recalling the day he and Mario had played gangster with the amiable American.

These reactions were not lost on Wettlaufer. He sneaked a quick look to the back of the room where Sweeney hid his mashed face, wallowing in shame. Never was Sherman more poignantly aware of his debt to that wastrel. To all these courageous people Sweeney had meant something. But Sweeney could not accept their gentle plaudits. Lower and lower he sank into the metal chair, his guardian sinking with him.

Whitlock thanked Father Frade. Then with professorial expertise he began to outline the goals of the foundation in forming the Legion. He said nothing about the outlandish birth of the organization. Indeed, Wettlaufer had never confided to him that night of horror peopled by lumberjacketed morons shouting *antichrist!* at him. Only Sweeney knew about this, and Sweeney had his own troubles.

"The world has heard much about the Eichmanns and Himmlers and Heydrichs," Whitlock said, "but it has not heard about that decent minority of Europeans who refused to co-operate with the SS and the Gestapo. We must learn about the true Christian heroes of Europe, the ordinary people who did extraordinary things—teachers, priests, housewives, farmers, workers, nuns, ministers, librarians—the people who with no wealth or power or arms or influence looked at the suffering of their Jewish neighbors. . . ."

Whitlock went on to explain that once the data had been assembled it would be submitted to a board of social scientists who would then evaluate it. They would look for motives, for reasons, for the factors that went into the creation of "an altruistic personality." Why did Willem Kruis volunteer to save a Jewish family when another Dutchman down the street turned Jews in for monetary rewards? What impelled General Pandolfo to risk his career, to defy Rome, Berlin, the Croats, by hiding Jews? When virtually everyone around her stood by idly or cheered the murder of Jews, why did Marushka Mezhnev protect her Jewish employers?

"We confess we have no answers. Perhaps we may never find the answers. Why is person A brave and compassionate, while person B is cruel and cowardly? Indeed, what would you or I have done knowing our lives would be in danger if we did the moral, humane thing? It has become increasingly evident that the tendency to look the other way in the presence of evil is growing in . . ."

Again, a rude noise issued from the Communists. "Americans look away when Negroes are murdered?" Whitlock ignored it although the interruption caused heads to turn.

Craftily Sweeney opened his unbruised eye. The lights were too bright. The air-conditioning made him shudder. He wanted to be on a warm beach beside a green sea, beneath a palm tree, sponging up sunlight. His companion, Tenente Carlo Plasmati of the Rome Questura, who had come to the Delicato Hotel the previous night to arrest Sweeney, was asleep.

Self-pity laved Sweeney. How he wanted to be up there with his friends. A seizure of new throbs fluttered within his skull. Those hoods had really given it to him. Thank goodness he had gone down battling, young urban sophisticate to the end.

"Wake up, Carlo," Sweeney whispered, "it isn't polite."

"Scusi," Officer Plasmati murmured. "Il professore parla troppo."

". . . You gentlemen of the press can help. Any information about people who were involved in this effort will be welcomed by our permanent offices in New York and Rome. These deeds . . ."

Whitlock concluded his comments and threw the meeting open to questions.

317

There was a moment of hesitation. No one seemed interested in asking questions. A well-groomed Italian wearing smoked glasses, his long black hair slicked down, got up and asked General Pandolfo for a comment on the behavior of Italian soldiers under his command. The query had nothing to do with the purpose of the conference, but Whitlock was glad that some interest, no matter how tangential, had been stirred up.

As Pandolfo arose the hissed *Fascisto!* again emanated from the leftists. This time Whitlock rapped the table with his pipe. "Gentlemen, this is not a political rally. Politics are irrelevant here." There was applause again. Pandolfo, stiffly at attention, spoke.

"The Italian soldiers I commanded were the bravest, finest men I have ever known," he said huskily. "We have suffered many slanders. Cruel, heartless lies. But I point to our actions in Croatia in saving the Jewish people. It was never consistent with the honor of the Italian Army to murder defenseless civilians, Christian or Jew."

The cheering and applause was louder, more sustained. Clearly Pandolfo was the hero of the meeting—except to the men gathered around the Communist belle-lettrist.

A woman reporter asked Reverend Munk to explain the Danish resistance to the Germans. Another asked Kruis of Amsterdam if he still saw the Meier family. He did; they were close friends. A third wanted to know if Father Latour had acted with the approval of his bishop. "*Mais certainement,*" the old man said faintly. "*L'evêque m'a donné des vêtements et des comestibles pour les enfants juifs.*"

Father Frade was questioned at length by the American newsmen about Bolli. The young priest said he would be delighted to put them in contact with the reformer. After the Americans had pumped Father Frade the conference seemed about to end of its own inertia. No one had asked the Eastern Europeans anything.

"The gentleman over there," Whitlock said.

318

"I have a question for you and Mr. Wettlaufer," a small, sallow man asked. "Of what religious persuasion are you?"

Sweeney jerked up in his seat, yanking Tenente Plasmati with him. No question about it: it was Emile Gevaert, his spook. Sweeney smelled the imminent nastiness. The Belgian appeared to be wearing the same soiled shirt and lumpy black suit, the same thick sweater beneath the jacket.

"I do not think that has any bearing on the purpose of this conference," said Whitlock.

"It has. I insist. I must know."

Huguette Roux, recognizing the journalist, whispered to Father Latour, who agitated his feathery head. There was an apprehensive shifting in the audience. The Italians smelled a good fight. The Communists grinned.

"Whom do you represent?" asked Whitlock.

"My name is Gevaert. I am associated with the *Atheist Journal,* an international publication."

"Not that it matters," said Whitlock, "but I am a Unitarian and Mr. Wettlaufer is Jewish."

"That man you sent to do the interviews, Sweeney," Gevaert persisted. "He is a Roman Catholic, is he not?"

"You're damn right I am!" bellowed Sweeney. He blundered to his feet, hauling the sleeping policeman halfway up with him. "Gevaert is a known atheist and socialist! Nobody pay any attention to him!"

"Good for you, Sweeney!" cried Reverend Munk.

"Bravo!" added General Randolfo. "Guarda il nostro amico!"

Sweeney's old friends were overjoyed. Huguette Roux applauded. Kruis and Munk joined in the tribute.

By now the entire assemblage was turning, craning necks to see this absent member of the foundation.

"Ah, there he is!" cried Gevaert. "Yes, the same man I met in Brussels. I am pleased to inform my fellow members of press, especially the Americans, that this man is a drunkard, a fool, a hooligan, and a secret agent of the Vatican!"

319

A wild roar went up from the Communists. They pounded the floor, whistled gleefully. Their star journalist, a tall glowering man with a rising mop of iron-gray hair, stood up and shouted: "*Avanti Popolo!*"

At the sound of this taunting battle cry of the left the anti-left journalists rose, gathered around the man with sleek black hair, and shouted insults across the room. General Pandolfo's eyes were bright with anger as he slammed the table, calling to the Reds, "*Vergogna! Vergogna!*"

"Carlo, turn me loose," Sweeney begged. "There's gonna be a first-class hooley, a brannigan. I got to have both hands free." But Plasmati had been to too many meetings, rallies, and conferences at which similar disturbances had threatened. Punches were rarely thrown.

When the shouting subsided, except for an occasional curse or rude gesture, Whitlock turned to Gevaert. "Now, make your point. Your attacks on Mr. Sweeney are without foundation. Unless you can prove them they discredit you a good deal more than they reflect on him."

"I base my accusations on personal contacts. But let that pass. I have much graver charges to level against this so-called Legion."

Wettlaufer gulped. His face turned a putty shade. He tugged at Whitlock's seersucker coat-tail, but the latter ignored him, convinced he was equal to the burgeoning crisis.

"I charge that this survey is a cunning attempt to whitepaint the historical sins of Christianity!" the Belgian shouted.

"For shame! For shame!" Father Frade sprang to his feet, his small white fists clenched around the cross at his chest as if to protect it from the journalist's abuse.

Gevaert ignored him and in a trembling voice ranted on. "The preponderance of Church figures and practicing Catholics whose deeds are being stressed should be evidence of this sly maneuver. It is an attempt to draw attention away from an historical truth—two thousand years of systematic, official anti-Semitic dogma per-

320

petrated by Christendom. Dogma and tradition, gentlemen, which provided the *moral sanction* for the mass murder of millions!"

"You lie! You lie!" shouted Father Frade. The Communists applauded. The conservative journalists hooted. "Dr. Whitlock, I demand the floor. I must respond to these terrible accusations!"

Wettlaufer lowered his head between his hands. So it had come to this—public disgrace, an embarrassing brawl sure to be fully reported in the press, making the Wettlaufer Foundation a laughingstock, canceling out the goodness of his guests. Huguette Roux was standing and shouting at Gevaert. Sweeney, yanking at his iron bracelet, was trying vainly to pull away from his guardian.

"I repeat, I repeat, I dare anyone to contradict me," Gevaert bawled. "The line from historical Christianity to the furnaces of Auschwitz is true and straight for all who are not blind to see! Look at the flames, listen to the screams—all of you—then deny that the victims are not the ultimate burnt offerings of our great religious impulse!"

Bedlam followed these embittered remarks. The shouting was general now. The dark-haired Italian journalist was being restrained by two of his colleagues from walking over to the Belgian and thrashing him.

The American correspondent from the network was saying to his colleague from the wire services that he was sorry he had not brought his cameraman along. The Communist writer strode across the room to shake hands with Gevaert, who did not seem interested.

"I don't like you either," the Belgian said, "I am a socialist."

Whitlock pounded his pipe against the table. As the hubbub subsided, he spoke firmly. "I hardly think the gentleman's wild accusations have any relevance here. Our survey is not aimed at examining old grievances. Yes, many of the members of the Legion of Noble Christians are clergymen. Some are with us today. But that has absolutely nothing to do with Mr. Gevaert's fantasies about a whitewash. Now if I may conclude this—"

Father Frade was still standing and fidgeting. "Dr. Whitlock, that man's comments cannot be allowed to stand unanswered. I must ask you to permit me to respond."

"By all means, Father."

"I address myself to the gentleman, but also to all who are present," said Bolli's friend. "No one denies the existence of historical religious anti-Semitism. Yes, we have erred. We would be less than candid to deny it. It has ebbed and flowed. If some popes were less than generous to the people of Israel many were kind and protective. They saw to it that actions of certain communities were stopped, that persecutions were denounced—"

"Persecutions by other Christians!" yelled Gevaert. "By bishops and priests who taught that Jews were well-poisoners! Christ-killers, spawn of Satan, children of Lucifer, deicides!"

The Communists guffawed. It was clear they too regarded the Belgian as a crank, an odd nut. But with typical cunning they were aware he was an oddball who could be exploited. The conservative Italians were angrily waving rolled copies of Whitlock's press handouts at the atheist.

"We concede much of that," said Father Frade plaintively. "But the middle ages are long ended. There is a new spirit in the world—"

"Your history teachers cheated you," mocked Gevaert. "Dreyfus did not live in the middle ages. The mass murder of millions could not have been accomplished without a moral spur, a conviction that the victims deserve to die, that the most horrible acts of torture and degradation were worthy and noble acts. And what could be more noble than killing the killers of God?"

"Blasphemy!" gasped the American priest. "A dreadful thing to say! Especially because you ignore the vast new changes in our Church, the work of our beloved Pope John! Oh, Mr. Gevaert, have you not heard the word aggiornamento? Do you not know that the Church is conveying a whole new attitude toward the Jews—yes, and towards Protestants, Moslems, nonbelievers of all variety? All the old historical antagonism will be abandoned . . . forever . . . put aside, forbidden. My dear friends, if I had the tongue to put in words the inspiring new insights the Church has found! Like Pope John, we open our arms to the Jews, Christ's people. 'Spiritually we are all Semites' said a great pope—"

"And what did Pacelli say?" sneered the Belgian.

Irate shouts and catcalls arose from the noncommunist press. There were cries of *Bravo!* from the Marxists.

Frantic, Wettlaufer grabbed Whitlock's arm. "Jerry, you must stop this, stop it at once." Huguette Roux and Father Latour were looking nervously toward the exits. They had had enough of the abrasive affair and were beginning to be sorry they had made the trip from Brussels.

"Yes, and we will be made aware of His Holiness' deeds and words," Father Frade continued enigmatically. "The Church changes, it learns . . . and it has vowed there will never be another Auschwitz!"

"Hah!" Gevaert yelled. "Can you bring back the little children murdered by the SS?"

"*But we did not murder them! We did not want them killed! We prayed for their lives, and we pray for their souls!*" Father Frade cried. "*Never, never again!*"

The Belgian made a rude lateral gesture with his arm, threw Whitlock's handouts to the floor, and scurried to the rear exit. He turned at the doorway. "You reform too late!" he shouted at the priest. "Who will ever believe you again?"

Then he vanished.

"Rat!" Sweeney called after him. "Sore loser!"

Whitlock tried again to bring things to some kind of conclusion—a goal that now seemed impossible with the rancor that had just burst upon them. "We thank you, Father Frade, for a fair and learned comment." He looked at Sherman for a signal to end the harrowing session and with Wettlaufer's nod prepared to invite everyone into the next room for refreshments. Most of the Italians were ahead of him, already moving noisily toward the bar.

"I have a question."

At the sound of that peremptory voice Sweeney spun around. It was Stonebreaker. The master of Villa Malerba had just made an entrance. He was standing at the rear of the long room in a checked sports jacket, smoked glasses, a gnarled walking stick in one hand. To Sweeney he looked like an elderly queen dressed for a night in Greenwich Village.

Wettlaufer also had seen Stonebreaker and tugged at Whitlock's jacket, knowing that his own ordeal was far from finished. He feared Stonebreaker, the latent power he represented, the cruel irrationality that motivated him.

"Yes, the gentleman in the rear," Whitlock said cheerfully.

"I am A. C. Stonebreaker, European correspondent for *Manifest Destiny* magazine. I have a question for the person calling himself Dusan Primich."

The black hawk, at the sound of his name, moved forward in his chair. Alert, watchful, his beak sniffed the air for plump rabbits, fat mice.

"Who will be translating my question into Serbo-Croat?" asked Stonebreaker—and his commanding manner at once gave him a dominance over everyone in the room.

A pudgy blonde girl in the front row got up shyly. "Please, I am."

"I want to make certain that the man calling himself Primich understands *precisely* what I ask."

"Please," said the girl.

Primich fastened his savage eyes on his challenger. Perhaps, Sweeney thought, he knew enough English to guess what was coming. Stonebreaker took a few steps down the center aisle, and Sweeney called to him: "Get lost, Stoney. Who sent for you?"

Stonebreaker ignored him. "I am not concerned with this man's alleged acts on behalf of Jews," he said.

The pudgy blonde girl proceeded to translate in a swift breathless manner.

"Perhaps he helped them, perhaps not. I would suggest that the foundation examine his story most carefully. It may find that all kinds of scoundrels are now claiming credit for saving Jews."

The translator kept pace with him. Primich listened impassively.

324

A mean one, Sweeney could see. The old hawk had flown through a lot of fire; a little heat would never ruffle his feathers.

"I'm concerned only with Dusan Primich's true identity," Stonebreaker went on. "I ask him to confirm that he is really the notorious Major Kraz, chief executioner for the Communist partisan bands who ravaged Croatia, the man known to the people of Croatia as 'Bloody Kraz.' I further ask him to confirm that he is the man responsible for the murder of forty-two Croat patriots in the village of Pleg on September 17, 1944."

The translator gasped between sentences as she conveyed Stonebreaker's queries to Primich. Toward the end she edged closer to the table, as if to put herself under the protective wing of the old partisan. Around the room Stonebreaker's questions were being translated into French, Italian, German, and other tongues. There were cries, moans, sighs, . . . and all eyes turned to Primich (or Kraz?) who was still thinking things over.

With a barroom veteran's sensitivity to violence Sweeney lumbered to his feet, dragging the policeman with him. Tenente Plasmati at last had awakened.

"Spring me, Carlo," Sweeney pleaded. "There's gonna be a St. Patrick's Day minuet and I got to have both pairs of knucks free."

An elated ripple agitated the Communists. With their leader in their midst chattering excitedly, they left their seats and began drifting toward the dais. Sherman saw them—eight or nine mean-looking fellows—and blanched. He grabbed Whitlock's elbow and whispered to him.

Now the rival party of Italian newsmen, grouped around their slender dark-haired leader, also rose. They, too, began moving toward the center aisle.

General Pandolfo stiffened in his seat. He turned his mournful countenance toward the Reds. "*Basta, basta,*" he said wearily. "*Siete ragazzi bravi.*" Unpredictably, the Marxists, sworn enemies of everything Pandolfo stood for, halted their advance. Some respect was due an old soldier.

325

Primich-Kraz had now started his response—it was a long one—banging a calloused fist on the table to underscore his points and never taking his eyes away from Stonebreaker. He spoke with guttural fury. Nothing Stonebreaker had said had embarrassed him. At the conclusion of his peroration he curled his lip at Stonebreaker, and for a moment it appeared he was going to spit at him.

"He-he-he says," the blonde translator stammered, "he says the gentleman is right. He certainly was Major Kraz, his *nom de guerre* during the war of the liberation, but his real name is Primich. He also is proud to confirm command of a partisan brigade. It is also true he executed Croats by firing squad, but not forty-two as the gentleman says, sixty-three. He denies, however, that they were patriots, merely *Ustashe* murderers who had killed several hundred of his Serbian comrades."

There was a frigid silence, then a pleasantly horrified murmuration.

"I congratulate him, Primich, Kraz, or whatever," Stonebreaker said. "An honest answer. Now, if I may give some honest advice to Messrs. Wettlaufer and Whit——"

But his words were obliterated in the ensuing madness. Far from making the Serbian partisan a pariah, a villain, a man to be hated and feared, the revelation of Primich-Kraz' guerrilla days suddenly touched off cheers and shouts. While the Communists led the tribute, racing to the dais, slapping the Serb on the back, and pumping his hand, a good many other Italians who simply did not like Fascists, or Croats, or to whom the words *partisan* and *guerrilla* had a heroic connotation, joined in this unforeseen paean.

"*Viva i Partigiani!*"

"*Viva Kraz! Viva la Resistenzà!*"

Overwhelmed by this Latin adulation (he was now surrounded by them) Kraz-Primich melted a little. A mountaineer's smile rearranged his predatory face and his lips parted to reveal a mouth badly in need of dental care.

The dark-haired journalist tried to rally the noncommunists

326

from running to Kraz, but he was only partially successful. In a matter of seconds he lost a right-wing Socialist, a left-wing Christian Democrat, and a very old deaf man, a Monarchist who had misunderstood everything and imagined the Serb to be a supporter of King Peter.

"Gentlemen! Gentlemen!" cried Whitlock. "The meeting is ended, over . . . now please stop the shouting and singing! Everyone go into the next room for—"

"*Bandiera rossa, trionfarà!*"

"*Bandiera rossa, trionfarà!*"

Sherman had given up. He sat frozen, waxen.

The man in the dark glasses, furious with his defectors, rallied his dwindling conservative legions. Shouting, they charged the long table, putting on their brakes in front of the Serb executioner, waving their copies of the Legion publicity at the Communists. Threats, rude gestures, intricate insults roiled the air-conditioned atmosphere.

Huguette Roux, guiding a shaking Father Latour, was crying. The crush around the table prevented their departure.

Some of the Italian Reds approached the Hungarian physician, Jekely, and Krakowski, the Pole. These two were also hailed as heroes although the doctor kept protesting he was nonpolitical and had saved Jews as a humane duty, not a political one. The potato-faced Pole sat stolidly and said nothing. He hated Communists and the Soviet Union in that order.

Their Protestant standards of decorum offended by such a circus, Reverend Munk and Willem Krijt were on their feet castigating the rioters. The Dane waved his cigar at them. "Disgraceful, shameful," he called out. "You men are journalists! Do honor to your profession!"

Munk was rewarded with several sets of cuckold's horns, deftly depicted by Communist fingers. The argument surged and billowed around the table, the conservatives and the Communists shoving, cursing, gesturing. At Whitlock's urging General Pandolfo left his seat and tried to mediate. Soon he, too, was yelling and being manhandled (gently, to be sure, no punches thrown) by the milling members of the press.

The bushy-haired Communist belle-lettrist prevailed upon Primich to leave his seat. He explained they would all go to party headquarters for a *real* Marxist shindig. There were more cheers. Moreover, he added, they would hold their own press conference and prove conclusively that the only people who had helped the Jews were people like Primich, dedicated antifascists. That would take care of all those others—priests, ministers, bourgeois poseurs. This notion pleased the Communist so much he repeated it in English for the benefit of Wettlaufer, Whitlock, and the American newsmen.

"Please be advise," he said, "please be advise we members Communist party and left-wing allies intend take full credit, full historical praise, for rescue of Jews. We have own conference, print own version. Only people like Major Kraz here deserve praise for full revolutionary engagement against *Fascisti.*"

"Oh no, oh no," moaned Sherman, "they'll ruin everything. They always do. They're taking all the credit!"

"They better not!" Sweeney yelled. "Who'd ever believe them anyway?" He turned furiously on Stonebreaker. "You lousy wrecker! You give them all the good arguments!"

"That's exactly what I intended to do," Stonebreaker said jauntily. He spun around, squat and formidable in his checked coat, raised his cane in a gesture of farewell, and walked out of the tumultuous room, a stylish saboteur, leaving his work of destruction behind him.

In a moment the room was empty except for the honored guests and promoters of the Legion. The Communists and their hangers-on had marched off singing *Bandiera Rossa* and carrying Bloody Kraz on their shoulders. The conservatives chased after them to pursue the battle through the streets of Rome. Even the curious hotel guests had left. The fun was over.

Frustrated, Sweeney turned his anger on Tenente Plasmati. "Yellow belly. Why didn't you stop them?"

"Not my job," he yawned. "Different cops for politics."

Sherman was swaying from side to side, his eyes unfocused. Even Whitlock, that imperturbable Unitarian, had been unsettled by the disaster. Around the room lay scattered his sedulously prepared publicity sheets—all those unselfish deeds, ignored, torn, crumpled, unread.

"I'm terribly sorry," Whitlock said to Sherman. "It's my fault for calling on that fellow Stonebreaker. I should have taken the high sign when you gave it to me. We'll have to give it another try." But his voice did not have its usual crisp confidence.

"Another try?" asked Sherman dumbly. He asked the question expecting no response; how could there be another try? The members of the Legion appeared to have little desire to prolong their participation. Huguette Roux and Father Latour were huddled in a corner. Kruis of Amsterdam was studying his airplane tickets. Reverend Munk was gazing out of a window, taking in a view of a Roman air-shaft. The Eastern Europeans sat stonily silent; perhaps the Hungarian and the Pole were concerned about the political implications of their trip to Rome. The old woman Marushka Mezhnev betrayed nothing, blinking her octogenarian eyes.

The ultimate symbol of the prevailing misery was the return of General Pandolfo. Attempting to mediate the melee, he had been swept out of the conference room by the rioters and propelled into the hotel lobby before he could free himself. He now returned, tie undone, a pocket of his jacket ripped. He fell into a chair, holding his head and murmuring, "Vergogna, vergogna." The general looked around at the remnant of people in the cold room. "Communists take credit. Always do. I apologize for my people."

Wettlaufer walked up to Whitlock. "Jerry, what have I done to these brave people? They are the finest people in the world, they remind us we are human. And look at the terrible way it ended."

"Damn that Stonebreaker," Whitlock said helplessly. "Suppose we—" He halted. He was adrift, planless.

Through bruised and burning eyes Buck Sweeney surveyed the

room. He was sad for his friends, for indeed he thought of them as beloved friends with whom he had shared some precious knowledge, some treasured awareness. The history from which another son of a Dubliner had tried to awaken surely was not all nightmare. Were not Sweeney's friends proof that a little of the dream was sweet?

And he would not let them down, would not let them suffer this humiliation, this descent into political argument and didactic bitterness. Raising his bandaged head, fixing his lumpy black eye on the members of the Legion, he started to walk down the center aisle still mated to Tenente Plasmati.

Sweeney looked poignantly at Huguette Roux. He thought of her fiancé dying with an SS bullet between his eyes while pleading with frightened Jews to escape from the cattle car. Beside her was Father Latour, a withered leaf of a man still rich with the sap of mercy. He had presided at the Passover seder for his orphaned wards, and the stern old God of the Jews surely must have smiled when the priest broke the matzoth. There was General Pandolfo holding his bald-fringed head in his hands—Fascist, opportunist, probably a bad general. Yet was not his honor greater than any medal, any citation? Sweeney looked at the tall clergyman Munk, and at Kruis of Amsterdam's prophetic head. By God, these were his people, Sweeney's people, Sweeney's friends. How he wished Father Louis had been able to come! And Ludwig Helms. And Bolli, that placid reformer living out his life on scorched hillsides mourning forever his murdered brother.

Yes, they were part of him. He hoped he was a little part of them—if only a memory, a fraction of their consciousness. How the Sweeneys of the world needed them. He blinked fiercely, stemming his tears. *I am not much of a man, but at least I have known them.* Euphoric, he yearned to hug and to kiss them, to tell them they were immortal, blessed, living witnesses to the hard-to-accept truth that it wasn't all bad.

No, it couldn't all be bad the way Stonebreaker insisted it was. There were people who hid the children from the sanctioned murderers; people who looked the horror in the eye and said, no, no, you can't do it any more, we're against you even if you kill us. Thus had Sweeney's friends acted, and they had redeemed belief and tradition for millions.

As Sweeney approached the dais an economy-minded hotel employee turned off the overhead lights and opened the drapes and blinds. The soft gold of Rome suffused the end of the room where the members of Wettlaufer's Legion sat in disarray. Drawn to them, Sweeney had a shivering vision of something Ludwig Helms had told him in Hamburg. With the clarity of a detailed photograph Sweeney saw in his mind's eye the engineer's last view of the bloodied Jews, their imploring hands reaching to the frigid sky, seeking a word, a sign. *Theirs is a very old God, much older than ours. . . .*

"Ah, I wish I could tell them," Sweeney murmured. Desperately he wanted to talk to the Jews of Poldarenko, to get the message to them. This same longing to speak to the dead had troubled him for several weeks after his father had died. All the good things he wanted to tell old Jim Sweeney! It was nonsensical of course, but the foolish desire persisted.

Studying his friends of the Sweeney Survey he was certain he had learned something worth telling Dr. Helms' Jews, those people who had reached for heaven in death. Perhaps it would not console them at all. Perhaps the telling would only console Sweeney.

"Oh, there's a little bit of God in *them*," Sweeney whispered. He glanced at Sherman's guests, at Mme. Roux, at Father Latour, the general, the others. "Yes, whatever God is He's in *them*. Not everyone. But in some people. He sort of doles Himself out a little, and He shows up in people where you'd never expect it. Huguette and Father Latour and Kruis and Mr. Munk. God gave a little piece of Himself to make 'em."

This knowledge pleased him. It would be splendid if he could find a celestial telephone somewhere, an angelic pay station, and ring up the murdered Jews of the Ukraine. His information would not bring back to life the old lady who sang about raisins and almonds to the little child, or the father who pointed to the sky when he reassured the little boy, or the young woman who told Helms she was engaged to be married. No, it would not help them. But it buoyed Sweeney; it might be valuable news for a lot of other Sweeneys.

Father Frade saw his acquaintance from Borracco standing hypnotized in the center aisle.

"Mr. Sweeney, you have been badly hurt," called the priest.

"Kid stuff, Father. Sweeney can take it. Hey, Father, I gotta ask you something. Tell me if it's blasphemy or heresy or just screwy."

"I'll try."

"A crazy idea I got. You see, Father, I just saw some of God. Bits and pieces of him. In our guests. And in your pal Franco Bolli and his brother. All of 'em."

"Well, they are indeed blessed people."

"More than that. The Real McCoy. I tell you, Father, and don't get sore at me. I'm going to communion tomorrow. And when they tinkle the bell I'll hear Huguette Roux talking to the children in the library, and when they raise the wafer I'll see Massimo Bolli, and the wine'll make me think of General Pandolfo. No, no, don't get sore at me, I'm not worth it, Father. . . ."

At the sight of the battered American, everyone in the room stirred happily.

"*Bonjour* there, Huguette," Sweeney called. "How's Pierre? And all those swinging cats in the Railway Workers' Band? I bet that's Father Latour. I want to shake that man's hand."

The librarian laughed. Vivaciously she began to tell the priest about the legendary Sweeney who had beaten the Communists *avec les moules*. The old man smiled. Sweeney kissed Huguette Roux, then spun about, wheeling Plasmati with him.

"Why, there's my pal Enrico Pandolfo!" he said. "Hey, General, remember when you and Mario put me on? Couple of tough guys from Chicago. Did I ever fall for that. What a sucker!"

332

Pandolfo rose, his melancholy face reassembling into a shy smile. "*Piacere*, Sweeney."

"Yes, you're all here, all of Buck Sweeney's friends, the best people in the world!"

In step with his captor he walked to the table and shook hands, with his free left hand, with Reverend Munk and Kruis of Amsterdam. "There's my buddy Mr. Munk. Boy, didn't you Danes give me a wild ride on the Puttgarden Ferry! And Willem Kruis. How's things at the zoo, Willem?"

Both men laughed politely, ignoring Sweeney's manacled condition. Munk stuck a cigar in Sweeney's mouth and Kruis lit it.

"Hey, Father Frade, come join us," Sweeney called. "You're Bolli's proxy."

All gathered around Sweeney. Sherman's eyes bugged as he walked toward them. Jerome Whitlock, confounded by Sweeney's unorthodoxies yet grateful for them, stood on the edge of the admiring group.

"Now, Father Hank," Sweeney said to Father Frade, "Father Hank, were you kidding when you say Franco got himself jugged? And I thought I was doing him a favor when I sprung him from the cops!"

They all laughed although many did not understand him. Sweeney winked at Plasmati. "Punk cops, Carlo. Not like you. Listen, in a little while turn me loose. Mr. Wettlaufer here, the *Americano* who's doing all the sweating, he'll vouch for me. Loaded. *Ricco*."

It occurred to Sweeney that the Eastern Europeans were being left out of the celebration. "Listen, you guys," he called to the Hungarian physician and the Pole, "get off those chairs. Stop looking so glum and join the party."

Father Frade translated Sweeney's order into German. The Hungarian obliged, but the Pole, a suspicious farmer, remained rooted to his chair.

"Ah, a hard case," said Sweeney. "*Yach shimash, Stash?*" He nudged an admiring Wettlaufer. "Didn't know I could talk Polski,

did you, Sherm? Well, I didn't get bombed at the Polish Falcons'
Eyrie Number Four on Brook Avenue for nothing."

The farmer Krakowski got up from the unfamiliar chair—he was
a man accustomed to a tractor seat—and shuffled toward the
assembled group.

"Okay, we're all here and Sweeney's in charge. As for the way I
look, please ignore it. My friend Lieutenant Plasmati will attest to
the fact that I was innocent, the victim of a frame-up. And now
that we all know each other we're going into the next room, where
Mr. Wettlaufer has laid on a great spread, and heist a few brews in
peace. Okay?"

Gallantly he offered his left arm to Huguette Roux.

"Huguette, you be my girl. Father here'll watch us to see we
behave."

The librarian laughed as she took Sweeney's arm. "*Il est très
drôle*," she said to the priest.

"You bet I am," Sweeney agreed.

They followed him into the next room, animated, pleased with
one another's company. Languages were tried, discarded, mutual
tongues agreed upon; a small concert of Europe developed. Wettlaufer beamed. He kept giving Whitlock hints on how best to
resume the survey, how to overcome the bad image the conference
would assume in the Italian press, the suspicions that would arise
when the Communists exploited their efforts.

"I wouldn't worry," said Whitlock. "We've got Sweeney."

"Goodness, we forgot the old lady," Wettlaufer said.

Marushka Mezhnev, the octogenarian from the Ukraine, the
shriveled woman who in the bloody days had sheltered Jews for
reasons she herself could not make clear, sat hunched in her seat.
A remnant from Chekhov's tender heart, she sat with eyes closed,
secure in her black babushka and shapeless dress. Withered lips
moved faintly. Was she praying?

Sweeney, impeded by the policeman who now thought of
himself as a member of the party, wheeled about when Sherman
spoke. He, too, looked at the ancient on the dais. Perhaps she was

334

mulling over eighty-eight years of hard work; revolution; war; sorrow, births, death; lakes of cabbage soup; oceans of hot tea. Generously Plasmati unlocked the handcuff and freed Sweeney. He and Wettlaufer walked toward Marushka Mezhnev.

An epiphany touched the two friends as they approached her. With the gentle agitation of old age her head bobbed slightly. She brushed a strand of white hair under the scarf. Surely, it seemed to Sweeney and Wettlaufer, she was the essence of the good deed unselfishly performed, the deed that could save the world if the world wanted saving.

Sweeney walked around the dais and helped her to her feet. "Come on, Gran'ma," he said. "We'll make you a nice cup of tea."

"Yes, yes," Sherman added. He thought of his own grandmother in the Bronx Hebrew Home for the Aged.

Sweeney guided her down the steps. Then he and Wettlaufer, like guards of honor, escorted her across the room. At Reverend Munk's signal all began to applaud.

Wettlaufer thought of all who had died because there had been no Marushka Mezhnev to hide them. Dignified tears coursed down his cheeks.

"Knock it off, Sherman," Sweeney said. "You'll ruin my party."

Wettlaufer stopped crying. It was the least he could do for his friend Buck Sweeney, who running true to form had rescued him again.

EPILOGUE

Epilogue

The Wettlaufer Foundation
European Office
Via Ostriana, 22
Rome, Italy

Mr. Sherman Wettlaufer
Copper Beech Lane
East Redfield,
New Jersey,
U.S.A.

Dear Sherman:

This letter will consist of a response and a headache. First, the response. You ask for a breakdown by occupation of verified cases. I've come up with the following, although it is not 100 per cent accurate because of multiple occupations. How classify an Army officer who was a lawyer for many years? A nun who has taught school? I have been arbitrary in many instances.

Professionals	213
Government service:	
Civilian	53
Military	31
Farmers	13
Industrial workers	36
Small businessmen, Merchants	20
White-collar workers	6
Business, Industry, Finance	
(Management Level)	3
Miscellaneous	4

The high number of professionals is due of course to the large numbers of Christian clergy who rescued Jews. Of the 213 professionals listed, 141 were priests, ministers, nuns, brothers, etc. The balance of the professional group were journalists, teachers, lawyers, physicians, and so on.

These are revealing figures but please do not publicize them until our sample is more complete. For your own guidance, however, we have checked 379 cases to date, so that the percentage of persons involved in rescue work who were of the Church is 37 per cent! This is a truly amazing portion when one considers that in relationship to the total population of occupied Europe the clergy was only a tiny fraction.

Now to our headache. As you may have guessed its name is Sweeney. Sherman, I did not argue with you when you insisted that he be retained as a "roving ambassador" for the foundation. I am not blind to Sweeney's talents and charm, and I know he is an old friend. But I sometimes wonder if he is the right man to be representing the foundation?

A case in point. As you know, I packed him off to Greece. After a three-week silence I learned about him through a complaint from the American Embassy in Athens. They were vague on the details but it involved Sweeney jumping or falling or getting pushed (no one is certain) onto the stage at Epidaurus during a performance of The Clouds. He was evidently full of ouzo. The Greeks were scandalized. I submit all this without comment.

Sincerely,
Jerome B. Whitlock
Chairman

P.S. As I finish dictating this I am in receipt of a letter from Sweeney. He makes no mention of his difficulties in Greece but includes some excellent notes on an interview with the Metropolitan Nikola, the old fellow who saved the Jewish population of Lapinas. I don't know—is Sweeney worth the trouble or not?